P9-DNU-552

EGG
&
SPOON

EGG
&
SPOON

+ a novel by +

GREGORY MAGUIRE

CANDLEWICK PRESS

The author thanks the usual coterie of early readers, in this case
Liz Bicknell, Betty Levin, and Andy Newman.

Special gratitude to Sophia Lubensky, author of
the *Random House Russian-English Dictionary of Idioms*.

Any infelicitous misapplication or dismissal
of their good advice is the author's fault.

For Matt Roeser's cover art, which inspired a passage
on page 435, the author is especially grateful.

This is a work of fiction. Names, characters, places, and incidents are either
products of the author's imagination or, if real, are used fictitiously.

Copyright © 2014 by Gregory Maguire
Damask pattern copyright © Nuttakit Sukjaroensuk/Veer

All rights reserved. No part of this book may be reproduced, transmitted,
or stored in an information retrieval system in any form or by any means,
graphic, electronic, or mechanical, including photocopying, taping, and
recording, without prior written permission from the publisher.

First edition 2014

Library of Congress Catalog Card Number 2014931834
ISBN 978-0-7636-7220-1

14 15 16 17 18 19 BVG 10 9 8 7 6 5 4 3 2 1

Printed in Berryville, VA, U.S.A.

This book was typeset in Minion Pro.

Candlewick Press
99 Dover Street
Somerville, Massachusetts 02144

visit us at www.candlewick.com

For

Maureen Casey

and

Brian O'Shaughnessy

"Society . . . has taken upon itself the general arrangement of the whole system of spoons."
— Charles Dickens, *Bleak House*

"Tell Polly she shall have half my egg."
— Jane Gardam, "The Tribute"

✦ CONTENTS ✦

PART + THREE
SAINT PETERSBURG, SAINT PETERSBURG

PART + FOUR
FIRE AND ICE, ICE AND FIRE

Was there ever a time when all of us had enough to eat?

Well, honeybucket, that depends on what you mean by "us."

Before.

THE HEELS OF MILITARY BOOTS, STRIKING MARBLE FLOORS, made a sound like thrown stones. The old man knew that agents were hunting for him. He capped the inkwell and shook his pen. In his haste, he splattered the pale French wallpaper around his desk. That will look like spots of dried blood, he thought, my blood.

He wrapped sheets of paper around his forearms, then pulled down the sleeves of his monk's robe. He threw on his greatcoat against the cold. He put his steel-nibbed pen in his breast pocket. Were he lucky enough to survive, he might leave record of how he had come to this.

◦◦◦◦◦◦

This is where I am inclined to start, with my own abduction. You will think me overly interested in myself. Or worse, melodramatic. I can't help that. If *you're* ever dragged from your chambers at midnight, blindfolded and gagged, without being told whether you're off to a firing squad or a surprise birthday party, you'll find that you turn and return to that pivotal moment. If you survive the surprise.

Sooner or later you realize that everything you experience, especially something like being arrested, is never only about *you.* Your life story is really about how the hands of history caught you up, played with you, and you with them. History plays for keeps; individuals play for time.

When soldiers broke down the door to my palace apartments, I thought I was headed for a rendezvous with death. The men were rough, the way young men frightened of their own strength can be. Their mutters, their coded syllables, I couldn't understand them.

I was rushed down a back staircase, I was hustled toward a carriage. Before they knotted a blindfold about my bleeding head, I saw ravens fighting over the corpse of a rat. Ravens aren't usually nocturnal, but hunger can be.

I wasn't shot. Instead, I was locked in a tower on the outskirts of the empire.

At first I scraped the wall with a sharp stone to mark the days. I bunched the scratches in sevens. Then I fell sick, and lost count while in a fever, and when I recovered, I was too discouraged to begin again.

But this story is not about me.

<O· ·O· ·O·

I should explain about living in custody.

From the start, food and medicine came up to me daily, in a bucket tied to a hoist. Right away, I began to send letters by return bucket. One letter a day, for several years. Begging the Tsar to forgive me my part in the plot, to release me. Explaining to him, as I do to you now, how it all came to pass. It was a gamble. Tsars resent insubordination. I was imprisoned for helping a prisoner escape from prison. Ironic, isn't it.

I didn't know if, at the bottom of the rope, my letters were laughed at and thrown away. Or if my entreaties were sent to the court of the Tsar. Now and then, however, more writing supplies arrived.

I was afraid that one day the Tsar might become tired of hearing from me and order me killed. I tried to keep my letters vivid so he would wait for each one daily. The Scheherazade strategy. Though I may only have been entertaining my anonymous sentries below.

In those years I didn't see a human soul, except through the gaze of my memory or my imagination.

I had a single narrow window. I could identify anything viewed from a distance: the celestial parade, the windswept barrens. Nothing near.

With my good eye, I saw birds and landscape, landscape and birds. The birds came close at first — larks, curious wrens, stupid pigeons, as I thought then. They soon learned that I wouldn't spread crumbs for them on my window ledge. I didn't have enough to spare. They stopped visiting.

At first I watched the birds against the sky, their shadows

against the ground. Then I followed birds in my mind. I thought of it as peering with my blind eye: seeing what the birds could see, or had seen in the past, about what had happened to bring me to this prison tower. I put together what I knew for certain with what my visions now told me. I wrote what I saw to the Tsar.

Take, for instance, those birds. Everywhere, birds. Have you stopped to think that on a sunny day, almost every bird casts a shadow?

It's true. When an eagle floats over the icy peaks, his shadow slides upslope and down, a blue cloth. The hawk and the hummingbird: big shadow and small. Even the duck in a millpond drags her ducky umbrage in the mud.

The sparrow in cities, on a spree with her thousand cousins. Have you noticed? As sparrows wheel over the basilica, they scatter shadows like handprints on the spiral wooden ribs and ribbons of those turnip domes. Sparrows even come between the sun and the high windows of the Winter Palace of the Tsar. How dare they, the Tsar said once. He had a headache.

I know this because he told me so. I once had the ear of the Tsar.

Anyway.

Yes, all birds cast shadows on bright days. Except for one. The Firebird, bright soul of all the Russias, casts no shadow.

You can't be surprised at that. What, after all, could the shadow of light be? No such thing. It is a trick, a paradox. It hurts to think about it.

However, they say any mortal boy or girl who can snatch a tail feather of this bird . . . well, that child can make a wish that will come true. Why a child and not, say, a robber-baron industrialist or a society dame? Or even some goofy naturalist collecting specimens in the badlands? I don't know. The stories are always about children.

Now, in his line of work, a monk meets few children. If any of them ever made wishes that came true, they didn't tell me about it. Why should they? I might not have believed them anyway. Not back then.

I didn't understand the business about Firebirds and children and wishes. I guessed the Tsar didn't either. So in this chamber haunted only by myself, I let my mind unspool. I suppose you might think I was going mad. Think what you like. In my raveling thoughts I flew away, as if my spirit were nestled in the breast feathers of some passing hornbill or waxwing.

I flew to observe children, their dark secrets, so I might better understand the origin of my own darkness. I also flew to understand my young accomplices in crime, to put myself in their shoes. In one case, felted peasant boots laced with rawhide cord. In the other, fine French slippers suitable to wear to a ball.

I flew to have something to write to the Tsar, to extend the number of my own days in light.

Those pages are now lost, along with so much else. Here is my effort to re-create them, before the darkness finishes its claim upon me.

PART · ONE

UNTIMELY THUNDER

The World in Curtains

The girl has never gone into a theater. But the doctor once told her what it was like, so the girl thinks she knows.

She thinks a theater is like this room in their home. This one room. There was another room once, a kind of shed, and that was for goats. But the last remaining goat was hungry and ate the rope that tied the door shut, and got out. Then something ate the goat. When the shed fell down because it was mostly sticks to start with, the family burned it for heat. So now they live in a one-room house. Simple, but it has a stage at the far end. So it is a theater.

Yes, it is, the girl insists to her two brothers. The nook *could* be a stage. Why not? Everybody thinks it's only a bed built into the wall, with curtains you can draw together to keep the warmth in. But you can make a world of the bedclothes. When the curtain opens, a stone can be a pig, a feather can stand for a whole bird. A crumb: a feast. Whatever you can think of—there it can be.

"Sit down, the show is about to start," says Elena. Luka and Alexei, the brothers, are older, and practice skepticism. "Shhh. The performance can't start if the people aren't paying attention." Maybe a magpie is perched on a windowsill, looking in. Trust me. It's possible.

"This is the best show I ever saw," says Luka, the firstborn. He has attended no shows but hers. "Look at those bed curtains. I'd pay good money to see these bed curtains four times a week. Look at those moth holes. Such drama." He makes a retching noise.

"I hope there's a dragon," says Alexei. He's the middle child, and more prone to tenderness.

Luka agrees. "A dragon diving at coaches on the high road to Warsaw. Terrifying the horses. He especially likes to eat fat rich old countesses. First he burns their double chins off with his breath, one at a time . . ."

"If you don't quiet down, there will be no show," says Elena. So her brothers settle. She pulls the curtains back to show them the world she has made.

Usually it's a world of brown hills, a blanket mounded around pillows. An edge of the sheet shows from underneath, and that can be the shore of the sea. The blue stripes on the mattress ticking, waves coming in.

Now and then Elena makes some old familiar folktale happen here. More often, Mama's magic nesting doll stands in a valley. Nearly round on the bottom, like a pear, and softly narrower on top. The shape of a slow teardrop: that's a mother for you.

The trick about this doll, the magic part? She opens in halves, and inside her is another mama doll just like the first, except smaller. Inside that one is a third, and if you keep opening mamas, you find a fourth and a fifth and a sixth. The seventh doll is a painted baby. It keeps its own counsel and doesn't open.

Sometimes the play is about six mamas searching for their lost baby in the mountains. They take turns climbing the hills and rolling down the slopes, calling, "Baby, baby," until one of them finds the infant in a cave of wrinkling blanket. The wooden chinking sound as they collide is chiding, kissing, scolding. It means the family can be put back together again.

Putting families back together again. Perhaps an impossible exercise. We shall see.

When the play is over, the boys clap nicely enough. Alexei admits, "I'd rather there were a dragon."

"Here's your dragon," says Luka. He's found an old sock that belonged to their father, back when he was alive and needed socks. Through the holes in the toe, Luka sticks his two fingers. The dragon flies above the world, snapping its two-fingered mouth and crying in a spooky Luka voice. It dives to snip at Alexei's nose. *Hard.* Alexei yelps and swears.

"Show's over," declares Elena, upstaged, and flicks the curtains closed. Annoyed. She doesn't like the story to get away from her. Luka stomps off to check his traps and snares. Alexei changes his clothes; he has a job as a houseboy.

That's what it used to be like. Once upon a time. Today, however, the boys aren't in the little hut. Elena has just come in from the village well. The room has a stillness that seems potent, if

11

tentative. The winter light on the bare floorboards is splotchy from the grime on the windows. It looks like residue, something having been washed away. Well. Much *has* been washed away.

The motherly nesting doll, called the matryoshka, watches from the shelf with the holy ikon and the cold unlit candles.

Elena sets down the pail of water. She draws near to the curtained side of the room. She pauses and she says a prayer, and then she opens the two sides of the drapes as quietly as she can.

Here is the world she sees. It looks a lot like the world she plays. A rolling landscape of upland meadows, sudden woolen cliffs. The world steams, and it smells of camphor medicine. It groans and turns in its bed.

"How are you feeling today, Mama?" whispers Elena.

The world does not answer.

"Would you like the matryoshka to hold?" asks the girl.

The world does not answer.

The World
in a
Graveyard

So Elena goes out. Can you see her? Over there, on the path by the fence made of wire and disoriented wooden rails. Now in the shadows of the juniper, now coming into the light. There.

She's about this tall. Her faded scarf is slipping backwards off her snarly hair because she's been running.

A few crows lift out of her way, but not far. A girl is no threat to them.

She pauses for breath. Her hand is at her side, she has a stitch. She leans against a stone wall that supports a rusty gate — the way to the land of the dead.

Two churchyard rooks look at her sideways, considering.

A red squirrel in a rotting tree scolds her. The creature is mangy, and it probably has rabies. Still, she mutters, "Please," and then, "Forgive me," and then she puts her hand in a hole in the tree. She takes out two acorns and sets one back on the wall. One for him and one for her. "Sorry, sorry," she murmurs. Three more, and she drops them all in her apron pocket. It's stealing. It isn't fair, but she's bigger.

Then she swings the gate open.

The churchyard is dank. What small snow there was this winter has been reduced to translucent mush. Last year's grass lies exposed, wetted down and combed all in one direction. The girl pinches a fistful of tatty pinks and whites hardly out of the ground. Then she walks past the few carven stones and worn obelisks to the meadow beyond, where the poor are buried.

She doesn't know how to find her father here, for there are no markers. Still, she has a game she plays with him. She closes her eyes and spins around and lets the blossoms scatter in a wheel about her. "Have I found you, Papa?" she calls. She doesn't bawl, for this is an old game by now, she is used to it. She hopes that, sometimes, some flowers fall on his grave. That's all she hopes.

Today, though, before she leaves, she drives her hand into her apron pocket. She grips a few acorns. "Look, Papa," she says. "I promised to help take care of Mama, but this is all I have to bring home. There's nothing else for us."

If the spirit of her father has an opinion about this, she can't make it out.

Any cemetery is already a ghost village, but this one is a ghost village planted within a ghost village. Outside the graveyard gates, there's too little sound of human bustle. The child just stands there amidst the silence of phantoms, fists clenched, in a wheel of scattered pinks. From up above it would make a pretty enough sight, peasant girl in a circle of torn blossoms. One might do a painting. Some colors and a brush, a square of flawless white.

Lifting away, the rooks drag their shadows across her upturned face. She sees them but she doesn't see them. She is thinking of her father and of her mother, and how hunger is like a shadow that makes everything wobble in its outlines.

I do not mean to make her seem pathetic. She is only a common child. Perhaps you already think a peasant child not worth your time and attention. Perhaps you are right. I shall lay it out for you, and you can decide.

The Doctor's Curse

That's how it is, that's how it was, that's how it was going. Every day was pretty much the same, until the day of the doctor's curse. That child's life and mine began to go awry on the same day.

Things can start happening anytime, anywhere. Prisons, gardens, palaces, woods. This particular stumble of fools began outside Elena's hutch of a house.

The doctor was shivering on the step, his back to the closed door. He was really a doctor for horses and sheep, but last fall the báryn, that local lord fancypants, had given up. He with his big house and his big mattress stuffed, it was said, with big cash — he had decided to move his flocks off the estate. Get out while he could. So work for an animal doctor, for everyone, grew scarce. "Too sad," said the báryn. "We'll meet again in happier days, if they ever come. Good-bye."

There'd been few people to reply. Some wives, several farm-workers, toddlers and teenage boys, old men and older women. Alexei, on one of the departing carts, had not waved farewell to Elena and Luka. He'd stared at the sky with his chin up to keep anything from showing.

Dr. Peter Petrovich Penkin saw humans now. He insisted that he wasn't qualified, but the remaining villagers of Miersk had no other doctor to trust, and Peter Petrovich was a kind man and a good one. Yes, a good man, despite his breath, which smelled as if he had inhaled all the animal and human germs he had ever met, and kept samples in the twin cabinets of his lungs.

The horse doctor was just leaving Elena's hut. He shook his cane at her. "Where have you been, with your mother so poorly?"

"I was looking for the last of the hens," replied the girl, "though I think the foxes got there first."

"The only onions left on my shelf are running to jelly. So I declare this Onion Liberation Day. I made a broth, but broth is not enough. On onion broth, your mother will not improve." The doctor spoke with impatience, as if he had a dozen more appointments. "She is failing to thrive, Elena. Show me what you found."

The girl brought out the handful of acorns. The doctor shook his head. "Split the meat from the shells and boil them soft. You can add them to the onion broth. It's better than nothing. Unless it poisons her. Remember, I'm a horse doctor, not a chef."

"She's better, isn't she?" But Elena sounded dubious.

"She's too weak to do anything but pray, so she is praying for a better harvest this year than last. Are you sure all the chickens have been eaten? Maybe they were just hiding."

"The last one was the black hen, and I'm afraid she's been carried off, too. Or run away. Doctor, what are we to do?"

He purred a finger against his lips. "Hmmm. It's too soon for cuckoo's eggs. I'm told that nothing has wintered over in the kitchen gardens of the big house. Miersk is barren. The soil is bankrupt. So sip away: it's Onion Liberation Day."

"We have nothing to pay you with." Elena fixed her gaze on the track that passed as a road. She couldn't look directly at him. In this she took after Alexei.

"No one in Miersk has a kopek to spare," said the doctor. "Once the serfs got their freedom, we earned the freedom to starve. Listen, my little chickadee: If your mother gets well enough to plant a squash seed, and if she waters it with her tears so it becomes a great golden turban, and then if she's strong enough to pick it and to bake it for me . . . well, then, I'll come and eat squash pie. That's a reward worth waiting for. Now: How about you, you fretful child? Are you eating enough?"

Elena didn't answer him. What answer was there?

The doctor observed, "Luka isn't much of a scavenger, is he."

Defending her brother, she muttered, "The world around Miersk is scavenged out."

The doctor licked his forefinger and stuck it out in the wind, to judge the direction of the cold. "May he go a bit farther abroad to find better pickings."

And that was the doctor's curse, though Elena didn't see it as such.

So the doctor pulled his tattered coat around him and left. He took with him his small climate of diseased breath. Elena could hear him puffing it out with each step. He was a big man, but like everyone else, he was thinning. While liberating his onions in their direction.

Maybe the doctor's presence had made Mama anxious. A doctor inside the izba usually means something is wrong. Mama turned her head on the pillow at the sound of Elena's footstep.

"Luka?"

Mama always asked for him first: he was her firstborn. And a boy. Elena knew that was not Luka's fault, just his luck. "Luka is checking his traps."

"And Alexei?"

Elena drew a breath. Alexei had been borrowed by the báryn. He wouldn't come back until the báryn's family returned to the district. Mama knew this. But just now Mama wasn't remembering. A sign of steeper decline?

Elena tried faking the truth. How easily lying comes to this one. Watch how she does it. "Alexei is busy with Grandmother Onna." Grandmother Onna was a childless old spinster, granny to no one and thus everyone. She lived in a room attached to the village shop, which did her no good now that the shelves were all empty. She was simple and she minded young children during the day, not for money but because they made her happy and kept her from throwing herself absentmindedly into the well.

Elena's mother should recall that Alexei wasn't with Grandmother Onna. But the lie worked, it calmed her mother, which both relieved and worried the girl.

"Where is Elena?" said Mama.

Now Elena smiled. This was a familiar game, not lying but make-believe. "Elena has gone to Moscow," she told her mother. "The Tsar invited her to a ball."

"Ah, how will she know the way? She'd better bring my magic doll for advice."

"Elena will dance all night and eat everything in sight —" But here Elena stopped; talking about distant food was cruel when there was none to be eaten nearby.

"Ah. I hope she doesn't come home too grand for us," said Mama. Her eyes closed. "Elena?" she whispered. "If I die, will you children take care of one another?"

"You won't die, Mama."

"Promise me."

Elena sat still. She thought, My promises aren't worth a swear word scratched on birch bark.

Finally she thought of something peaceable to say —"Would you like me to bring you your doll, Mama? Mamenka?"— because recently when Mama was half asleep, she would hold the doll and it seemed to soothe her.

As Elena waited, a roll of thunder cleared its throat. Thunder is a summer sound, usually. It's all wrong for midwinter. Still, lightning was cooking in those clouds. Mama, startled from her thoughts, cried out, "Luka."

Elena slammed out the door. She was running to find her brother, this is true. But she was also running from the fact that, in a crisis, her mother called for her oldest child, for her first son. Luka, almost always for Luka. Rarely for Alexei. Never for Elena.

Perhaps I make her sound petulant. The girl was aggrieved, she was running. A coward, or a sensitive urchin? Draw your own conclusions. I'm just telling you what happened, not what it means. Perhaps it means nothing.

Farther Afield

Look again, before things go wrong.

Ha. As if they're all that right to start out with.

What do we have so far?

Here's a girl running through this place. What kind of a place is it? An old-fashioned one. Some distance away in custom and in geography, too. Examine it as you would a stage set when the curtains open. The larches near the village well, the tumbledown farm buildings empty of livestock, the stubbly fields and the pale ravaged pastures and the woods all around.

The world had gone upside down. Midwinter, and the snow already melting off, draining away. Elena didn't even need her mittens. And above the ridge of hills, beyond the known neighborhood, cloud armies bumbled and massed.

She hurtled along the track to find her big brother. Mama demanded it. Elena could resent Luka and rely on him at the same time. With Papa dead and Alexei in Moscow, Luka was her touchstone. As for this unpeopling village, its alleys and stricken yards — it was like running through a bad dream.

Then, past these trees and those, she saw her brother. His sack was tied at his belt, slapping too freely. Little or no weight in it. No food. No supper. "Luka," she called.

He looked beaten, but he straightened at her voice. A show of strength, anyway. "Have you checked for eggs?"

She didn't want to admit that the last black hen was missing, presumed dead. A raw chicken dinner for some lucky fox. So she replied, "The doctor came. He thinks Mama is not getting better yet."

Luka sneered. "He couldn't diagnose a wart on a warthog. He's a big fake." But he stopped as he and his sister became aware of another sound, unearthly but of the earth: at ground level. They shouldn't have paused —

But children have a hard time imagining dangers they've never met before. They turned, with that curiosity to know. An instinct that betrays children and their elders every day of the universe's long life. Lot's salty wife on her road, Pandora's itchy imagination.

Upon them, around them, a drumming of horseshoes on frozen ground. Seven, eight, ten angry mares, cropped to the task by their riders. One of the horses reared and whinnied, a rumbustious *hnbree-eee-eee*. Elena thought she and Luka would be stamped off balance and trampled to death.

"Whoever they are, they won't get my catch," muttered Luka. "I won't let them." He stood his ground.

The commander of this sortie took off his cap. "Another gosling to join the few we found in the fields," he said, not to the children but to his men. Then, to Luka: "Lad, is your father out with

22

the other village men who were felling dead trees for firewood? And if not, where will we find him?"

Luka replied, "You will find my father in his unmarked grave. If you can."

"Your brother, your uncle, your grandfather, then?"

"I am my family's man."

The commander paused, and might have passed on. But an underling said, "Sir, shall we leave him be? He's just a boy...."

At this, the commander flinched. No enlisted man criticizes a superior officer. "We were told to bring fifteen men from each estate, and we have fourteen," declared the commander. "Take him."

From the chapel of Saint Veronika across the way, two women came running. Their scolding roused the doctor in his study. Peter Petrovich Penkin saw disaster through his window. He roared from his doorway, "You can't — he's a child." The flopping pocket of his big coat caught on his door latch. He worked to free it. "I'll come in his stead." His voice confident and false.

"You're too ancient to be useful," said the commander.

"I'm a doctor; doctors are always useful. Take me. Besides, that boy has infections that will bring down a battalion." Lies, lies, kindly but useless. The doctor shook his cane in the air, ripped his pocket stitches, and almost fell off his doorstep onto his face.

"We take fifteen men from this village," shouted the commander. "That's our charge, and I require it. Company, onward."

The women began to understand that their men were being impressed into service. They shrieked to raise their sisters. They rushed at the horses to scare them away. In the flurry of their whipping skirts and aprons, Elena couldn't quite see what happened.

23

Luka's feet were lifting off the ground. He was being slung like a saddlebag on the back of a horse, behind a horseman with a pistol in his hand.

The rider aimed it at the doctor, and then turned to menace the emboldened women, who fell back.

From the porch of the shop tumbled Grandmother Onna, wobbling under the weight of a rifle. She raised it to her face. "My aim is unsteady and I don't intend to kill anyone, but I might," she cried. "Let the boy go."

"Grandmother Onna is loose," announced the doctor. The ruse of nonsense. "Usually we tie her to the chair for her own safety. Don't mind her, she left her mind along with her youth in the back alleys of Novgorod. Onna, give me that thing, no one is after your virtue anymore." He swiveled her way.

The frisky horses shied and were cropped with hard *thunks*. The commander said, "Put down that rifle or I'll arrest you."

The doctor's bad leg slowed his approach. Elena was nearer the mad old pepperpot. Without thinking, she grabbed Grandmother Onna's gun out of her hands. A shot cracked out, more whip-snap than musical zing. Elena didn't think it was from the old woman's rifle, but she tossed the weapon in the well just in case.

The gunshot was the commander's, firing into the air to frighten everyone.

The horses capered and nickered. The only human sound was Grandmother Onna grumping. "That was my best husband. Now he's drowned. You little stinker." Her other remarks were lost in the pummel of horse hooves as the company wheeled about.

Before he disappeared, Luka managed to wrench his sack off

his belt and toss it on the ground. After the party of ambush cantered away, Elena snatched it up. Inside she found the carcass of a baby hare. One of the horses must have stamped on it, for the creature now was a handful of bloody guts, fur, fractured bones.

That evening Elena scraped two mouthfuls of meat from the remains. She added the stewed acorns and scrappy flesh to the onion broth, and fed a cup to Mama. She couldn't bring herself to taste even a sip of it. She was a child of stone that night.

Now: Remember the curse? The doctor's wish for Luka to go farther abroad to find food? Farther he was going, farther every moment, abducted, on the back of a horse. What good might come of it, if any, we shall see.

There was a blessing, though, of sorts. By sundown Mama was too lost in fever to be able to count the people in the room. She didn't take in anything: that Alexei was gone away into domestic service, that the soup was horrid, that Luka was missing, too. Elena sat at her bedside holding the matryoshka baby.

I always think a weeping child makes a sweet picture, don't you? I see this in a dim, crepuscular light, a little greenish. A fiddle playing a long note, heavy on the vibrato, would punch the effect up a little. But I have no idea if anyone in Miersk can play so much as a squeezebox. You'll have to add the melody yourself.

Tea Brewed from
Salt Tears

The good doctor came by just before dawn to look in on Elena's mother. "I couldn't sleep, so why should you?" he demanded of Elena. He brought some tinder and banked up the fire, and he clucked over Mama and rubbed her hands to warm them. That was the only medicine he had to offer today.

Natasha Rudina didn't stir under his attentions. He stood back. "So have you made a decision, then?" he said to Elena's mother. "Come now. You have to *want* to live your life."

He nodded Elena out of the house to confer. They stepped off the threshold and began to stroll, keeping their voices low. The world was darkness, inside Elena and out.

"How is she taking the abduction of her luckless boychik?" asked the doctor.

"I haven't told her about it."

The doctor glanced at her. "And she hasn't asked? Child, you shouldn't carry all this on your own shoulders."

"Who is going to help? Who is left to ask? Saint Nicholas? Saint Nobody."

"Don't be withering. Grandmother Onna might pitch in, and it might do her some good, too. I'll ask her."

"I heard more carts going by last evening. What's left of the Rudetsky household was clustered around the shafts of their wagon, pulling it themselves."

"So the wives of the conscripted men are leaving to harbor with relatives elsewhere. Can you blame them? First their daughters taken, now their husbands."

"Are you going, too?" The girl's voice was cold.

"And leave you all alone with a bed-bound mother? What kind of doctor would I be if I abandoned those who need me most?"

You're not much of a doctor to begin with, thought Elena, but she kept that to herself. "Why did that commander scoop up Luka and our other men, too?"

The doctor held up his hands, palms out, as if he were on trial. "Who can say? There isn't any military need. No Crimea in the offing. I'd have heard. A doctor can make out quite well during a war. I'd have sent back rations from the front, anyway."

"What are we going to do? Such a bad harvest last summer and too little snow now to irrigate the fields come spring . . ."

"The world is protesting. It feels like a summer cloudburst coming, yet the hymns of the high holidays still ring in our ears. Can the calendar turn inside out? Can a year run backward?" But the doctor could never stay down-spirited for long. "We could break into the báryn's big empty dacha and chip the plaster angels off the ceiling. Roast putti *du jour*."

"Is starvation making you mad?"

"We are together," said Peter Petrovich. "When we have nothing left, we'll divide it in half and each take a portion. We'll fill the samovar with tea brewed from our salt tears. Grief is hard to swallow; you have to take it slowly. I declare this One Sip at a Time Day."

"That's not enough." They had reached the place in the path where the old combine had broken down, never to stir again, and was rusting into eternity. "You should go to the Tsar and find out why he has stolen Luka and the others." She spoke as she thought Luka might, with nerve. "Maybe the Tsar plans to send them to war against some country that had a better harvest last year."

"With my bad leg, I'd be dead of exhaustion before I reached the first crossroads. And anyhow, which way should I turn? Who knows the way to the door of the Tsar? Ambition without direction is like milk without a cup." He shrugged. "But if I got there, I would bring him a flask of our tea of salt tears and say, 'Try a sip, dear Tsar: it is One Sip at a Time Day.'" He laughed at his own conceit, laughed until salt tears came out of his eyes.

He almost didn't hear Elena say, "Then I'll have to go see the Tsar myself." But little by little, he stopped laughing.

"Very well. And for directions, you will ask whom? The spirit of your dead father, maybe? Don't look at me like that, child. I'm trying to make a point —"

Though a tender nonsense of the doctor's, and meant without malice, this hit like a slap. "I'll ask Baba Yaga, the old witch of the woods, if I have to," she cried. "Don't think I won't."

Chastened, he pawed the air toward her with one hand, and she reached out and found his hand in the dark. They walked in silence for a few moments. "I hope you don't leave," said the doctor.

Was this another curse? Pay attention now.

"If you *should* go," he said at last, "I'd look after your mother until you get back. As best I could. But you are a better helpmeet to her than I could be. I can't easily trot through muddy woods finding wild turnips or berries, if they even choose to come back this year. My bad leg is made of concrete. And my good leg gets tired of dragging the bad leg after it."

She knew the doctor was apologizing for teasing her. She said, neutrally, "With all those stars in the sky, why isn't there enough light for us to see by? We stumble like blinded sheep."

"As you can see, it is clouding over. The stars can't pierce that gloom; they just wait it out. That isn't the stars' fault. It is their custom to stay heavenly."

"They should come down closer to the earth."

"Well, ask them politely."

He was humoring her. He thought her simple, a younger version of Grandmother Onna. He didn't think she would ever have the courage to leave. She'd prove him wrong.

"Ah, now you're not talking to me," he said. "That's all right. Sometimes there's nothing left to say."

Double Lightning

They got as far as the fields of rotten rye. There they turned and, starting back, looked down on what was left of life. Miersk huddled under onrushing clouds. Miersk in an uncertain dawn.

In the center squatted the chapel. A pagoda in stained timber.

To one side, along the edge of the settlement, the station where trains had once stopped, long ago, but no longer bothered. A study in the science of decay.

The doctor's house, with no more medicine. The schoolhouse where no one studied since there was no teacher. The shop where no goods waited to be bought. The henhouse where no hens clucked. Abandoned homes. Isn't this depressing?

The clouds parted on cue, a certain stage business of the deity. A wedge of solar blue between scoops of cloud. Then a crack of thunder. The air felt green and filigreed with grit, plates of atmosphere scraping together.

As if the overlord of the heavens had a campaign against Miersk, the lightning that had threatened for days finally snipped across the clouds. It started out crosswise but arced earthward, to the north. Lord save the Rudetskys, out on that road, thought Elena.

"Run," said the doctor companionably, and swatted her on the behind. She wouldn't let go of his hand, and dragged at him to hurry, even with his bad leg.

Another sickle of lightning was readying itself. You can feel that kind of thing. This one meant business, as if there really is no such thing as mercy in the universe.

They were almost to the doctor's house when the second bolt struck the top of the chapel steeple. A scorched note, a sound of wood ripping like paper. The bell in its wooden wheel dropped through the belfry, bringing with it most of the timber cladding of the front wall.

The bell thudded six feet away from their heels. They felt the vibration of overtones into their skulls. The roof of Saint Veronika's began sparking, and the lightning crackled backward along the roof beam. Then the tortured javelin dove earthward and finished in the graveyard, turning the ground over as a giant mole might. Coffins and rot and sulfurous smells burst through the nap of ground-level pinks and whites.

Elena grabbed the doctor's lapels. The sweat on his eyebrows was like jelly. In a moment Peter Petrovich opened his eyes.

"Is this heaven or hell?" he managed to say.

"You're still alive," she said.

"Hell," he replied.

"And so am I," she answered.

31

"Well, nearer to heaven, then, so I might as well sit up." He tried to. "This is Second Chance Day, and I didn't see it coming."

"Second Chance Day? Good, another chance to suffer."

Day after day in the season of disaster, it can be hard to recognize a change in fortune when it comes. Elena was untried at hope. Still, the doctor was right. It was Second Chance Day, and the chance was coming.

Thunder on the Rails

What a worthless trade, thought Elena. All those clouds brashing down the sky, bellowing their opinions and knocking down church steeples. And the only thing that matters to the people of Miersk? A sensible snowfall befitting the season?

Not a flake of it. Full of static and sizzle, the clouds swagger on toward the Urals. They drag the dry tails of their purple greatcoats behind them.

She spent that day hunting through the cupboards of the Rudestkys and the Popovs and other departing families, hoping to find something left behind by mistake. Only crumbs between floorboards, dust in the larder.

With nothing to offer her mother for supper, she stopped in to see how Peter Petrovich was faring.

His light was low. Conservation of lamp oil. The old man lay flat in his bed, raking his beard with a broken comb. Grandmother Onna was heating towels over his tiled stove and then trying to push them under his lower back with a poker. He had twisted the ropes of muscle that supported his spine. His hip wasn't much better. His mood was nasty. "Doctors are supposed to help the sick, not lie around like women in the birthing bed," he snarled.

Grandmother Onna replied, "They say a shoemaker has no shoes for himself. Doctor, you can't help the sick until you recover. Lie still or this poker will do some interesting damage."

"You're trying to finish the job the lightning couldn't manage. Oh, Elena, you're here. Good. Hit that old woman over the head with a shovel."

"Tell him to stop flirting," said Grandmother Onna.

"Are you alive?" Elena asked the doctor.

"Do not ask for whom the bell tolls," he replied. "The bell is broken. With no bell to chime the holy hours, we're unclocked. Time itself can't tell what time it is."

"It's time to eat," said Elena, hoping they would have something to spare. The doctor spread both his hands, meaning empty left, empty right.

"Is that the rain I hear?" asked Grandmother Onna.

They stilled themselves to listen. This noise was more orderly than wind. More like muffled drums. "Our men come back, and all turned into soldiers already?" wondered the doctor.

"No." Grandmother Onna wagged her forefinger, thinking. "I do believe it might be a train."

A train. In all of Elena's living memory, no train had ever come through. The Miersk line wasn't much more than a siding.

A little-used byway of the great Moscow–Saint Petersburg rail network, serving dachas and grain dispensaries on a capricious schedule. It was often abandoned for years at a time: Miersk wasn't exactly a holiday destination.

"Help has come," said the girl, though I think she had little reason to expect largesse from the world. "Food, maybe, and milk." She ignored their protests, she bolted outside.

"A nice world you imagine. It's fun to believe in magic, but help doesn't travel by train," called the doctor. "If I'm wrong, I'll take five fresh eggs."

Elena joined the few remaining village women, who had gathered in hope or curiosity as sounds grew distinct. A percussive huffing. A shrieking of metal upon metal. Then a steam whistle, which can sound like a piccolo being tortured unto death.

The engine emerged from behind fir trees. It drove ahead of it a tumble of saplings and bracken plowed down by its cowcatcher.

The older women remembered the train from their childhoods. They brassed up a high-pitched traditional greeting. They thought their folklore hello might be heard above the noise of industrial advance. They had no potatoes to sell or fresh baked bread, not like in the old days. They waved junk. Wooden spoons, nearly clean shawls, tin ikons torn from the holy corners of their huts. Anything for a trade, for a few pieces of fruit, for oats or black bread or maybe a wedge of bacon.

"Hello," they cried. They looked like what they were: starving peasants in the outback of an endless country.

Don't take my comment as criticism. Starving peasants can be attractive and well behaved. I believe they also sing nicely from time to time.

In any case, the train paid them no attention. As it passed, it spun black lace curtains of sooty exhaust.

"Five eggs," begged Elena, choking on indigestible hope. The younger children and the older women, expecting less, didn't waste their tears. They turned away, muttering about the good old days.

"I'm not surprised it passed by," said Peter Petrovich when Elena went back to tell him what had happened. "Though I do wonder why the service is being revived after all this time."

"We'll never know," said Grandmother Onna.

In this, she was wrong. The train — the very same train — returned about an hour later, slowly backing up until the lighted windows of the final carriage lined up with the platform of the abandoned train station.

Fuss from the engine — mechanical farts and groans, the like. I'm not technical.

Look at it there for a moment. Ever since I lost an eye, I've loved to picture things clearly when I can. Winter dusk in Miersk comes hard and fast even when the winter is being irresolute. The wheels are lost in shadows all plum and black, like rising water. The light from behind drapes, an alluring rosy tangerine. Brass fixtures on windows and doors. There are only four cars to this train. It is a private experiment in luxury, perhaps. Someone important may be on this train. The Tsar himself? We could look closer and see. Shall we?

The Accidental Guests

The doctor was the only man distinguished enough to greet travelers on the iron horse. But his back was a torment and his hip no better. So he wasn't going to make formal inquiries as to the reason for its visit. He couldn't get up.

Grandmother Onna had little interest in wrestling a train and trying to throw it down the well. She was too busy harrying the doctor.

At rest in the theater of the sickroom, behind the bed drapes of her own infirmary, Elena's mother, frail Natasha Rudina, never heard the train arrive. She couldn't forbid Elena to go find out what the commotion was about.

So the girl, alone of the villagers, ventured forth. As Elena drew nearer, she could see the train more clearly than I've described so far. Earlier, the iron-wheeled enterprise had been a smudge of speed and noise. Now, at rest, with steam clearing like mist on the rise, Elena caught glimpses of greasy pistons and twisting valves that resembled the architecture of a trumpet. Above the massive wheels, four separate carriages. The last one was grandiose with shiny finials, ornamentation like shoe buckles. Every window was cloaked with drapes.

The train seemed like a creature on its own accord; Elena half expected it to speak. She had a fanciful side, given to drifting in and out of reason. But she also had a no-nonsense grip on things. What can I say, the child is not a symbol: she's a child with a messy mind.

A voice from the head of the train: "For the love of old Mother Russia! Is this place even alive?" Elena turned toward the sound, not sure if she should run away or stand her ground.

Before she could decide, a door swung open just behind her, and another man's voice replied, "Temper, temper, my good man. Let us greet adversity with manners."

The first speaker materialized in tendrils of steam. At the sight of Elena, he stood still. Shreds of steam clung and coiled to him. I imagine they looked like strips of detaching skin. At first Elena thought him a body exhumed from the bedeviled graveyard, or a ghost. The ghost she most wanted to see, were she ever to see one. He was the right shape and size. But his voice was too earthly and his accent not the local one. "A pint-pot of a girl, that's the ambassador they send?" He pointed at Elena and frowned.

"At least they haven't welcomed us with pitchforks and torches," said the other speaker, the calmer one. Elena pivoted to watch this second man step down from the elegant carriage. He was the tidiest man Elena had ever seen, cleaner even than the absent báryn. This fellow's beard wasn't long and dense, like the doctor's, but trimmed to fit his chin as neatly as a stocking fits a foot. His hair was clipped and silvered. Against the starched whiteness of his shirt climbed a row of ivory studs.

Elena knew at once that the visitor was the Tsar of All the Russias. He could be no other. She gave a curtsey as best she could.

"Up from your knees, child," he ordered her. "Adoration only gives one splinters." His accent was softly bruised, perhaps from a lifetime at court. She could but obey.

The ghostly conductor came no nearer. "Do you think the wretched of this village might be sending a mere daughter as a decoy and a diversion while they summon an ambush?"

Mere daughter, thought Elena. But what else was she?

Mere is an interesting word. A safe one. One can never be less than *mere*. It is someplace to start. For instance, I am a mere storyteller. But who knows what I might accomplish from such a humble platform?

The Tsar inched white gloves off whiter fingers. "Ambush? That would be ambitious of them. I doubt them capable of such a strategy. Though I have not made a study of the subject, I believe peasants come in two varieties. Either they are pokingly direct, or they disappear because they can't find words to say what they want."

Elena found her words just fine. "We have no men left to protest your arrival." She curtseyed again to the Tsar and, for good measure, to the phantom conductor. "By your order, Your Highness, our men have all been hustled away like sheep to the cattle fair. Except for one smelly old man with a white beard."

"By my order." The Tsar, amused, was going to say more. The conductor interrupted him.

"Without help we'll be here at least a few days, maybe a week."

As the conductor stamped his foot on the ground to make his point, several other men appeared, massing upon ladders and ledges at the front of the train. "Sure, we're six able-bodied men. And we work as hard as any illiterate muzhiks. But it will take time."

"We have time," said the Tsar. "We have enough supplies to see us through. You will do whatever it takes."

"I wasn't hired on for this sort of labor," began the conductor. The other attendants began to murmur in agreement.

"You would like an interview with Madame?" The Tsar used a tone that came close to sweetness.

No one answered him.

The conductor spat on the ground. The last of the steam dissolved around him. He was no ghost, just a working man in a blue coat with a dirty yellow kerchief around his neck. He swiveled his jaw as if trying to loosen a wodge of tobacco from under his tongue. Then he spat again. "Very well. But there's nothing doing now, not till the sun is up. We'll get a better look at the size of the job tomorrow."

"It's a blessing that it was still daylight as we approached that trestle bridge," said the Tsar. "We'd all be dead at the bottom of the ravine if you hadn't spied the damage. What's a few days' work with your axes? You are still alive to use them. Celebrate through labor."

He twitched a finger without looking at Elena. "Bring us fresh water in the morning. If you're lying, and if the men in the district are lurking to attack us in our distress, tell them that the Madame in her apartments would not appreciate such an entertainment."

The Tsarina? "I couldn't lie to the Tsar," she told him.

"Admirable policy." With this he retreated into the elegant

carriage and pulled the door shut. Elena heard an ostentatious, well-oiled *click* and the turn of a key in the lock. A little bit of theater. She loved it.

The other men grumped among themselves. But now that the Tsar had given Elena a job for the morning, she knew that they wouldn't dare harm her.

So she wandered toward the conductor. He groused; she listened. After the train had passed through Miersk, it had traveled some versts out of town. Then, slowing down with the effort of climbing a knoll, it had come to a gorge. The conductor had seen how the track curved onto a trestle bridge reduced to a henge of blackened timbers.

The bridge had been hit by lightning. He'd stopped the train just in time.

"Oh, yes," said Elena. "That was this morning. That first bolt. I could tell it had struck something. You could feel the contact from here."

About a third of the trestle was compromised. The supports could give way under strain. The bridge would have to be examined and its bad limbs replaced with new.

"The work starts tomorrow," said the conductor. "If your village can supply a crew of woodsmen to fell trees and strip them, and oxen to haul them into place, we shall make easy work of it."

"If the Tsar hadn't already commandeered all our men, I'm sure they'd be happy to help," replied Elena. "As for oxen, they've moved on to starve elsewhere." This was as tart as she dared to be. The conductor spat once more, nearly in her direction.

The crew turned to caring for their halted iron steed. Elena picked her way along the platform. The carriage to her left was near enough that she could draw tracks with her fingers in the frosty soot, the sooty frost.

Her hand ran across the window frame and onto the glass. She thought she saw another hand on the other side of the glass. Maybe it was just her reflection. But didn't the drape twitch, just now?

She ran to tell Grandmother Onna and Peter Petrovich that the Tsar and his retinue were spending the evening as their accidental guests.

Grandmother Onna wasn't impressed. She'd just come back from scouring the Rudetsky house by lamplight, and her old eyes were sharper than Elena's. She'd found a cupful of oat mash hidden in a tin matchbox, and she shared half with Elena. "The Tsar to his veal, and we to our meal," she said, smacking her lips.

Mamenka's Gift

Elena had always felt like the center of her own world — who doesn't? The world arranged itself around her like petals around the stem of a flower. This way the meadows, that way the woodland. Over here, the báryn's estate, out there, the hills that hug the known world close and imply a world beyond.

Tonight — with the presence of the Tsar hardly a verst away — for the first time Elena felt what it meant to be a subject. To serve as a bit of rude local color, decoration on the edge of someone else's amusing world.

This wasn't a sorry thing to feel. But it was unsettling. Everything new is.

She lay down near her mother's bed. She could sense the emptiness of Alexei's and Luka's mattresses, tied up and stacked on the chest like deadness itself, as if they might never again give off the warm boy smells of her brothers. She felt the drifting sadness of her mother. Natasha Rudina, unmoored, nearly unreachable. She tried to summon the memory of her father, but it was too dark, he wouldn't come to her.

What she lay at the center of tonight: emptiness. Emptiness all around her.

In the morning, Elena heated up some water for her mother and steeped the flakes of powdery oats in a clay cup. Natasha Rudina stirred and opened her eyes but could not sit up. "Who's there?" she called.

"It's me, Mamenka," said Elena. "Your mere daughter."

It was as if her mother couldn't see or hear Elena. "Maxim?" she said.

Maxim was the name of her dead husband. Elena's father.

"Mama." Elena let annoyance mask her worry. "Don't you know where we are in this life?"

"I don't have long," her mother managed to say. "Call him here."

No Maxim. No Luka. No Alexei. Only Elena. "Have some of this oat mash first." She was brusque of tone, gentle of touch.

A spoon, then another. Some liquid dribbled out. Elena caught it and returned it to the parched lips. After the fourth swallow, Mama's eyes closed again. She looked as if she were asleep, but she said one thing more, to the ceiling. "My mother gave the doll to me, and now you should have it."

"Are you talking to me, Mama? To Elena?"

Only silence in return.

There was no tincture or tablet left in the doctor's apothecary to help Mama now. Elena waited until her mother's breath was regular — long shallow swoops, like winds too high up in the air to feel, yet still the high clouds pass by.

She stepped outside so she could hear herself be alive. Her breathing was more like gasping. The sun made a white hole in the blue sky, too sharp to look at directly.

Here comes the doctor, along the rutted road. He had managed to get hold of a cane for one hand and a chair for the other, and he was heading for the train platform. The steps would defeat him. But the Tsar appeared, in close-fitting gloves the color of a dove's breast feathers.

The Tsar lit a cigarette and leaned over the edge of the platform to talk to the doctor. He didn't descend. Well, he was the *Tsar.*

Other women and small children stayed their distance, but Elena drew close. After all, she had already met the man.

She listened. Peter Petrovich was confirming that there were no men to help to repair the trestle bridge. "In my younger days, I might have swung an ax to help. But it would more likely have gone into someone's leg than the trunk of a tree." The doctor laughed; Elena could hear shame in his joke.

The Tsar: "I'm told there is no parallel branch line to which this train can repair. We can't locate an alternate route unless we retreat nearly to Moscow. And we haven't the time. So it seems we must be neighbors until the bridge is fixed."

"We can't be as generous as we would wish. The scrappiness of our own circumstances in these hard times, you know. The general insult of rural life."

"It is a wilding world, is it not," agreed the Tsar. "*C'est la vie.* A train journey that ought to take a day or two lasts a week, what with upheavals, strikes, floods, and lines out of service. But don't concern yourself with us. The train carries its own ovens and supplies, flour and sugar, dried fruit and hothouse flowers, cured meats and salted nuts, wines and cordials and juices of every variety. All we might require is fresh milk and eggs."

"You, too? That's all we require ourselves. But milk and eggs are in short supply in Miersk. Had we any, I'd trade them for something in the way of medicine."

"How sad we have none to spare."

"Anything? A tonic, even morphia to ease the pain? Not my own, I add."

"Ah. *Désolé.* But I am called. I leave you to supervise." Then, to Elena's surprise, the Tsar stepped off the platform to where members of the crew were gathering with ropes and axes. "Gentlemen?" he said to them. They began to stride away, presumably toward the troubled bridge.

When they had gone, Elena said, "A magnificent man."

"Thank you," said the doctor. "I do try to make an impression."

"I mean the Tsar, of course."

The doctor laughed as he scraped and lurched, beginning to retrace his steps. "He's magnificent, all right," managed Peter Petrovich. "A magnificent butler."

"What's a butler?" she cried.

The doctor paused for breath and called over his shoulder to Elena, "A butler is a servant who opens doors for others. But not for us."

"But he left you to supervise."

"I am supervising myself home to my chair and its wife, the little footstool. I decree this to be Supervise Yourself Day."

So Elena felt sadder, but a little more at the center of her own world. Back to normal. A butler might be a novelty, but he wasn't a Tsar.

So few are.

She walked around the train from front to back and then to the front again. It was such a brief train, she could circle it in moments. First the sentinel engine with its funnel smokestack and its iron belfry. Then the tender car, for the carrying of fuel. Next, plain as stale brown bread, the utility carriage and rolling bunk-house, with a row of little windows running high up along each side. A swinging walkway spanned the coupling between the third and fourth carriages.

The last car, the fancy one, was lined up with the station plat-form. It looked like a toy of the sort Alexei had described from the báryn's house, but life-size. Elena admired it even more today. Upon its lacquered evergreen paint glowed gold numbers and some words in a golden foreign script. Wooden slats paneled the sides. The polished copper roof was bowed, and a row of scalloped spikes ran along the center.

The silence of this car seemed a decided policy.

A central door, bolstered with iron braces, was flanked by draped windows. Today none showed a hand on the glass, not even a finger.

"Come along," called Grandmother Onna, out on her morn-ing rounds. "Elena, I have discovered an old bagel from before the Crimean War."

Elena waved the old woman by. Yes, the girl was hungry. But her hunger was curiosity. She wanted to see if a new door on the edge of her world might open to her. After all, a hand, but for glass, had almost touched hers. After all, the butler who blocked the way had walked off with the crew.

She didn't have long to wait. At midmorning the door near the center of the magnificent carriage swung halfway open. A figure looked out.

The shadows were too deep for Elena to make out details, but she was pretty sure it was something that she hadn't seen in some time. A girl her own age.

"Are you going to run away?" asked the girl. "If not, then talk to me quickly, while the others are at their morning devotions, and I am free to disobey them."

The Apple

The girl inched partway into the light. A fold of white serge skirt with blue piping. Showing a length of stockinged calf that would have scandalized the grown-ups. The glamorous newcomer: "Why are you the only child who comes to stare?"

"The few other children are infants, or toddlers at their mothers' aprons."

"How can that be?"

Elena took a breath. This was her private world, after all. Its sorrows belonged to her, they weren't to be aired out like merchandise for examination by the Tsar's family making a tour of the provinces.

She gave a half-answer. "All the older boys in the village, and the men, were rounded up by your Tsar." Too late, she remembered that the man in the trimmed goatee was a butler, not the Tsar; she hurried on. "Our settlement here, it's hardly a village. An outcropping of houses to support our báryn's household and farms, no more than that. But our men and boys were taken away a few days ago, and no one knows where they've gone."

The girl produced an apple from the shadows and crunched into it. Elena's stomach turned with greed. The newcomer continued. "What about the village girls?"

"A few years ago, the other girls my age, older and some younger too, went out to pick berries."

The stranger waited.

Elena continued, "They didn't ever come back."

"Lost their way, I guess?"

Elena hurried past the hard part. "They couldn't. So now there's only me, only me and some runtlings and babies. My older brother was taken away by the soldiers, who also took the celibate village pig."

"Celibate?"

"Ah, there was only the one pig." Grandmother Onna's joke, meant to distract.

"But what happened to those girls?"

Elena held her ground. "I'll tell you another time."

"Who knows if there will be another time? Tell me now. I never get to talk to anyone my own age, and I'm tired of my books."

"Don't you have any sisters or brothers?"

The girl didn't seem to mind that Elena had asked a nervy question herself. "No sisters and no brothers," she replied, taking another big bite, and another. A chunk of apple skin and flesh fell to the floor of the doorway. Elena felt like a dog, wanting to lunge for it, but she stayed herself, and managed to say, "Is the butler your father?"

"Monsieur d'Amboise? No, no, he's a servant."

"Servant? Whose servant?"

"The old witch." The girl twitched her head, indicating someone else in the carriage with her. "She thinks she's praying right now, but actually she's asleep. So I crept forward. How old are you?"

Elena said, "I can't remember. How old are you?"

"The same age as you," said the girl. Elena wasn't sure if the visitor was being saucy or agreeable. "I'm the same size, don't you think?" the newcomer continued. "So perhaps the same age."

"I can't see all of you," Elena pointed out. "You could be stout as a barrel."

"Hardly. I watch my fork and I leave most of my dinner on the plate. I must be trim to appeal to admirers." She sounded disgusted, superior. A little like Luka.

Dinner on a plate. Again, Elena struggled to speak about something other than food. "Do you need to escape the old witch? Do you need someplace to hide?"

"There is no place to *hide*," said the girl. "For the preservation of my virtue, I'm watched by any number of beady hawk eyes. The butler among them. Also Miss Bristol, my governess. But Monsieur d'Amboise is out on an emergency mission with the crew, and Miss Bristol has the vapors. So this is my escape from chaperones. This is as far as I can go." As if to prove it, from inside the carriage a hoarse voice began to cough and carry on in an aggravated *moo*.

"Ekaterina?" demanded the voice. "Where have you slipped to?"

"Bumblebees and bumbershoots, she's back among the living," whispered the girl. Ekaterina. "I must disappear. *J'arrive*," she trilled over her shoulder into the carriage. Then she hurled what was left of her apple toward the dead weeds fringing the tracks.

Diving, Elena caught the apple.

The girl called Ekaterina laughed. Elena would give a lot to be able to toss off a laugh of such loftiness.

As she pulled back into the shadows of the carriage doorway, the visitor said, "What would you want with my half-eaten apple?"

"The half you didn't eat," panted Elena; that's who she was.

So that night Elena cut what was left of the apple in four pieces, and she and Grandmother Onna each had a slice. The third was put aside for her mother, who was dozing, or something like dozing. The fourth quarter was set in a cloth for the doctor.

Grandmother Onna: "It is not the season for apples."

"That train is a magic train," said Elena. "It has a butler in it, and he serves Baba Yaga. She is riding in the carriage. She has a voice like a crow with the croup."

"Yesterday the Tsar, today Baba Yaga. Tomorrow the train will house Saint Nicholas. Let me tell you, if Baba Yaga gave you this apple, it's probably poison. Never eat any magic food, or you must serve the underworld for seven years. Yum, this is good." Grandmother Onna licked her fingertips.

Then she put on her shawl and pulled it tight. "I need to go see how the doctor is faring. I'll bring him his portion. Bar the door when I leave, Elena. With strange men in the village, one can't take any chances."

"There's nothing to steal in here," said Elena.

"You heard me," said Grandmother Onna. "What men might

steal from girls, girls never miss till it's gone. Do I hear you promise to bar the door?"

"Yes."

"Till tomorrow, then. Think about what you would like to ask for, since there are no eggs or milk. I'd accept a saddle of beef without a murmur of complaint." Elena could rarely tell if Grandmother Onna was being amusing or just stewing in the vagueness of old age. She hobbled away into the dark, saying her prayers aloud.

> "Old Saint Nicholas, young Saint Mark,
> Keep me safe in the pesky dark.
> Saint Olga of the High Himalayas,
> Send me a set of cashmere pajamas."

The Porridge

The next morning, Elena loitered in the shadows as the crew assembled with axes, flasks, and coils of rope. The butler carried tiffins of porridge. The smell was substantial and regal. To a hungry child, the aroma of a hot meal can be diverting, can swipe away all conviction. Elena swore she would not shame herself by begging, but she couldn't be sure she could resist that strategy if need be.

When the men were gone, Elena headed for the platform. Ekaterina waited for her in the doorway. Something unfamiliar organized the girl's expression. Her very eyelashes seemed combed and contented. Elena didn't know the word *privilege*.

Though Elena's chief interest was food, she didn't want to appear greedy. "You're free to come out?" she asked the witch's girl.

"It's a morning for hair-washing," said Ekaterina. "Mine is accomplished. But it's my great-aunt's turn. So with Miss Bristol whipping soapsuds in the china basin and Monsieur d'Amboise off playing woodland hero, I am released from French and English grammar for a while. A relief, *c'est vrai.*"

She stepped forward onto the platform. The sun adored her on all sides. She fanned her hair in the light, drying it further. Longer and somewhat lighter than Elena's, and full of verve. Corn silk dipped in beeswax. It almost hurt to look at.

"I didn't know that Baba Yaga ever washed her hair," said Elena.

"What has that got to do with anything?"

Elena believed that Baba Yaga had rather little hair, so it couldn't take long to wash. "Isn't Baba Yaga the old witch you mentioned?"

"Heavens, no — that was just an expression," said Ekaterina. "I must have been talking about Miss Bristol or my great-aunt. They can both be nasty when they are crossed. Baba Yaga is only a story-book creature."

Here Elena found herself stuck. It seemed a long time since the tragedy of the village daughters. She was out of practice with talking to girls her own age. She didn't remember how much disagreement is considered tolerable in talking to a friend. Still, the term *friendship* didn't apply here, so she dared insist, "You're wrong. Baba Yaga is fatally real."

"She's a storybook character. I even have a book with her in it."

"Show me."

This was a nervy demand. But though she could hardly read, Elena had a hunger to look. After the disaster, the schoolteacher had left for a position in a more populated settlement, taking the village storybook with him.

"Show you?" The rich girl sounded appalled. But apparently she didn't want to risk losing Elena's company, for she admitted,

55

"That's easy enough. It's in my chamber, which is separate from my great-aunt's parlor. I can sneak in and get it."

Ekaterina crossed to the open door of the carriage. Such elegance in how she slipped away into the dark. Your own chamber, thought Elena.

When the girl reappeared, she had a book in her hands.

"Come here and see." She sat on the doorsill of the carriage, patting the floor next to her.

"I mustn't," said Elena.

"What's the harm? There's no one to mind. You can't look at a picture from that far away, nor from upside down. I insist."

She sounds like someone used to getting her own way, thought Elena.

Conscious of the tatters in her shawl and the holes in her stockings, Elena climbed to the station platform but crouched as far from the doorway as she could get. The high-toned girl sighed and came forward. She knelt down opposite Elena so that their knees were almost touching.

"This is a book of Russian legends. I received it as a gift on Saint Nicholas Day."

Ah, gifts, thought Elena, but leaned forward eagerly.

"We want the story of Vasilissa the Fair." The girl turned the pages too quickly, passing other pictures that Elena wanted to look at. "This page always frightens me, but look. Here, the only witch on *this* train. Baba Yaga. Only four inches high. A drawing in a storybook, nothing more."

"Saint Nicholas is in the prayer books, and *he* is real," argued Elena, but she pressed the matter no further. She leaned close.

"I hope you don't have lice."

"I do not." Elena couldn't afford to act offended if she hoped to be thrown some more uneaten rubbish. A flowery, tallowy scent wafted from the carriage. Soaps and lotions. Also the steam of hot water, which can smell like iron. Beneath that moiled an aroma of wheat porridge and perhaps some fruit stewed with cinnamon.

Her stomach announced itself. She was mortified. That creak of hunger, another kind of thunder.

The girl asked, "How do you know you don't have lice?"

Elena puzzled to answer in wit rather than anger. "Lice would find little reward in my hair. They hop elsewhere." She examined the page with greedy eyes. "Baba Yaga wouldn't be a sensible home for lice, either," she said, pointing to the balding scalp of the famous old witch.

Oh, but what a portrait. The hag flew through the forest in something of a lurch. Her carriage was a narrow wooden bucket. She leaned forward, swinging a stout stake, hitting the ground with it to propel herself along.

As a man might pilot a small craft by nudging his pole against the bottom of the lake, thought Elena. But men have no magic spell to cry out when their raft unsettles.

If Baba Yaga had come along to save the drowning. *If, if.*

The fragrant, glossy girl: "She flies in a mortar. And the pole is a pestle. Like for grinding herbs."

"Everyone knows that. Oh, but look at her vicious eyes. She's the worst witch in all the Russias. Even were I to starve to death, I wouldn't ask her for a lump of bread. Or for a little cup of wheat porridge." Elena paused, sniffing the air. "Or stewed fruit with cinnamon."

"I hate wheat porridge. Miss Bristol knows that. She served

some this morning anyway. I scowled at her. I won't give her the satisfaction of watching me take a single bite. She said I'll have to do triple the number of pages of French translation today unless I eat it, but I just can't."

Elena couldn't stop herself. "What did you do with your portion?"

"I left it to turn to stone on the table. And there it still is."

The clearing fell silent. Someplace, someone was doing something. A chunk of an ax on a tree trunk, a command of a mother to a disobedient child. Wind tousled the bare branches at the tops of the eternal forest. A small militia of common wrens stormed a bush for berries and found none; most of the wrens disappeared. One stayed behind, lost in thought or maybe curious about humans. Curious to hear what the peasant girl would say next.

Slowly Elena brought out her thought in words: "I'll eat it for you."

"Would you?" Ekaterina turned her head and looked at Elena. Their eyes were close. They both had green-brown eyes, deep water in a working well. I don't know if they saw the similarities at once. You can, because I'm telling you.

Ekaterina said, "You're not trying to help me out. You're just greedy, aren't you?"

"I'm both," said Elena. "Also," she added, "I'm truthful."

This made Ekaterina laugh. "Take my book and I'll fetch the horrid muck."

It was frightening to hold Baba Yaga on her lap. So Elena closed the book. She half believed that Baba Yaga might emerge from the picture, right here in Miersk.

In a moment Ekaterina was back with a bowl and a spoon. There was no way for Elena to bring the porridge home to her mother. She had either to eat it or to let it go to waste. A cramp of guilt gripped her as she swallowed the slippery sweetness of it.

When she was done, she licked the bowl as far as her tongue would reach.

"You would not meet with approval in *la salle à manger de ma tante*," said Ekaterina.

Elena didn't know French, but she understood dismissal. "What are the other pictures like?"

They peered through the rest of the volume. The pictures showed figures frozen in a bookish world as foreign as it was familiar. Forests and pink skies, birch groves, lunar light upon snow. Magnificent palaces and crisply neat izbas. A Firebird here, a dragon there, and Baba Yaga's hut, standing on two giant chicken legs.

All too soon, though, a voice came from inside the railway carriage. It was a word Elena did not recognize. "Yes, Miss Bristol," replied Ekaterina. "I am coming."

"What did she say?"

"She called me 'Cat.' It is a word in English." As it happened, a starving local cat was sitting not far away, twitching its whiskers at the ghost of wheat porridge. "Cat," said Ekaterina, pointing at it.

"Why are you called that?"

"Cat," called Miss Bristol again, more fiercely.

"She calls me that because it sounds like part of my name. Ekaterina. *Cat.*"

Elena tried it. "Cat. Cat." She waited for Cat to ask what *her* name was.

"You'd better go," said Ekaterina, said Cat. "You can't have the book, though. It's mine."

"I don't want it. I don't want to have a picture of Baba Yaga in my home. It might attract the real Baba Yaga in the middle of the night."

The other girl stood up and began to hasten a brush through her hair. "You are some superstitious turnip. There is no real Baba Yaga. That's only a story."

"You might have your own chamber and you might have a book," said Elena, "but you don't . . ." She was going to say, "You don't know a thing about the real world," but she didn't want to offend this strange girl. She also wanted more food if she could get it.

She just let the sentence trail off.

Ekaterina twisted her hair upon her head and plunged a comb at a wrong angle. It looked as if she had gotten her head caught in a windstorm. Elena laughed.

Cat: "Why are you snorting like a little celibate pig?"

"I'll see you tomorrow, I hope. Cat."

"All right. We're not going anywhere in a hurry." The girl brushed invisible lint off her forest-murmurs skirt. "Do you have a name, by the way, or are you just Peasant Child?"

"Yes," said Elena. "I have a name. Good-bye."

Pay Attention Day

That morning, what gnawed at Elena wasn't hunger but shame. She'd been too distracted by the drama of book illustrations to ask for some food for her mother. So she stumbled along the edges of her world. She looked for nettles for soup, borage, mushrooms. Nothing. Only twigs for soup, and old filthy snow.

Odd, don't you think, how the hunger of children is so much more affecting to consider than the hunger of a more elderly member of the human family? When the elderly are so much more likely to be humble, loyal, devout? But enough about me.

Elena found the hut empty but for her sleeping mother, who lay on her side. Such a look on her face, as if she were turning to candle wax. Under the blankets, she'd drawn her knees up. Only the rising and sinking of the blanket showed that her mother was still alive, still breathing.

"Can you even hear me anymore?" asked Elena.

Elena pulled the curtains wide. She got the matryoshka and opened it. The great mother's first offspring, who was also a mother, came out. Next emerged mothers three, four, and five. Then the last of the mothers, the size of Elena's thumb.

She shook out the seventh doll. This one was a baby, in clean white swaddle. Eyes closed, smiling. It must be dreaming of breakfast, with all those mothers nearby.

Elena tried to tuck the baby doll into her mother's hand, but the hand had gone crooked and wouldn't take it.

She sat there at the base of the motherland plateau, looking up and down from the headlands to the foothills. There was no play to invent here. She sat matching her breath to her mother's, one at a time. The dolls held their breath.

The door opened. The doctor and his cane, poking.

Elena fit the dolls together and slipped them into her apron pocket. "I'm glad you've come. I've had nothing to feed her today, not a scrap."

The doctor hobbled over, grunting. He felt her pulse. "Unlike me, she seems to be in no pain."

"She's getting worse, isn't she?"

Peter Petrovich Penkin put his head to one side as if trying to shake the right words into place. "There isn't much worse she can get now. You understand this, I think."

Elena's words came out *chock-chock,* iron leaves off a sterile tree. "I had a bowl of porridge." Hatefully: "The girl on the train gave it to me."

"It was right you ate it. Your mother would have insisted you did, and she'd have taken none of it even if she were able." From a pocket the doctor fished a small square of paper. He unwrapped it.

Inside, look, some wet tea grounds. "I'll heat this up again and see if I can get your mother to sip something."

As he fussed about the house, he began to cry. It was horrible to see a man cry. Elena thought she should leave. But where could she go? She sat stiffly upon her stool and looked at the ikon. We need Saint Nicholas, we have a horse doctor.

Peter Petrovich blew his nose. If that noise didn't wake Natasha Rudina, only the last trumpet would get through. He said to the girl, "When your mother is gone, you and Alexei and Luka will come and live with me."

She had no reply for this. Alexei was in Moscow with the báryn's family, and who knew where Luka was?

Peter Petrovich: "Did you hear what I said?"

"Is there really a witch named Baba Yaga?"

"If I ever meet her, I will ask her if she is real. But listen. I declare this Pay Attention Day. I am telling you about something else. About what happens next."

"Cat said Baba Yaga was only in storybooks."

"Cat?"

"The girl on the train. She has a great-aunt, and a governess, and a butler. She has a book with pictures of Baba Yaga in it. But she says Baba Yaga is pretend."

"Moscow girls know Moscow facts, and rural girls know something different. You need to stop talking nonsense and listen to me."

"Who are you to scold me?"

"Dr. Nobody, at your service."

Grandmother Onna came in then, blowing on her hands. "How is our martyr to poverty tonight?" she asked the doctor.

"Which one?" he replied, which made the old woman angry.

"Your soul of goodness betrays your common sense. We should attack that train. We should break its windows and climb inside. We should find ourselves something to eat. It isn't fair."

"No need for violence. They should offer. They can see we are starving."

"They aren't looking our way," she snapped.

"Is Baba Yaga real?" asked Elena. "The girl on the train says she isn't."

"Stop your nonsense." Grandmother Onna in a rage. "You give me kinks in my patience."

The doctor picked up his cane. "You heard me, Elena. You will have a home with me when the time comes."

"Have you forgotten? I am going to Moscow to plead with the Tsar," she reminded him. "The real Tsar, not some butler."

"You've spouted too much nonsense as it is. Pay Attention Day," he snapped. "I forbid that."

"Pay Attention Day yourself." Yelling at him. "You're not my father or my mother, or even one of my stupid brothers. Go jump in the well." She picked up the broom. There wasn't much straw in it to be threatening with.

"Save room in the well for me, I'm right behind you," said Grandmother Onna to the doctor as they both got ready to leave. To the girl, she said, "I'll return when you've come to your senses, if I haven't died first."

Everyone angry at everyone else. Through the commotion, Mama descended ever more steeply into sunless caverns of sleep.

The Ghostly Daughters of Miersk

Elena didn't dare leave the hut until the doctor came in the afternoon to sit with her mother and read the psalms of heaven aloud. It was heavenly to escape.

"The old lizard is having her beauty rest," said Cat in a false whisper. "As if it could help."

"It's Pay Attention Day," said Elena. "I truly, *truly* need some bread."

"I can't distribute our food. What if we run out, here in Nowhere Forest?"

"I don't know. But we have nothing to eat, and my mother is very sick."

"Well, even if we could spare something, I can't just give it away for nothing. That would be charity, and demeaning to you. You must work for your food."

Alexei was a houseboy picking up things for the báryn's son, whose legs wouldn't hold him up. At least Alexei got fed. Elena stared at the girl. "What can I do for you?" Her tone is hard to characterize, except to say it wasn't lilting.

Cat put a finger to her lip to chew her nail. "I suppose you could brush my hair. Miss Bristol usually puts it up for me, but she's malingering in her cabin with *Wuthering Heights* and a cup of spiced tea. She blames the bad air of the provinces for her congestion."

"I don't know how to brush hair, really."

"I can tell." Cat produced a hairbrush and showed her how. "Start up here, and then long straight strokes, pulling away from my shoulders. Ow."

Elena practiced. She learned how to pull Cat's hair up top and arrange it with the comb. "Underneath, your hair is darker," she said. "More like mine."

"Fancy that," said Cat with a yawn. She disappeared into the carriage and returned carrying a looking-glass with a shiny engraved handle. "Not dreadful," she said, examining her locks. "For a first try."

"May I look?" asked Elena. She'd never seen herself in a mirror before, only the shadowy silhouette against window glass. "I'm not so bad."

"You could do with a good scrub. Several good scrubs in a row."

"That day will never come. But when the weather warms up, we sometimes bathe in the stream. If there is a stream this year. What do you call your great-aunt?"

"Her name is Madame Sophia Borisovna Orlova, but I call her *tante* Sophia. *Tante* means 'aunt' in French."

Elena tried it out. "*Tante* Sophia."

But here were the butler and his crew, returning earlier than usual that day. Monsieur d'Amboise wasn't happy to see Cat sitting on the floorboards like a common peasant. He foraged for a blanket upon which he insisted Cat sit.

Cat introduced Monsieur d'Amboise to Elena. He didn't say hello to Elena and answered Cat in French.

"That's rude," said Cat. "Don't speak over the girl's head."

The butler, in Russian with a French accent: "You are taking advantage of this situation, Miss Ekaterina. Have you worn your worthy governess to the bone?"

"Miss Bristol is busy keeping my great-aunt diverted. They are playing cards. They sent me outside for being coltish."

"It won't be long now. We finished the bracing today. Luckily the steel beams don't seem to be damaged. Hoisting them up with ropes was some heavy labor, believe me. All that remains is to secure the tracks to their footing. Don't give me that look. The conductor will test the supports before allowing the train to venture across. Now you should come inside."

"But I am learning why this child is the only girl in the village."

"I'm too tired to argue," said Monsieur d'Amboise. "You will be ready to sit down with your aunt when I call you." He moved past Elena without acknowledging her. Burrs and shreds of splintered logs clung to his smooth leggings. He smelled of normal sweat and of rope and grease, but there was a hint of cologne there, too.

"You were explaining why you have no companions of your own age," said Cat.

"Why do you care?" asked Elena.

"Look," said the visitor. "Do you see me surrounded by schoolmates and sisters and girl cousins? No, you do not. Great-Aunt

67

Sophia summoned me from my boarding school in London, where I actually have *friends*. Monsieur d'Amboise chaperoned Miss Bristol and me across the English Channel to Paris. There we were joined by my *tante* and traveled to Moscow. From there we engaged this private train, to make an *impression*, don't you see, as we approach Saint Petersburg. I've had nothing but adult company for weeks and *weeks*. I've been like a pretend adult, paralyzed in right behavior. Here I finally find an accidental playground. Such relief. A week frozen in time between my leaving school and all the festivities and challenges awaiting me. And, and, and . . . *is* there a supply of girls to play with, to sing with? Or race, or dance, or gossip? No. All I get is one stiff-faced, hollow-eyed, knock-kneed skeleton in a patched skirt."

"How would you know what my knees are like? I don't fling them around for anyone to see. And my eyes are not hollow." Elena would have liked to burst into tears just then, to prove it, but pride forbade her.

"I'm sorry," said Cat. "Forgive me." She didn't sound sorry.

"You have friends at *school*. I have only two brothers. One of them is in domestic service as a houseboy, and the other has been kidnapped by soldiers. I have no friends and no chance for friends."

"But why not? You keep hinting, you keep halting." Cat looked as if she were going to hit Elena.

So Elena told her. The whole thing. Two years earlier. How the disaster began, with the boys in the village being sent up to the hills to gather wood. Luka and Alexei among them that day.

How one of the girls noticed that a billy goat, who had gotten loose and tramped through a marshy lowlands to a dry hillock, an island, and had managed to pick his way back, lingonberry juice staining his pelt.

Lingonberries? So early in the year? Well, better than nothing. All the girls in Miersk gathered baskets. Sloshed their way across the mud to harvest what they could, and who cared if it was out of season?

All the girls except Elena, for her mother was nearly ready to deliver the new baby. Finally, someone for Elena to be big sister to. Elena had to tend her mother, for her time was almost near, and Papa was at work on the estate.

How the girls promised they would share lingonberries when they got back. But they never got back.

You see, up on the estate, the báryn had noticed his fields drying. He'd decided to open some sluices at the edge of his ornamental lake, to drain off some reserve into a channel that could bring it nearer to the rye. But when the workers inched open the floodgates for a controlled trickle, the wood proved to have rotted and couldn't hold. The whole barrier collapsed.

The lake drained in a gargling rush. It gathered force as it coursed downhill through narrowing channels. The panels arranged to direct a slight flow toward the fields couldn't withstand a torrent. They were slapped akimbo, like this, *pffft, pffft,* one after the other. So the water sought a place it could settle, lower down, and that was the swampy muckland near Miersk. Through which girls loaded with lingonberries were making their way home. Mired in unseasonable mud even before the deluge.

"And the girls . . . drowned?"

"Not all at once. Not at first," said Elena. She spoke out the tragedy roughly now, like dealing out cards, *slap slap.* "Up at the estate, my father was nearest the broken floodgate. He didn't know about the goat and the lingonberries, but he had a mind for worry. He ran home to Miersk, outpacing the other workers. Heard the cries of the girls — few of them could swim. Dragged an old raft to the rising waters. Kept pulling waterlogged bodies onto the raft in the hope that someone might be alive. Maybe he dove and hit his head on a stone. By the time the other men had arrived, he was gone too, as well as the girls. My other friends." The ghostly daughters of Miersk.

And this, though she didn't say it, was the beginning of her mother's decline. In Natasha Rudina's shock, the baby came early. That infant girl had nursed at first, but she hadn't strengthened. She was laid in the paupers' field.

The goat couldn't be recaptured and was eaten by a wolf, or something.

That's where Elena stopped. She didn't say that her mother was ready to follow her husband and youngest child to the village of the anonymous dead beyond the churchyard. There was a limit to how much could be said.

"Wait here," said Cat, and disappeared into the cabin.

Elena heard drawers opening. Madame Sophia interviewing Miss Bristol on the weather. Monsieur d'Amboise reporting on the day's progress in bridge repair. At least that is what Elena assumed they were saying. They spoke in Russian mostly, but time and again slipped into English or French almost as if they weren't paying attention to their own words.

When Cat returned, she had a bundle in her hands. "Here," she said. It was a hard cheese but still good; and three brown rolls; and a pot of some sort of jam.

"I don't want you to get in trouble," said Elena, reaching for it anyway.

"They won't notice this, at least not right away." Cat paused. "I'm sure you would rather have your father back and your drowned friends. Cheese and bread is sour comfort, no substitute . . ."

"My father would give me cheese and bread if he could," said Elena, but that made no sense. She stopped talking. She knew she ought to add, "Thank you." More words that wouldn't quite come. She wondered if she should curtsey to Cat, but that seemed false. Cat didn't notice; she'd turned to run to her obligations.

Elena walked home slowly. She'd been paid for the story of all those deaths with bread. It seemed wrong, even unholy, that the bread, that evening, tasted so wonderful.

The Egg

Grandmother Onna gobbled down half of one of the rolls and some cheese. Peter Petrovich Penkin had some. Natasha Rudina couldn't take any in. Elena ate the rest. "If they think that throwing us some rolls and a cheese will quiet us," soused the old woman, "they're right. But only until we get hungry again."

That night Elena discovered that when you fill up your stomach after a long emptiness, it still hurts. Just in a different way. Whimpering in her sleep, she woke herself up. A few feet away, Grandmother Onna was resting on Luka's mattress, and she heard Elena's distress. "What is it, child?" she whispered.

"Why are you staying overnight?" asked the girl.

"I don't want you to be alone if . . . if . . . if you're alone."

That was too mixed up for Elena to understand. In her mind were waters and bread, and friends, and a father. But as she tried to arrange words to enquire, everything rearranged, became ordinary, not worth saying.

"The morning is wiser than the night, my dear," said the old woman. "Hush now, or you'll wake your mother."

If only I could, thought Elena. She lapsed into a cold, characterless sleep.

Is the morning wiser than the night, as the old saying has it? In the morning, Elena remembered that her mother had given her the matryoshka. Before walking to the train, Elena slipped the doll into her apron pocket.

She felt a new determination. The train would leave soon, get somewhere else before long. It could restock on supplies there. If Cat were anything like a friend, she might leave some food behind. Elena would pay for it by giving Cat the matryoshka.

Was Cat a friend? If so, maybe Cat would ask the Tsar to release Luka and the grown-up men from Miersk. For, despite her bravado, Elena couldn't leave her mother now. Not like this.

She neared the station. The train had uncoupled, and the engine was returning from a short run. Perhaps to keep its parts from seizing up like the doctor's legs, thought Elena. She watched the crew reattach the back two carriages. As soon as Cat appeared, Elena pressed her request. She explained about the galloping hunger that cursed Miersk.

Cat regarded the doll Elena had thrust in her hands, Cat's expression quizzical, not quite a sneer. She said, "Miersk isn't the only place with crop failure. Your mild winters and dry summers? Ever since we began this trip, trouble is all we've heard about. All down the line. *Everyone* is suffering."

"I'm giving you my mother's doll," said Elena. "Please. We need more of your supplies."

"Aren't we a bit beyond dolls?" said Cat. "You're so full of fancy, with your tales of Baba Yaga and Saint Nicholas and your enchanted brooms and such." She wagged the doll in the air, an exhibit of Elena's naïveté.

"If you won't help, just say so. I'll go to the Tsar myself, after my mother dies. And when I get to Moscow, I'll tell the Tsar the truth about our suffering and your stinginess. If I meet up with Baba Yaga on the way, I'll tell her the truth, too. That's all that poor people own, the truth."

"Well, you'd better carry your truth in the right direction. For your information, the Tsar isn't even in Moscow. He's in Saint Petersburg. That's why this private train is headed north. Didn't you know?"

"The Tsar doesn't inform me as to his whereabouts."

"I can't *imagine* why not." Maybe Cat regretted her gibe at Elena, or maybe she liked lording it over the girl. She went on in a blasé manner. "The Tsar is having a *ball* to celebrate the availability of some remote cousin, his godson, to marry. It's called a Festival of All the Russias. In his godson's honor. That's why I've been hauled all the way from London: because Madame Sophia is a distant friend of the court. Along with several hundred other girls, I'm to be presented to the young princeling."

Elena thought, I might have gone all the way to Moscow only to find the Tsar was at the other end of the country. I owe Cat for this information, at least.

Her irritation began to dissolve. "You are presented at court — as a present?"

Cat looked guarded and angry. "No. I am *not* the present. At least I don't want to be the present. I shall be polite but chilly and hope he doesn't much like the look of me. I don't want to be engaged to be married."

"You're too young for that, surely."

"At thirteen, not a bit too young to be betrothed, and neither are you. No, I'm going simply because my great-aunt insists."

"What do your parents think?"

This was the first time Elena had dared ask about Cat's parents. But Cat just waved her hand as if dismissing flies. "They are in Venice, I think. Or Buenos Aires. Or, let's see . . . Manhattan? Vienna? Take a guess. They sent a wire to approve my traveling with my great-aunt."

"What are they doing in those places?"

"I don't know, really. Going from here to there. Hotels and restaurants. Dinners at the Russian ambassador's mansion. Taking a cruise, taking the waters, taking a bath. Taking it seriously, though it seems to me quite a dreary life."

To Elena, Manhattan was more fantastic than the country at the back of the moon. "You'd better watch out, Cat, or you'll find yourself being a present to the Tsar's godson."

"No, no. We brought an actual present to leave with him. My *tante* had it made especially to her design." Cat looked this way and that. "Would you like to see it?"

Elena would rather have seen several loaves of fresh bread, but she was working up to that. Cat hadn't rejected the matryoshka as a trade. "Yes."

"It's a perfect time. My great-aunt is having her toenails trimmed by Miss Bristol. A long operation involving a footbath with scented oils. They won't notice."

"Is Monsieur d'Amboise out on his campaign to rebuild the bridge?"

"Not today. The men are having a day off, I think. But he's up in the front, busy with the engineers. Wait here."

As if I'd follow you into that cavern of luxury, thought Elena.

In a few moments, on tiptoe, Cat returned. She'd put on a hip-length lambswool jacket against the cold. She had left the matry-oshka inside, Elena noticed — good, the start of a bargain for food. Or perhaps she'd just put it down so she could carry the gift. She held a wooden box carved with flourishes of flowers, stems, and leaves.

Cat said, "Madame Sophia had this made in London. It's fragile and valuable. I'm not supposed to know that my great-aunt hides this box under her bed. She sleeps with it there, for safekeeping. But she's too stout to kneel down and check on it. Since I can't give you all the food in the train as you ask, and I can't pester the Tsar with petty complaints, I'll show you this instead. A compensation."

Elena didn't intend to take this as Cat's final answer, but she was too curious to argue.

Cat turned a small key in the box. The lid lifted with ease, a backward hush. A smell of faraway places. "Cedar and sandal-wood," said Cat. "Draw closer. I don't dare show this outside in the sunlight. Come, where's the harm?"

Elena sank to the station platform, nearer the door of the train than she'd been before. Inside the box were folds of patterned silk, blue and gold swirls. "I've never seen such fabric."

"Cloth from Florence. But that isn't the gift." Cat unfolded the top layers of the cloth. A dull gleam beneath. She put her hands

76

into the box, as gently as one might lift a baby out of a cradle, and she pulled the gift into the light.

It was an egg. An artist's artificial egg. It took both hands to hold. About the size of two hands clasped together. It could cradle in your arm like a small cozy hen. Made of porcelain, Elena guessed and, if so, quite fragile indeed.

"Fabergé," said Cat. "That's the artist's name. Madame Sophia directed the design. She had it made in his London studio rather than in his main salon in Saint Petersburg so word wouldn't slip out to his other customers and give them ideas. She wants it to be a surprise and to attract the Tsar's attention. He loves this kind of thing. It's a music box, too. It comes with a stand that plays a lullaby."

"Hold it up so I can see it," said Elena.

"No, I don't dare. No one must know it is here. If you want to see it better, sit next to me in the doorway."

Elena hesitated.

"It's all right. They're only at the second toe. It'll be a long time yet."

So Elena stepped over the threshold, across the space between the platform and the train. Such a small step, across that crack. Into a vestibule that crossed the car to the opposite side. She squatted upon the matting to see the egg.

The thing was even more fabulous close up. Painted plaster furbelows, like curling bits of ribbon, were applied to the outside. Jewels bulged from the sides. The skin of the shell was painted rosy pink and pale grey and a luminous, silly yellow that made Elena want to laugh. Every inch of the shell of the distorted globe was covered in design.

Even more wonderful, though, was the interior.

Three different openings were cut into the egg. They were like windows. You could see one after the other if you carefully spun the egg about. A theater in an egg.

Inside were carved scenes, like tiny paintings but alive in porcelain. You might run your finger in and feel the edges of things if you dared. Elena didn't dare. She peered close, though. "Look," she said. "Baba Yaga."

There she was, a tiny image of the famous old witch. She was staring out the window of her house on chicken legs. She didn't look ancient and bony as in Cat's storybook. She looked serious and bright and strong and dangerous. Her house had the teensiest eaves, all in scarlet, with the head of a dragon carved onto the roof beam. A dark forest was painted onto the curved wall behind the house. Above the treetops, a sun glowed in gold leaf, its identical flames like the petals of a sunflower.

"What else?" Elena, hungrier to see than she'd ever been to eat, or that was how it felt just now.

Cat turned the ovoid globe. The next opening showed the magic Firebird flying at midnight. A full moon on the back wall of this niche was painted in silver leaf, and it made the black sky look soft as old paper. The Firebird was a jeweled figurine in red and golden flames. The artist had put two birch trees on either side of the clearing, as if the Firebird were flying just behind them. Between them a metal thread was strung, holding up the extended wings of the magic bird. Its lovely feet trailed behind it, sparky twigs.

"This is the very egg of *truth*." Elena remembered to keep her voice low. In her excitement she forgot not to let their shoulders touch, but Cat didn't seem to notice. "What else?"

Cat turned and grinned. "How could any princeling care about me with this to admire? I'll wind it up, and as the music casts its charm, I'll slink off back to my school." She revolved the egg one more time, a third of the way, to the final opening.

In this window was a creature Elena didn't know from the legends of Russia. A huge albino dragon hunched on a plain glistening with new snow. How did the artist *do* that? The dragon's eyes were mere slits. Behind its head was a blue circle near the horizon, a moon or a frozen sun, either rising or setting, slightly blobby. "I don't know who this is."

"An ice-dragon, I guess," said Cat. "Whatever story that's from, it's not in my book."

"Well, if you ever needed proof that Baba Yaga exists," said Elena, pointing at the egg, "there you are. How could the artist know to make it so true?"

"The artist made what my great-aunt told him. That's all."

Elena didn't want to argue. The common matryoshka must seem pretty shabby to Cat. Elena wanted to ask for it back. "You'd better put this thing away. But would you wind up the music part so I can hear it, just once?"

"And let the whole village know about it? Are you mad?"

Just then, from inside the cabin, a shriek accompanied by a wail. The voice of Miss Bristol. "Oh my. Good heavens."

"You clot!" cried the voice that Elena had come to identify as that of Great-Aunt Sophia. "You are trying to kill me."

"Miss Ekaterina, come quickly," cried Miss Bristol. "Bring a towel."

"Child, save me from this murderess!" insisted Great-Aunt Sophia.

Cat had turned pale. She went to thrust the egg into Elena's hands and leap up, but Elena reared back, her palms up in the air. "I can't touch that, I'll ruin it. I'll dirty it. I'll drop it. I'll give it lice."

"She's stabbed me with her scissors. I'm dying." For a dying woman, the great-aunt had a voice that was full of vigor.

"It's just a little blood," insisted Miss Bristol. "Oh, my smelling salts . . ."

"Don't you dare faint at the sight of blood, or I'll stab *you* with the scissors."

A loud *clunk*. Apparently Miss Bristol had disobeyed her employer and collapsed upon the floor.

"Open the box," hissed Cat. "I can't run in there with this in my arms."

Elena fumbled at the key to the lid. The lock jammed, and the key hung at a funny angle. It wouldn't turn.

"Child!" bellowed the great-aunt.

"Oh, *merde*. I'm coming, *tante* Sophia." Gently Cat set the egg on the sisal matting that covered the floor of the entranceway. She was up on her feet, and Elena was gathering her skirts and preparing to leave, when the disaster happened.

Yesterday had been Pay Attention Day. Today Elena had paid too little attention, and the engine jerked, causing a shudder to travel through the train.

Despite the porcelain bits and jewels appended to its outside, the egg began to roll. Not in the direction of Elena, or she'd have caught it. In the other direction. Only then did Elena notice that the door on the far side of the entranceway was also open. The egg was making a break for it — lurching to escape out the opposite door.

"Cat." Elena, venturing forward on hands and knees, pointing.

Cat turned and saw with horror that the egg was trembling on the doorsill. Beyond, the village was beginning to slide by. Cat dove through the air and grabbed the egg as if it were the ball in a game of scrimmage, on the fields of some boarding school in London. With both arms, she clutched it to her breast, and ducked her head down to protect it further.

Then she disappeared out the open doorway, an acrobat in a somersault, rolling. Leaving Elena kneeling on the sisal mat, in her place.

Next.

I'VE HEARD IT SAID THAT THERE ARE ONLY TWO KINDS of stories.

One type of story is when the hero goes on a voyage.

One of the few times I ever met the Tsar's children, they were all nattering about a play they'd recently seen in a London pantomime, of children flying off from their nursery beds to a fabulous island called Neverland. Who doesn't like going on a little journey?

All of those stories end with people coming home.

Then there is the second type of story. This is the type when a mysterious stranger comes to town and changes everything for everyone. It could be a fairy godmother coming uninvited to a christening with a nasty surprise as a gift. It could be Elijah coming in disguise to deliver a blessing. It could be, oh, an anarchist with a secret past and a bomb in his viola case.

The person who comes from afar usually goes away, too. Elijah never stays to rent the dacha next door, the anarchist often blows himself up by accident, et cetera.

So far, *this* story I'm writing out for you has been about a stranger coming to town. That girl who calls herself Cat. Quite by accident, and out of boredom, she's just gotten herself and her peasant friend Elena into trouble. She's changed everything. What happens next?

When we last saw them, the train was moving. One girl was not on the train, but another one was. So perhaps this story I'm telling is both kinds at once: a stranger comes to town *and* a hero goes on a journey.

Not that Cat is a mysterious stranger. She's just an ungrateful child. So far.

And Elena as a hero? A single match cannot light a landscape. Still, watch her. She's a simple child but a serious one.

All but forgotten in my tower, I thought: In the absence of heroes, we might as well watch children. I studied with my blind eye how my imprisonment had come to pass. My fate was sealed on the day those two girls changed places.

PART · TWO

IRON HORSE,
CHICKEN HOUSE

Two Girls Misplaced

Elena Rudina lunged toward the open door, as if she might be able to grab Cat by the ankles and haul her back inside the compartment. Too late — Cat was already well beyond reach.

Elena craned to the right, looking beyond the end of the train. She could see skirts and sashes and suddenly unruly hair: Cat was rolling and flopping down the embankment on the far side of the tracks like a life-size puppet. When the train obeyed some law of geometry having to do with curves and angles, Elena saw only the bone-grey woods and a covey of pin-tailed snipe.

For her part, as she fell, Cat sensed the train sliding forward like a carpet being pulled out from under her. If she'd tossed the porcelain egg aside, she would have been able to scramble to her feet, to grab hold, pull herself up. But Cat had the egg cradled in her arms, hoping it hadn't gotten smashed. She couldn't endanger it now in order to regain the train.

She is at least consistent.

When she could draw breath again, Cat fumbled to her knees. The carriage was moving only at the rate of a stroll. She could hail the conductor. But the train gave a great whistle and accelerated just as Cat screamed, and no one heard her voice — not even herself.

The final car on the train, with its little balcony where she had sometimes liked to stand and watch the forest pass in a swoosh — it grew smaller. Disappeared. Nothing left but clouds of smoke and steam. They were like theater curtains about to pull apart, to Cat's mounting dread. Exposing a world turned peculiar about her, a world unlikely and unlikable.

Trapped

In the train, Elena was beside herself. Her throat was locked, and her fingers turned to stone. She had barely ever been in a farm wagon. This iron horse moved with a drive that seemed both animal and industrial.

She was glad that she was near the open door, for she was able to stick her chin out and throw up without making too much of a mess. No one heard her. The whistle of the train sounded just as she was making those unlovely noises.

When she was done, and the whistle left off and a new kind of hustling silence grew in its place, she managed to get to her knees. A voice raked the vestibule from the rear of the carriage. "Ekaterina, *are* you there? *Why* aren't you coming? Monsieur d'Amboise must be engaged or he'd have closed and locked those doors; I can feel the draft. Come at once. Miss Bristol needs a hot towel to her forehead, and my feet are submerged in bath salts. Child, *j'insiste.*"

Elena let out a wordless throttle of a cry.

"Yes, I know we've started up again, I can feel it! Are you indisposed? Travel tummy again? Oh, what indignities the saints and demons march upon me. Well, take care of yourself, *ma chérie,* and when you are cleaned up, come in. It does feel good to be off and away, at last."

Elena lurched to the doorway. Best to tell the old woman what had happened, and let her shriek in alarm and arrange a correction. In the wall of the crosswise vestibule, through a door swinging to and fro on a hinge that went both ways, Elena caught narrowing and widening glimpses of the parlor. Upon the carpet sprawled a pale, drawn woman — Miss Bristol, to be sure — a tumble of grey skirting with high-buttoned shoes sticking out. Laid out senseless.

From this angle, the look of a faint wasn't different from the look of death. Elena was minded of how she was racing away from her mother. She rushed a hand to her chin to catch vomit should it spill again. She turned back from the parlor chamber.

Beyond the transept vestibule where the girls had changed places, Elena found a narrow corridor. It skirted the far edge of the carriage, against the windows, running forward to the other cars. Four doors opened off this passage, and one of those doors stood ajar. Some luck at last. This was clearly Cat's chamber, for her clothes were everywhere a mess. The precious storybook slid on the floor, the matryoshka was tossed upon a daybed. In the corner stood a copper sink built into the wall, so Elena rinsed out her mouth.

Even the water from the tap tasted rich.

As she was spitting into the basin, she heard footsteps hurrying along the passage from the utility car ahead. Monsieur d'Amboise's voice said something in French, and he closed the chamber door.

He must have thought she was Cat. He was giving her some privacy. He followed the plaints of Great-Aunt Sophia, and his voice was soothing. The old lady seemed to calm down.

What to do, what to do!

Elena pulled aside the drapes hung at the window. Bars fastened against the glass would prevent her from climbing out and escaping that way. The world slipped by. After a few moments, after a final field with three abandoned heaps of last year's bad rye, she saw no more evidence of Miersk. Elena was already farther from home than she'd ever been before.

If she told the great-aunt and the butler and the governess what had happened, they'd have to stop the train and go backward. But what if they had Elena arrested? What if they thought she had *pushed* Cat out the door? And the precious egg had surely shattered in the fall. All of Miersk, pooling every kopek, couldn't hope to pay to replace such a treasure. Not in a century of servitude.

No. Better to escape on her own and to go find Cat. Make sure she was all right. Take care of her until her disappearance was noted. Eventually the train would have to come back to retrieve their castaway. And by then Elena and Cat could have invented an excuse for whatever had happened to the porcelain musical egg. It surely must have smashed to shards.

Elena opened the door of Cat's chamber an inch. Along the passageway, she could hear the muttering of the butler and the great-aunt. They conferred in the parlor chamber at the end of the car. Elena tiptoed out.

Monsieur d'Amboise must have closed the two outer carriage doors. But a key still trembled in each. It would only be a matter of opening the door when the train slowed. She could throw herself out — and follow the tracks backward.

And what luck, for just now the train was entering a curve, slowing down.

Elena reached the door through which she'd arrived. She pushed the curtain aside. Through the high narrow glass, she could see nothing but a distant slope of ropy larches.

She heard Monsieur d'Amboise call something in French. He said again, as a question this time, and yes, that was her title, Cat's title. "Mademoiselle Ekaterina?"

She turned the key in the door. Over the clattering of the wheels, she didn't think it could be heard in the parlor beyond.

"Venez, Mademoiselle Ekaterina, immédiatement, s'il vous plaît!"

Elena put one hand on her throat. The other hand gripped the door latch. Then she pressed the door open.

Wind rushed in. Just as she feared, a throttle of machinery and a cloud of grit. As she flexed her calf muscles to push, she glanced down to see how far she would go, to ready herself for the impact. But there was nothing there.

She had nearly jumped to her death. The train had slowed down because it had reached the repaired trestle. A narrow, dried-up streambed far below winked up like a tarnished necklace of stones.

Of course. When the engine had left, earlier today, it must have been testing the bridge to make sure it held.

She crouched to think what to do next. The draft caused the parlor door to swing open. Three grown-up voices cried out in

annoyance, because smoke, dead leaves, and detritus funneled farther into the parlor at the back of the carriage.

"What are you doing, you mad child?" cried Miss Bristol, up
on her elbows by now. Monsieur d'Amboise strode toward the
vestibule, toward Elena. She could see his shape like a dreaded
Cossack. He would pitch her out the open door, and then she
would fly through the air to her death. . . .

She scurried back into Cat's room. She slammed the door,
rammed home a bolt. She leaned her back against the door. She
could hear Monsieur d'Amboise locking the outside door she had
opened. Such silence returned as there could ever be on a rattling
train.

He was at her door, knocking. "You are not allowed to open
doors in this train, Mademoiselle. Have you picked up habits from
that ragamuffin child with whom you were wasting your time?
Your great-aunt has a dreadful cold, and you will catch one yourself! What have you to say for yourself?"

She had nothing to say for herself. She had nothing to say
for Cat.

Another voice: Miss Bristol at the door. "Let me in, young lady."

Elena couldn't help it. A vacuous weeping poured out of her, as
wordless and wet as sobs in any language.

Monsieur d'Amboise: "She is distressed over leaving the peasant child."

"She is poorly behaved. She needs castor oil or a proper
caning."

"Her voice is hoarse. She's caught a catarrh from that dreadful
draft."

"We will all die miserable deaths. But we must live our miserable lives first. Miss Ekaterina, do you require a mustard plaster for your chest?"

Elena could not refuse to answer. They would break the door down. She muttered through her sobs, "No!"

"Yes, her voice *is* hoarse. She *has* caught the cold her great-aunt had." The governess spoke with something like satisfaction, as if she quietly hoped it might just develop into pneumonia.

"I shall fix you a tray, Miss Ekaterina," called the butler.

"And you would do well to brush your hair," said the governess. "I caught sight of you tumbling upon the floor. You looked like something the cat dragged in."

Having secured their authority, or so they thought, they went away mumbling. Elena couldn't hear their voices anymore.

She sat on the bed. She didn't know what to do next. So when she saw Cat's brush upon the nightstand, she picked it up and began to brush her hair.

Surprise Day

Cat must have stood there awhile. By the time she accepted that the train wasn't shrieking to a halt, not backing up to retrieve her — not yet anyway — a pall of evening had begun to shroud the eastern sky. It provoked a fit of desolation.

I don't know if you've ever experienced such a thing. It's an apprehension of dread. Anything can bring it on: a bad notice in the press, a dubious oyster, an unwarranted accusation. For Cat, it was usually tripped by a certain look the sky can take on as it tends toward dusk. A brooding, tentative aspect. It only occurred when she was alone in a place she didn't know.

When you're young, I think, being vulnerable to desolation comes from your not being able to imagine the world beyond you. If these are streets you traveled with your governess at noon, going from elocution lessons to a fork luncheon at your uncle's, it is easy to imagine what these same streets might look like at dusk. But if they are streets you've never explored, and your governess has been carried away by anarchists or hedonists and you are unsure which way to turn, then dusk itself seems to signify the potential danger of the secret world.

Being vulnerable to desolation also arises from being unable to picture a set of choices with which to change your lot in life.

Cat had no choices right now. That she was scraped and bleeding from her fall didn't make things better. She couldn't *command* the train to notice her absence and reappear.

But she also couldn't wait here in the bracken. She couldn't just freeze on her feet, clutching the gift for the Tsar. She had to keep it safe, and herself safe in the bargain.

The train's distancing whistle was being lost within the wind. *So far away* is the loneliest of sounds. Cat began to climb the bank up to the railroad tracks again.

She circled the shabby train station of Miersk. Beyond the platform, the huddle of cottages pretending it was an actual village.

One of those huts had to be less hostile to a visitor than the rest. The hut that belonged to that girl and her family. But Cat didn't know which one it was.

The wind became brisker by the moment. Cat tucked her head down and wandered across the half-frozen ruts of the dirt road toward the nearest hut.

A man's voice called, "Did you manage to get your hands on any food for us?"

Cat didn't know what to do. The lane was empty; the man must be talking to her. She supposed she had to admit herself to someone, though she had hoped it would be some kindly grandmother.

She turned a little and shrugged. The man wasn't looking at her, quite. He saw she was cradling something in her arms. "A useful size of whatever it is, black bread or cured salmon," he cried. "Bravo, my girl."

He came closer and continued, "But you're not my girl."

She dared herself to look at him. It was the doctor with the limp. An older man with fretted skin around his eyes. He smelled, and I don't mean of hand-milled soaps scented with lavender. But his eyes in their nest of wrinkles were deep, and not unkindly.

"Fair maiden," he said. Cat didn't care if he was being courteous or silly. At least he was talking to her. "You seem to have missed your connection."

"The train left without me," she managed to say.

"So I see. Have you run away from home?"

"It was an accident. And—" She knew she had to tell him about the mishap. She studied his face and lost her courage. She had met so few truly kind people that she didn't know how to trust one when he stood right before her.

The old man stroked his beard with obscure purpose. "Well, they will return for you in moments, but you can't just stand here and let the birds roost on you. I am on my way to look in on Elena's mother, who is failing. As you may know. You can wait with your friend until the rescue brigade arrives. Elena will be glad to see you."

"Oh, is that her name." This just slipped out.

His eyebrows raised. "*Close* friends, I can see."

"But Elena—"

"Yes, she *will* be surprised. Come along. Dr. Penkin, at your service."

And the desolation lifted a little. Though her companion smelled like a walking stable that hadn't been mucked out since the fall of Constantinople, there was something consoling in the dedicated stab of his cane against the ground. Even his ability to dismiss her problems as uninteresting while he was taking care of them was a relief. Cat felt she was walking into a certain drama unlike anything she had seen in the Christmas pantomimes Miss Bristol took her to in Shaftesbury Avenue.

"Doctor," she tried again.

"As I'm not *your* doctor, call me Peter. Peter Petrovich," he supplied. "Don't dawdle, child."

"I don't know how to tell you . . . there's been a dreadful calamity—"

"And here we are," he said, pushing the door open. "Elena? Shall this be called Surprise Day? A friend has come to call."

Cat stumbled inside. The entire hut was hardly larger than the parlor in which, even now, her great-aunt was hurtling away from her. One small lamp cast a fitful glow through thready, shapeless laundry drying on a cord strung diagonally across the room. In a gap between an apron and a kaftan, Cat saw a bed nook with raked-back bed curtains. A wasted figure, as good as dead, under blankets. A zigzaggy old woman hunched near the invalid with a rag of a towel, wiping her brow. This was the grandmother type Cat had been hoping for. But she looked weary and anything but buxom.

"Have you brought supper?" asked the old woman.

"Grandmother Onna, your eyes are tricking you," said the doctor. "This is the young train traveler, stopping awhile as a guest. Where is Elena?"

"She's not come back with her takings. What have you got

there?" the grandmothery creature asked Cat. "I hope if it isn't ripe, it's neither stale nor *very* maggoty."

"I'm trying to tell you," said Cat at last. "Elena is gone."

The old woman straightened up as much as she could, wincing at a pinch in her spine. "Gone where?"

"Gone on the train."

"Gone to Saint Petersburg." The doctor hit his forehead. "Surprise Day for me. That naughty child. And clever. Why didn't I see this? Hitching a ride with a steam engine. She'll go far. I mean in life, also on the branch line. But why did she leave you here?"

"She didn't. It was an accident. I fell just as the train was leaving."

"Then the train will come back for you." The grandmother must have seen a lot of the world, thought Cat; she's taking this in stride. "Elena, *bon voyage* and Godspeed and don't forget to wash under your arms, all that. Meanwhile, Miss, I hope that whatever you carry will do for supper."

Cat didn't want to reveal the magnificent gift for the Tsar, but she was both guest and prisoner. She saw that she had to offer a glimpse of the Fabergé egg. Reluctantly, carefully, she unwrapped a corner of her shawl.

"Saint Nicholas and all the saints." The doctor turned pale. "It is too impossible. They will think we have kidnapped you to steal this priceless item."

"We are yesterday's dung," agreed Grandmother Onna, reaching out to touch the egg, but Cat wouldn't let her.

"Miraculously, it's not broken," said the girl. "Should it break now, for whatever reason, you *are* doomed."

"Don't threaten me," said Grandmother Onna. "This is no egg at all, just silliness. What else have you got?"

Cat found some salt biscuits and a handful of figs wrapped in a handkerchief in her pocket. She'd been intending to give them to Elena. Now she presented them to Grandmother Onna.

The old woman cut up the figs with a knife into four portions.

Cat couldn't eat her portion and left it on the table. Once it had lived in her pocket, it was peasant food.

Eventually the doctor said good night to Cat and went home. Grandmother Onna indicated Elena's pallet. "You might as well lay your body down there," she said. "Keep that jacket on for warmth. Don't worry about anyone stealing your precious stupid item. The good doctor is too smart to tell anyone it is here. I'll sleep on the floor next to the bed, to tend to the poor invalid in the night should she need help. She's sinking."

"But what will I do?"

"Go search high and low, and see if you can find the golden Firebird. If you can inch forward and clip one of his tail feathers, you can make a wish and put all your problems to rights."

Another devotee of folk magic? Or was she being sardonic? "I need some advice I can *use*."

"Advice? Don't waste your energies fretting. The morning is wiser than the night, my ducky. The train will be back in the station by dawn. If not, you're welcome to starve with the rest of us. But don't worry. If it gets too much for you, just outside this cottage is a convenient well. A more efficient method to drown yourself is hard to find. Splish-splash."

Cat thought of the drowned daughters of Miersk. Perhaps that had unsettled the old woman's mind.

The desolation followed Cat into her sleep. She was in an unrecognizable world that bore almost no resemblance to the world she knew. Even though the world she knew was wide indeed. The Happyweather School for Young Ladies in Kensington, London. The boulevards and bistros around her great-aunt's Paris apartments near Saint-Germain-des-Prés, where Cat spent the shorter of school breaks. The Manhattan town house where her parents sometimes lived; she had been there once. And scraps of Moscow, and Villefranche-sur-Mer on the Mediterranean, and Biarritz on the cold Atlantic.

The landscape of her dreams, though, resembled her known world only to the extent that the sky was still above the earth. Everything else was so imponderably different that, tossing and waking for a moment, she could find no words to describe the differences, and drifted off to sleep again on a sort of raft of dread. A raft that threatened to overturn, and make her the next drowned girl of Miersk.

The Hand
at the
Window

Miss Bristol, one of life's pests, was at the bolted door again. She knocked and said something in a language—French, English, Italian—Elena didn't know or care to know. In a voice made throatier by her weeping, she replied in Russian, "Go away."

"I *see*," editorialized Miss Bristol in Russian. "You are speaking the mother tongue out of some benighted sense of association with your little serf friend. Very well. Your dinner is on the rolling cart. Your great-aunt excuses your attendance at the dinner table for this evening. I have persuaded her you are ill. I should recommend that as you have your meal in silence, consider your cruelty in depriving your great-aunt of your company." She sniffed a long elastic sniff, as if a bit of damp material in her sinuses couldn't decide whether to drop or be sucked into her brain. "Conduct your toilet with care, and say your prayers before retiring. I shall see you in the morning. I am still suffering with the very cold you

seem to have, or else I should insist you come bid me good night."
She coughed convincingly and moved away.

Elena waited for full silence — silence heard over the noise
of the iron horse dragging its carriages along the rails. She would
make a second attempt to escape.

When she guessed it was safe, she unbolted the chamber
door and opened it a crack. In the corridor she found a little table
on wheels. The top was bordered with brass rods to keep things
from sliding off. A blue plate with a gold rim sat centered in the
middle of a thick white cloth. A dome, its handle in the shape of a
disgruntled swan, covered the plate.

Elena dragged in the cart and bolted the door again.

She gripped the swan and lifted the dome. The most heavenly smell in the world clouded up in soft rounds of steam. For a
moment she couldn't see; her eyes were watering almost as much
as her mouth. She swiped at the steam as if opening the curtains
on a miracle.

She ate the food so fast she couldn't stop to think what it was.
Flaps of pale simmered meat of some sort and peeled, unblemished potatoes, cut into chunks and boiled till their hard edges
were blunted. Two small perfect onions so identical that one could
wear them as earrings. Ha. She'd never thought of earrings before
in her life. But, oh, the fragrance. Spooned over everything, a sauce
of gravy and cream and some aromatic herbs. A crisp pillow of
bread, a scoop of butter melting upon it. A glass of water with
some wine mixed in.

Elena ate and drank everything in three minutes.

She licked the plate and then the inside of the dome as far as
her tongue would reach. Minutes later she threw up into the basin

in the corner. But her stomach was more satisfied than it had been since — since ever.

The dinner revived her. She was braver, ready to make her escape. At the moment, the train was keeping a serious pace. Sooner or later, it would have to slow down at some station, to take on water or tinder. Or other passengers.

While waiting, Elena peered in a cupboard and found a dozen clean and perfect outfits. Full skirts and less full skirts, bodices attached or separate, shawls and ribbons, bonnets and shoes. Items she couldn't name or imagine how to wear. A bleached blue parasol with imbecilic ruffles. Some matching shoes with the same ruffles.

She was so far from home now. Who knew if she might meet strangers in the forest? To appeal to their sense of obligation, she would exchange her own rude clothes for some of Cat's. The items looked to be the same size, or near enough, for Elena to wear.

She undressed, pushed her commoner's threads out the window into the dark, and chose a crinkly beige frock with crimson trim.

Elena in the mirror. Her calves shone back at her, shocked. But with her hair brushed, in this half-light of dusk, she could almost pass for Cat.

She put her hands to the back of her head and tried to heap her hair up top, the way Cat wore hers. The resemblance was even stronger. The nape of her neck felt naked and shaming; she endured that.

She prowled. Opened drawers. Books, diaries, a bottle of ink, a few pens made of polished wood. Opened low china jars filled with a flowery powder. Sniffed vials of liquid that smelled like heaven but tasted like poison. Perfume, perhaps. She washed out her mouth again.

She looked under the bed, where she'd stashed the ornate box in which the Fabergé egg belonged. Nothing else under the bed. No trapdoor under the carpet. No hatch in the ceiling. No turn screw to undo the bars on her window. No way out.

With every moment spent nuzzling the luxury in which Cat lived, Elena saw more clearly the danger into which she'd stumbled. Before she could become paralyzed by temptation, though, she felt the train respond to the resistance of brakes. The carriages jolted.

She glanced out the window. The world had gone mauve and silver, indistinct in the dusk. The light behind her in the chamber cast a gold reflection only a few inches deep. She saw her hand at the edge of the curtain, mirrored. She put her hand out flat against the glass to touch a glass hand from the other direction.

Now or never, she thought, and gathered her courage. The passage looked empty, and the door to the parlor was closed. Perhaps the others were eating an evening meal. She slipped to the transept and reached one of the outer doors. Through the high slit of glass, she could see the tracks describing a gentle curve. The halftone twilight was partly because of fog, though fog is not a winter phenomenon in Russia. They must be passing through a steppe of some sort, she thought. A grassland worn into flatness by the wind. She slid open the door and leaned out as the train slowed further to enter a curve. Ready, steady . . .

The world shifted, as worlds will do when you travel. A turning wind parted the mists. Elena discovered a double train. An upside-down train, its reflection. An iron horse rolling along on the wheels of its overturned cousin. The tracks laid out on clusters of pilings.

The mists were the result of evening light upon water, and the lake was broader than any prairie Elena could imagine. It might not be deep — it could not be deep — but there was no telling, and six feet deep was too deep.

Elena couldn't swim. Ever since her friends — ever since her father — she'd never been able to look out across a stretch of pond without feeling that it had the hands of devil-maids waiting to drag her under. She could not jump now.

Still, she got to her knees and inched herself forward until her head and some of her shoulders were cantilevered out the train door.

She didn't know what she wanted to look at. Perhaps, as this vacant fog-scape seemed so otherworldly, she might see her drowned father below the surface of the still, still water.

Whether that was a nightmare hope or a sweet terror, she couldn't tell. In any case, his face didn't appear. However magical the world might be, the dead do not regularly return.

She saw her own face. At least she thought it was her own face. From this distance, Elena was examining her own expression of surprise. Without a shawl of the sort she usually wore in Miersk, with her hair piled up, Elena saw again that she looked like Cat.

Not exactly. But close enough. Put that together with the wonderful smart clothes that fit so well, and from a distance, someone who only knew them a little might not be able to tell them apart.

She sat up, stunned at the possibilities.

Maybe the world had gone magic on this endless stretch of water. Perhaps she shouldn't try too hard to escape the train. It was, after all, going to Saint Petersburg. To the Tsar. Once it arrived, she might emerge from the bedchamber and slip away from Cat's family and minders.

This was an opportunity, not a curse. She'd told the old doctor she would go see the Tsar. And here she was, keeping her promise by accident, not design.

She pulled herself back into the carriage, closed the door, stole to her chamber. The cloudy coverlet settled over her with comfort and warmth as if approving her revised strategy.

So. That's our heroine. Snoozing away. I suppose you could say she has initiative. You have to give her credit for trying to make good of her dilemma. That's the beginning of heroism, the decision to *try*.

The Morning Is Wiser Than the Night

It was morning, of sorts. The air seemed heavy with cold dust. The invalid in the bed twitched her hand once or twice. Had she just murmured "Elena"?

Cat sat up on her pallet. That superstitious old crone with her eyes rolling in opposite directions was nowhere to be seen.

So Cat went over. The sick mother's eyes were near to closed. She couldn't lift her hand, but she slid it along the coverlet. Cat didn't care to touch a dying person, or any person who was so poor and unkempt, but her hand reached out anyway and let the woman feel the warmth of her clean, well-manicured fingers. The woman gripped Cat's hand, not tightly. "Elena." Not even a whisper, just a half-breath.

Cat couldn't speak. She didn't return the squeeze. But she didn't pull her hand away either.

"You rest," said Cat at last. "I'll fix you a *petit déjeuner.*"

She patted the woman's hand again and then set it down farther away from her, like a paperweight on a desk. She stood up. She wasn't Elena and had not tried to pretend she was, but the sick woman seemed comforted anyway. Soon her eyelids stopped fluttering and just stayed still.

Cat realized that she wouldn't know if Natasha Rudina had just died. She'd never seen death close up. The breathing was so shallow that it might not be breathing at all anymore.

She just couldn't tell. She turned and made her way to the door. When she opened it, she came upon a surprise.

The old woman, Grandmother Onna, stood on the threshold with her back to the chamber. Her arms were folded, a posture of belligerence. The doctor rocked back and forth on his feet next to her, wringing his hands in distress. "But you don't know what you are saying," he insisted.

In the muddy lane, facing them, stood some other women of the village. Silent, staring. A few of them carrying young children, several accompanied by rickety old fathers or uncles with pox or palsy. The women were shoulder to shoulder. Cat thought they looked like fishwives at Bermondsey or Les Halles, ready to start slapping their enemies with spoiled trout. "Peter Petrovich Penkin," said one of the women, "get out of our way. This isn't a question of medicine, so your opinion is of no account."

"It's a matter of public safety," he replied. "She is only a child. I can't let you abuse her."

"We're the ones who need safekeeping. She's an intruder. She must go."

"I tell you, the train will come back for her. Why wouldn't it?"

"Here I am," said Cat, more bravely than she felt. "What is the matter?"

The doctor turned. "Well, good morning. This is Grand Inquisition Day, I fear. They think your presence here puts all of them in danger. That they — me too, I suppose — will be accused of kidnapping. That our sorry life will get sorrier, and we will die in prison, or be rounded up and shot, and our homes set on fire. Finish Me Off Day, I suppose. Aren't they a cheerful sort, our village goddesses. You can hardly blame them, Russian luck being what it is."

Cat could see the bare tracks off to one side. "Why hasn't the train come back yet?" she asked.

"So it can kill us all?" The agitated spokeswoman shifted her baby to her other hip, the better to have a fist to shake at Cat.

"So I can be rescued. You won't be persecuted. I can promise you that. You will be rewarded for keeping me safe." Cat spoke slowly and clearly. She could tell her accent was too polished for this population.

"Oh, we'll keep you safe, all right," growled the leader. "Safely silent. When they come back, you won't be able to point to us and tell lies." She picked up a stone. The baby clapped and wanted one too, though probably only to put in its mouth. Breakfast.

"Don't be rash," said Grandmother Onna. "It will be a simple exchange. The train will return and exchange Elena Rudina for their little lost fairy princess. We'll bargain. The train has more food on it than we have seen in our village in a month. This is a godsend, the one we've been praying for."

"You're growing mad with hunger," said the doctor to the gathered mothers and wives. "Understandable, but beware. You're not

110

thinking with love and with concern. What if this pesky girl were your own daughter, lost?"

But the mention of lost daughters only agitated the women further. "Who has concern for us?" cried the spokeswoman. The others nodded and cursed. "Did those visitors share of their abundance with us? With such little kindness they showed us then, why should we expect it later?"

"Sweet nameless child of the train," continued Peter Petrovich to Cat, "go get your things and wait on the station platform. The kind of reasoning I want to present to these good women I must deliver in language unsuitable for your ears."

Cat returned to Elena's hut. She pulled on her lambswool. Moving softly, she wrapped the fabulous Fabergé egg in an old towel and tied that bundle into a worn apron. She knotted the strings to turn it into a satchel. Then she slung it over one shoulder. At least the villagers didn't know what a valuable item she carried with her.

Everyone was silent as she slipped back into the sunlight. She walked with her head down as if in single file in her London school yard. She was afraid someone might throw one of those stones when her back was turned. She was less afraid of being hurt than she was of hearing a stone crack the delicate egg.

When she got to the train station, she didn't stop. She just walked along the side of the tracks. She took the direction that train had taken. She kept the same steady pace with which she walked in Kensington Gardens for her daily exercise, two by two next to taciturn Susanna von Stockum, her marching partner.

She didn't need that busybody doctor's help. She didn't care about that old biddy's advice. On her own, she would hail the conductor of the train as it returned for her. She could do this any-where north of here.

Before anyone noticed, she was leaving Miersk behind. The last thing she heard was the doctor cajoling the small crowd toward charity to strangers, who were still having none of it.

Finish Me Off Day. She almost laughed.

You're Not Yourself Today

E lena didn't know where she was, or that she was waking up, until she heard her own voice saying, "What? What do you want?"

Then she opened her eyes and remembered. The cunning little bedroom was still rocking. A magical, diffuse light filtered past the edges of the draperies.

She realized that she'd been responding to a summons. She'd forgotten behind which door she was sleeping. She'd thought it was the one-room home in Miersk, with her mother and brothers, and maybe even her father still, slumbering adjacent.

Through the locked door, the voice of Monsieur d'Amboise: "You are insisting on speaking in Russian. Again." More amused than angry. "You were late for breakfast with your great-aunt. Bad habits, Mademoiselle. Shall I bring it to you on a tray?"

She panicked, and put her arm up to her face, and found her teeth nibbling on the perfect sleeve of the perfect dress that fit, well, perfectly. Though it had wrinkled overnight. "No," she said. The shortest response she could think of.

"You do not sound like yourself. Perhaps you have the same cold that has forced Miss Bristol to take to her bed for the day?" Monsieur d'Amboise seemed a bit tight in that comment, as if he disapproved of Miss Bristol, or perhaps of colds.

She thought to say, "I am not myself today."

"Very well. Still, I cannot bring your croissant if you do not return my cart."

The cart. Yes. "I'll put it outside the door in a moment," she ventured.

"Your voice is husky indeed. I shall bring lemon and honey with your tea. I suppose you have a swollen throat, too. I shall let your great-aunt know that you will join her presently."

"I need to stay here today," she said.

"You need, just once in a while, to do what you're told," he replied. "After I finish with your breakfast, I must go forward to confer with the conductor and the engineer about our progress. We have a lot of lost time to make up if we are not to arrive late for the proceedings. I will be engaged with the engineer and his charts for most of the morning. With Miss Bristol indisposed and taken to her bed, you will have to distract your great-aunt in cards, reading, or conversation. At her age she cannot be expected to amuse herself." There seemed a whole history of resentment in that remark. But how neatly compressed, Elena noted.

She could hear him stalk away and leave the carriage. The kitchen and storerooms must be forward. Elena rose, rushed the tray out into the hallway, then tidied up the coverlet and pillows onto which she had fallen, senseless, the night before.

He was back shortly. He remarked through the closed door, "If you're presentable, I'll enter with your tray."

"No," she said.

"Touchy this morning. Perhaps you are getting a case of jitters about meeting the Tsar and his godson?"

"I told you, I have a cold. I don't want you to catch it."

"If I didn't catch my death from those diseased peasants, I shan't be afflicted by some well-bred virus of yours, Mademoiselle Ekaterina. Now, mind you don't pester Miss Bristol. I shall be forward till luncheon, but I hope your breakfast affords you some pleasure."

"Thank you," she thought to say, but she wasn't sure if he heard it. When he was gone, she dragged the cart back into the room. A funny little curved puff of bread, airier to chew than anything she had ever had before. And a lump of butter and a pot of jam made of bitter orange rind. She ate the butter in one bite and drained the jam out as if it were thickened yogurt. This time she did not throw up. And she felt a little sharper, for the first time in weeks.

Miss Bristol was in her own private room. Monsieur d'Amboise was gone for the morning. She had time to think. To plan.

She brushed her hair and tried to pin it up again. With more of her neck exposed, the way Cat wore her hair, she looked more like Cat than ever. She changed her clothes, an outfit of green, soft rain on willows in summer.

The pretty shoes were too large until Elena stuffed into their toes some filmy items of apparel, the use of which she couldn't imagine. Then she tried walking in small steps about the chamber, holding her hands the way an elegant lady from Saint Petersburg might.

"Oh!" came the voice of the old great-aunt. She called out something in French, and then again, and finally in Russian, "On my word, Ekaterina, come here at once! I am in grave need of your assistance."

Elena creaked open the door and peered to the right. Down the passage, through the vestibule. The door to the sitting room was swung wide open, and the room was sunk in a gloom darker than the rest of the carriage. Elena saw one stockinged foot resting upon a bolster of dark velvet, and an old hand like a thick bloated crab patting about the skirts. "I have lost my eyes, do come at once."

Perhaps the breakfast gave Elena a courage she didn't usually have. Or perhaps it was the spirit of her father encouraging her. The morning is wiser than the night, as Grandmother Onna always said.

The worst, Elena supposed, was that they would discover her and push her off the train into the next lake, and she would drown. At least then she would be with her father again.

Drawing a deep breath, Elena put her hands on her heart and then on her head, to check the arrangement of her hair, and she stepped forward into her mirror life.

Now that she needed to see this new world, she took the time to look.

The parlor room occupied the entire back half of the carriage. It felt like a giant carved cabinet turned inside out. Wood scrollwork on every wall and door, flourishes of flopping wooden foliage that I imagine were acanthus leaves, though Elena wouldn't have known that. Most of the furniture was secured in place with bolts through the Bokhara. The room clearly served as the great-aunt's bedchamber too, as an Empire divan was beached in one corner, blue velvet pillows heaped upon it.

The room chattered to itself. A great many prisms, hanging off loops of ormolu, shivered and knocked. They cast no rainbows; the drapes were drawn tight as the gates of the Kremlin. In one corner, a canary tried to sing a complaint about her dusky incarceration but gave up after a few bars.

Great-Aunt Sophia hunched in her stuffed chair, which was one of the few liberated items. She was a huge leathery bellows of an old cow wallowing in silken circumstance. In the gloom, she said, "There you are. What is all this about, speaking Russian? Don't you know that the imperial family prefers to speak in French? That's all they've spoken for two hundred years. Russian is for the servants."

"Russian is the mother tongue of Russia." Elena spoke softly.

"Harrumph. A conceit. Well, I suppose you're bored, all that long delay. And there are worse ways to misbehave. In any case, Monsieur d'Amboise told me you had a cold, and I hear that it must be true. You have a frog under your tongue today. Now, *ma chérie*, I have misplaced my spectacles again. They have fallen on the floor, and as the lamp has just run out of oil, of course I can't see to find them."

Elena knew what spectacles were because the doctor had had some until he sat on them one day. The old woman's spectacles were right there on the side table, laid beside a book. The oil lamp hadn't run out; it just wanted trimming.

The girl approached the old woman, who was squinting and

117

grunting and trying to feel between the cushions upon which she was planted. As she was stout, there wasn't room to get her hand in between her hip and the upholstered side of the chair. She wheezed and winced and swore in French.

Elena circled behind the chair. While Great-Aunt Sophia was leaning to the left, Elena came up behind her on the right and covered the spectacles with her hand. She slipped them into the pocket of Cat's cloud-green dress.

"I wanted to pick out a book for you to read to me," said the old lady. "But you know my eyes. It is too dark to see, and my eyes are not good in any case."

"I can increase the light a little."

"Very well. And then take this book and read at the marked page."

But Elena couldn't read well in any language. She put her trembling hands upon the dial of the hanging lamp. She turned it a fraction, raising the wick, so the room brightened but by a feeble amount. The mound that was Great-Aunt Sophia took on a highlight of sulfurous yellow. The old woman waited, laced and lassoed in a dark tufted dress, one hand splayed across the bosom like an infant pup trying ineffectually to nurse through the napery. Her hair was industrial nickel, swept up to the crown of her head and nailed into place with hairpins. She smelled of a root vegetable as dressed with an attar of roses.

In her heart Elena applied to the spirit of her father to give her inspiration, and perhaps it did. She moved across to the swinging door and said, "If you wait a moment, I'll get something from my room."

"I shall remain here. I have no intention to go air-ballooning at present."

Elena slipped down the passage. She returned with Cat's colorful storybook in her hand. "I will *tell* you a story," she said daringly to the great-aunt.

Madame Sophia had put her head back on her pillows, and her eyes were closed. She waved her hand as a sign for the story to start.

Elena pulled up a low stool and sat at the old lady's knees. She turned to the story she knew best, the one about Vasilissa the Fair and her visit to the old witch in the forest, dreadful Baba Yaga.

She began to present the history as she might have arranged it in the bed-nook theater. Vasilissa was sent into the woods by her wicked stepmother to petition the old witch in the woods for help. The witch lived in an izba that stood on two enormous chicken legs. Around her house was a fence of stripped saplings, topped here and there with the skulls of children she had eaten. A wicked light spilled through their empty eye sockets.

Elena had just finished with the description of Vasilissa meeting the witch when the old woman spoke up. "Very luscious in the telling, Ekaterina. Did you learn this story from that child on the railway platform?"

"Yes." This, at least, was hardly a lie. And then Elena dared to add, "Yes, *ma tante*."

"I suppose the joy of conversation and story made Russian the more appealing tongue for the moment. I'll grant you that you tell it well in Russian, all those little slips of grammar. Very convincing. Well, go on."

By the time Elena had reached the end, the old woman had nodded off to sleep. The girl turned the lamp down low again and tiptoed back to her bedchamber — she was already beginning to think of it as hers — with Cat's storybook in her arms and the great-aunt's spectacles still in her pocket.

Two Cats

The truth was this: despite promenading in Kensington Gardens, rain or shine or British bank holiday or, Lord help them all, Mothering Sunday with nary a mother in sight, Cat wasn't the most energetic child.

She'd had so little practice. She'd never been allowed to scuffle like the urchins she saw in the mews of London. She had envied them their freedom to roam, those guttersnipes straight out of Dickens. Skulking, nicking apples off market stalls. Caps down, heels worn. Eyes, when you could catch them, canny beyond their years.

Nor had Cat been allowed to roll hoops or chase yipping lapdogs through the Luxembourg Gardens like Gavroche or some other liberated gamin in Le Quartier Latin. She'd only learned to pace the garden paths, shoulder to shoulder next to her assigned partner — most often Susanna van Stockum of Sneek, a broad and wheezy Frieslander who wept at the very thought of exercise.

Still, traveling the Russian hinterland by following the rail line wasn't tough. No steep climbs, for one thing. A train prefers to zig and zag along a gradual incline.

She reached the trestle bridge and saw where it had been repaired with new green-blond logs. She crossed it, left it behind. She was surprised not to come upon other towns or farmsteads. Either Miersk had been the last tiny village before the great forest or the forest had become enchanted.

What a droll notion. She must be more tired than she realized.

Walking kept her warm. Only when the sun began to hover westward did she realize she didn't know what to do next. She'd expected the train by now. Or at least someone useful to emerge and offer help. She'd even be glad to meet the peasant girl, what was her name?—*Elena.* Maybe she'd have jumped the train and even now was nearby, wandering home.

As the woods lost their pleasant particularity, and as a return of the desolation threatened, she tried to imagine company. Here was Susanna van Stockum of Sneek, dragging along beside her. No, hours ago Susanna would have sat down by the side of the tracks and died.

How about her great-aunt? But Madame Sophia was too fat and old and weary of ankle. And Cat didn't want the governess. Miss Bristol had no gumption.

For a short while, she tried to pretend her parents were with her. One on either side, how is that? Pater with his moustaches, Mother with her lapdogs. The lapdogs would have fallen off the trestle bridge, though. Without the lapdogs, Mother was impossible to conjure. And Pater. Cat knew only his knees and the back page of his racing forms; his face was less distinct. Even in her imagination, they wouldn't come to her aid: they were otherwise engaged.

Cat then went back to Elena. She had some spunk and minded the world.

But poor Elena, really? That's the best you can do, Cat? Elena hadn't shown the guarded alertness of streetwise brats. Instead, a rural vapidity. Sweet, if dim. She seemed actually to believe in witches. No doubt she'd have bought the whole gamey portfolio they peddled to kids in England: Father Christmas, as they called him in London. Jack Frost. Little Cinderella squatting in a rotten pumpkin shell. And fairies at the bottom of the garden, if Elena could even recognize such a fantastic concept as a garden. Now, if Cat ever saw anything that looked like fairies at the bottom of the garden, she'd set her great-aunt's Russian wolfhounds upon them. Cat laughed, imagining Ivan the Terrible and Ivan the Even Worse loping through the Jardin des Tuileries, corpses from the root-and-hedge society bleeding out of their slobbery mouths.

But maybe, thought Cat, maybe Elena isn't as innocent as she looks. Why hadn't she instructed the engineer to turn the train around and return? Maybe Elena's naïveté was a ruse, and Cat had fallen for it.

Oh, for *company,* she thought. All right: I'd even accept Miss Bristol, plagued with alarums as she is. Then Cat began to sense movement to one side, in the woods.

She whistled to herself. She wasn't a robust tunesmith, but perhaps whatever she was sensing objected to atonal whistling and might skulk away, offended.

"Elena?" she called, just in case the girl *had* actually escaped the train and gotten lost in the woods to one side. Though following tracks seemed elementary.

She called again, louder out of a growing fear. "Elena! Elena?"

A voice came back: "Elena!—lena?" Cat understood the logistics of echo. Still, alert to a nameless energy on the prowl, she felt unmoored. She *wasn't* Elena, no matter how the echo voice addressed her. Though by now her skirts were dirty and her stomach growling, and her hair unknotted and brambly as a peasant's.

She was Cat. Cat! she thought. "Cat!" she cried.

"Cat," returned her voice, panicky. By now she was all but running.

Why had she let her great-aunt talk her into leaving London and traveling halfway across the world to meet a distant scion of the imperial family of Russia? Now Cat would be devoured by a beast as ravenous as those grubby villagers. No one would find her body. No one would ever find the Fabergé egg near her well-chewed bones. Tinkling a little funereal lullaby.

The world was flinching, rippling in place. A local wind, revising the law of gravity, shirred the gluey shreds of last autumn's leaves and pine needles into the air. Though she wasn't a religious child, she called upon Saint Nicholas to help her. Saint Nicholas didn't oblige.

The leaves resolved into a shape she began to understand. Whatever it was, it was . . . it was . . . cat-like.

She had summoned it. She had called "Cat!" and it had come into being.

A real cat, a large, wild thing. Its pelt scarred by a scrabble with another creature. A look of golden longing in its eye. It hung low to the ground, like all cats on the prowl, and it moved toward her and then stopped, growling.

Its face an exotic blossom of fur. She didn't know what species might haunt the Russian woods. A mountain lion, a snow leopard, a tiger. An Abyssinian ocelot.

"You don't want me," said Cat.

The cat wasn't convinced. It paced slowly, driving Cat off the tracks and into the woods.

"If it was whistling that annoyed you, I'm sorry."

The cat was playing with her. It was pushing her farther from the safety of the rail line. Paper birches and spruces closed in, rock skittered underfoot. Thorny brambles at hip and elbow. The ground skipped and rose as if it couldn't make up its mind on a preferred surface level. Almost at once she lost her bearings.

For a length of time that, later, the girl could never name, the soft-padded monster drove her through the forest. Finally it seemed to tire of the game, and capered directly at her, picking up speed as it neared.

She screamed and turned her back, imagining its claws driving into her scalp. She raked her way through a stand of cane, through translucent slush and puddles the color of mud.

Quite suddenly she came upon the edge of a small bridge. In the middle of nowhere, no path leading up to it. The span was painted in green and red, carved with totems she didn't pause to examine. At the end of both railings, on near and far sides, stood a pole — four poles in all. Each pole was capped with an ivory sculpture shaped like a human skull. A jaundiced light flickered from the eye sockets of each skull.

Cat threw herself upon the bridge and fell on all fours. The egg in its apron-satchel thumped against her spine.

The cat stopped, hissing. It didn't step foot on the bridge. Perhaps it wouldn't.

Cat straightened up onto her knees. The bridge was a walkway to an independent island of private climate. Before her, a landscape of perfect old-fashioned winter. How could it persist adjacent to the mess of the thaw all around it? Heaps and drifts of snow coated the branches of trees, outlining them, pressing them down.

Underneath the bridge gleamed a frozen stream, clear as glass. Behind her, in the woods through which she'd come, the big cat paced back and forth.

The light was lowering still. Her desolation hour. She glanced over the side of the bridge, in her hysteria expecting a cousin tiger, or perhaps trolls. What she saw was her face in the ice. Scratched, smudged with dirt and a little blood. Her hair had come loose from its pins. Her lambswool collar was awry. She looked like a peasant — indeed, almost like Elena.

She paused, halfway on the bridge from here to there.

Discovery

Elena managed to spend the rest of the day in her chamber.

Cat's chamber.

Her chamber.

Monsieur d'Amboise came by with lunch, and then again with some supper.

"Your great-aunt says your voice sounds like death stew on the boil, but she told me you felt well enough to come read to her," he called through the closed door. "Why won't you come out and join her for her evening meal?"

"I've taken a turn for the poorly," she said, a phrase that Grandmother Onna used when she was getting ready to go on an all-day ramble for medicinal mushrooms.

"Hmmmm," replied the butler. He didn't sound convinced. Still, he left her yet another sumptuous tray. This time the dome revealed a plate of sausages, fennel, and white beans, all swimming in a savory juice of herbs and wine. She cleaned the plate so thoroughly, she could see her face in it as she licked the last morsel and splash.

When Monsieur d'Amboise came to take the tray away, he called through the door, "Miss Bristol remains under the weather. Has the meal revived you enough to grace us with your company?"

"No." She tried to sound faint, though she hadn't felt so healthy in months.

"I must remark that for a girl who feels iffy, your appetite has tripled. I've never seen you finish your meals like this before."

"Hmmmm," she said, throwing his skeptical one-note melody back at him. Still, she took stock. She'd have to mind herself carefully or she'd make an error, and all would be lost.

It must be said that her plan was vague. She intended to improvise her way from the train once it arrived at Saint Petersburg. She'd find the Tsar somewhere. She'd ask him to release Luka from military service. And, while she was at it, why not release all the other men of Miersk? That couldn't be too complicated.

Elena discovered a drawer with a set of loose shifts in warm girlish colors. She guessed that they were sleeping gowns. Carefully she undressed and hung up the clothes she had been wearing, then washed her hands and her face and brushed her hair. It was starting to like being brushed, she thought. Then she climbed under the quilts and blankets and extinguished the lamp. She could hear Miss Bristol snoring softly in her room along the passage. As Elena drifted off to sleep, she wondered how long she could maintain this charade, how close to Saint Petersburg they were at this point.

Her father, pointing: *Go home*. Where could he be, that he still came to her in her dreams?

In that certain black-and-grey half hour, before dawn starts to lend pinkness to the world, she woke up. Why? Something had changed. Oh: the train was standing still. She peered out the window and saw nothing but an airy leafless birch woods stretching as far as definition held.

She couldn't hear the tympani of Miss Bristol's aggravated sinuses. Everyone was asleep so deeply that it felt as if they were gone.

Perhaps that dream had made her silly, but the longer she lay in bed, listening for some sound or another, the more she felt that something had happened to the entire train. A spell of some sort had fallen upon it. Everyone else was dead, or spirited away, or sleeping a hundred years. She alone was left to perform the task that must be undertaken to break the enchantment.

She pushed the covers back and tiptoed to the door. She turned the key slowly so as not to allow for a single creak, and then she opened the door about four inches to begin to peer out.

A foot slammed into the doorway, and an elbow. "Open up."

She threw herself against the door. To no avail.

"Open, I say, or I'll scream Monsieur d'Amboise out of his *dormez-vous.* Miss Ekaterina, *open.*"

Miss Bristol hurled herself against the door from the outside. She was bigger and stronger than Elena. She gained enough space to wiggle her shoulder and then her hip into the breach. When Miss Bristol's knee began to show, Elena gave up and retreated to the bed and pulled the covers over her head.

It was a feeble gambit. It didn't stop the governess for a moment. She lunged onto the bed, sat on Elena's legs, and yanked at the covers. "You've taken a scissors to your beautiful hair to escape being forced to the Tsar's ball, is that it? You're ashamed of yourself, as you ought to be — let me see you, you ungrateful child —"

What she saw startled her into speechlessness. Her mouth just gaped.

"Don't . . . don't . . ." stammered Elena, but she didn't know how to finish the sentence. *Don't hurt me? Don't scream? Don't faint?*

For a moment that lasted a month, Miss Bristol stared at Elena. Perhaps she didn't believe what she was seeing and thought she was having a nightmare. It gave Elena a chance to study the governess. The grey eyes, wide with shock, bulged, but elsewhere the woman's skin was tight, as if she hardly had enough to cover her body. Her face, rather like the flank of a cone, began at the chin as a fat carrot and flared out to a turnip forehead. A furze of chestnut-grey curls was largely smothered by a sleeping bonnet. The white nightgown featured a repeating arrangement in blue, a lion and a unicorn dancing some sort of polka.

Then the governess slapped her. Miss Bristol, hissing: "You are doomed. *Where is Miss Ekaterina?*"

"It was a mistake." Elena sat up and scooted backward on the palms of her hands until she hit the headboard.

"Where is she?" Miss Bristol arose, tearing open the cupboard as if she thought she might find Cat's dead body hanging from a hook among the gowns.

"I don't know."

"I'll find her." Down on her knees, Miss Bristol peered under the bed. Then she gave another sound, a sort of inward huff, a backward cough. She pulled out the beautiful wooden box and opened it. She felt the empty space where the Fabergé egg should be as if she could not believe it, as if it must still be there, though invisible.

Then she sat back on her heels. "*I* am doomed," she said.

"She left with it, back at Miersk," began Elena.

"And she left you to serve as a decoy. You were in collusion with her. But why? You must have known you'd be found and thrown into prison."

"It was an accident. She didn't mean to leave. I didn't mean to stay."

It was as if Miss Bristol couldn't hear. "But what does she think she can do with that egg? She'll be murdered for it, out in the lawless stretches! And the thieves who take it from her won't be able to sell it. It is one of a kind. It will lead the authorities right to their door. And they shall be sent to Siberia, never to return."

"I tell you, she didn't mean to leave."

"I will be held accountable." Miss Bristol began to weep. "I will be deemed unfit as a chaperone. I will be tossed out of the train. *I* will be sent to Siberia, never to return. They will think I was an accomplice."

"I will tell them the truth."

"No one listens to peasants. I tell you, I am ruined. You have ruined me."

Elena could stand it no longer. "You think you are the only one with troubles? My father is dead and my mother is dying, and Cat is left behind, and my brother Luka is conscripted in the Tsar's army, and my brother Alexei is off in Moscow and doesn't even *know*. According to Cat, half of central Russia is dying of starvation, and *you* are *worried* that *you* will be turned off the train? I'll tell you what to do. Tell the conductor and Monsieur d'Amboise and that old walrus about what happened just now, and turn the train around, and go find Cat."

Her father's form in her dreams: *Go home.*

She leaped out of bed. Miss Bristol reared back and didn't try to stop her.

Elena ran out of the chamber and turned to the vestibule. The key to the outer door was still in the lock. She didn't know if she flipped down the folding steps or jumped. She just flew away. She heard her pretty nightgown flutter like wind through the wings of a bird. Away from the stopped train. Into the black-and-grey forest in the black-and-grey dawn.

The going wasn't hard. In only moments she'd left the train behind. She wasn't *really* flying, of course. It only felt like that, being able to run on solid ground after several days trapped in a chamber.

I know how she felt. Even old men miss running, once they can't.

The forest floor was relatively shy of undergrowth. The birch woods went on forever, a thousand uprights, dalmatian-spotted. All the eyes in the trunks of birch trees watched her. Some of the trees trailed ribbons of bark, where deer had torn away their papery white leggings, exposing an underside the sometime color of flesh.

The bark didn't quiver as she passed. The transparent leaves still clinging from last year — they didn't rustle when she passed. Maybe she was still dreaming.

At length the ground began to slope up, but the rise was so gentle she didn't slacken her speed. As soon as she got to the other side, she'd have put a hummock between herself and the train. Then she could stop and draw breath.

The trees at the summit seemed gilded with a pink-gold light. The sun must be coming up above the horizon. Daylight would make of this black-and-grey forest a buttershine woods, rapturous even before spring had breathed green mist among the birches. She didn't know much, our Elena, but she knew the moods of forest.

Then Elena reached the crest of the hill. She meant to slow herself, but gravity tumbled her over the side. The descending slope was steeper than the rising one had been, and more thinly populated with trees. It joined with slopes beyond and to the sides to form a natural basin. She saw that the source of the light wasn't sunrise, after all. In the center of the bowl trembled a thread of shining sun, nearly too bright to look at.

Though Elena lived in full faith about matters fabulous, she'd never expected to come upon evidence. She suspected that exposure to holy magic was the exclusive right of royalty. It takes a princess to come upon the wise man in the wood, or the talking wolf with a thorn in his paw, or something else useful and good. Even if a princess is switched at birth and raised humbly by starving stepparents, she deserves the luck she inevitably finds. Her diadem may be invisible, but magic always notices it.

Yet here was a Firebird, no more, no less, in Elena's own grubby life. It was basking on the ground in a circle of birch trees.

She caught at slender tree trunks till she was stilled. Then she inched forward. If you could snatch the tail feather of a Firebird, you could make a wish and you would get your wish. Had she the courage? Had she the deserving wish? To console Miss Bristol;

to recover Cat and the Fabergé egg; to heal her mother's wasting sickness?

To bring her father and those girls back to —

That was the hugest wish, but —

And what about when wishes backfired? As so often, in stories, they did?

She was nearly there. Her eyes were getting used to the glare. The creature was about twice the size of a swan, its proud head capped with a froth of sparks. It wasn't made of fire, she now saw; it simply glowed from inside, like a flame in a glass chimney. It was poking in the ground for breakfast like any common bird. It didn't hear her coming . . . not yet . . . not yet.

Please excuse this interruption at what I hope you are finding an agreeably tense moment. I must explain. Hitherto I have been saying "it" in referring to the Firebird, because Elena wasn't clever enough to wonder about the creature's gender. But the probability is that the Firebird is male. Yes, the Firebird lays an egg; I know that. But the Firebird is *a magic bird.* The maleness of him isn't material to the various legends, true, but there you are. Think about it. If a Russian nesting doll can find in her own womb six other generations of children without a male doll's involvement, a Russian male Firebird can lay his own egg.

In any case. Elena was almost upon it — him — when she set her foot upon the inevitable twig put there by a very Russian sense of fate. Tragedy, comedy, and what you might call sardony, all at once. Of course the twig snapped — Elena wasn't royalty. Of course, the great bird whirled about, crying an alarm that sounded like burning bells. His tail whipped out of the reach of Elena's fingers. She feared that the bird would rush her and peck out her eyes.

She put her hands over her face but peered between her fingers, and saw the most amazing thing — less a fairy-tale miracle than a hectoring folktale about the constancy of defeat.

Out of the woods behind the bird exploded a common black hen, bouncing and fluttering as hens do when fussed. Hot upon her bounded a fox, jaws open and eyes trained upon his chicken breakfast. Elena could only imagine this was the last hen of Miersk. Out in the barbarous wild, having outpaced a hungry fox for a week now. The hen's progress was ungainly. By accident, by instinct, she careered near the sweep of the Firebird's tail. To correct her course, she opened her beak and grabbed at the nearest beak-hold. Which was the tail feather of the Firebird.

Outdone by a barnyard cluck.

Distracted by the appearance of Elena, the Firebird hadn't seen the emergence of the hen. His shriek at the sight of Elena became shrill, a volley of sweeping octaves, as the hen bounced away with the Firebird's tail feather in her beak.

The Firebird's gold turned a white that made Elena squeeze her eyes closed. A tempered explosion, lightning in a vodka jug. The fox couldn't swerve away quickly enough; he ran into the blaze and then retreated, yelping, the way he had come. Singed perhaps into sagacity, I don't know. We won't see him again.

When the girl opened her eyes, the fox was gone. The hen was gone. The tail feather of the Firebird was gone. The Firebird was gone, too. All that was left was a small blaze upon the ground, hardly up to her knees. The fire subsided a few moments later.

In a rash of embers and black ashes remained an egg. If you have ever seen an ostrich egg, you can picture this one. About the size of the head of a newborn human infant, or two hands clasped together.

Elena waited until it was cool enough to touch. Then she picked up the warm souvenir. She would do with it what she could. She would repair one thing at a time. She would walk back to the train and see if it was still stopped on its tracks. She would take the Firebird egg to Great-Aunt Sophia. It could replace the missing Fabergé egg, and Cat's *tante* could give it to the Tsar. That much being repaired, Elena could then decide what to do next.

Go home, as her father had told her. Or had he meant, *Go get the feather, make a wish?* If so, she had failed him no less than she was failing her mother.

Still, there was a change in her. She was no less frightened than she'd been before, but she was something other than frightened now. She was a girl in a life in which something amazing had happened. She hadn't gotten a wish, but she wasn't empty-handed any longer.

I hardly know what to think about why she was granted an audience to magic. Access to real magic is vouchsafed to very few individuals. In my opinion, such individuals ought to deserve the honor, not win it in some accidental lottery system of luck. Maybe Elena deserved the honor. We shall see.

I myself, in all humility, have been waiting to witness magic my whole life. I am still waiting. But why feel sorry about me? You're probably wondering what happened to Cat, there on the bridge in the middle of the nowhere woods.

The Hut in the Woods

C at was a realist. Breathe, breathe. Till her heartbeat came back to normal.

The great lynx or whatever it was hadn't been willing to follow her onto the bridge. It must have slunk back into the woods while she was on her knees, awaiting its pounce, the electrified pain, the blood, darkness.

She took stock of her situation. Here she was on a footbridge. Behind her, the slop of an early thaw. Before her, the chilliest sort of winter landscape. It could have been a stage set for a panto production of Andersen's fable "The Snow Queen." A night scene on a stage, which actually has to be lit well enough for performers to move about.

In the gloaming, the drifts shone with a sequined gleam. The fir trees straight out of Bavarian Christmas cards. A certain snap to the air, the pungency of balsam and also, was it, improbably, cinnamon?

Through the crowding treetops, what Cat could see of the sky looked black and starry. Already. Dusk seemed to have snapped to a close, in one instant.

Cat didn't want to back off the bridge. She feared the great cat. Nor did she want to go forward, yet. While she was on the bridge, she was suspended between past and future, and, perhaps, as safe as she ever would be in her life.

Another shimmer, as of sleigh bells, very far away, and then the haunting sound of children's laughter. Cat didn't believe in Saint Nicholas, but she was willing to change her mind if given a reason.

Cat knew she couldn't stay motionless for long. Hers was a rueful moment, yet on the other side of trauma sizzled a spit of pleasure. She was still alive, after all. And she had held the Fabergé egg intact through her trials. She could go on.

She crossed the bridge and began to traipse through the snow. She followed that hint of icy melody. The surface was crunchy but gave way under her weight. In a dozen steps, her feet were drenched. In two dozen steps, they were stiff, ice forming like metal socks around her toes and heels.

Still, she had the sense that no great cat stalked her now. So she kept on.

She was overjoyed and not so surprised when, a moment later, she spied a light in the forest ahead. She'd be able to make it that far, she was sure. One foot, then another. Come on, Cat! You can do it.

Her calves had nearly turned to marble by the time she

rounded a hedge of red-berried holly and arrived at a clearing. What she saw made her wince with relief.

A little house, hardly larger than the carriage of a train, but of more regular proportions, sat in the clearing of black pines and white snow. Its snow-heaped roof was steeply pitched, like that of any izba in the Russian countryside. Low cribs and sheds extended to each side like outstretched arms. The roof beam was painted a military crimson and finished at the front end with the carved head of a dragon. Above perched a kind of cupola. It looked like a silly hat cocked over a brow, like Napoleon's bicorne. A squat little head on the warm broodiness of the cottage below.

Around the windows, more carved trim: diamonds, lozenges of dark blue amidst others of yellow and Chinese red. A carved sash, imitating fringe, ran below each windowsill. The door in the center of the hut was framed in a dense rank of yellow and white twigs worked to look like bones: femurs and tibias, if she remembered her anatomy lesson.

The front of the house welcomed callers with a small roofed porch. Facing benches allowed visitors to rest while they waited for someone to answer the bellpull. And the rest of the place was no less homey. Cheery bays in front, with casement windows dressed in lace. In one of the windows, a kitten sat licking itself.

The kitten swiveled to watch as Cat, stumbling through snowdrift, approached to knock.

She needn't have bothered. The kitten mewed once — Cat could see its little mouth with those pretend fangs — and the front door swung open. In the steam of cider and cloves that billowed out, Cat could hardly see who greeted her. "Oh, look what the cat dragged in," said a kindly voice, a female voice, old and quavery but vigorous, too. "Just when I was feeling hungry for a visitor, the goodness of fate brings a peasant girl to my door! Come in, my child, before you catch your death out there."

"You can just as easily catch it in here," said the kitten on the windowsill. But cats don't speak, so Cat thought she might be suffering frostbite of the mind.

"It's nothing short of a miracle to find you here," said the girl. She nearly fell over the threshold into the close, cozy quarters of the homestead.

The door shut behind her. Bony fingers helped brush the snow from Cat's hair and shoulders. The lambswool slipped to the floor; Cat kept hold of the knotted apron.

"First, let's wrench off those frozen stockings, or the meat on your bones will be spoiled rotten." The old woman came around from behind. Her head was astoundingly large for such a thin, twiggy body. Cat didn't know how her shoulders and spine could support such a monstrosity of a skull. But that smile, thin-lipped and broad, was madly convincing. "You'll want some tea at once. Some soup to follow, and some bread. What's your name, and what drove you to my door?"

"Cat," she replied, and the one word seemed to answer both questions at once. "May I have the honor of knowing the name of my hostess?"

"I should have thought everyone knew me already," said the old woman.

"You're so vain," said the kitten. It was a yellow scrap of a thing, and its ribs showed. It began to leap about, trying to bat at a hummingbird who was taunting it. Cat had never seen a hummingbird inside a house before.

"I've been walking. I don't recall that I've met you before. Perhaps I caught a touch of fever," said Cat. "I'm imagining things."

"Dreadful habit. The imagination is a curse and must be removed, like an eyelash in the soup."

Cat sat down suddenly on a carven bench. The old woman squatted and grunted and pulled off Cat's shoes. They were ruined. The stockings, too. "You'll want to warm up those piglings," she said. "Look how nasty they are, all white and pink and crunchy with the cold. I prefer them at room temperature. Come, my child, lean into the warmth." The little old woman took hold of the bench and yanked with surprising strength. Cat found herself in front of a ziggurat of a wall stove in the corner, ceramic tiles lining it from floor to slanted ceiling.

"Oh, lovely," said Cat.

"Thank you. I admit, I've kept my figure, after all these years, but I'm pleased you still notice."

Cat turned again. The woman was preening with a hand on her hip and another stroking that chin, so prominent as nearly to be exoskeletal. "I can't possibly have met you before," said Cat. "Can I?"

"Nothing's impossible," said the old woman. "I get around."

"But who are you?"

"I should have thought you knew, honeybucket! Why, Baba Yaga, the very same."

She is an insane old woman, thought Cat, but at least I'm safe in the warmth, and she knows how to cook. The old woman was ladling pink broth into a bowl whose sides were etched with obscure runes. "Drink up, my dear. I find borscht a wonderful marinade when applied from the inside."

"I'm as hungry as sin, but I find I'm not ready to dine," said Cat. Her words surprised her. She was ravenous, nothing less.

"You're not more clever than you are hungry, or you're the rare child, indeed. Sip up the soup."

Cat demurred and said, "Who are you really?"

"I'm Queen Victoria. I'm Nellie Bly. I'm Columbia, the Gem of the Ocean — what difference does it make? I'm hungry and I want to eat, so do my bidding."

"I couldn't dare take your supper. I have nothing to pay you with."

"You're not taking my supper, you're supplying it."

Cat sat up. She realized she was in grave danger from this old coot, who was at the very least deluded.

"Don't worry about the soup," remarked the kitten, getting up and stretching in front of the fire. "It's only lightly poisoned."

"The mouth on him! The mouth on you, Mewster," said the old woman cheerfully. "For that, you get squat for yummers, and double squat for afters."

"You can't be serious," said Cat. Her spoon went *plonk* in the untasted soup. "You're playing with me."

"Ah, I do play, but only for the higher stakes," said the old woman pretending to be Baba Yaga. "What's that great rutabaga you've been clutching since you arrived? It must be valuable if you haven't set it down."

"If you give me back my stockings and shoes and my coat and let me go," said Cat, "it's yours."

"A present?" The voice turned gruff, suspicious. The eyelids of the old woman narrowed, the purple irises darted. "*That's* a novelty. Give it here. I want to see what kind of bargain you're driving."

Cat unwrapped the Fabergé egg meant for the Tsar. She handed it over. It hadn't suffered a scratch or a fracture, as far as she could see. Every figurine and filigree, every jeweled inch and scrap of gilded appliqué glittered in the light of the stove. The old woman: "Oh, look, the Firebird. Spirit of All the Russias. Ha! It looks like a canary wearing wing extensions."

"Just because *you* favor feather boas . . ." mewed the kitten.

The witch — as Cat was beginning to imagine her to be — turned the egg. "And second, let's see, who do we have? Saint Nicholas? Kublai Khan? Or maybe his aunt Gerdie?" The witch peered. "No, it's the ice-dragon, of all things. Hardly a reputation to equal the Firebird's. Or mine."

"Look, there you are," said the kitten, pointing a paw at the final opening.

"How cheap. I'm much prettier than that. And I've taken better care of my hair. I give this a two out of three. Thanks for the tchotchke." She tossed it in the air.

"No!" cried Cat. But the egg didn't fall and smash. It drifted in an updraft. Relaxed as smoke, revolving like a little local moon. The old woman flexed a forefinger. *Come, come.* From a rafter descended a broad and ancient bird's nest — floating in the air, without cords or pulleys. The Fabergé egg settled in the hummock of straw and string and whatnot.

"Oh," said Cat. "That's a fine trick, better than anything I've seen on the stage."

"I don't do *tricks*," said Baba Yaga.

143

"I thought you were out of your mind, but it's me. I am out of my own mind." She felt oddly calm as she said this. "I've stepped sideways out of life."

"I *am* life," Baba Yaga corrected her. "You've stepped nearer. For good or for ill, for inspiration or for indigestion, I don't know yet. We'll see how you get on."

Onward to Saint Petersburg

Sideways out of life, Cat had said. This applied to how Elena felt, too. She held all the possibility of happiness in the crook of her arm. It retained a remote warmth, that cinder egg. More leathery than ceramic to the touch. Hefty, if dull to look at — the color of first flame from paper.

She would have it, she would have it: she would *have that wish*. She would keep the Firebird's egg safe in the box on the train. Under her bed. She merely had to wait. Hoard the egg until it was ready to hatch. Keep her thumb and forefinger primed for pinching its tail and making a wish.

She had a reason to return to this stolen life. To that carved box under the bed, that little private chamber with the locking door. But what if the train had left? Between some trees, around a turn in the tracks ahead, she saw the train, paused, still waiting. As if for her. She was the center of her own life, still, but her life was getting bigger.

Maybe the engine had just overheated. In any case, Elena hurried toward where it stood, steaming in the dawn cold. The butler and the governess huddled a few feet from the door, conferring in whispers, faces close.

Something interesting then happened that made Elena feel she was only now waking from a dream. The ordinariness of it: Miss Bristol shivering in a coat thrown on over her nightgown, that neat Monsieur d'Amboise with his shirttails out and his hair a thicket. She almost doubted what she had just witnessed: the Firebird's immolation. I'm not the kind of person who gets her wish to come true, she thought. I'm the other sort. I have to make my own way. Don't I?

She shifted the egg from one arm to another; it seemed faintly cooler.

When they saw her, they paused. Miss Bristol put a forefinger to her lips.

"The most amazing thing happened," Elena started to say.

"Get on board the train before Sophia Borisovna Orlova wakes up and sees you," hissed Miss Bristol.

"But I saw an extraordinary thing. You won't believe it."

"*You* won't believe the inside of a prison. Child, you imperil all of us. Miss Bristol has told me everything." Monsieur d'Amboise's enunciation so keen that his words almost left knife marks in the air. "Quickly now."

She struggled to keep the Firebird's egg safe as she was lifted into the train carriage. They hustled her down the passageway to the room adjacent Miss Bristol's — her room, Cat's room. Her room. They followed and closed the door with seditious gentleness.

Monsieur d'Amboise: "I want to know who your accomplices are. Your scheme, your ransom price. Everything."

"I'm not smart enough to have a scheme." Elena explained to them how she and Cat had changed places accidentally. "I don't know if the fancy party gift smashed as Cat rolled out the door with it, but it doesn't matter now: I *have a replacement.* It's an even more wonderful gift for the Tsar than something expensive from London." She held up her boon. She saw in their expressions that they were thinking, A big ugly egg. So what? "The egg laid by the Firebird in his moment of dying," she explained.

"What tosh," said Miss Bristol. "I never."

"There's no such thing as a Firebird," added the butler. "That's only a woodland find of no significance. Though how you've made it glow, I can't imagine. Some peasant trick having to do with grease, no doubt."

"There is a Firebird. Or there was," said Elena. But now, back in the architecture of authority, she doubted herself. So does the magic world tiptoe away from us while we quibble and fret. "There must be a new Firebird waiting to be born in this egg," she continued. "Really. We have to keep it safe. When Cat rejoins us, she can present this to the Tsar. Whatever else he has in his treasury, he can't have something as magical as this. A magic thing belongs to royalty."

"Give me that," said Miss Bristol. Elena would not. She stooped down and pulled from under Cat's bed the bespoke box that had held the Fabergé egg. The lid closed neatly upon the plain old egg from the wilds of dawn, boxing it in the dark.

"And now," said Monsieur d'Amboise, "we must plan. Listen,

Mademoiselle Faux-Ekaterina. The justice of Russian princes and boyars isn't known for its mercy. The past few days spell disaster for all of us — for you, for your village, for Miss Bristol, and for me. We'll be accused of conspiring with villagers to kidnap Mademoiselle Ekaterina and to steal the gift made for the Tsar. We'll be thrown into prison."

"Or *worse*," said Miss Bristol.

"Our only hope is to continue the fiction that you are Mademoiselle Ekaterina until we arrive in Saint Petersburg. There, Miss Bristol and I can escape into the crowd and try to make it out of the country to Sweden before our absence is discovered. You have ruined our professional lives."

"Also my digestion," said Miss Bristol.

"Therefore, you are going to continue on this train to Saint Petersburg. You are going to continue to visit Madame Sophia, pretending to be Mademoiselle Ekaterina. With a cold. You've already convinced her so well that we never guessed the substitution. I suspect you've purloined her glasses, by the way. It wasn't necessary; she's nearly blind as it is. The lenses are a fiction of competence for her. You may return them without fear of discovery."

"But why don't we turn the train around, even now, and go rescue Cat?"

And to think Elena had once taken the butler for the Tsar! Now he looked stricken. Uncertain. There was feeling for Cat in his face, and in Miss Bristol's, too. But cloaked by sharper apprehensions. "It is too late to turn back," said Monsieur d'Amboise. "Your villagers will have killed Mademoiselle Ekaterina and stolen the egg."

"That's outrageous."

"I heard the muttering in Miersk. The starving lose all sense of proportion. I speak," he added, "from experience."

"You're wrong. They'd protect Cat. Grandmother Onna would cut a raisin in half to share it. The doctor will do everything to return her to you."

"Let them prove their goodness. Now, listen, child, you don't understand anything about the Russian suspicion of foreigners. Miss Bristol and I are from England and from France, respectively. We're here on sufferance as it is. If Cat's disappearance is discovered — *when* it is discovered — we will, at least, be deemed criminally negligent in not having noticed the switch before this morning. More likely, we'll be considered accomplices in the loss of that precious, idiotic item. As it was intended for the Tsar, made for the Tsar, its theft would amount to a theft from the Tsar's coffers."

"Plip-plop, we've stolen a trinket. Chip-chop, off with our heads!" sang out Miss Bristol. Her eyes were running.

"As I say," continued the butler, "we are ruined. But perhaps we may escape abroad instead of dying in a work camp in Siberia."

"You have confidence in no one," said Elena. "The doctor will declare it Save Ekaterina Day. Or Cat will be following the train tracks. Just as I was thinking of doing. She'll catch up with us. She'll return the Fabergé egg, if it's still intact. Then we can exchange places. Madame Sophia will never know. All will be well."

She was not sure how much of this she believed. She was only saying it.

"Your doctor fellow cannot heal this wound. And Cat is not that competent," said Miss Bristol. "Oh, my poor girl, lost in the wilds of some misbegotten oblast. I cannot allow myself to think of it. Or of the misery she has brought upon us. She is irresponsible, headstrong, unmoored."

"She is lost. And you, Mademoiselle Serf, are a fool," said Monsieur d'Amboise, nearly kicking the box with the Firebird's egg in it.

"And have I mentioned that we are doomed?" said the governess.

The butler turned away from Elena. Over his shoulder: "And so are you."

And Onward to
Saint Petersburg

So you see I am trying to keep my comments to myself. I don't always manage. Although I have been known to find girl-children tiresome, something about these two captivates me. Is it because they have both become prisoners, and I'm alert to that hardship? Cat is trapped in a folktale she never believed in. Elena is caught in a web of wealth and luxury that seemed to her more fantastic than magic.

I might say here that I don't pretend to understand everything the witch says. Her references are often obscure. I suspect stratagems of a darker magic, codes of enchantment in her remarks. I present what I deduce to have happened, communing with my dead eye through the visions of birds. Perhaps I am an unreliable scribe. In any case, here we are, back in the woods.

The witch inched toward Cat, indicating the borscht, and said, "You're not going to drink the Kool-Aid?"

"I don't know what you're talking about. I have to leave. Thank you for letting me warm up."

"I wouldn't *hear* of your leaving in this weather! It's a blizzard out there, honeybucket," said Baba Yaga. She put a bony hand on the drapes and pushed them aside. A wind picked up as if on demand. Out of the black night, a swirl of flakes smacked the window. Icicles formed on the casements as they watched, growing a foot long in a matter of seconds.

Iron bars on a prison cell, thought Cat. "If you harm me, they will come after you. They are looking for me even as we speak."

"They? *They?* Who they? All the Cossacks and hussars and Tartars and Mongols and Georgians the great motherland of Russia can muster? All the schoolmarms of the land, with their rulers and their little iron bells? Maybe all the singing little rabbits and squirrels of the woods? Get real, child. No one finds Baba Yaga without her invitation. Not until she sends her familiar to chase them in. Right, Mewster?"

"Meow," said the kitten. His face suddenly ballooned up, turning into the head of the feline brute that had threatened Cat. The girl shrieked, fell backward off the bench.

"My great-aunt," said the girl. "She'll save me." It was hard to imagine Madame Sophia getting out of her chair without help. "Or the villagers from Miersk, where we stopped. They took an interest in me." That was true enough.

"Miersk? That greasy squattlehold? I've had truck with folks from Miersk before. Pifflestew. Now, you shut up for a moment. I lit up my welcome lights for you. I offered you soup. I said funny things to amuse you. Enough. It's time for my supper. I can see you've been plumped up on Parisian pastries and British cream teas, and that's fine. I'd have preferred a hot pastrami on rye, but I'll settle for a steak-and-kiddo pie." She reached into the rafters and withdrew a broad, curved knife with toothy serration. It looked capable of sawing through skin and bone.

"Those were the heads of real children on that bridge," said the kitten. "And you thought they were holiday decorations of some sort."

"Yes, like All Hallows' Eve in London, or Hallowe'en, as they call it in the Benighted States of America!" The witch cackled, a horrible sound you might hear in an asylum of unseated minds. "Come here, my ambulatory cutlet, my sanguine savory, my sentient supper. It's time for munchies." She whisked the knife above her head like a saber.

"Of course, like me, *those* children didn't bring you a present," observed Mewster. "This one did. I don't imagine you've forgotten the custom?"

"Getting legalistic, are we?" But the witch paused, picking at her iron teeth with the scimitar. And then they all heard a sound you might describe as the crack of dawn, if the cracking of dawn could mean that the dome of the sky had been struck from above with a sword mightier than the witch's.

The hut tumbled over onto its side. Cat rolled up against a wall with her knees in her face. Baba Yaga fell on her sword, but it didn't hurt her. "What in the devil's handbag?" She pulled the sword out of her leg. "Mewster, what's happened?"

"Meow don't know," said the kitten in a fake little child's tone.

"What's that horrid light?" The witch rolled around until she

153

found her feet at last. A wall had become the new ceiling. Its window was now a kind of skylight, no longer showing blizzard conditions but rather a caramel glare of sunshine.

"What offense against magic and manners is this?" demanded the witch.

"I think it's called an early spring," said Cat.

"Not in my backyard, it isn't!" She was furious and, Cat realized, perhaps frightened. "Mewster, go investigate!"

"I'll help," said Cat, seeing her chance.

"Oh no you don't, you little pain-in-a-pinafore. You stay put."

The witch used her sword to open the window latch on the ceiling. The panel of glass swung inward. A few jonquils and hyacinths and some green leaves of grapevine fell in. The witch recoiled as if they were poison ivy or, worse yet, blooms from a wedding nosegay. She shrank back into a corner of her izba as the kitten bounded from a toppled wardrobe to the leg of an upended table, and from there to the window and out into the springtime.

The table legs were real hairy human legs. They seemed happy to be freed from their job of holding up the tabletop. They were all bending their knees and kicking out their kinks. "Stop that cavorting!" cried Baba Yaga, and hit the nearest leg in the knee. It kicked her in her own knee. "Ow! Call social services! That's downright abusive!"

Then she turned and looked at Cat. "This is all your fault, isn't it?"

Cat wasn't sure if she should claim credit. That might only make things worse.

"Or is it that stupid frippery-finicky egg you brought me?"

"I'm beginning to think it's cursed."

"If it were cursed, I'd like it. I'd cradle it to my withered bosom. Look, it's the only thing that didn't get broken in the collapse of my own personal housing market." True enough, the egg was serene in its floating perch, remaining upright even as the house had tumbled about it.

"That's some remarkable nest." Cat hoped that small talk might distract the witch from her hunger.

"Once belonged to the Firebird, but I stole it right out from under him. Where *is* that darn cat?"

Mewster returned. "It's worse than you feared." He sounded pleased.

"Give me the skinny straight or you'll never grow up to sniff your own sandbox."

"Something has broken the hold of your magic." The kitten interrupted his report to lick his front paws free of wet. When finished, he said, "Spring, it seems, has sprung a hole in your winter."

"I don't see how this could be. Why have we fallen?"

"Because the snow melted all at once while your house was hibernating."

"Well, it's time to wake up."

Cat now realized that the low sound she'd been hearing since she arrived wasn't a wind in the eaves but a gentle snoring. Baba Yaga found an iron frying pan and began to smack the walls of her hut, making half-circle dents in the wallpaper. "Dumb Doma! Rise and shine, you silly cluck!"

Wonder of wonders, the house began to right itself. Cat and the witch both tumbled face forward as the room reasserted itself into traditional orientation.

"All my nighties will have gotten wrinkled," said Baba Yaga.

She hurried to the open window. "Egads, Mewster, you're right. A horrid stink of springtime. Ferns and folly in every direction. My private weather has been canceled."

"It's all her fault." The kitty hissed at Cat.

"No, it's not," said the witch. "She isn't strong enough to break my spells." She peered through the woods. "I can't see my bridge from here. Hut, make tracks!" She rapped on the wall. The house began to lurch back and forth as if in a swing. It couldn't be true, but it seemed to be true: the little house lifted up eight feet in the air. It trudged through sudden mud into the clear light of morning. Its sheds and bins slapped against its hips like saddlebags.

"Look." The kitten rolled his head toward the windowpane.

"I *am* looking."

Cat came up behind her to see what they were talking about. She spied the bridge over which she'd walked. It now appeared little more than an ornamental structure in a Japanese garden, going from nowhere to nowhere, each end descending into early spring posies. The skulls mounted on the poles were rotating, inspecting the mess.

Baba Yaga drew a breath between her big iron teeth. "*Zut alors,* crikey, gee willikers, and Bob's your uncle," she exhaled. "It's worse than I thought. My winter's been abolished. The nerve. Mewster, go get my souvenir skulls."

"I live to serve, and I serve to live." The kitten darted out the window.

"Something is wrong with the world," said the witch, almost to herself. "It appears to be broken."

"You'll have your work cut out for you, setting it to rights," whispered Cat. "Don't want to be in the way. I'll let myself out."

The witch: "Well, it's true, I've been put off my lunch, but you're not going anywhere without me. If I've lost my magic protections, I need a hostage. Consider yourself invited on the trip."

"What trip?" said a skull at the window. The kitten was wearing it as a helmet.

"We have to go tell the Tsar. I mean, if the world is ailing, he should know. Perhaps his wise men will have some theory or other about it. Wise men often do. Myself, I don't dabble much in logic."

"How are you going to find the Tsar?" asked the cat. "You can't even find the powder room."

"We could head for Saint Petersburg, if I were any good with maps."

"You couldn't find your way from *A* to *B* in an alphabet book."

"True. I don't even know where we are starting from." At Cat's expression, she added, "What? You think Baba Yaga lives by ordinary coordinates? *Not.* The latitude and attitude of magic require me to change my address frequently, often in the middle of the night when the local welcome wagon comes to call with torches and pitchforks. I rarely know where I'm going to wake up in the morning."

"I know how to get to Saint Petersburg," said Cat. "Just cross your bridge and keep on through the forest until you come to the railroad tracks. Then turn to the left and follow them. That's the line to Saint Petersburg, and that is where I was going anyway."

"Isn't that convenient," said Baba Yaga. "I adore having a personal navigator, as I'm bad with directions. Fasten your seat belts, honeybuckets — it's going to be a bumpy walk."

The Reluctant Student

So far the ruse was working. For several days now, Elena had kept to her room, complaining of a rheumy chest and dribbling nose.

Monsieur d'Amboise continued to bring her meals, though less formally arranged on the plate than before.

Miss Bristol proved a sullen chaperone. She painted the heels of her shoes with gutta-percha so as to be able to run more swiftly, without loss of grip, away from the authorities when the moment came. The unguent stank, but Miss Bristol, so thin, felt a chill whenever the window was cracked a smidgeon for fresh air. So Elena had to put up with it.

They looked out the train windows as the shapes of the land changed. They chatted. Elena told Miss Bristol about Luka, Alexei, their mother. Out of habit or maybe only to busy herself, Miss Bristol corrected Elena's grammar and comportment. She shared her portfolio of arcane knowledge, like it or not. How one holds a fork. How one sits up straight so one's spine does not look as if it were made of wool. How one keeps mindful of the drape of one's hem. How one speaks French.

Though she tried and tried at this, Elena couldn't speak French.

She accepted lessons, though, on how to speak Russian like a townsperson and not like a mud snipe.

"If someone asks you about London, you must answer in English, just this one line. It will make them laugh and will relieve their anxiety about your insistence on Russian," said Miss Bristol. "You must say, *Ah, London! London, it is veddy, veddy grand indeed. Cheerio, what?*"

Elena practiced this repeatedly.

"As for Paris," added Monsieur d'Amboise, who had stopped with cups of tea, "you might say, *C'est vrai, la Ville-Lumière, elle vous enchante comme aucune autre.*"

"I might not," said Elena.

She didn't like being improved, but it helped to pass the time. Elena pretended to listen and learn. Sometimes she accidentally took something in.

Daily Elena would wait until the drapes were drawn against the afternoon sun. Then she'd steal into the parlor chamber where Great-Aunt Sophia was often nodding asleep in her chair. The canary would nap with sympathetic exhaustion. Elena brought the picture storybook with her and prepared to tell the old lady a story when she woke up. This worked well until once when the great-aunt said, "I'm tired of this peasant drivel. Read to me from Thackeray."

"But I have my heart set on this 'Tale of the Golden Cockerel,'" said Elena. She'd learned to be more forthright; everything depended on her getting safely to Saint Petersburg. Talking to the nearsighted old lady was good practice for approaching the Tsar.

"You go more native every day," complained the old woman. "I don't know why I spend so much money on that school in Kensington. Young lady, I've noticed you're avoiding my favorite texts in English and French. I want to know why."

"I prefer the old Russian tales."

"You must have misheard me. I didn't ask you what you preferred. I have no interest in what you prefer. Imagine if you are to behave with such dread arrogance when you meet the Tsar's godson. Don't forget you must woo him with docility, my child. None of this 'I think' and 'I want' and 'What it seems to me'! It's unseemly for a young woman to express opinions."

She added, perhaps to herself, "You have to become old and ugly before anyone listens to you, and then they don't, because you're ugly and old."

The train shuddered on a crossing. Elena put the book down. "The truth is that reading in a moving train makes me feel sick. It's easier to tell stories."

"Yes, I have noticed you're good at telling stories. Scant talent *that* is. Well, have your way this time, *ma chérie*. But don't think you're going to make it a habit, having your own way. No good comes of such indulgence. Where *is* that blasted butler with my afternoon sherry? Standards are going to the dogs."

Elena told the "Tale of the Golden Cockerel." In the pictures, the world of Russia was antique and clean. The Tsar looked a little like Peter Petrovich, but not as fat. He wore embroidered sashes at the waist. His throne room was dignified but largely empty. Elena tried to imagine walking across that space, among the colorful pillars, bowing to a man swamped in a colored bedspread. "Dear Tsar. I am here on behalf of my starving village, my missing brother, my sick mother . . ."

"I'm not following. The story has taken a false turn, it makes no sense," snapped the great-aunt. "You're not on your mettle today. That's enough." Elena slammed the book shut with a guilty wince. "Pull aside the curtain on the far window, and let's see what we can see. The light is changing, and I feel we are closing in on Saint Petersburg."

Elena did as she was told, but she took care to stand in the shadows.

The afternoon sun had slid down the bowl of the sky. The long night was almost upon them. The world was filled with a pearly light. The great-aunt: "Oh, for my spectacles! Is that what I think it is, my dear?"

"I don't know what you think it is."

"Confound your adolescent contrariness. Is that flooded fields, at this time of year?"

Elena shaded her eyes. "Yes, *ma tante*. Some wide meadows underwater. One can tell by the rows of trees that mark out boundaries and tracks."

"Bizarre. Is that Saint Petersburg in the distance? Oh, these old eyes. Would I could see in light what gleams so bright in memory. We're almost home, I think, but my child, can you remember?— home doesn't look like this."

"I don't remember," said Elena, daring the truth. The old woman didn't seem to notice.

"Canals and lakes and rivers. Saint Petersburg was built on a swamp, *ma chérie*, by Peter the Great. An Asiatic interpretation of

161

European finesse. He ordered canals to drain the water away so he could have a northern capital city that faced Europe. For part of every year, it would enjoy easier access to France and Prussia and England. What could have happened, that the canals are overflowing? Is Saint Petersburg drowning? Have you brought your rubber ducky in your kit bag from school?"

Elena didn't reply. She'd learned that not to reply to what she didn't follow was seen as an act of subservience, not stupidity.

"And look, look; are these old eyes playing tricks on me? Were it not confounding, I should call it beautiful. A prospect laid out in duplicate. The most elegant city on the continent above, and its reflection in the accidental mirror below."

Elena was silent, awed not by its splendor but by its size. At this distance, the city of Saint Petersburg spread across half the horizon, coherent as a form of nature.

Elena had imagined that the Winter Palace would be directly across the road from the train station. She'd simply dash from the door of the train to the door of the throne room. Which would be empty of anyone but the Tsar and the supplicant (herself), like in that picture in the storybook. Once there, she'd curtsey in the way she'd been practicing. She'd present the Tsar with her gift of a Firebird's egg, if that's what it was — she was beginning to doubt her own recollections about finding it — and she'd ask for his release of Luka. She'd be in and gone, just like that, and beginning the long walk home along the railroad tracks.

Now she wondered if it would take her days even to identify which of these magnificent buildings was the right palace.

As the train continued its rickety approach, Elena and Great-Aunt Sophia watched the mirrored city, above and below the water line, growing at the same rate. An escarpment almost porous with blue and ocher light. Structured water, liquid stone.

"I don't know what the crisis is," muttered Great-Aunt Sophia, "but have you ever noticed that the world can hardly fail to be beautiful even when it is falling apart?"

The Progress of
Dumb Doma

B aba Yaga's hut was called Dumb Doma. *Doma* means "house" in Russian, Cat knew. As to why it was called *Dumb*, Cat didn't take long to guess. Baba Yaga treated the house like a kind of stupid cluck, beating it from the inside, sticking her head out a window and talking to it from the outside, whispering when she didn't want it to overhear what she was saying. The house *was* a sort of cluck, standing as it did on two giant chicken legs.

A certain odor. I'll leave it at that.

Without ceremony they prepared to evacuate the melted island of winter in the middle of the impossible early spring. Baba Yaga told Dumb Doma to pause on the bridge. The witch then leaped out the door and sprang onto the railings. For an old withered dame, she was mighty spry, thought Cat, watching from the porch. Baba Yaga sniffed the air in four directions. "Smells like we're lost already," she announced. "Well, let's get more lost."

As Dumb Doma lurched along, and the floors of the little house tilted about like the deck of a ship in a high wind, the witch began to pitch the four skulls toward a basket near the fireplace. "Skittles, come play skittles!" she shrieked to Cat. "Whoever gets her two skulls in the basket first wins. Here, you can take Caligula and Richard the Third, and I'll keep Robespierre and Tamburlaine."

"I don't want to bowl with skulls," said Cat.

"Mind your manners or I'll have your head to complete the set."

So Cat played. She landed Caligula almost at once, but Richard the Second proved traitorous and wouldn't settle.

Dumb Doma paid no attention to the game going on within its walls. It picked its way through the woods with jaunty tread. Tree branches brushed its porches with a sound of tulle skirts. When that sound stopped, Cat could tell that they'd arrived at the railroad tracks. The veering and listing of the cottage subsided.

Baba Yaga opened the front door. The front porch was no longer a rustic portico but a little Iberian balcony in wrought iron. "When did you manage this renovation?" asked Cat.

"Dumb Doma remodels itself. A nasty habit, like binge shopping. But what can I do? I'm only a tenant."

They stepped onto the balcony. The tracks stretched in both directions.

"Which way?" said Baba Yaga. "Directions confound me, as all ways are one to me."

"Left," said Cat, and pointed. The house obeyed.

"Time for elevenses," said Baba Yaga, pushing Cat back inside before she got any bright ideas. The witch slammed the door. "Are you hungry, child?"

"A little," said Cat.

The kitten commented, "Don't eat anything the witch gives you, or you'll have to serve her for seven years."

"That's a filthy lie," snapped the witch. "You just want more for yourself, Mewster, because I'm such a good cook. Take it back."

"I never take anything back," said the kitten. As the witch picked up a frying pan and began to swing, the creature continued, "Though I do declare, her Munchy Mouse Buttocks aren't to be sneered at."

"Old family recipe," said the witch.

"You don't have any family and you never did," said the kitten. "You're all by yourself, come from no parents and yielding no kits."

"I invented the recipe a long time ago; I'm my own family; I'm old: so it's an old family recipe. What, you want me to send you to law school? Be quiet, I'm trying to concentrate. Let's see what we have in the larder. We have eye of newt and toe of frog, carbon-crisp residue of manticore loin, a beaker of all-natural belladonna extract, some wolfbane, some romaine, a poteen of ptomaine, and a few limp radishes in butter, pinched from the platter left out for Marat after his bath, which he never got to since he died therein. Let's have Cheerios."

"I don't know what Cheerios are," said Cat.

"They haven't been invented yet. You'll love them." The witch brisked up three bowls of some dry, light brown circlets. "Here. *Bon appétit.* They're better with milk, but we're out of milk. Mewster, why are we out of milk? That's odd."

The kitten sneered. "This looks like cat food." At the witch's glower, he added, "And lady, do I love cat food. I'm a cat."

166

"Me too," said Cat, trying to be polite. "I mean, my name *is* Cat."

"Oh, she has a name. How affected," said the witch. "I was going to call her Little Drear."

Despite being dry, the food was not too bad. And now Cat could see why the table stood on human legs. As the room rocked back and forth, the legs took turns standing on tiptoe or bending at the knee, to keep the surface level and the food from spilling out of the bowls.

"Yummers. I *am* a good cook," said Baba Yaga when she'd finished. "All done, Little Drear? I mean, Cat? Look, Mewster, our guest has finished up every morsel of toasted oat goodness. Now she's obliged to be my slave for seven years."

"For Cheerios?" asked Cat.

"I'm just *kidding*. Children are so literal. It's a penance."

The house was slowing down. "Are we there already, Dumb Doma?" The witch ran to the front window and peered through the lace curtain.

"No," said Cat, "it looks as if we're coming to a village."

"Drat. This'll slow us down."

"She doesn't like her house to be seen by human eyes," said the kitten to Cat.

"I saw it, and *my* eyes are human."

"Yes, but she intended to eat you. That's different."

"Why didn't she eat me?" whispered Cat.

"Maybe because you brought her a present? No one does *that*," replied Mewster. He nodded his little furry head to the Fabergé egg, still hovering in the Firebird's nest. "Only children can see

Dumb Doma, thanks to some ancient spell the witch can never remember nor revise. Sometimes children tell what they've seen. And sometimes their parents remember seeing Dumb Doma when they were young, and then, oh la! Quite the chase. Children shrieking and pointing, adults following blindly with catapults filled with burning oil, and a roundelay of curses."

"You're spoiling my digestion," snapped the witch. "Still, I can't be bothered with buboes today. They're too finicky. We'll have to sit here and wait until everyone is asleep. We can continue by moonlight." She hit the wall with her pestle. "Dumb Doma! Settle down and roost in some copse not too near a school yard. The rest of you campers, it's time for beddy-bye! Lights out!" She reached into the wall and somehow withdrew, like a drawer opening, a comfy bed with pink ruffles and a princess canopy. It was littered with heart-shaped pillows saying things like BE MINE, VALENTINE and ET TU, BRUTE? She threw herself in a heap upon the coverlets with her bony rump up in the air and started to snore instantly.

"Do we have to retire?" asked Cat.

"I find it easier to sleep in the daytime anyway." Mewster chose a spot where sun slanted in through a high window. He licked himself to slumberland in a matter of seconds.

Cat, however, wasn't tired. She tiptoed around the one-room hut, opening drawers and cabinets. She saw a lot of things she couldn't recognize. Obscure medical instruments, or maybe they were cooking devices. She found scraps of writing in several languages. Spells, perhaps. She found bottles of vile liquid and deposits of powder in husks of paper. She found three dead parrots in a basket, yoked together at the talons, half covered with gold glitter as if they were a failed attempt at a holiday decoration. She found a jar labeled UNEATEN MACADAMIA NUTS. She found where the hummingbird lived, in a Tyrolean cuckoo clock carved to resemble a gravestone. A script over the front door read, TIME FLIES WHEN YOU'RE DEAD.

Above the settee, a whole shelf of masks. Some she could recognize and some not. A beaded Venetian plague mask with a beaky nose. A papier-mâché mask of someone a lot like Diderot. A mask of Comedy and one of Tragedy and a third one that cringed. Cat thought it might be named Malady.

She found a bookshelf. She found a Bible, which surprised her. It fell open to the Book of Job. She found a complete set of the works of Edgar Allan Poe, with little tabs of paper sticking out. They were scrawled over with the witch's comments to herself. "Fun!" "Try this, but with exploding feathers!" and "Gotta love him — deeply sick." She found a book of black-and-white etchings called *The Far Side*. Also a set of flat cardboard sleeves printed over in English, each containing a black dinner plate etched in thin concentric circles. ORIGINAL CAST RECORDING proclaimed each sleeve at the top of its front cover. The titles were things like *Annie Get Your Gun, The King and I, Damn Yankees,* and something called *Cats.*

Then there were drawers dripping with jewels, and other drawers deep in assorted jawbones, and a complicated kitchen labor-saving device that promised to slice and dice mice. A miniature guillotine.

Cat felt dizzy. She'd only barely scratched the surface. How could all this fit in a room that was hardly ten feet square? This was surely an enchanted home. When she returned to a drawer she'd already examined, she found this time that it was stuffed with unmatched socks.

She found a rocking chair and pulled up a cozy blanket over her shoulders. Maybe the meal was having a soporific effect. Or maybe the witch was singing a lullaby in her sleep. Cat felt her head nodding on her shoulders. Was this normal tiredness, or had she really been enchanted into servitude? True, it would be one way to get out of having to preen in front of the Tsar's godson as a prospective bride, but she hadn't bargained for such a commitment. . . . In seven years she'd be twenty.

When Cat came to, the witch was already awake. Her fancy bed had disappeared. But for a few candles, the room was steeped in darkness. It was juddering slightly. It took Cat a moment to remember what this motion felt like, but then she did. Like being on a train.

Cat, politely: "Good evening."

"Is it? Well, we'll have to do something about that," snapped the witch. She was doing a jigsaw puzzle on a card table. It appeared to be a picture of a wreath of dead skunks. She picked up a pair of pinking shears, trimmed a piece, and smacked it into place.

"We're moving again."

"Oh, yes," said the witch. "A cargo caravan was going by in the middle of the night, and when it slowed down for a curve, I instructed Dumb Doma to make a flying leap for it. Dumb Doma landed on a flatbed and settled down nicely. So we're taking the train the way hoity-toity folks do."

"Baba Yaga." Mewster was nosing about in a cabinet. "Did you finish the biscuits while we were sleeping? You hog."

"I did not. If they're gone, she must have taken them." The witch grunted in Cat's direction.

"I never did," said Cat.

"Well, we're all out," said Mewster.

"It's a magic cracker tin," replied the witch. "There's no such thing as *all out*."

"I think we're running through our provisions," said the cat. The hummingbird came out of the cuckoo clock and pretended to drop dead, but when Mewster tried to pounce, it flew back up and slammed its little door.

The witch put down the snippers. "I don't understand," she said. "It's a very slight spell, a magic cracker tin, but it has never failed before." Absentmindedly she began to nibble on the puzzle. Then she turned to Cat. "You're human. How does it feel to be hungry?" she asked.

"Well," replied the child, surprised at her own answer, "I suppose I don't really know."

Two Moons
in the
Long Wet Night

It's been so long since I've seen Saint Petersburg. I hope I'm equipped to present it to you as marvelous as it truly is.

It was the most enchanting thing Elena had ever seen. Often this feels true about whatever we are seeing for the first time, whether it be a newly discovered best beloved or steep mountains. Or justice. Whatever *that* is.

How appreciation for any of these things arises in the young, I don't know.

As the sun set, it seemed to Elena, the horizon became a ridge of black shapes, lights above staining the flood below, wavering strips of gold and silver.

These were lights in the windows, though Elena couldn't imagine so many lights in all the world, let alone in one city. They looked like stars. She tried to imagine walking among them, stars at eye level, stars within the reach of her hands.

Then, bronze as dried orange rind, a gibbous moon appeared behind a cathedral. The torqued domes looked like paper cutouts across her bosom. In a few moments, she found her sister bobbing beneath the waves, looking more diffuse, the white of a poaching egg.

"I never knew the night to come in so fast." Elena let out a breath between pursed lips, as if she might disturb the prettiness by being too urgent.

"I've *told* you all about this," said Miss Bristol. "You've done your geography. You know how close to the Arctic Saint Petersburg is. Even more northerly than the farthest of the Hebrides, and about equal with the southern tip of mighty Greenland. We're only five hundred miles or so from the Arctic Circle. You remember."

"You forget," said Elena. "Cat knows all about this, not me. Cat knows about miles instead of versts."

"Oh, yes. Well then. I suppose I'm bewitched by the sight, too." Miss Bristol fussed at her nostrils with a handkerchief.

"It got dark so fast," said the girl. "Has the Tsar commanded it, to make the city shine so?"

"Don't be fanciful. It's not magic nor is it imperial taste," said Miss Bristol. "It's astronomy, no more than that. You see, the world is tilted, so, and the sun is a golden melon, so, and the earth floats about it, so." Miss Bristol made fists of her hands and shook one and then the other, apparently under the delusion that she was the earth and the sun. "In winter, the sun is here and its light falls like this, so the nights are long and the days are short. In the summer, it is in reverse, and that is what makes the White Nights of the summer, when the sun hardly seems to set for longer than it takes to give your teeth a good brushing."

"I have no idea what you're talking about."

"Neither do I, but dental hygiene is important. If you aren't to be clapped in chains for halitosis, you'd better come with me. You'll thank me for showing you a thing or two about rinsing with sodium bicarbonate and rubbing your teeth with pulverized chalk. You have a portion of tinted abrasive for your use — I mean, Cat had a portion for her use. You may as well avail yourself of it."

So Elena was dragged away from the window and inducted into the care of her choppers.

Though the city seemed close, the train had slowed to a crawl. Monsieur d'Amboise reported that most of the tracks into the central rail station in Saint Petersburg had been flooded, and trains from other directions had been rerouted onto a single approach. A queue of trains waited to arrive on this line. It might take a whole day until it was their turn.

The larger grew this brilliant city of the north, the more Elena remembered how far she was from home. And why she had not run away when she'd had the chance. She was beginning to be more nervous. Her father was dead and her mother was dying, and her brother had been impressed into military service by the Tsar's generals. Her village was starving, and she was starving herself, most of the time. (Only not tonight. She could feel Cat's gown across her stomach pinch a little.)

She thought of the old doctor back in Miersk. Acting like a Tsar of fate, naming days! As if he had that right. From this distance, he seemed parochial. Still, what sort of day would he have named this one? Run for Your Life Day?

Once an hour or so, the train groaned and started to move,

and inched for ten minutes until it came to a halt again. The twin moons swam in tandem.

"Up, up." Miss Bristol was shaking her. "We arrive today, and the wheezy old calliope wants you to have breakfast with her. She won't take no for an answer."

Elena groaned. She was afraid that the excitement of returning to Saint Petersburg might bring the great-aunt some sharper faculty of awareness. Elena couldn't afford to risk discovery now, just as she was about to flee. "Tell her I didn't sleep well last night and I'm ill."

"That's a filthy lie, and I won't be party to it. She insists, and if I don't produce you this time, I'm not doing my job, and she will wonder why. We aren't safe yet. Get up, and put this on." Miss Bristol fussed in the wardrobe and selected a dark-blue dress with white stripes along the hem, and a white sailor bib-collar with blue stars in the corners.

"This shows my ankles!" said Elena.

"And a sorrier pair of knobby fetlocks I've never seen. You'll wear stockings. And these black shoes. Wash your hands."

"And brush your teeth," said Elena in a singsongy way. She had gotten to know Miss Bristol.

"And your hair," added the governess. "And mind your manners. And your tongue. Govern yourself. We aren't out of the woods yet."

It would seem we are, thought Elena, as the city crept closer and closer in the rose-green light of dawn.

Madame Sophia Borisovna Orlova was dressed and wolfing

down a hearty breakfast. "Well. Brisk is as brisk does," she said. Briskly. *"Jus d'orange?"*

Elena had learned enough to say, "Yes, please."

"Are you ready for your return to my home, my child? It's been so long since you visited, and you were quite small. With winters in London and summers in Brittany or the Riviera, that scandal strand, I expect Saint Petersburg will seem tame." The words said one thing, the tone of voice quite another. "But manners in all the European capitals serve as your passport, and you will find yourself quite at home here."

"I should be very happy if that happens." Another truth, and said in the kind of tortured sentence of which Miss Bristol would approve. Perhaps, Elena thought, I'm not quite as stupid as I look.

"I must confess that all this"—Madame Sophia waved her hand about, indicating the wet world beyond the windows—"all this *splash*—well, it does worry me. For this I have dragged you across Europe? I cannot imagine what damp catastrophe is going on here. Perhaps we'll discover that the Tsar has had to cancel the ball to introduce his godson to society."

"Perhaps." A safe word. Perhaps the safest.

Madame Sophia: "If I find I've ruined your season on a wild-goose chase, my dear, I shall be very cross with myself as well as with the Tsar. And with the floods. That great moon last night no doubt made things worse, dragging in heaps of extra water from the Gulf of Finland. Oh, my dear. I can see this trip has worn you out. Your voice has lost its youthful fluting. Though your carriage has improved, your carefree tone hasn't returned. You are guarded. I have frightened you with the anticipation, and perhaps all for naught. Perhaps the Tsar will send all his guests away."

"Maybe his godson drowned in the floods."

"Hardly a cheery thought. I expect he can swim. Can you?"

Cautiously. "I rarely get the chance to try."

"Yes, I know; the Atlantic waves are too rough, and the Mediterranean too lacking in smack to bother with. Nonetheless, my dear, to the point. Should we discover that the great event of the season has been canceled, I shall compensate you for the disaster."

"You needn't worry about me," said Elena. I will be out of this train in an hour, she added to herself.

"My Persian rubies," said the great-aunt. "You always admired them, and why should your irresponsible mother have them? The lavallière in the diamond-crusted pendant and the matching earrings. Your face isn't yet mature enough to do them justice. Do you think the emerald brooch would accord nicely with the rubies, or is that gilding the lily? Not that I believe there is any such concept. Any lily can do with a little gilding against the next frost. Myself, I enjoy a little lavender-scented powder upon my Roman proboscis." She turned her head this way and that, displaying the squat nose planted among the pleated quilt of her wrinkled cheeks. "I'm being humorous."

"You're looking very beautiful."

"I think so, too, especially since I misplaced those cursed spectacles. Thanks to myopia, in the mirror I have come to resemble Aurora, Goddess of the Dawn. But do you accept my suggestion about compensation in case the Tsar cancels his festival? About the rubies and diamonds? Of course this is all speculation, but even so."

"I suppose it is," said Elena, and began to speculate.

⋄ ⋄ ⋄

She was going to run away. She was. She *was*. What if she didn't, though? Could she somehow pass off that old egg as a Firebird's egg long enough to get the Tsar's attention? She no longer quite believed it was magic; she now wondered if she'd been sleepwalking off the train and found it in the woods that dawn, and if her dreamy imagination had filled in the indistinct fiction of a Firebird, a fox, and a chicken.

The old leathery thing in its box wasn't quite as warm to the touch as before.

She pictured herself presenting it to the Tsar, curtseying, asking for clemency for her brother and food for her poor mother. She would look almost regal in the rubies, and he would have to pay attention.

Miss Yaga

pparently Baba Yaga had told the truth about her house being visible only to the young. No one on the freight train seemed to have noticed that Dumb Doma had climbed aboard and was hitching a ride for hundreds of versts. "Did you enchant your house to be invisible to all but children in order to preserve the sanity of adults?" asked Cat. "Like the laborers caring for this train?"

Baba Yaga: "You mistake me for someone who spends her time worrying about other people. I don't. If someone wants to freak out over seeing Baba Yaga's hut on his train and spend the rest of his life babbling in some sanitarium, why should I care? I enchanted Dumb Doma to screen out nosey parkers, always coming around to borrow a spoonful of salt so they could get a glimpse at my lifestyle choices. I use my magic for my own purposes. To protect myself from the misery of normalcy, mostly."

"Being normal isn't that miserable."

"Try it for a thousand years in a row, and you'll be grateful for a little zaniness." The witch cut a caper the likes of which Diaghilev would have approved.

"But you can't approach the Tsar as you are," said Cat. "You'd never be allowed anywhere near the court."

"What's wrong with me?" The witch shoved her chin farther out in the air, and her eyes flashed. "I take my vitamins."

Half the time Cat didn't understand what Baba Yaga meant. She had learned to just keep gliding toward whatever shared meaning might be possible. "You aren't exactly presentable."

"I'm the very glass of fashion and the mold of form. Aren't I, Mewster?"

"You look like a walking hairball," said the kitten.

Baba Yaga clapped her hands. A wardrobe shuffled forward abjectly, reluctantly. The witch yanked open one door, on the inside of which hung a full-length looking glass. From where Cat sat upon a three-legged bench, she could see both the witch and her reflection. The one scowled at the other, and the other scowled back.

No one in her right mind would call Baba Yaga a spray of loveliness. She was no taller than Cat. Her legs and arms, clothed in tight black undersleeves, were spindly, rickety. Atop this she wore a belted black tunic cinched tight around her tiny waist. The way the fabric flared up toward her neck and down as far as her knees made her look like an all-black hourglass with arms and legs. How her scrawny neck carried her monstrous skull?—laws of gravity didn't apply to Baba Yaga's head. Her pallor was the dead white of snow, though she had trailed a few smudges of crimson paste across her lips, which wobbled from cheek to sunken cheek, string from an untied knot.

Her coiffure was her crowning ghastliness. Her tresses seemed neither black nor white nor grey nor silver, but perhaps a kind of dry marsh-grass color. They rose from her forehead like a hairy soufflé, reversed direction, and dove down her neck. Halfway down her back, they were gathered tightly in a cord. Below the cincture, the hair sprang out again with agitation.

The witch turned this way and that. "I think I've kept my figure, don't you?" she asked Mewster.

"Who else would want it?"

"Don't be snarky." She batted her eyelashes at her reflection. "I do believe I have my mother's eyes."

"Maybe it's time to give them back. Your mother's been dead since the reign of Oleg the Incontinent."

"And everyone says I have the sweetest smile." She cracked open her lips. A few flakes of orange rust flew out of her mouth. Her teeth were made of iron and did not line up with conviction. "When a Russian maiden smiles, the balalaikas of the Volga boatmen strum in tune."

She smiled. The balalaika hanging on the wall snapped all its strings at once, a tangle of catgut and atonality, prefiguring Stravinsky.

"Are you trying to tell me something?" she asked the instrument. The wardrobe tried to close its door and back away, but the witch said, "I'm not done with you, you!"

"Perhaps you should ask our visitor what she thinks," said Mewster. "She comes from the world of the temporarily sane."

"Well?" said Baba Yaga. "Go ahead, girl. Give me your opinion."

Cat almost found herself wordless. Still, it was in her best interest to keep the peace. If she could help the witch pass through the court of the Tsar, she'd have a better chance of returning the Fabergé egg safely and of escaping the witch's clutches at last.

"Among witches, there is no one I admire more than you," said Cat. "But you may find that you draw more attention to yourself than is useful."

"Explain yourself."

"Well." Cat thought before she spoke. "When I discovered you, you were hidden away in a sort of private snow globe of your own invention. You seemed to like to keep apart."

"Human behavior is so tawdry," admitted the witch. "Present company included. I keep to myself. As the lady poet said, 'The soul selects her own society, Then slams the door.'"

"You've been able to display your own particular . . . glamour . . . in the refuge of your Dumb Doma. In a great city," ventured Cat, "one wants *not* to draw attention to oneself. It's not only safer, but more convenient. You wouldn't want your progress to be slowed down by mobs of people coming after you."

"To burn you," whispered the kitten.

"To admire you," insisted Cat. "You have business to conduct with the Tsar, you said. To warn him about the death of your personal winter, and press for an enquiry? You'll make your way to his court much more easily if you can pass among humans as an ordinary person."

"How revolting a notion. Still, I see what you're getting at. So what do you propose?" Baba Yaga turned and stared at the mirror again. "Shall I arrive as an infanta from Prague or Seville?" The reflection in the mirror showed a huge-headed toddler in a golden gown, Baba Yaga's face pivoting above a stiff white lace ruff.

"Babies don't often travel on their own," said Cat gingerly.

"You can push me in a perambulator. I shall wave like a queen."

"I'm not old enough to be your governess."

"Perhaps I should be a performer of some sort." In quick order, the mirror organized images of Baba Yaga as Columbine without Pierrot, as Judy without Punch, and then as a chanteuse in a slinky black shift with a single dead rose in her hand.

"Better," said Cat, "but still, a performer wants attention. What you want is to avoid attention."

"So I could be, what? What kind of person gets the least attention in society?"

"Peasants?" offered the kitten.

"Oh! Slumming. What fun," said Baba Yaga. The mirror worked up a new outfit and showed Baba Yaga sporting a head scarf and a pair of spectacles with elongated, translucent frames that came to a glittery point on each end. She was sheathed in a slurry-colored coat that plunged cylindrically to the floor, a fulsome tree trunk shorn of its bark. Drooping from her hands, two overladen paper sacks with handles. On their sides, in English, the sacks said BLOOMINGDALE'S.

"I haven't met many peasants," said Cat, "but those I *have* met don't look like that."

"You're awfully fussy."

"The girl knows the current world better than you do," Mewster reminded Baba Yaga.

The witch shrugged. "If not a peasant, then what?"

The kitten turned to the girl. "What if she was your governess?"

"I take every second Saturday off and a week in the summer, and I refuse to sing stupid songs to make you behave!" shouted the witch.

The mirror struggled to get the outfit right. First, a black skirt rushed to the ground beneath a pale apron with grey stripes. Then the skirt retreated to mid-calf length, and sensible stout black shoes with laces appeared. A tight acid-citron waistcoat with big buttons. Cat thought it looked like the jacket of some hunter going out with hounds to catch a fox. Still, it could be a lot worse. "We're getting close. What about that hair? Can you manage it in a bun?"

The mirror gathered Baba Yaga's hair up onto the top of her head. There was so much that it looked like a giant bundle of shredded laundry. On the top perched a small green loden hat with a feather in it.

"I'm not loving it," said Baba Yaga.

"The bun is too big."

"Where am I going to carry my necessities?"

"A little reticule of some sort?"

The mirror shrank the hair and provided a carpetbag.

Baba Yaga snorted. "I look like a woman of a certain age."

"You are," said Mewster.

"Oh, no," said the witch. "I am a woman of every age. What shall you call me, Cat, if you need to address me out on the pavements of Saint Petersburg?"

Cat thought of Miss Bristol. "Is Miss Yaga too personal?"

"If this is going to work, we're all going to have to suffer," said the witch. "Miss Yaga it is."

I think, thought Cat, Baba Yaga is rather enjoying this.

184

A Grey Rainbow

I will only say this: As the private train bearing Madame Sophia and her retinue began its final approach to the capital city of Russia, a cloud of migrating grey wagtails, who favor marshes and wetlands, arose from where they rested. In concert, they made an ashy swerve in the sky. Elena saw them and gasped.

I have talked a little bit about the Firebird. He is a living torch, a kingly flame. But here I point out numberless forgettable, nameless serfs of the breeze, turning this way and that, searching for a new way.

They shouldn't be here. They winter in West Africa, I'm told, and usually return to Scandinavia and the great northern lakes, Ladoga and Onega, only in springtime.

They are too early. They are impertinent.

But the common grey wagtail came in a number of hundreds of thousands. Maybe millions, flying a grey rainbow above its grey reflection.

Next Next.

I USED TO SIT AT THE WINDOW OF MY PRISON. THE HORIZON, the sun and moon, all that tiresome flotsam. Haven't I told you this before? I must have done. The birds, they were my unwitting allies. I borrowed their freedom and their sight. I flew with them over the landscape of the past, trying to discover what led to my downfall. I may have been muttering to myself all the while, but there was no one to tell me to just shut up.

I could see this train, loitering outside Saint Petersburg, one silver snake among many, waiting for permission to approach.

I could see this other train, hundreds of versts to the south, on which the hut of Baba Yaga sat, swinging its chicken legs.

All I could see had already happened, though. I couldn't see forward, to the moment when someone came up the steps and unlocked my door, carrying either a writ of freedom or a pistol. Birds, alas, can't fly to the future and bring back hope.

Except, I suppose, that bird in the Old Testament, who brought Noah a green signal, an olive branch of peace from the reviving world. I could have done with such a dove, such a branch.

No doubt Noah offered his wife that olive branch. Forty days in a boat with those animals to clean up after? A peace offering likely all that stood between their marriage and bloody murder.

Maybe she put the sprig in a clay jug of water to see if it would root, in case this little stem wasn't the promise of a new world, but the last scrap of life in the old one. Women are smart that way, husbanding. Of course, Noah was husbanding, too.

I think about that branch, about that jug. About what we have and how we husband it.

Think of egg and spoon. If there is an egg, well, fine. You eat. Unless you use your spoon to hold the egg out of my reach. Does being in possession of a spoon give you more right to the egg? How about a knife? A throne? A purse full of cash?

Or maybe the spoon is what you use to share with. To lean over the bedside of someone's ailing somebody and tuck a little soft egg into her mouth.

Egg and Spoon, I've learned, is the name of a children's game. One version was played at Queen Victoria's Golden Jubilee in London. Children carrying raw eggs in metal spoons raced to see who could get over the finish line first without dropping and cracking their egg. Another version has been featured on White House lawns in those far United States; this contest involves children pushing their eggs across the grass with long-handled wooden spoons. Both varieties involve winners and losers. Neither game mentions what the winner does with the egg. Or who consoles the crying children who are clumsier, or unlucky, or merely younger.

The dove flies and spies a sprig of olive; we earthbound mortals are chained by horizon.

If we are high enough to see the train bearing Elena and, hurrying along behind, the hut of Baba Yaga with Cat inside, we can't help but see evidence of other people. Other dramas on other trains, probably. Other hungers, solitudes, incarcerations. If we dare notice. I bet the Firebird notices.

We can't see into the future, no more than Noah and his wife on the high floods could. A certain enchantment indeed, could we learn to see into the present. Most days I do not, personally, manage this very well.

PART · THREE

SAINT PETERSBURG, SAINT PETERSBURG

Sharing

The disappearance of stock items from the witch's larder was becoming habitual. "Are you running some sort of a cooking consortium behind my back when I'm asleep?" the witch demanded of Cat.

Cat: "I don't cook. That's the job for Cook."

"Cook and Butler, Butler and Cook. I suppose you had someone to soap you in the tub too, lest your hands come in contact with your own personal grease."

"Don't be disgusting."

"Don't dare me. I majored in disgusting at Gulag Community College. Lucrezia Borgia taught cooking, and Madame Defarge taught knitting. Emperor Nero taught violin and also led the cheerleading squad. I skipped all my classes and failed with distinction."

"I never know what you're talking about. I hear the words, but you spout only nonsense."

"She's mad," said Mewster. "Haven't you noticed?"

"I'm not mad," said the witch, rooting through a cabinet. "I'm a scad loose in the head, true, but redeemed by the genius of my personal glamour. If you must know, I'm hungry, that's what I am." She tossed out dusty hardtack, sacks of dried herbs, and an empty mousetrap. "Not much of a hunter-gatherer, am I," she said.

"Conjure something," said the kitten. "A babka of some sort, or blini with caviar. How about a nice bird-and-nest cake?"

"Enchanted supper is all empty calories. I'd dish up my famous porcupine stew, but I'm fresh out of porcupine."

"Improvise," said the kitten. "Do I have to suggest everything?"

"Are you volunteering? Kitty kebabs on a charcoal grill?" The witch opened a hinged panel in the wall and pulled out a stone fire pit, above which hung a battered copper basin.

"I never saw that before," said Cat while Mewster leaped to the rafters.

"This house. Dumb Doma is always into self-improvement. Every time I turn around, behold, another airing cupboard or root cellar. Once I opened a door and there was a closet of the sort that the Americans call an elevator. If I'm not mistaken, it was invented by a man named Otis Elevator. Have you seen one? The English call it a lift and the French, *l'ascenseur.* I think the Dutch don't believe in it; the Dutch are a low-lying people. The whole chamber rises to another floor. I took it up and found a penthouse done over in pickled birch wood, with a tiger skin thrown over the baby grand. Not to my taste, and maybe Dumb Doma caught on, as it's never appeared again." She threw a pinch of cayenne pepper onto the stones, and a roaring fire resulted at once. The house filled with smoke. Dumb Doma opened its own windows and flapped the shutters to clear out the stench.

"I just remembered," said the witch, and drew a salted cod-fish from a purse beneath her clothes. "I was using this as a kind of personal sachet, but the time has come to sacrifice my vanity for the sake of dinner." She threw the fish in the pot, and it began to flop around as if it had just been hooked. In a minute it was charbroiled. The meal seemed mouthwatering to Cat. I must truly be hungry, she thought.

The witch flipped the fish on a plate, picked up a fork, stabbed it, and swallowed the entire thing whole.

"Hey! What about sharing?" called the kitten from above.

"I forgot. I didn't think you'd want any. I can bring it back up."

"No, thank you. Is there truly nothing else?"

"Well, I sent *you* out to scare up a delivery of fresh meat," said the witch to the kitten, nodding at Cat. "Instead of some peasant, you brought in a debutante armed with an ugly party gift for the hostess. Vexing, but there we are."

"I hope you're not going to change your mind and eat her now," said Mewster.

"Don't put notions in my head. A little princess stuffed with her own *foie gras?* Yummers. I'm still ravenous, by the way. That fish was only an appetizer. "

"You're scaring the child," said the kitten.

"It's too late for that," said Baba Yaga, and Cat realized that this might be true. She was getting used to Baba Yaga. Crikey.

"Aren't there some onions in a basket somewhere?" asked Mewster.

"Of course not," said Baba Yaga. "No, we have no bread, we have no meat, we have no cheese, no milk. None of my famous Granny Yaga's Frozen Tater Tots, made from real tots. As the great sage put it, 'When she got there, the cupboard was bare.' And so what was there, they all had to share: *Nothing.*"

"You can't share nothing. There's nothing to share," said Cat.

Unaccountably, she thought of Elena at the side of the tracks, glaring at Cat eating the apple. That green, green apple. She'd thrown half of it away, mindlessly.

Baba Yaga looked at Cat sideways. Sometimes when the witch was speaking like a loopy old bird staggering out of a gin parlor, she wore the keenest expression. "Listen, honeybucket. Kindergarten ethics. As far as I know, there are four ways to share. Count 'em with me."

"Do I have to?"

"Let's say you and I are in a nursery that has a couple of toys. We both want to play. One toy is a pretty doll, one of those nesting dolls, maybe. The other is, say, a little pearl-handled revolver with repeating action. What do we do?"

Cat sighed. School again. Miss Yaga was becoming Miss Bristol, always improving her charge. "We play together. We share."

"All right. First rule: *Everyone owns the treasure together.* No one owns a part; we all together own all of it. In other words, sharing in ownership. So we play together. You take the doll, I take the gun. I shoot the doll. Fun for all. Then we trade. Your turn for the gun. You say to me, 'Hand over the doll.' I throw the doll out the nursery window. So now we only have the gun to share. What do we do now?"

"I guess we take turns. You have the gun for a while, then I do."

"Good enough. That's sharing, too. Second rule: *Everyone owns the treasure in turns.* In other words, sharing in time. Though whoever gets the gun first gets the advantage."

196

"I understand," said Cat.

"And I just enjoyed that codfish. You can eat it next. Doesn't work for you?"

"Not when sharing it wrecks it."

"Which brings us to the third rule: *Every person singly owns an equal part of the treasure.* Preferably before it's worthless. In other words, sharing in portions. One part of a freshly prepared, edible codfish for me. One part for you. Better?"

"Yes. That's better. That's true sharing."

"Okay, but rule three doesn't always work, either. As Solomon said in the Old Book, if two women squabble over which of them is the mother of a certain infant, the way to solve the problem is to cut the baby in half and share the baby in parts."

"That's revolting."

"Is it? I always wondered if that baby was a colicky brat and both women were really trying to pawn it off on the other one. But what do I know from babies? I never had one. Anyway. Sharing in pieces doesn't always work, either, if the treasure is ruined. So on to rule four: *The stronger party gets the whole treasure.*"

"That's not sharing. It's unfair."

"The one with the gun always invents a reason why he deserves to have both the gun and the treasure. But, good, you're listening. It isn't really sharing, no. And so we get to the real rule four."

"Which is?"

"Rule four: *If there are no rules that work, no one gets the treasure.* In other words, sharing the suffering." At this the witch pulled from her sleeve a gorgeous chocolate *gâteau* with cream filling and glazed berries on top, and she tossed it out the open window.

"Why did you do that?"

"It was an illusion. It wasn't really a cake. I was trying to make a point."

The sight of the fake pastry enraged Cat. "This is silly. If there's nothing to share, there's no point in continuing the conversation on how to share it."

"Exactly," said the witch. "That's where we began. What's easiest to share is precisely nothing. We all get an equal part of nothing, if nothing is to be had." She brisked her hands together, clapping imaginary chalk dust off them. "I like being a governess."

"What about *that* useless egg?" Mewster twitched his whiskers toward the Fabergé egg still suspended in the air. "What a fancy omelet that would make."

"It's not edible. It's porcelain, with gold leaf and jewels," said Cat.

"That's all right, I have iron teeth," said the witch, plucking the egg out of the floating nest.

"You can't eat that." Cat was beside herself. "It's not a snack."

"You gave it to me," said Baba Yaga. "I can do what I want with it. If I cut this egg up into three perfectly equal pieces, which slice would you like? Destruction, Creation, or Life as she is lived these days? By which I mean the ice-dragon, the Firebird, or the beautiful young witch in her stylish country getaway?"

"Please don't. It's Solomon and the baby again," said Cat. "You'd ruin it, taking away its value. I'd rather you have the whole treasure than smash it for the sake of a schoolroom lesson in goodness."

"Oh, it's too late for that," said Baba Yaga. The tone of her voice had changed. "It's ruined already."

"What do you mean?"

The egg was so close to the witch's face that it looked like a jeweled carbuncle sprouting from her nose. She peered with one eye, then the other, and rotated the ornament to examine the scene in each of its three apertures.

Finally she handed the egg to Cat. "Tell me what you see, so I can be sure I'm not going all loosey-goosey in the noggin."

Cat examined the glorious impracticality. "Well, in the first window, here is a huge dragon lounging on a snowy steppe. Is that what you mean?"

"Keep looking."

"The second window shows you in your little house. You don't look much like yourself. You look much —"

"Better in real life. I know. It's called charisma. What about the third window?"

The girl turned the egg one more time. The third window showed a spring forest of white birches. For a moment Cat was confused; what was wrong with this? Boring, but pretty enough.

Then she realized. "Oh, my. The Firebird. It's missing."

"No wonder I can't even rustle up a skillet full of sticky buns," said Baba Yaga. "I *knew* the world was ill; my little Russian winter melted without my permission. I thought the Tsar or his advisors might know why. But where has the Firebird gone? He was there when you first gave me the present. Now he's flown away."

"What does it mean?" asked Cat.

It was hard to imagine that white-as-egg-yolk face growing whiter, but Cat could swear that it had. The witch wobbled and began to poke about for a chair. Her little wicker rocker slid forward just in time. She spoke tentatively, working it out. "The soul of Russia is sickly. Even a fancy-schmancy bibelot made by some suck-up in London knows the truth. Perhaps the Firebird, wherever he is, is dying? He needs to lay his egg, as the classical phoenix taught him to do, and resurrect himself? If he won't complete the cycle and emerge, then maybe Russia is dying, too?"

"Why should you care about that? Baba Yaga only cares about herself. She eats the whole fish, remember?"

The hummingbird ventured out of the cuckoo clock and did an un-hummingbird thing. It perched on the edge of a wineglass, perfectly still. Mewster did a thing that cats rarely do: paid no attention to an available bird. They both looked skeptically at the witch.

Finally Baba Yaga turned to Cat. I'd like to say she was stricken lovely with wisdom. She wasn't. She looked as if she'd swallowed an assortment of her own hangnails. "All this talk about sharing. We will share starvation if we learn to share nothing else. If Russia is dying, then magic is dying, too. And I do care. I have to. Don't you understand? I am Mother Russia."

She stood up. She looked no different. Still like a misshapen marionette figure, newly liberated from its strings, uncertain of its strength. Her wicked old face was full of a complex curiosity.

Cat was old enough to know that worry is one of the functions of love, and the witch looked worried. What Cat didn't realize was that *she* was worried for the witch.

That's all they had to share tonight. A big stew of worry.

Vitebsky Station

The approach to the station in Saint Petersburg was most exasperating. The train moved so slowly. But the delay gave Elena the chance to study what of the great capital she could see from the window of the parlor.

She gaped at the heaps of architecture. So much plaster and marble, all in untroubled colors. She watched the lucky citizens in the streets. It was nothing to walk about Saint Petersburg, so what might people on a train be looking at? That's what they said, their shoulders like that, their spines so erect.

The streets were skinned with water. Passersby raised their skirts or trouser legs, sometimes picking their way along board walkways. Not much use when horses and carriages kicked up a dirty fountain. The wealthier people, Elena guessed, stayed dry by being driven about in droshkies or troikas.

As if thinking the same thing, Madame Sophia said, "If he has managed to keep in touch with the stationmaster, Korsikov will meet us with the carriage. Are you excited, Ekaterina?"

Elena was so excited that for a moment she forgot that the great-aunt was addressing her. "Oh, yes, I am, *ma tante*," she finally said.

"It seems so long since you've been here. I expect you'll find it quite —" She lifted her eyebrows at the prospect. "Quite wet."

Miss Bristol appeared in the doorway. She was flushed. "I'm told we are cleared for a platform," she said. She drilled a look of instruction at Elena. *Get ready to flee,* said the look.

The train put out a final burst of steam and slid into a great shed. It came to a halt beneath a glass canopy resting on iron columns. Elena checked the fastenings on her high-buttoned shoes, the ones with the red leather linings. She didn't want to risk falling over her own feet and being apprehended by railway security officers.

Miss Bristol and Monsieur d'Amboise had worked out a strategy with Elena. Miss Bristol and Elena would dismount and walk with the matron to the carriage halt, where it was presumed that Korsikov somehow would still be waiting with the trap, even though the journey had been delayed by a week or so. Just before boarding the carriage, Elena would run away. She would have to find her way to the Tsar on her own. She would ask for directions.

She had her mother's doll in her purse. She would forego the rubies. Pity.

Her departure would distress Madame Sophia. But there seemed no other way. Sooner or later the great-aunt had to discover that the Fabergé egg had gone missing. Elena and the staff would be accused of conspiracy and theft.

So when Elena made her break, Miss Bristol would lunge after her, calling, "Miss Ekaterina!" and she, too, would round the corner, out of sight. There, Miss Bristol would regain her breath and consider herself dismissed from service.

Monsieur d'Amboise, meanwhile, would escort the luggage to Madame Sophia's home by hired cart. After seeing the steamer trunks delivered into the butler's hall, Monsieur d'Amboise would liberate himself. He'd rejoin the governess in the lee of the famous basilica, the Church of Our Savior on the Spilled Blood. With luck, they'd make it across the Grand Duchy of Finland to the border of Sweden before Madame Sophia discovered that the Fabergé egg was missing, too, and raise the alarm.

"Ah, Vitebsky Station." Madame Sophia clapped her hands as they prepared to dismount. "At last. 'Mid pleasures and palaces though we may roam, be it ever so humble, there's no place like home.' Now, *where* is the box with the bespoke present for His Imperial Majesty?"

"It is in your hat trunk, where you placed it ten minutes ago, Madame," said Miss Bristol. "And your hat trunk is in your left hand."

"Then you hold my right hand, Ekaterina, and help me alight," said the great-aunt. This involved negotiating a rolling wooden staircase steadied by a porter. Should she take a tumble, there was quite a lot of her to descend.

The old pomaded battle-ax hadn't been out of her rooms in the private carriage for nearly a month. "Ouf," she said, and "*Zut* alors!" and *"Mon Dieu!"* and "That extra croissant I had on Shrove Tuesday last, it seems to have settled," and also "When I was a circus acrobat, this was a good deal easier," but Elena could tell by now that she was joking. She wasn't such a bad sort, *tante* Sophia.

Finally they were squarely on the rail platform. All around them people were rushing to leave or disembarking from other trains. Shouts of welcome and shrieks of anguished farewell, and *flap-flappity-flap* of the wings of pigeons circulating under the roof, studying the pavement for crumbs.

"Madame," called a man's voice. Here came Korsikov, it seemed, a bandy-legged little man with a hump on his back and a frown creasing his brow. "Eleven days behind schedule. I had feared the worst. I'd seen you sinking beneath these tides. Or attacked by Tartars or disenchanted muzhiks, or marauding bands of elk deranged by starvation. Or you'd become indisposed and been buried in some unmarked grave of Muscovy. I'd all but given up hope."

"Ever the optimist. Delighted to see you, too, Korsikov. And sorry to have kept you waiting. Look, here is Miss Ekaterina! She's grown so since her last visit! Do you recognize her?"

The driver looked at Elena, who kept her eyes trained on his muddy boots. "My," he said in a voice that had darkened considerably, "you *have* changed a great deal, Miss Ekaterina. Haven't you."

"Hello." Elena let her eyes slide toward Miss Bristol's boots.

"She's been under the weather; the trip did not agree with her," snapped Miss Bristol. "She hasn't been herself, and we should get her home, Korsikov. Don't look so gloomy. We survived."

"Call up the army, it is the return of *Mees Bresstollll*," he replied.

"Right this way. You can wait in the front of the station while I collect the carriage."

He led them through the great hall to a plaza beyond. Much commerce and traffic, people coming and going and having unimaginable lives.

Madame Sophia gripped Elena's hand tightly. "It is so easy to get lost here, and Saint Petersburg is not Kensington. Were we separated, I'm not sure you could find your way home, so I mean to keep you safe. Excited, my dear?"

"Very," said Elena. And she was. Her insteps flexed in her tight boots, readying.

"Good. So am I. The thought of my own pillow fills my head with sleep. Miss Bristol, have you got the hat trunk?"

"You have it, Madame. In your left hand."

"Oh, yes. Look, here's Korsikov already. Yoo-hoo! He'll be pulling up next. I must ask him what he has heard about the Tsar's festival. He will know everything. I do hope it hasn't been canceled, but then if it has, there are rubies sooner than your eighteenth birthday for you, so I suppose you will be happy either way."

The great-aunt let go of Elena's hand so she could reach up and haul herself into the carriage. Miss Bristol shoved from behind as elegantly as she could. She turned as Madame Sophia's bottom was negotiating the doorway of the carriage and indicated with her eyebrows and a swift jerk of her head, *Now! Now!*

But the great-aunt had entrusted the hatbox with the big old egg in it to Elena. If she ran now, she'd be running away with it. It made no sense for her to run off with Madame Sophia's hatbox. Even though Elena had begun to doubt her memories about the

Firebird, the great-aunt thought the Fabergé egg was still inside the box. The hue and cry of the chase, the accusation of robbery. Guilt by implication.

Not to mention the rubies, which also caused her to pause.

Miss Bristol broke the paralysis by grabbing the hatbox from Elena and making even more menacing expressions at the girl.

"That hat trunk, Miss Bristol, where is it; have we loaded it yet?" called Madame Sophia from the carriage.

"It is *here,* Madame!" Miss Bristol replied with unusual emphasis. She all but shoved the hatbox into the carriage, and she mouthed at Elena, *Are you mad? Think of your mother! This is your chance! Flee!*

Her mother. Of course. And Elena curtseyed, to thank Miss Bristol for reminding her what she needed to do, and why. As she turned on her heel, her upper arm was clamped as if by iron. "Let me help you up, Miss Ekaterina," said Korsikov.

"I . . . I . . . I believe I left something . . ." she began to stammer.

"What's lost is always found," he replied through gritted teeth, and more or less forced her into the carriage. "I shall see to that. Miss Bristol, you next." And he impounded the governess in the carriage as effortlessly as, weeks earlier, the Tsar's soldiers had abducted Elena's brother Luka.

The ride through Saint Petersburg, a certain torment for Elena.

On the one hand, she'd missed her opportunity to escape. This may have condemned the governess and the butler to persecution. Miss Bristol clearly thought so; sitting opposite Elena, she was busy shooting daggers of hatred from her beady black eyes.

On the other hand, Elena was that much closer to a treasure

of rubies should the Tsar have canceled the festivities. With rubies, perhaps, somehow she might locate Luka and ransom him from military service. He could go back to Miersk. They could try to nurse their mother back to health, hold on till things improved and the báryn's household returned with Alexei. Then they could be reunited. Live ever after, happily enough, not too happy — they were, after all, Russian.

"Look at that! Will you look at that!" said Madame Sophia. Elena peered out the window. She saw hundreds of young men, their shirts off in the winter air. Working up some sweat. Wielding shovels and sledgehammers in the earth. Over on this side of the road, over that direction, too. As if mining for salt. "Whatever could they be up to, making such a *macédoine* of our elegant city?"

"No doubt they're being punished for theft," snapped Miss Bristol. "The hungry in Russia are numberless as the stars. Theft is rampant. Punishment is merciless." She almost sobbed.

Madame Sophia seemed not to notice. "I suspect these criminals are a prison detail assigned to dig new canals to help drain off the floodwater. I shall ask Korsikov when we arrive. Now, that parcel, Miss Bristol. Where have we put my hatbox?"

"No earthly idea," said the governess. "For all I know we left it on the kerbstones."

Elena took pity. She picked up the wooden trunk and handed it to the old lady. When Madame Sophia wasn't looking, Miss Bristol stuck her tongue out at Elena.

Curses and Penalties

One morning, while Baba Yaga was exploring a sudden-onset conservatory that had appeared like a huge glass bustle on the rear end of Dumb Doma, Cat asked Mewster how he happened to come to be Baba Yaga's familiar.

"Mind your own business," he replied. "You think you're the only one who made a mistake and has to pay the penalty?"

"Let me guess," she said. "You're really a prince cursed into service to the witch for seven years, and if someone kisses you, you'll revert to your handsome form. Don't hiss. Trust me, I have no interest in princes. You can stay trapped."

"Whoever tries to kiss me, sweetheart, gets my claws hooked in her upper lip. Listen, we're all trapped in our own lives. You, me, everyone we've ever met."

Baba Yaga, who found potted palms bourgeois and so was tossing them out the window, disagreed. "I'm not trapped in my life. *You're* trapped in my life. And Cat is trapped in the life of that cursed peasant girl she keeps mentioning."

"Am I?" said Cat. "Were you expecting Elena to come along and be supper?"

"Elena Schmelena. Some peasant child or other. That's why I put on the porch lights. And look what the cat drug in! A selfish prig who gave me a present so I can't eat her. Give me a hand with this aspidistra; it's a bruiser."

"I'm not a selfish prig."

"You *are* selfish. Have you given a single thought to what has happened to your alternate number stuck on that cursed train?"

Cat didn't answer. The aspidistra sailed out with a brave flailing of fronds.

Now, perhaps you will think Cat cruel. All this time, hilarity and high jinks on chicken legs, and the girl hadn't spent a moment wondering about the problems that must have beset her new friend. The witch was right. If by stepping sideways, Cat thought, I've escaped being trapped in my own life somehow, so has Elena. Like it or not.

Mewster settled down for a snooze, high up on the wardrobe where he couldn't be subjected to an attack kiss. Cat rocked in the witch's chair and, for a moment, thought about her mirror twin.

As far as Cat knew, Elena was marooned in an accident as surely as she herself was. It hadn't been Elena's fault that the train had started with such a jolt that the Fabergé egg had escaped, more or less bringing Cat with it. What kind of friend was Cat, after all, not to have thought of the distress visited upon Elena?

Not much of a friend, she concluded. I agree with her. Shame, shame. Then again, Cat was the unwilling houseguest to the greatest figure in Russian folk history, and she was distracted by magic.

Now Cat wondered. Had Elena been trapped on the train, hauled away? Been frightened out of her mind? Suffered her own desolation? Or had she jumped off Great-Aunt Sophia's train a few versts on? Perhaps on the far side of the tracks, and that's how Cat had missed crossing her path?

There were people to worry about in every direction, Cat was learning. Prior to the delay at Miersk, she'd had only one concern: how she would duck the attention of the godson of the Tsar without bringing dishonor upon her great-aunt. To whom the presentation at court seemed to matter a great deal.

Crash, bash. The witch had discovered a trove of asparagus ferns huddled under the harpsichord, and they were sailing out the window now. Someday would she tire of Cat and toss her out, too?

Though starting late, Cat now practiced worrying. What *about* Madame Sophia? Had she suffered at the disappearance of her beloved great-niece? Perhaps had a cardiac seizure? Maybe, when Cat's absence had been discovered, the old lady had ordered the train to return to Miersk. If so, would the villagers admit to having seen Cat? To having ganged up on her and scared her away?

That's what the patchy villagers had done, terrified her right into the arms of Baba Yaga. Though the villagers weren't to blame for Baba Yaga. No one was to blame for Baba Yaga except, apparently, Baba Yaga.

Warmed up, Cat now moved on to fretting about Elena's mother, too. Having seen little of her own parents except for brief and brittle visits, Cat had found Elena's mother tender, if uncommonly limp. Were that kindly old doctor and the busybody grandmother still tending her, or was Natasha Rudina beyond help now?

We're all imprisoned in our own parallel lives, thought Cat. Yet Elena and I, without quite getting to be true friends, have accidentally shared our lives. Now I can't even help caring about her mother. It's a kind of curse, friendship.

A Fresh Enchantment

One of the differences between Miersk and Saint Petersburg was posture. The izbas and the chapel and barns of Miersk, all hewn logs and twig-work and tilting roofs, appeared drifted into place. The effect was of a pleasantly organic mess as built by myopic Canadian beavers.

Here, in Saint Petersburg, the buildings had been drawn with rulers and built to an arithmetic precision not guessed at by peasants or beavers.

Look: a statue centered in a perfect dial of a plaza. So lifelike that Elena thought it really was an officer about to plunge his steed off the marble plinth into the city traffic. But only a bronze hero, and pigeons were paying little attention to his nobility.

Damp boulevards and damp parks. Avenues slicing between high facades of imperial stucco, all facing one another without blinking. Elena was disoriented at once. When she fled Saint Petersburg via the rail lines, she'd have to ask for directions.

Finally the equipage turned into a narrower street and stopped at a house the color of new mint leaves. Madame Sophia said, "I will lean on each of you, my human canes." At the top of granite steps, breathing heavily, she let go of Miss Bristol's arm but kept Elena's tightly clenched. She put a hand on her side, breathing through the pain. "Worth the effort, though. Now, Miss Bristol, the gift for the Tsar?"

"In your hatbox."

"I knew that. I was just checking in on your memory. I sometimes worry it is failing you." She winked at Elena while Miss Bristol pulled a cord and rang a bell.

Was this the palace of the Tsar, with all its carved marble and sparkling windows? When the great-aunt entered, however, she slung her gloves on a table. In aprons and caps, a couple of bowing maids and a swaybacked cook greeted Madame Sophia with warmth but formality. "You remember where your room is," said the great-aunt, waving Elena up the interior staircase.

A few cubicles in a train carriage were one thing. But this! . . . A collection of rooms more ornate than she had ever imagined. Beyond pairs of doors, all flung open for welcome, she saw herds of furniture everywhere. Chairs and sofas upholstered in feverish silks. Tables and mantels carved unto the final inch with restless scrollwork. And everything tricked out in gold. Gold cloth, golden flocked wallpaper, gilding on every architectural punctuation point.

Tall pier glasses doubling the golden light.

Wherever Elena glanced, she saw herself in this space. She saw Elena in the garb of Miss Ekaterina. She saw her shoulders pulled back, as Monsieur d'Amboise had hectored her to learn. She saw her hair clean, brushed, upswept.

She saw someone for whom self-contempt was not the foundation garment worn every living day and slept in every night. This child in the mirror — a mystery, but a welcome one.

Did she think of the girl whose life she was stealing, of what misery Cat might be going through just at this moment?

I regret to say she did not.

At this moment, on the landing of the second flight of steps — the brightest part, for skylights let in aqueous light — she saw herself in yet another mirror. Clearly again, for the first time in a long time.

Was she Miss Ekaterina? Or was she a peasant girl stumbled into an accidental warren of comfort and magnificence? There was no witch here, unless Madame Sophia was a witch in disguise. There was no magician, no spell, no enchantment.

Was there?

Had she ever really seen a Firebird? Surely not. But if she had, if she'd grasped his tail feather, is this what she had wished for? Suddenly she felt uncertain. Really, how else could she have made her way to the top of this set of circumstances, standing in such pure elegant light, *without* the help of magic?

She'd dismissed that dawn vision as a dream. But if real magic — somehow — then how far would it take her?

She was still planning to run away. She thought she was. But what if she didn't? What if she let Madame Sophia take her to the ball to meet the Tsar's godson?

What if he fell in love with her? What if hers had become *that* sort of life?

So much impossible had happened up until this moment. Perhaps it was leading somewhere. Perhaps she wasn't at the crest of her adventure, about to career back down the slope, back into that other life of want and woe. Perhaps she was merely midway, and the possibilities would continue to expand.

Approaching from below, Miss Bristol: "Govern yourself. You look like the cat that ate the canary."

Elena turned. "I don't know what you mean."

"It means you look like a hungry peasant girl who has stuffed herself full of stolen marzipan and gingerbread. Exceedingly pleased with yourself."

"Is that so?" For once Elena didn't feel cowering. "Which is my room?"

Miss Bristol rushed up the final steps and swooped upon her at once. Her eyes looked wild. Her bony hands grasped Elena's wrists. "You have no *room* here, missy. You have no *rights* here. You were to run away, and I to follow, and you lost your nerve. I am here to find it for you. Have you become bewitched by all this glamour? Prison will not have such pretty appointments, I promise you that."

"Get off me, you're hurting."

"I see the greed in your eyes. No good can come of trying to trick life. Cook and the servants may not recognize that you are not the young Miss Ekaterina, whom they haven't seen in five years. But Korsikov does, and so will Miss Ekaterina's flighty parents, should they ever visit their supposed daughter, engaged to the Tsar's godson and living a purloined life. You've decided to play with fire, child, and you will be burned. And you mean to hurt me as you play. But I will not have it."

"You can leave," said Elena. "Go down to the doorway where Monsieur d'Amboise will deliver the luggage. Run away with him right now. No one will put it together with me. They might think

215

you have had romance, if they have enough imagination. If there *is* that much imagination in the world."

Miss Bristol looked as if she'd been lanced. "You are a wicked child."

"I am not. I'm tired and I want to rest. Where is my room?"

Miss Bristol sat down on the top step and put her face in her hands. She began to weep. She said some things that were unintelligible. Elena left her there and opened doors until she found a pretty room in the front of the house. It must be her room. A girl's nightgown was laid out upon a chair covered in olive velvet, and fresh white roses nodded from a silver vase on a table in the middle of the carpet.

How very nice, she thought. How appropriately welcoming.

There was a book on the table. She opened it up to see if, enchanted with possibility, she had learned to read. But this proved not yet to have happened.

The Hunger of Children

"Why has this train slowed down so? Dumb Doma could walk faster in high heels," complained the witch. "Even the table could walk faster."

The table, which rarely got a compliment, began to do a traditional peasant dance that involved bending at the knees, leaping up, and kicking out, all in unison. Mewster, who'd been napping on the tablecloth, was flung toward the ceiling, where he caught hold of a rafter. Baba Yaga doubled up in laughter, while Cat tried to coax the creature down. Mewster hissed, "I'm warning you: I'm no house cat."

"We're on the same side," said Cat, pouting, but turned back to Baba Yaga.

The witch threw open a window and leaned out. Her black-clad derrière stuck up like a cushion in a mortuary parlor. "Wheels, put on some muscle, or I'll roll you all to kingdom come!" The wheels didn't obey.

"I wouldn't draw too much attention to yourself by screaming out the window," said the kitten, who had inched down and was now planning revenge on the table. "You've slipped by unnoticed for quite a while, but don't push your luck."

"Luck is for peasants. Baba Yaga doesn't have *luck*. Baba Yaga has fortune. *Destiny.* Still, it might be my destiny to be burned at the stake, even at this late stage of my career, so I take your point." The witch swiveled her head, sniffing with her shark fin of a nose. "Lot of water in this world, Mewster."

"Join a swim team." The kitten was stalking the table, which was inching away.

"What are you saying?" asked Cat, who had crossed the English Channel on the boat train from Dover to Calais and had seen big water before. "Move over — let me see."

It was late in the day. The spires from villages across the reaches looked like the tops of bottles of cologne. Cat guessed they were entering the outskirts of Saint Petersburg at last. The world, though, wasn't drifted with snow but leveled with the sheen of glass.

"What in heaven is going on here?" asked Cat.

"Heaven has little to do with it, I'd warrant," said the witch. "This is the work of confusion. I don't have too much congress with God, myself; we stay out of each other's hair."

"Silent partners," suggested the kitten, pouncing, claws out. The table jumped up on the sideboard.

"As the old proverb goes," continued the witch, "if anything ever happens to God, we always have Saint Nicholas. Though how Saint Nicholas would deal with a winter more damp than icy is beyond my ken."

"Has this thaw anything to do with your sense of the death of magic, do you think?" Cat asked of the witch.

"I have no sense, so I can't say. What *is* that sound of rabble?"

The cargo train was pulling to a stop in a small town. It was the first time they'd entered a station during the daylight. "I hope your house isn't discovered," said Cat. "What would they do to you?"

"I told you. Dumb Doma is invisible to adults," said the witch. "That's why we've had no trouble from the crew of the train. But, bad cess upon us, it *is* visible to children. With any luck, the local children are languishing in a schoolroom or some other prison."

"With any luck? I thought you don't *have* luck," the kitten taunted Baba Yaga. "Only destiny." Such proved to be true, for by the time the train came to a halt, first three, then seven, then ten, then eighteen children began to surge toward the windows of Dumb Doma with their caps in their hands.

"One polushka! One denga! One kopek! Any coin of any size!" cried the children.

"Oh, the peskiness of brute childhood! I always detested it!" remarked the witch.

"Nonsense," replied the kitten. "You ate children for a living and loved it."

"Yes, but by invitation only. A mob is an ugly thing, and the younger, the uglier."

"What do they want?" asked Cat.

"Kopeks!" yelled the children. "Money for food! And food! We want food!"

"Who doesn't?" the witch hollered at them. "We don't have a morsel. Go away."

But the children didn't. They could see Dumb Doma, and they

loved the look of it. As Cat craned farther, she could tell that the house was sitting with its two big chicken legs stuck out, like the stiff legs of a porcelain doll coming straight off a bench. The children were reaching up to grab on to the legs and swing on them. The house was ticklish, and shivered its timbers.

"You better do something," said Mewster, "or your house is going to collapse on its back, and then you'll have to find rooms in this village and live here."

"This is outrageous. I have never been under such an assault, even when Bajazet and Roxane came for dinner and trashed the place. If worse comes to worst, I'll move to the Bronx and spend afternoons playing bingo in some church hall, cheating like the other old hens. Stop that at once!" she screamed again. "Urchins have no manners."

The house was rocking back and forth in mirth. The table fell off the sideboard.

"Dumb Doma, if you don't settle down, I'll give those hoydens some giant barbecued chicken legs for supper!" bellowed Baba Yaga.

"Give them *something*," said Cat. "Anything. Attention, even."

"Oh, is that all it takes?" The witch used a soupy voice. "So glad I have a high-level security advisor on board." Still, she changed her tone when she returned to the window. "Children, your old babushka doesn't have two coins to call her own."

"Give us gold ingots, then!" shouted some wag, and the other children laughed.

"I'll give you what for," muttered the witch, then: "Old Granny Greasy-Hair doesn't have a smidgen for you, much less a side of beef."

"Milk and bread!" they chorused.

"Not a chance. Would you like me to sing you a song instead?"

The response was deafening. "No!" They were beginning to climb Dumb Doma's legs the way children climb apple trees.

"We'll be overrun by the vermin any moment," hissed the witch. "We're lost."

"Tell them a story," said Cat.

"You tell them a story, I'm busy," she snapped. She went to sit in her rocking chair and suck her thumb. The kitten was pretending to forgive the table. He was rubbing up against its hairy legs and purring.

Cat leaned out the window. "My babushka's gone to have her afternoon nap," she said. "You must be quiet, or she'll wake up and eat you all."

The children screamed with joy and fake terror.

"This is intolerable," muttered the witch. "I've lost all credibility."

"I'll tell you a story. Why not," said Cat.

"Better be a good one!" shouted a little girl.

"It's the best," said Cat. She searched in her mind for legends from the elegant storybook that her great-aunt had given her. She settled on the wonder tale of Tsar Saltan. She began to tell about the three beautiful sisters, and how the youngest one married the Tsar, but all her children were kidnapped by Baba Yaga and hidden in a chamber underneath a tree.

"Slander. Actionable offense," muttered the witch from behind Cat.

Outside, the hungry children had quieted down. "What next?" they asked.

So Cat continued, about how the Tsar eventually threw his young bride into the sea, in a casket made of wood, which floated away to a magic island.

"Now, that was foolish," muttered the witch. "The casket ought to have been made of stone, so it could sink. Like a stone."

There was a magic squirrel, it seemed, who cracked nuts of gold with his teeth. And a cat who lived in a magic crystal mansion.

"A distant relative, I think," mewed Mewster.

"Magic cats! And squirrels! Ha. And magic ladles, no doubt," hissed the witch, "and . . . and . . . and magic buttonhooks. Oh, and a magic telegraph pole, and magic, um, muskmelons. And enchanted piles of donkey manure. Very magic." She was having fun, pretending not to listen.

Cat paid her no mind. She told the tale as well she could recall it. Catastrophe followed catastrophe, but eventually the Tsar was reunited with the young bride he had tried to murder, and their marriage resumed with peals of delight.

"No wonder they call these fairy tales," said the witch. "Tolstoi would know better, and a fast train coming into a station would be involved. Blood, tears, regrets. All the fun stuff."

But the children seemed satisfied. They might have preferred a basket full of dinner rolls or a fistful of rubles. But the story would see them through the coming night until the morning brought new promise. The story fed one hunger, anyway. And, really, thought Cat, how much more can we reasonably ask than that?

That night when everyone else was asleep, Mewster scratched the table legs till they bled. That kitten enjoyed a talent for revenge.

The News
of the
Evening

Sitting by her window, Elena watched the sun set through taffy-pulls of cloud stretching in from Scandinavia. The lengthy dusk in Saint Petersburg, she concluded, had to do with the use of electric lamps and gas lamps, inside and outside. The foreheads of buildings across the way glowed against the sky.

Playing plays in the bed nook. A landscape of sere woolen hills. The world outside this window looked artificial, too. Orderly, candied, ready for drama.

She felt a touch of what Cat would have known as desolation, but shook it off.

Miss Bristol appeared at the doorway. "Madame summons you. You'll have been expected to change from your traveling garments. You'd best hurry."

She helped with the blue sash and redid the buttons that Elena had done wrong.

"You are carrying out an errand of madness. I would have your impersonation revealed at once but for its consequences upon my life." Miss Bristol took out of her pocket the great-aunt's missing spectacles, which she must have retrieved from Elena's bedchamber on the train. "Before, I was a hostage to your insolence. Now I am forced to become an accomplice. I hate you." She set the glasses on the vanity.

Elena didn't reply. She ignored the glasses and descended with as much poise as she could manage.

At the bottom of the flight, a maid stood waiting. She preceded Elena into a parlor and announced her. Elena walked in on toes, for added grace.

Madame Sophia said, "Ah, and here, Deputy Sub-Lieutenant, is my young charge, Miss Ekaterina Ivanovna de Robichaux, newly arrived from school in London after our unfortunate delay en route."

The Deputy Sub-Lieutenant, a man with yellow hair oiled just so, was standing at a mantelpiece with his hands behind his back. He clicked his heels together, bowed, and spoke in English. Elena curtseyed as best she could and replied in Russian, "You have very bright buttons."

Madame Sophia's laughter, perhaps a little forced. "The campaigns of childhood! She has decided to pretend she is not being schooled abroad, and instead has affected a rude country accent."

"Perhaps she thinks she can charm the young Prince Anton with it. She has charmed me," said the Deputy Sub-Lieutenant, posing. His lurid hair is one thing, but he has very little chin to be charming with, thought Elena.

"Do sit down, both of you," said Madame Sophia. "Ekaterina, a swallow of sherry, a thimble's worth? No? Well, mind your posture, my child. I have news for you."

The guest's shoulders were thrown back so far, it looked as if he were trying to pierce the wallpaper. Elena rotated her shoulders like his. She felt that this made her neck more swan-like.

"I wait to hear the news, *ma tante*." She chose simple words that she hoped she wouldn't mispronounce and perched on the edge of a chair.

Now that the strain of travel was behind her, Madame Sophia appeared revived. "Our guest reports that the canals of Saint Petersburg are all flooded. Lake Ladoga has spilled its banks. The highland lakes of the Grand Duchy of Finland have risen to form an inland sea. Should this continue, we will all be drowned in our satin sheets, unless we take our rooms on the top flight, with the staff." She spoke merrily, as if this sounded a great adventure for someone at her ripe old age.

"Do not frighten the child," said the Deputy Sub-Lieutenant, deigning to speak in Russian for the sake of household protocol. "Though I do hope you can swim."

He chortled. Elena felt a chill up her straight spine. She couldn't swim.

The Deputy Sub-Lieutenant continued. "The Tsar has called up soldiers from all the Russias to dig new channels. Canals, lagoons, reservoirs, in the interest of flood control."

"But what about the wars?" asked Elena. "Who will conduct them?"

"There are no foreign wars scheduled at present," replied the military man with, perhaps, a touch of sadness.

Elena didn't understand.

"All the men we saw from the train," said Great-Aunt Sophia, "they were soldiers, conscripted by order of the Tsar to help in the emergency."

"I see." Elena twisted her hands in her lap. Then perhaps Luka was *here*, digging nearby somewhere. She must find out. "Very exciting news."

"It's lucky we have such abundance of strong young men in the Russian heartland, but that's not the news, *ma chérie*. With the Neva River flooding beside the Winter Palace, and the ballrooms three inches deep in ice water, other arrangements have had to be made. Wait till you hear! The Tsar has had floating pavilions built to house the festivities. Despite our delay, we've arrived just in time. The opening ceremony is tomorrow evening. The Deputy Sub-Lieutenant has delivered our formal invitation. Just think, Ekaterina. Had our crew not repaired that scorched bridge with dispatch, we'd have been late."

"Perhaps I will have a sip of sherry after all," said Elena. They didn't hear her. The news too thrilling. The Tsar approaching the capital. The great and the good come from throughout Russia, and from many other countries besides. All to meet the Tsar's godson and distant cousin, Prince Anton Antonovich Romanov. Displays of fireworks, military parades. Fresh fruits from the South of France, and flowers from Holland, and champagnes and whatnot, and the titled families of Europe all sending treasures.

"We hardly qualify as a noble line," Great-Aunt Sophia was saying as Elena got up to leave the room, "but we *have* managed to bring a very special bibelot indeed, all the way from London. The Tsar will be gratified. I shall say no more."

In the corridor, Elena put her face in her hands. So close to the

Tsar, already, and perhaps to her brother. Yet so close to danger, if Madame Sophia decided to inspect the Fabergé egg for breakage before she had it wrapped up to present to the Tsar of All the Russias.

Then, from a door under the staircase, Monsieur d'Amboise emerged, arrayed in a formal waistcoat and grey gloves.

"What are you doing here?" whispered Elena in a whisper.

"I delivered the luggage, as was my duty," he replied, neither warmly nor coldly.

"But . . . you were to have gotten away as soon as you did that! Nothing could keep you locked in this house. You are the butler, after all — you must have all the keys."

"I do keep the keys," he replied.

"I don't understand."

In a low voice he said, "I learned from Miss Bristol that you did not flee the train as planned. Thus Miss Bristol had no opportunity to follow you and make her own escape. I could hardly leave her here to face alone the penalties of your loss of courage."

"I have plenty of courage," she said. "But you have the keys. You can both leave, right now. Tonight. Nothing is stopping you. You owe me nothing."

"You," he said, "have begun to think highly of yourself. But you are a child still. What sort of people would leave a child on her own, and in such a mess as you have made for yourself, for us all?"

"You owe me nothing," she repeated faintly, "and I owe you nothing. You stay behind by your own choice."

He walked away to his next chore. "I have already made that point."

Landfall

The freight train had come to a halt. On the raised track bed, the rails ran between plates of unorthodox lake. Wind-rippled diamonds cut into one another.

Cat: "They're taking cargo off the train and putting it on small boats."

"Go find out why," replied the witch.

"I can't just climb out of a witch's house and appear out of nowhere on the tracks and talk to strange men. Anyway, I don't talk to laborers."

"You're my houseguest, so if I tell you to help, you help."

"Houseguest, house cat," said Mewster, stirring from a half-nap. "Same status. Aren't you afraid she'd run away?" he asked the witch.

"Not really. But if she does, so what? She's only auditing my life; she's not doing it for credit. She can drop out whenever she likes."

Cat passed over her lambswool jacket and settled herself into a belted serge coat that looked as if it had once belonged to a welder. She crossed the threshold of Dumb Doma for the first time in what felt like weeks but was probably mere days.

Making her way along the side of the freight train, she called out to the first pair of workers within earshot. "Ho there, my good men," she said. The phrase sounded false in her mouth. But she'd never talked to workers before.

The men were Uzbeks or Kazakhs or Armenians. Their tongue was thick to her ear, but little by little she understood what they were saying. The tracks ahead were underwater, but the cargo was needed immediately. The festival was beginning tonight.

"Tonight!" exclaimed Cat.

Yes. Events had been delayed, but they would be delayed no more. The final guests were arriving on a makeshift relay of barges. And the material being transported from the cargo train, firework powder from Novgorod, was needed for the festival's opening ceremony.

Cat returned with the news. Baba Yaga paced back and forth with her hands running over her long, trowel-shaped jaw. "So," she ruminated, "the Tsar of All the Russias won't let the misbehavior of the world interrupt his schedule any longer. He'll be busy. It'll be hard for us to get an audience tonight. But he's the big daddy. With the snap of his fingers, he can rouse an expedition of discovery and salvage. He may learn what I cannot: why the world is turning so ornery. Assuming his wise men advise him where to look. I don't have a clue. Navigationally challenged."

"Your talent at magic won't reveal where you might hunt for a clue to the mystery?" asked Cat.

"Are you drawing attention to my shortcomings? I'm a governess now, remember? I know my place."

"Regardless, if the party starts tonight, I need to get this gift to my great-aunt."

"You gave that garish knickknack to me, remember? A little house gift."

"I gave it to you in exchange for your releasing me. But you didn't."

Mewster harrumphed a little *murr-wang*, and the witch shot him a dirty look. "Well, Cat, we'll go now. Both of us. And take the stupid egg and regift it to the Tsar. Why not? For one thing, it doesn't match my décor, which I like to call Scythian Revival with a touch of shabby-chic Silesian Provincial. For another, the egg is Exhibit A: Firebird Disappearance, as enacted in porcelain."

"How are we going to get to Saint Petersburg if the train is stalled and washed up here for good? In any case, I have nothing to wear."

"Take your pick, honeybucket." The witch opened the door to her wardrobe. It exploded, jack-in-the-box fashion, with a tsunami of lace and crinoline, paisley and tartan, purses, stockings, sashes, and little hats capped with feathers and fascinators.

"What kind of service is this? She's expected to go barefoot? We'll take our custom elsewhere!" the witch screamed. The cupboard responded with a veritable hail of shoes; Cat had to hide under the table to keep from being kicked to death by flying footwear. The table legs, however, immediately began to try on the new stock.

In short order Cat selected two outfits. A demure blue worsted for traveling into Saint Petersburg. Then, if an audience with the

Tsar proved possible, a green silk number that fell like a waterfall, all moss and silver.

"You'll look like a trollop. That's probably good," said the witch. "You know the rules, Mewster. Don't answer the door to anyone while we're gone."

Regarding the world from the windowsill, the kitten said, "I think the last emergency barque has sailed away."

Indeed, the boats had cleared the train tracks and were halfway across the ersatz lagoon, being poled like Venetian gondolas. A few mergansers swam alongside them, quacking for bread.

"I'm not beat that easily," said the witch. "Table, kick off those high-heeled slingbacks. We're going wading."

Reluctantly, if furniture can ever be said to exhibit reluctance, the table angled itself out the door of Dumb Doma. It shivered in the westerly breeze, its four knees knocking.

"So lily-livered. Get in the water," said the witch. The table tip-toed in.

"Don't forget your little hello for the Tsar," said Mewster, passing along the Fabergé egg. Around the fabulous thing Baba Yaga folded the edges of the nest so it looked like a packet of brambles. "I don't suppose I can come, too?"

She didn't reply. Slamming the door behind her, the witch urged Cat off the stalled flatbed carriage and onto the table, which waded away. It felt like being on a raft, and reminded Cat of punting on the Cam, only without a pole.

In the daylight, Baba Yaga appeared smaller and less menacing than in her own home. More like a real governess than Cat had expected. Her garb was almost convincing. The clothes were serviceable, not flashy. Her head still looked like a slab of pale granite capped with weeds, but the extremity of her visage seemed less noticeable when set against the width of the whole world.

Which, Cat had to admit, had a magic of its own that even Baba Yaga's allure couldn't match.

"First things first," said Cat. She felt it was time to take over a little, if Baba Yaga was going to play the nanny. "We'd better locate my great-aunt and tell her I'm all right. We can show her that the Fabergé egg is safe, too."

"So *she* can unload *my* gift on the Tsar?" The witch looked miffed, but continued, "Oh, who cares? I hate that thing. Looks like something laid by Andersen's mechanical nightingale."

"I only hope my *tante* is here and not still looking for me back in Miersk."

"I'll present myself to her with credentials in hand." Baba Yaga patted her purse.

"Um," said Cat. "I already have a governess. Actually."

"We can take care of *her*."

Cat and Baba Yaga followed in the wake of the emergency flotilla that had carried the festival fireworks toward the city. Only when Cat turned around to see how far they had come did she notice the stalker.

"Oh, my. Baba Yaga?"

"Miss Yaga to you, honeybucket."

Cat pointed. The witch turned and bared her teeth. A verst or two behind them, the house was tramping along, splashing like a toddler in a big puddle. Several side sheds had lengthened and narrowed, and they were pushing at the water like oars.

"When I left home to accept a position in domestic service, I didn't expect my home to follow," said the witch. But Cat noticed the change in tone. Baba Yaga wasn't quite as shrill out in the open air. Maybe she was alarmed at the disobedience of Dumb Doma.

The flood deepened. The table legs began to kick and swim.

"I hope Dumb Doma can swim, too," said Cat.

"It's made of wood. It'll float."

"I've been meaning to ask. How did it get such large chicken legs?"

"I was reading a little something by Gregor Mendel about the hereditary characteristics of pea plants. I decided to try a little do-it-yourself genetic engineering in the privacy of my own home. It went rather badly wrong. I don't like to talk about it."

"But I've studied Gregor Mendel. My seminar called 'Great Men of Science and Madame Curie.' Gregor Mendel did his work only fifty or sixty years ago. According to the stories and your own asides, you've been around for a millennium."

"And I've still got my own teeth." She gnashed her iron dentures.

"I mean your house on chicken legs precedes that famous monk by centuries."

"Haven't you figured out anything? I joke when I'm nervous. Leave me alone," said the witch. "Did you know the great Janáček played the organ at Mendel's funeral? An improvisation on 'Pease Porridge Hot.' We all sang along."

When they made landfall, the table lay down on its back and kicked its legs to dry them off. Then it folded its legs underneath its top, which dwindled to the size of an attaché case. A handle sprouted on one side.

As the izba paddled up near them, Baba Yaga said, "I'm making a house arrest. Dumb Doma, stop in your tracks." She climbed into her home, cursing. She emerged with a length of rope. "Of all the dachas in all the Russias, I had to get the one with a case of wanderlust." She tied one end of the rope to the horny talons of one of Dumb Doma's legs and the other to a lamppost. "If you follow us through the streets of Saint Petersburg, you'll provoke a riot among the schoolchildren. Now, wait right here in case we need a quick getaway. Pretend to be a houseboat."

"I'd like to come, too," said Mewster from the doorsill. "I've been good."

"You know the rules. You have to stay and guard my set of nutcrackers. And don't eat the hummingbird. And don't let anyone in." Then the witch picked up the table by its handle, turned to Cat, and said, "Miss Ekaterina, as your governess, may I propose that it is time to go kick some imperial butt?"

Apologies here are tended for Baba Yaga's irreverence. There is nothing I can do about it. She says what she says. I suppose she is the original anarchist. Statements made by characters in this rendition in no way reflect the opinions of the writer. I should have said that earlier, perhaps.

In any case, Cat was distracted by her own concerns. She hadn't been to Saint Petersburg since she was seven or eight, and remembered it poorly. Next, to locate her great-aunt's town house and set the poor woman's heart at ease. Return the egg to her.

Then there was the matter of the other girl. Elena. *She* must have jumped off the train at the earliest opportunity and run home. Cat could ask her great-aunt to send a basket of supplies, maybe medicines for the mother. In her relief at Cat's return, Madame Sophia would surely rush to help.

Traffic

Tonight!" said Madame Sophia. "Go try on your gown, and let me see."

Upstairs, Elena became immobilized in a gown heavy as upholstery. It wanted to stand in place when Elena preferred to pace. The fabric was printed with a repeating pattern of some blossom she didn't recognize. Miss Bristol dismissed it as a chrysanthemum. "A filthy foreign flower."

"I like it," said Elena.

"Blowsy. Showy. I should have preferred you in prison stripes."

Downstairs, surveying the display, Madame Sophia sighed. "Even with my sorry eyes, Ekaterina, I find your hair an ordeal to contemplate. I'd engage a hairdresser to come to us, but every woman in Saint Petersburg is having her coiffure done today. I shall have to take you to someone's home on the far side of the Fontanka River. It's a dubious district, but we shall pinch our noses, shan't we? Go change. I'll meet you at the front door. Miss Bristol, you'll join us. I'll need your beady eye to assess the repair work done to Miss Ekaterina's tresses. We will require Monsieur d'Amboise as chaperone in case the rabble misbehaves. Given it's such a fine afternoon. One never knows if Korsikov would sell us to the first mob we meet."

The cook and maids had already departed to join the crowds in the Nevsky Prospekt, hoping to catch sight of the Tsar's procession into the city, so Monsieur d'Amboise drew the drapes and locked the house up with a big iron key. He climbed up front with Korsikov. They didn't talk. The party set out from the kerbstones, snaking through the carriage and the foot traffic, all that tintinnabulum of a city on the eve of a holiday.

"*Tante,*" said Elena as a stout woman named Olga washed her hair with lavender lather, "what is Prince Anton actually like?"

Madame Sophia: "Are you getting nervous? Please don't. I hear he's very"— she searched for a word —"nice."

"How so?"

"Princely."

"Is he old?"

"Heavens no. He's hardly older than you, I should expect."

"Is he pleasant to look at?"

"In point of fact, *ma chérie,* I've never met the young man, or I'd be better able to advise you. However, I know you'll do just fine. You may want to switch to French, of course. In the royal courts, French is still the most elegant tongue."

"But I am Russian."

"That's what Catherine the Great said, and *she* was German. Well, you'll give up this fancy for the vernacular when you hear the great buzz of French. A divine frottage upon the eardrums, as someone said. Presumably someone French."

"Will we meet him tonight?"

"Or tomorrow night, or the next. Mind, there are hundreds of eligible daughters of privilege for him to meet. I do hope you won't slump, as you're doing now."

The great-aunt allowed her own head to be soaped. When wet, her silvery hair plastered itself against her scalp like threads of metal. She looked masculine. She might as well put on armor, thought Elena. "How is our darling's hair coming along, Miss Bristol?" asked the great-aunt.

"This hairdresser is a magician," replied the governess. "Of that nest of eels, she has made a rather fetching chignon."

"Wonderful. Now, if she can only tease my hair up to make me look like Lady Godiva on a windless morning, we'll be satisfied."

Several hours later, they descended the narrow wooden staircase to find Korsikov and Monsieur d'Amboise guarding the barouche. The chauffeur offered no compliment. The butler intoned, "Dreams of loveliness, both."

"I wonder what a nightmare of loveliness might be like," replied the great-aunt. "Something by Fuseli or Bouguereau, no doubt. Or Goya. We'll go home now and force down a little something, and dress in our finest. I hope you have wrapped the gift in Nanking silk as I requested."

"The box is fully wrapped," said the butler.

Notice the care he took not to speak a lie.

The carriage turned into a demure street off the Bolshoy Prospekt, where Madame Sophia kept house. In swerving around a couple of pedestrians, it splashed them. Korsikov cursed their insouciance, walking where he wanted to drive. "Silliness, to trample in these wet gutters," muttered Madame Sophia. "What are people *thinking*?"

Elena craned to see. One figure, a scrabbling ferret of an old woman, had leaped with vigor. The other person was a young woman near Elena's own age: Does she seem familiar? Could it be —? Or maybe I'm beginning to feel guilty, thought Elena, noticing people who look like Cat in this great city. Just as I start the exercise of impersonating her.

So I can get to the Tsar and beg for his mercy, she reminded herself. But she also thought, And so I can meet the prince. Once in her life, peasant or no, every girl should have the chance to meet a prince.

"An intolerable offense," said Baba Yaga. "Were I feeling a bit more like myself, I'd turn that carriage into a haunted calabash and send it hurtling toward its vegetable graveyard." She shook the wet from her clothes.

"I didn't imagine my great-aunt would be there," said the girl flatly. "But I thought *some* staff would be in residence, waiting for her. For me. They knew we were expected from London. Yet the house is locked tight as the Tower of London."

"Perhaps your great-aunt is out bobbing on the canals on the back of some hogshead. *We* had the benefit of a swimming table, remember. She might have caught a nasty current and been swept out to sea. What? I'm being consoling."

They had rounded the corner already. They didn't see the great-aunt's carriage pull up at the very steps they had just left.

The Floating Pavilions
of the Tsar

"I hope they play a great many waltzes that I can sit out," said Madame Sophia. "Ekaterina, *ma chérie*, are you nervous? You're so quiet."

The girl did not speak. She felt for the shape of the matryoshka, which she had put in her evening purse for courage.

"The nearer we have gotten to this festival, the more retiring you've become. I do realize the delay in that peasant village alarmed you, for you've not been yourself ever since. But, my dear, the Happyweather School for Young Ladies in London has prepared you well. As long as you let the Prince see your natural ebullience, you shall avoid disgracing the family, and perhaps do a good deal more."

"What do you *want* of me?" asked Elena. The carriage, lolloping along broad avenues, splintered the frozen puddles. A dreadful sound. Elena had always been afraid of dropping through the ice on a pond and drowning.

Madame Sophia took her hand out of an ermine muff. The dry evening air made the fur stand up. The great-aunt patted about Elena's knees until Elena supplied her own gloved hand for the old woman to clutch.

"I know something of the arithmetic of likelihoods. The chance that you, of all the young women drawn to Saint Petersburg from all over Russia, and its colonies, and its allies — that *you* might be the one to secure the signal interest of the young Prince Anton — well, that is a slender chance. So slender that I pay nearly no attention to it."

Elena sighed.

"*Nearly*," emphasized the great-aunt. "I didn't say I pay *no* attention to the matter."

"No one can descend from a carriage and just walk in and become engaged to an heir to the throne," said Elena.

"You have forgotten my lessons in genealogy. Silly girl. Prince Anton is not in direct line for the throne. He would never become Tsar unless the extended royal family was struck simultaneously by an impossible series of epidemics, revolutions, intrigues, and peculiarly accurate comets. But by custom, any consort of the Prince would become a member of the court and would have a palace of some sort in which to live, sooner or later. Wouldn't you like that?"

"A palace would require a lot of sweeping."

"If you flaunt and flirt, you will mortify us with forwardness. But if you relax and exhibit your natural charm, who knows? At worst, we shall have had a glorious time. You won't wonder, later in your life, if you might have appealed to the Prince *had* you met him. You *will* have met him. When I am dead, recall this night and bless my soul. Heaven knows this exercise has cost me half my annual income. Now, to draw the Tsar's eyes upon you, I trust in this wonderful present reclaimed from the safe." She patted the silk-wrapped box on the seat next to her. "Monsieur d'Amboise wrapped it beautifully. I only hope that the Tsar is not presented with eight or ten ornamental eggs from the same studio, or if so, at least that he sees ours first."

That thing, thought Elena. That oversize duck egg I found someplace. I hope he breaks it. But not until I get a chance to talk to him and meet his godson.

They neared the river. "I've never known the Neva to remain in thaw at this time of year. They say the world continues to change as one ages, but I hadn't expected so much change at this late date in my long life."

They turned a corner to join a queue of carriages dispersing their passengers. And then Elena rushed her hand to her mouth in case some crude word from her former life in the fields slipped out.

Upriver and down, across from the Winter Palace, eleven pavilions floated. Anchored in place and linked like beads on a necklace. Against the south bank, the black water glittered with the reflection of lights shining in the palace windows. On the north side, from which direction they were arriving, a covered gang-plank funneled guests across the water to a central salon roofed by a pale silk dome.

Madame Sophia: "Oh, Ekaterina! It outshines the Brighton Pavilion. It rivals the Crystal Palace in Chicago a few years back. Even these tired old eyes can see how luminous, and they tear up at the sight."

Each open room bobbed on pontoons. Each was linked to the

next by lighted walkways. Together they looked as if they might easily house the population of Miersk: every soul going back centuries since the day of its founding.

Evergreen boughs roped the railings and the white cast-iron pillars. Set out on tongues cantilevering around the edges, iron kettles burned tinder, shaking the air in aromatic, heated curtains. Under the canopies, whose various elevations and bulbous profiles were painted in patterns of cobalt, gold, and aquamarine, oil lamps flickered behind spheres of frosted glass.

It was the most magical thing that Elena had ever seen. Crowned heads do throw a good party.

Madame Sophia handed the gift parcel to the governess to hold while she alighted the carriage. "I do not think staff is included in the invitation."

"Certainly not," said Miss Bristol. "Where would you like me to freeze?"

Elena looked at the abrasive Miss Bristol. So beleaguered, not knowing if this was her last evening as a free woman. Why wouldn't she flee? Behind the great-aunt's shoulder, the girl made the same shooing gesture she had once made at hens, back when there were hens in Miersk. *Go. Go!*

"I shall send for you when we are ready to depart. It could be dawn, for all I know. But there will be a room nearby, and benches, and gallons of hot tea, no doubt. Perhaps some decks of cards, or a sing-along. Jolly chatter."

"Very well. My teeth shall jolly well chatter. Till dawn," said Miss Bristol.

She straightened the shawl on Elena's shoulders, then settled her hands there, lightly, and looked Elena in the eyes.

"You are a brave child," she said. "Foolhardy, but brave enough. Whatever fate you walk toward, and however far you walk away from us, you will not be forgotten."

Elena was inclined to reply: *I do not need your blessing.* But something stopped her. The woman looked like a little old lark about to be squeezed to death in the fist of a gorilla. Life was too strong for some people. What was it the doctor had said to Natasha Rudina? *You have to* want *to live your life.*

"I appreciate your kindness," said the girl. It came out sounding more dismissive than she intended. Miss Bristol almost controlled the flinch in her eyelids.

"We shall be waiting for you." Korsikov jumped down from his perch with the reins in his hand. The horses shook their heads, releasing the shattery sound of small bells.

"Come, *ma chérie,*" said Madame Sophia. With the gift for the Tsar in one arm, clutched tightly to her well-padded bosom, she linked her other arm into Elena's. "Let us see what enchantment this night shall bring."

The Treasury of Marvels

A s Madame Sophia was of great age compared to some of the other guests, she and Elena were ushered to the head of the line. They came to a halt at a podium set upon the granite embankment of the Neva River.

The Deputy Sub-Lieutenant was wearing a red sash and a pince-nez. He was too busy to recognize them. "Madame Sophia Borisovna Orlova," said the old woman, only slightly testy. "Accompanied by Mademoiselle Ekaterina Ivanovna de Robichaux."

The officer found their names on a list and made two check-marks. "Please proceed to the reception salon, where you can leave your wraps if you like. You will be surprised by the warmth supplied by the fires and by the crowd itself." He patted his hair affectionately.

Another officer rigid with pistols unhooked a velvet rope from a brass stanchion. He stood aside as Madame Sophia ventured aboard. The ramp was slatted, and the gangplank swayed. "A caution, a trial," murmured Madame Sophia, "but worth the vexation. I shall try not to pitch headfirst into the brink."

Once inside the central pagoda, the great-aunt and the girl decided to liberate themselves from brocaded coats and ermine muffs. The weather was indeed comfortable. Almost like being in a ballroom, Elena guessed, in the Winter Palace itself.

Another adjutant told them that they should make their way to the final pavilion, farthest downriver — to the right from the broad reception area — and deposit their gift to the treasurer. Good, thought Elena. I shall be shot of it. But Madame Sophia said, "Oh, I had planned to have my great-niece present it herself."

"His Imperial Majesty is not yet arrived. In any case, you cannot be expected to carry a parcel while you dance and feast."

"Of course not. I'll deputize Miss Ekaterina to consign our gift to the treasury. Ancient ladies need to sit down at once."

"You will find many cushioned chairs for your comfort."

They stepped farther into the press of guests. From downriver, a floating orchestra began to play. "What a delight. Heavy in the woodwind and brass sections, whose sound carries better in the cold, I should think." Madame Sophia sank into the first love seat she came upon. "Do deliver that package. And carefully, *ma chérie*. It would do us no good to have you drop it at this late date in the campaign."

Elena accepted the silk-wrapped parcel and held it close to her heart. She passed from chamber to chamber, across the linking walkways. Relief suffused her. Some lackey guarding the treasury would have to explain how a plain if substantial specimen egg from the wild had been substituted for a bespoke confection. As long as Miss Bristol and Monsieur d'Amboise kept their mouths shut, no one need ever know.

About halfway along, she came upon a dining chamber. On one side, champagne was being poured. Extra bottles were tied in groups of a dozen and submerged in the river for chilling; she watched waiters haul them up and pop the corks. Opposite this station, behind more velvet ropes, stood an exceedingly long table covered in lace of black, gold, and ivory. A narrow silver tray, the length of a railway carriage, sat upon them. When Elena pushed for a better view, she saw that the tray held edible maquettes of the eleven different pavilions. Spun sugar columns; platforms of biscuit and cream; decorations of candied berries; canopies of tinted meringue. The dark river was represented by the blackest liquid chocolate.

"Dinner will be served in due course," said the Guardian of Imperial Pastry, shooing people away.

In a state of subdued panic, Elena reached the floating treasure-house. This final pavilion was a tented caboose of sorts. Its sides were not open but paneled loosely in canvas. Behind yet another velvet rope to divide the gift givers from the chamber of treasure, seven handsome soldiers stood at attention, receiving the tribute and recording the names of the givers.

Beyond them, when the drapes parted, Elena caught a glimpse of the bounty. She'd never heard of the riches of Babylon, the glories of Troy or ancient Rome, or even Ali Baba's cave. She just thought: Ah, the Tsar's playground.

As the drapes fluttered, she spied gifts standing about in heaps, on tables, some too large to be wrapped. A six-foot bejeweled rooster made of hammered precious metals, inset with cloisonné.

A glass globe at least as tall as she was, encasing a colorful model of a grand cathedral. A set of nesting dolls, like her mother's own humble set, but life-size. At those proportions, the smile on the superior mother, the matryoshka, looked not so much devoted as demented.

Elena regarded the soldiers. They seemed stamped from a common press. Erect, handsome, aloof, precise. Only the colors of their hair and the shapes of their beards and moustaches differed. All, that is, except for the beardless one at the end, the seventh, who looked a little younger, more relaxed. Possibly a troublemaker. His eyes were more alert. He reminded her of Alexei. She went up to him.

The youngest of the soldiers bowed solemnly to Elena. "The Throne of the Tsar of All the Russias receives your tribute." He reached out for the wrapped parcel. "Please let the Commissar of Gifts know what the gift is, and from whom it is given, and their homeland."

"Yes, sir," she said.

"I mean, tell me," he continued, not unkindly.

"Oh. Well, I'm informed that this is a Fabergé egg specially commissioned from the factory of the artist. It comes from Madame Sophia Borisovna Orlova, of Paris and Saint Petersburg."

"You look young to be called Madame."

Elena supposed she had to give the name. "Oh, no; I am Madame's great-niece. Mademoiselle Ekaterina de Robichaux." She raised her chin with what she hoped was elegance, not fear.

". . . of . . . ?"

"Well, a school in London."

"I see." The soldier said something in English.

Elena had practiced her response in the pier glass. She drilled her eyes into his. "Out of respect for the Tsar of All the Russias, I speak only in Russian."

He laughed. "Well. Imagine that, someone who doesn't like to show off. You're at the wrong party. But thank you for the gift." He made a note at his podium, and then he handed the gift to a fellow soldier standing at attention behind him. When he turned back, he was surprised to see that Elena was still standing there.

"Have you another gift? Trying to get in good with the Romanovs?"

"I have a question."

"If I can't cadge another gift out of you, I might as well take a question." He grinned as if he thought his remark clever.

Elena felt bold because the young soldier seemed less abrasive than she had come to expect in a military man. She leaned forward and spoke in a low voice. "I was wondering if you are familiar with someone I know in the army. I was wondering if you could tell me if he is in Saint Petersburg tonight."

The soldier pouted. "Oh. The secret beau. I might have known. I'd hoped you wanted to gossip with me about all this *houp-là*."

"I wouldn't waste your time, but my question isn't frivolous."

He drew himself up into military strictness, though at his most erect, he still looked the runt of the company. "I doubt I can supply the answer you require. But I'll try."

She felt her cheeks coloring and expected the soldier was getting the wrong idea. Yet she couldn't tell him she was asking about her *brother,* because Mademoiselle Ekaterina de Robichaux didn't have a brother. "The boy's name is Luka Maximovitch Rudin. He comes from the village of Miersk. That's in the oblast of Tyer, south of here."

"I know neither the fellow nor the location. However, I could send an envoy to hunt for the answer to your question, if it can be found easily." The soldier's face became more impassive than ever.

"I'd be glad if you did. Shall I shall meet you back here?"

"I may not still be at this post. But if I find out anything, I shall see that the information is registered here for your retrieval."

"You are too kind." Elena nodded her head. She felt like Miss Bristol, starchy and opinionated.

"I hope I'm able to locate news of your . . . your *acquaintance*. Next, please."

Back in the shadows of the great-aunt, Elena flumped upon the love seat. She felt exhausted already. The great-aunt said, "I hope you've eaten enough not to faint. The dancing will begin soon, I expect."

"I'm hardly undernourished these days. But I'm not inclined to dance."

"Oh, I *am* so sorry. But I have been filling up your dance card. You will dance."

Elena looked at the great-aunt and shook her head in objection. Before Madame Sophia could remonstrate further, a burst of singing shot out across the waters. Forty bearded Russian monks standing on a separate barge were droning in voices lower than Elena would have thought possible. All throughout the pavilions, everyone said "Ohhh!" A few messy starbursts, outlines of peony blossoms in gold and purple light, exploded in the sky — so these are fireworks, thought Elena. The fancies bloomed but faded too fast. She held her breath. Would that their stars could fall all the way to the water, surrounding us in light . . . what they might suggest to us!

But then the boom of their thunder made her think of rushing horse hooves, of double lightning spilled upon the steeple and striking the trestle bridge. All the trouble of a season sprung loose from the annual schedule.

"The Tsar approaches," said Madame Sophia. "Haul me to my feet, Ekaterina. Even at my tough old age, hoary at the temple and hairy at the chin, I stand for our blessed guardian."

Admission Denied

The witch and the girl paced to keep warm, trying to think what to do.

Cat: "I am worried out of my skin about my great-aunt."

"Stay in your skin; it gets sloppy otherwise, and I didn't bring a pail."

"But if she's not here in Saint Petersburg, she may still be looking for me in the forests around Miersk. And what if she found Elena on the train and accused her of conspiracy to steal the gift for the Tsar? What trouble Elena would be in. And who knows what wrath *ma tante* might have called down upon the villagers of Miersk?"

"I never got the sense you cared a whisker about your so-called friend. So why should you care about those lumpen people that spawned her?"

Cat shrugged. The truth was too simple and ugly to say out loud. In the few hours since she'd been released from the spell of Dumb Doma, the memory of that good doctor, the ancient nurse-maid, Elena's sick mother — it had all taken a firmer hold. Those folks had come to seem as much like a family as any she had ever known. She didn't have a strong basis for comparison.

The witch picked at a whitehead on her nose, trying to agitate it into greater repugnance. "Don't romanticize the rurals. Those villagers wanted to turn you out of their cozy little Heritage of Serfdom village display."

"They have a right to protect themselves. What other rights do they have?"

"Oh, so now you're going to prattle like a whining broadside circulated in a student ghetto? I'll amuse myself in song." Baba Yaga began to warble:

> "Sunrise, sunset.
> Unwise, upset,
> Peasants gotta sing.
> Nothing's so bad it can't be funny,
> Nothing's so good it doesn't sting.
> Sunrise, sunset,
> Uprise? Not yet.
> Peasants sing away.
> Justice is scheduled for tomorrow.
> Business as usual today."

"Very funny," said Cat. "I think you're nervous."
"I sing to drive my cares away. So go away already."

Cat kept still. All the trouble into which she'd plunged Elena! So what if Baba Yaga was right — Cat really hadn't given Elena much thought. There was still time. Maybe. Where was that child now? What if she'd leaped off the train, hurt herself, starved in the woods? Or been attacked by a beast the way Cat herself had been herded and hounded by — well, by a terrifying kitten?

"Let's go to the railway station and see if we can find out any information about my great-aunt's train," suggested Cat. A place to start, anyway.

Off they went, clopping and splashing, two pedestrians navigating through the display of imperial muscle. "They don't make cities like they used to!" the witch fussed. "All this mausoleum marble, all these bronze swans and other municipal gewgaws. What are they trying to prove?"

It occurred to Cat that Baba Yaga was less comfortable when lost in a throng than when she was queen of her own superior society out in her secret woods.

Yet her disguise seemed to hold. To Cat she still had a face as high as a medieval shield, but the passersby on foot and in carriage didn't turn their heads to gape. Children stared, but children always stare. Baba Yaga stuck her tongue out at them, but that was a simple curse. More than once she received a curse in return.

The doors of the Vitebsky terminal were closed. ALL RAIL SERVICE SUSPENDED DUE TO FLOODING, said a sign. No one answered their knocking.

As night began to fall, Baba Yaga got directions to the Winter Palace from a beggar huddled near a fire in a brazier. "At the very least," she said to Cat, "we can walk in and ask the Tsar if he knows about the missing Firebird."

"At the very least," replied Cat, "we can deliver the present to the Tsar that my great-aunt brought from Paris. Then, if the authorities have accused Miersk or Elena of theft or conspiracy, they'll have to let the charges drop."

"You maintain a juvenile belief in due process. Still, I'm in the mood for a party. Or a dust-up."

Behind a soldiers' barracks, shivering in the cold, Cat changed into the gown that Baba Yaga had magicked up for her. Baba Yaga didn't adjust so much as a button on her governess uniform. "I am getting to like this martinet drag," she admitted. "It brings out my inner Mary Poppinskaya."

"It's not too late to call upon the Tsar?" asked Cat.

"You said the fireworks were for this evening. If he hasn't invited friends in to watch, he'll be sitting in front of the fire in his comfy slippers with his slobbering borzois nearby. He'll be grateful to grant an audience to a subject like you."

"And you."

"I am not his subject."

When they approached the river, they caught sight of the pavilions. So: This was the grand festival. Not in the palace, but outside. The Tsar wouldn't be home answering his doorbell; he'd be here, presiding. And they were punctual. By the time they approached the checkpoint, most of the revelers had arrived. The pavilions were filled with hundreds of the lofty guests, their laughter skimming upon the icy wind.

"Name?" asked the guard. It was the Deputy Sub-Lieutenant.

Cat gave her name. The man regarded his manifest and turned a few pages. Then he stroked his waxen moustaches and said, "You'd better remove yourself before I have you arrested."

"What is the meaning of this?" asked Baba Yaga.

"Miss Yaga," said Cat to the witch. "Please. Not above your station."

"What are you talking about? My station is at the top of Chomolungma! Move aside. Let me at this regrettable bit of sour sausage. His hair is unnatural. A crime against the Crayola company."

"You'll have to excuse my governess." Cat kicked the witch, silencing her. "She's overexcited at the prospect of this festival. Can you check again? I'm sure there is some mistake. I've come all the way from London."

"If you don't have papers to press your suit, I must assume you're giving a false name. I wouldn't care to take into custody a young woman as neatly turned out and well-spoken as you, but I suspect you are a rebel of some sort. Begone before you leave me no choice."

"But I *have* used my own name. I do insist that I am the great-niece of Madame Sophia Borisovna Orlova."

The officer checked the list again and shook his head. "Madame Orlova and her ward have already been admitted."

"Fraud," said Baba Yaga, hopping on one foot and then the other. "Fraud and chicanery, naked flimflammery, charlatan trickery, knickknacking knavery!"

"But we have a present — a present from Paris!" Cat hardly knew how to proceed. In London, she could plead painful shyness and blush a gentleman into submission; in Paris, she might flirt, up to a point. But she didn't remember the best strategy for getting her way in Russia. Bribery?

The soldier was impassive. "Judging by your crony's discomposure, either she has to use the comfort chamber or your gift is a bomb with a lighted fuse." He pulled out a whistle and blew upon it. Just at that instant, though, the fireworks and the bass singers began, respectively, to explode and to rumble, and all heads turned to the sky. In the mêlée, Cat turned away from the entrance desk, pulling Baba Yaga by the horny hand.

"Why are you giving up? I can take young Colonel Suno-vavitch!" cried the witch. "Both hands tied behind my back! I'll *comfort chamber* him."

Cat muttered, "If we press our cause, my great-aunt will be summoned to answer questions. For all we know, she'd be charged with harboring an enemy agent under a false alias. At least we know she's *here*."

"If someone's impersonating you, someone could be imper-sonating her, too. Or maybe your doddery aunt has scared up another great-niece."

"With the same name? Anyway, I have no cousins. But it couldn't be Elena Rudina — she hasn't the . . . the . . ."

"The moxie."

"The wit. But how are we going to find out?"

They looked upriver and downriver. From the eastern approach, perhaps launched off the Palace Embankment by the Summer Garden, and guarded by a line of ships from the Russian navy, a barge was emerging. Lit by smoking torches, it fluttered with pennants. The gold of Russian wheat, the crimson of Russian beets. The blue of Ural valleys and white of refined Ural salt.

In the center of an armored guard of forty soldiers with rapiers aloft stood the Tsar of All the Russias.

A magnificent sight. I well remember, through both my working eyes. I had been watching from the Winter Palace. No one had thought to invite me to the party, but I was coming closer to involvement in this mishap.

From the western approach, nearer the sea, another rank of great ships stood shoulder to shoulder. An impenetrable hedge of naval might. Access to the pavilion across the water, from upriver and down and also from the northern armlet of the Neva River, was blocked.

"We are lost," said Cat.

"Fiddlesticks," said Baba Yaga. She put down the briefcase she'd been carrying and said, "Excuse me, I see the establishment is full. But surely you have a little table for two somewhere?"

The table unfolded itself. Its legs reappeared. Happily enough it walked into the river. Baba Yaga stepped upon it and beckoned to Cat. Then the tabletop became a raft. Under a sky of pyrotechnic explosions, as the table legs churned the waters of the river, the girl and the witch floated toward the festival from which they'd been turned away.

The Tsar of
All the Russias

very head turned to regard the advent of the emperor.

The Tsar stood upon a podium behind a rank of forty soldiers with rapiers, who held box formation, facing outward in four directions.

He was dressed in the Prussian style: tight leggings in high boots, a snug waistcoat glinting with knots of gold braid. He was made to look taller by the crown of slender silver finials studded with jewels, from which a pouf of purple velvet emerged. His beard was clipped tight in the modern European style.

The roar of the crowd nearly eclipsed the cannon sound of the fireworks. Trying to sing over the racket, the bass choir became hoarse, but that didn't matter — few notice hoarseness in a bass voice.

"Oh, my," said Elena, rising with all the others at the progress of the imperial barge.

Madame Sophia: "Worth the trip from London, assuredly? Worth missing a month or two of walking two abreast about the Round Pond in Kensington Gardens? With Susanna what's-her-name?"

"Worth more than I can say."

"What *is* her name? I forget."

"I can't think — it's the Tsar!" This was the first time Elena had been asked to supply information that Cat would know and she didn't. The luck of timing was with her, though. When the Tsar hies into view, all attention rivets to him.

The barge tucked against the eastern end of the floating court. The Tsar appeared at the head of a carpeted gangplank. The fireworks sputtered to a halt. The basses rested their tonsils. The Tsar said a few words to open the festival. No doubt they were magnificent words, but few could hear what he said.

Then he stepped onto the pavilion at the opposite end of the chain from the treasury. The hum of comment began to blur the air.

Elena: "What's going to happen next?"

"I don't know," said Madame Sophia. "Why don't you get a plate of food, Ekaterina? It could be hours before we're summoned for an audience. Or we could wait all night and find the Tsar has suddenly decided to retire, and we'll all be called back tomorrow evening. I can't predict, but you need to keep up your strength."

"I don't think I could eat a thing." A remark Elena hadn't often made.

"*Ma chérie.* Any eligible gentleman of breeding knows that she who flirts before her marriage may well flirt after it. Ask Tolstoi.

But few men are interested in women who are too demure to look at them. Child, you will have your whole life to examine those shoes. For now, pick up your chin. You will never be so young as you are tonight. Live this evening fully. The slippery moment will pop like a bubble soon enough."

Elena supposed there was some truth to what Madame Sophia said, even if she thought she was speaking to the real Ekaterina, not to an impostor.

She looked at the great-aunt and replied, "Your advice is sound."

"Besides, with my eyes, these days I can't tell a white diamond from a black bean. I want you to regale me with descriptions of all this when it is over."

Elena glanced this way and that. She hadn't learned the rare language of Paris couture. She couldn't tell an Empire waist from an S-curve hourglass. Frankly, she didn't know passementerie from pastrami. Her crammed education on board the train had covered only so much.

But under assignment, she began examining the dignitaries. Some grey-bearded and beribboned, others clean shaven and foppish. Black evening coats. Military men in dress uniform so trim they looked as if they would squeak if poked.

And the confident maidens and their stale mothers and beaky chaperones. A catalog of net worths, or net needs, in jewels brokered or borrowed. Diamonds, opals, pearls.

As she watched the crowd flow by, Elena tried to make an inventory of costumes for Madame Sophia. Gowns with fringe. Gloves with buttons to the elbow. Bodices of beaded jet. What else would the great-aunt want to picture?

Hats. Platforms for fruit, ribbons, and feathers from the birds of every continent.

And the shoes. And fans. And boas. And purses. And parasols.

She grew dizzy trying to name the colors she saw. Ivory, amethyst, oyster, cabernet. Gold silk, silver bead, copper thread.

In trying to drag these visions into rich language, Elena suffered a perversity of the soul. It came upon her like a cramp: sudden, sharply. She found herself missing the chromatic scheme of home. The thousand browns of forest bark. The blues of cloudless January mornings. The whites of winter, from new snow to pale ice.

And then the first greens of the year. New ferns in old bracken. Fresh emerald needles on venerable conifers. All the colors from that shocking rash called springtime.

But Elena gave up. More colors in the world than words to name them.

Is it odd that thinking of color, of all things, should have released her homesickness at last? I think I understand. As I've mentioned, my own sense of color has become compromised. In any case, Elena suddenly saw the rank of pavilions as if from a distance: as arrayed in a bed nook, say, a certain play of elegance, nothing more. And in recalling the palette of her ordinary world, she was attacked by nostalgia: faces of Miersk bloomed. In value and light, they eclipsed even the fireworks that had announced the advent of the Tsar.

The doctor, Peter Petrovich, with his sour-jelly cheeks. What would he name this day? Pinch Yourself to Make Sure You're Not Dreaming Day?

And old Grandmother Onna, that scorched soul, a bole loosed

from a chestnut tree, refusing to rot, refusing also to root. Chased by the winds of her mild detachment from one house to the next, dispensing slightly deranged attention and comfort. Taking care of Elena's mother.

Her mother.

Elena wiped the corner of her eyes with the tips of her pinkies, flicking away wet, and diverted her attention to Luka and Alexei instead. Luka. That was why she was here, why she'd braved so much. Standing here in this floating market-garden of prospective brides, at last she felt snapped free of the perilous spell.

Still, she argued with herself. Look, if I *did* happen to attract the young Prince, I could call upon his power to find my brother, to petition for his release, to pay for proper food for Mama, to pay for fresh potions for the doctor to administer.

But she caught herself in that snare. She thought: Wait. You've already gotten yourself here, and you've already asked for help to find Luka already. That young guard who collected your gift for the Tsar: he promised to help. Waste no time. Go back and find out what he has learned. You weren't flirting, but he liked you anyway. He might have sent someone to enquire.

Find out, and then flee, before the wolves arrive, before the lightning. Before it's too late. "I shall walk about," she said.

"Oh, no," replied the great-aunt. She had been speaking to a beribboned emissary of some sort. "You have left it too long. We're being required for an audience with the Tsar." She gave her arm to the envoy and allowed him to haul her to her feet. "Come, my dear. The great moment has arrived."

"But . . . but . . ."

"Incredible, I know. *We* are scarcely counted among the

crowned heads of the continent! But the Tsar has taken mercy on the elderly at this late hour. He's called for the oldest to have their audiences first."

"You aren't the oldest. I've seen more ancient hags here in their greasy painted faces than you could find in a cemetery vault!"

"I never question what a lady says about her age. Should someone want to cling to the notion of being younger than I, let her so cling. I have no pride. Come. By accident or by God's design, we are promoted to first place. And first impressions are important, my girl. The young Prince Anton may fall in love with the first girl he sees. Your storybooks and the novels of Miss Austen rarely suggest that true love strikes at Candidate Number Four Hundred Seventeen. Hurry along; don't drag your slippers so."

Elena wasn't ready. But enchantment, having brought her this far, now abandoned her. It had no more to offer her.

What in the world had she thought she was going to do once she met the Tsar? She was only a country hound, snuffling along a golden carpet on her way to meet the eminence of the continent.

"Keep up," said Madame Sophia.

Even if Elena could swim, the waters of the Neva looked too cold to jump into. Besides, at such a stratagem, Madame Sophia would probably have a fit. *I couldn't do that to the old lady,* Elena thought, *even if I've lied and taken advantage of her and prevented her from searching for her lost great-niece.*

Every decision she'd made since the train began to pull away from Miersk looked boldly, coldly like what it was: self-interested calculation.

She'd been under a spell, all right: a spell of delusion. She'd forgotten right from wrong. She hadn't set out to replace Cat with herself, not originally, but she'd become sleepy with luxury. She had lost herself.

She couldn't reclaim herself fast enough, not as she walked across the swaying links from pavilion to pavilion, heading to the salon in the center, the one at which they had first arrived.

The murmuring crowds parted on either side of them. Elena heard people murmur about them as they went past.

"The Duchess of Haut-Saxony?"

"One of the Montmorencys, surely . . . the branch from Dijon. Their family's in mustard."

"I believe she is the Princess of Hesse-Messenburg."

"How amusing that our Tsar requests such an obscure duckling for his first course."

The whispering fell away as they neared the golden carpet in the center of the central pavilion. Elena could only see the carpet. She couldn't look up.

"Wait here," said the envoy. He pivoted across the carpet and announced in a blat, "Madame Sophia Borisovna Orlova of Saint Petersburg and Paris, with her great-niece, Mademoiselle Ekaterina Ivanovna de Robichaux, arrived from London."

At least that is what Elena guessed was being said. It seemed to be in French.

She followed a few steps behind her great-aunt, her eyes still cast down.

"Madame," said a deep, kindly, tired voice. Elena held her breath. He sounded almost ordinary.

"Your Imperial Majesty," replied the great-aunt, in Russian, "may I present Miss Ekaterina de Robichaux. She is the daughter of my niece, Izolda Robichaux, née Orlova."

"*Enchanté*," said the Tsar.

Perhaps that means "charmed," thought Elena. How did he know? She was just about charmed out of her wits.

"Through a surfeit of love for her mother country, she speaks only in Russian. Spending so much of her childhood in England, she suffers a flush of patriotic fervor upon returning to Saint Petersburg after a long absence."

"May I welcome both of you to the festivities," he replied in Russian.

There was a silence as Elena tried to count the number of colors on the patch of Turkey carpet on which she stood.

"She is not usually reticent," said the great-aunt, just a little less smoothly. "Miss Ekaterina, your sovereign addresses you."

But all she could think of to say was *I am not who you think I am.* And as she couldn't say that without betraying the great-aunt, she couldn't speak at all.

"I believe," continued Madame Sophia, rushing, "she has for so long thought that she would present our gift to you and to the Prince that she is tongue-tied. It is a wonderful gift, you see."

"How kind." The Tsar murmured an aside to his attachés. "Next set of guests."

"We had been hoping to present it to your honored guest. But I see he is not here."

This was when Elena realized that the famous Prince was absent. She felt a little safer. She began to think perhaps she could look up and curtsey. Then they would be done. Then she could escape. Maybe locate Luka.

"The gifts are so many, and some of them so large, they are established in a well-guarded treasure tent," replied the Tsar. "The Tsar thanks you for your kindness to his family." It was a dismissal. They were almost free.

Madame Sophia pretended not to understand. "It is specially made for you by the London studio of the great Fabergé." The great-aunt was gabbling as she gambled; the Tsar's love of Fabergé eggs was common knowledge. "The lore of all the Russias is exquisitely featured. I shall say no more."

She stood her ground. In rapping her bosom with her closed fan, Madame Sophia exercised long dormant wiles. The Tsar continued after a moment, "Still, if it is portable . . ."

"It is exactly portable. All the way from England, by hand." The great-aunt smacked her lips as if just having set down a fan of winning cards.

The Tsar dispatched the attaché; a drink was brought; the Tsar and the great-aunt spoke about much nonsense. One thing led to another. Armies in Austria-Hungary. The Lippizaner stallions. Tennis at Wimbledon, Odessa watering holes. The miracle of the Victrola. On and on. Elena lifted her brow enough to slide a glance at the sovereign close-up.

He was more firmly packed in person than he had looked in profile: a well-kept and sturdy torso. Shoulders tossed back like an oxen yoke. The eyes danced, and the tone was bright and sober at once. The moustache was more white than brown, though, and the mouth did not smile.

May this be over soon, she pleaded with all the saints in heaven and her drowned father, too.

But here came the cheery foot soldier who had taken the gift from her and who had promised to ask after the whereabouts of Luka. He carried the parcel gravely but grinned at Elena when he saw her.

The Tsar: "May I present my godson, Prince Anton Antonovich Romanov."

"You?" said Elena, her first remark.

"She is surprised. But the Prince wanted to see the guests incognito, before they put on their formal faces to try to appeal to him. A party game among royalty; we do it all the time. Except me."

"How do you do, little Russian girl," said Prince Anton. He was almost scampering with fun at the surprise. He didn't notice the discomfiture of his guest.

"And now," said the Tsar, glancing at his pocket watch, "let us have a look at this wonderful thing, because there are hundreds of other people to greet. Anton Antonovich, will you please do the honors?"

Something that had started to give way in Elena, under the pressure of this strangeness, continued to crumble. Finding the egg in the dawn forest — that had come to feel like a dream. This was now a nightmare, the type that accelerates toward a scream you try to make but can't.

"I bet it's a model of the imperial crown made out of marzipan," said Prince Anton. "I'd rather a cowboy outfit, with spurs." He untied the ribbon and let the silk cloth fall away from the box, which still said in golden letters, *House of Fabergé, Dover Street, Mayfair, London . . .*

Meanwhile
on the Other Side

As the barge of the Tsar was floating toward the eastern end of the linked platforms, and the heavy-lidded Russian eyes of Saint Petersburg played upon the progress of the emperor, the table of Baba Yaga was kicking industriously, approaching from the other direction.

No one saw the witch and the girl float by.

Cat: "What are we looking for?"

"Well, the Tsar, of course. We're going to give him that gift. And then I'm going to ask him about the Firebird. He has advisors who know something about everything. Except me, hee-hee-hee." The witch looked about at the crowd, all focused forward on their sovereign. "Goodness, I'm underdressed."

A minute later she added, "Luckily, no one looks at staff."

Another minute later she said, "Who do they all think they *are*?"

"Shhh," said Cat. The fireworks and the basses had stopped. "I believe the Tsar is addressing the crowd."

"Yoo-hoo, honeybucket, I'm over here." The witch spoke in a whisper; she was only kidding. She was learning.

They floated so close to the platforms that anyone glancing from the interior might have imagined that Cat and her retainer were gliding on tender toes along the very edge of the pavilion. They went slowly so as to draw little attention to themselves.

"The hoity are very toity in this town," said the witch.

"Governesses should be seen and not heard, Miss Yaga."

"*Miss Yaga* stands corrected." She minced a little, but then clamped her mouth shut. As they drifted, the Tsar alighted somewhere beyond them, to cheers.

Perhaps the only creature that noticed a tiny independent platform sidling along the great linked pavilions was an old raven. It had mangy wings and was blind in one eye. It turned its head to follow the progress of the gate-crashers.

A Divertimento

"Oh, Madame," said Elena. She put her hand on the great-aunt's elbow. "I should've done this long ago. I —"

Watching the Tsar's face, the great-aunt was readying to burst into blushes. "Hush, child, your timing! You've chosen to speak at the wrong moment."

"You should sit down. Perhaps someone could bring a chair?"

"One does not sit in the presence of the Tsar." Her voice low and impatient. Elena glanced at the Tsar, but apparently he agreed with his elderly guest. He was standing, after all, so why shouldn't the entire continent?

Elena turned from the box and looked instead at the young soldier, who was really a prince. Just like in a fable. The person she'd come all this way to meet.

That *Mademoiselle Ekaterina* had come all this way to meet.

Frankly, he didn't look worth a trip to the nearest grain crib. Which is to say, he didn't look like Elena's idea of a prince. Though what ideas did she have but those from the silliness of fairy stories?

For one thing, Prince Anton was young or short for his age, or both. His unguarded eyes danced more like a spaniel's than a boy's, and nothing like a potential husband's. His hair went in several directions, as if he'd started to run a race and fallen in the process. Grandmother Onna had more hair on her upper lip than he did. His cheeks, two scuppers of borscht, as Peter Petrovich had been used to saying.

After this short while in the household of Madame Sophia, Elena had picked up some standards. She wasn't impressed by the boy's manner. His interest in the gift was unseemly.

All this occurred to her as his fingers gripped the lid. "May I?" he asked his distant cousin, his godfather, his host, his Tsar.

"Please."

The lid came up. Madame Sophia gripped Elena's hand.

In this amber light of imperium, behold: a plain eggshell. No longer pale brown, but chalky grey.

The pressure of Madame Sophia's fingers lightened. She made a sound as of air sucked into a wooden recorder — a peasant *dudka* in mid-melody, catching its own breath. The stiffness of her skirts slowed her descent. At the Tsar's nod, a slender sofa was rushed forward. The gilded palm fronds carved on its legs and back trembled as the great-aunt was lowered senseless upon it.

Prince Anton lifted out the egg. How had Elena once imagined that it glowed? It looked like an outsize quail egg. Admittedly, an egg from a big-boned quail, a portly quail; a quail with a bit of heft to it. A quail of magnitude.

Elena giggled. Hysteria. She'd mistaken a biological anomaly for an artifact of magic. How impressionable she'd been when young — a week or two ago.

A quail of means. A quail of quality. A landed quail, with property in three provinces. Sir Quail of Upper Quailistan.

The Prince was laughing, too, until he saw the Tsar's face. His godfather said, "This is not Fabergé unless Fabergé's London office has been taken over by revolutionaries and sent this as a rebuke to the throne. Who *is* this woman? Why is she languishing?"

"Maybe it's going to detonate," said the Prince.

"That joke suggests furiously poor taste, and I shall chastise you in private. Awaken this woman. Remove this offense." The Tsar swept his hand as if at a gnat.

It was all over now. Send away the basso profundos, bring on the firing squad. Elena dropped a curtsey, then a series of them. "It's not her fault. I can explain. I'm not who she thinks I am. I'm, I guess, a substitute."

Prince Anton Antonovich Romanov would have clapped his hands if they hadn't been full of egg. Such readiness to be intrigued. "Let her speak, if you please? Oh, but this is excellent fun."

Elena, rushing on: "She's not to blame. She's horribly old, and nearly blind, and so thick that she hasn't realized I'm not even her great-niece —"

"An impostor. A traitor." The angrier the Tsar grew, the more mellifluous his voice. But as he didn't overrule his godson's request, his men held still. "Speak, then, while you can."

"Go on," said Prince Anton. "Why have you done this?"

"I didn't . . . you weren't . . . . it wasn't . . . and I thought this was the egg of the Firebird," said Elena.

"The Firebird. And you?—a limb of Bolshevism," said the Tsar again, but in a quieter voice.

Madame Sophia was coming around thanks to smelling salts uncorked near her broad old nostrils. Her first syllables were in the tongue of the lost, but they arranged themselves into language soon enough. "Miss Ekaterina, what has happened? What is this foul old thing? . . . And where is our precious, precious, full-of-preciousness gift for the Tsar? Have I gone entirely mad? Oh, that's it; I'm having a dream. Very well. I like this sofa." She squinted at Prince Anton. "I can't see him well, *ma chérie,* but in this fantasy he's rather a lightweight. I hope the real one has a bit more heave-ho."

"Madame." Elena spoke as softly as if to her own sick mother. "I must confess. I'm not your great-niece."

Prince Anton to the Tsar: "Is this an entertainment you've arranged to surprise me with? You are such a dear godfather!"

The old woman sputtered to Elena, "What do you mean, you're not my great-niece? You're certainly not my maternal gypsy grandmother, who was known as the Scourge of the Carpathians before she was carried off by my grandfather. Though I've always suspected *she* carried *him* off."

Elena knelt on the carpet. She fed her hands into the old woman's palms. "You must listen to me. I'm not Miss Ekaterina. I'm the girl from the village of Miersk, where the train stopped for days. Miss Ekaterina fell off the train as it departed, and I was trapped inside. I've been out of my mind with worry. With something: I've been fully out of my mind."

Madame Sophia, dubiously: "This is a most peculiar dream."

Elena finished: "And the gift for the Tsar was lost, but while we came north, I happened upon a freak of nature. An accident at sunrise, a trick of the light. I thought it was a Firebird in its final throes, and this must be the egg it left behind." In a smaller voice, then: "I told myself too many stories."

"It's a pretty egg," said the Prince, without conviction. He turned it about, trying to think of something else to say. "It has a nice eggy shape. We used to throw eggs off the balcony at school in Rome, until we hit a monsignor one day."

The great-aunt was blinking, confusion giving way to alarm.

"You thought I had a cold," continued Elena. "It isn't that I had a cold. I just don't sound like Ekaterina, even if I look like her a little. I don't speak French. Nor English. Whatever decent Russian I have, I learned from the doctor in the village, who studied in Moscow when he was young."

Too late brave, she turned to the Tsar. "I beg for mercy. Remember, for all my crimes and mistakes, I did briefly believe I was bringing you a Firebird's egg in place of the Fabergé egg that Madame Sophia arranged for."

The Tsar: "In the tales, the Firebird lays its egg in flames, and like a phoenix it hatches at once, from its own ashes. So it is never dead. So even were the Firebird real, this couldn't be its egg. And frankly, this thing looks like papier-mâché."

Madame Sophia clucked, "I am beside myself."

"You are all excused," said the Tsar. "Take the egg to the treasury. I shall have Brother Uri examine it later."

Anton put the egg back in the box, and the envoy marched off with it.

"But if you *aren't* Ekaterina, then where *is* Ekaterina?" Madame Sophia sat bolt upright. "What have you done with her?"

Elena's throat had thickened. She couldn't answer. She was distraught. The Prince handed her his handkerchief, but she felt too lowly to sully it. She put her sleeve to her eyes instead.

"Unless you prove to be involved in some campaign of treachery, Madame, I shall find your great-niece for you," said the Tsar, without warmth. To his retinue, he continued, "Take the young offender into confinement. Escort the matron away. Haul her on that piece of furniture if you must." His men did a few squat thrusts to prepare for the hoist of their lives.

Madame Sophia held out her hands. By her gestures, she might have been a fine opera singer. "I have died at the feet of our excellent sovereign and plunged into a pit of hell! None of this can be true! I have never seen the like!"

"Really?" said an approaching member of the court. "Then you haven't seen anything yet, Madame Avoirdupois."

Elena turned. Across the very floor of the river stepped Cat, at long last. The real Ekaterina. Not, as last seen, in a lambswool traveling coat cut to mid-calf, but in a gorgeous gown, with jewels like snow crystals at her ears and throat. By relativity of glamour, Elena was even more fully proven an impostor.

Cat was accompanied by a shriveled-up, grinning old harridan in a tight black skirt and generous bodice, with a jaw shaped like the shovel used by the Miersk gravedigger. "It's been so long since I've crashed a party," said Cat's miniature chaperone. "Puts me in the mood to cast a curse or something."

Cat walked up to Elena and looked her unblinkingly in the face.

The Presentation
of the Gift

L isten through the pause. Small waves are slapping at the sides of the floating reception platform. Elena is sniffling. The great-aunt's breathing is labored, a leather bellows with a rip along one pleat. A raven on a post rearranges its torn wings.

"I don't believe it," said Cat at last. "You have stolen me."

"You'd better pay your respects to the Tsar before you finish ruining my life," replied Elena. She thought coldly, This is the only time I'll ever have the chance to criticize Cat's manners.

The other girl flushed. Anger or shame, maybe both. She turned and made a curtsey so deep that the skirt of her gown puffed out on all sides. "Your Highness," she murmured, "I am the real Mademoiselle Ekaterina."

Prince Anton applauded. "This *is* profoundly ripe drama. And who are you, the humble nanny who stole her away at birth?"

"I'll humble *you*," went the little woman, but Cat interrupted.

"Your Highness," she began again, "I am Mademoiselle Ekaterina de Robichaux, great-niece of Madame Orlova. May I present my governess, Miss Yaga."

"Glad to meet you, guv'nor." Miss Yaga weaved and pranced, and jiggled her fingers at the Tsar's court, which had drawn closer to this impromptu theatricale.

"Nothing of moment here. Take the lot away." The Tsar managed a nod. His men came forward.

"But wait! We've arrived in time to deliver to your stable this fresh new bride," said Miss Yaga. The Tsar's men paused at the chaperone's reply, momentarily elevating her authority over His Imperial Majesty's. (Imagine.) "Is *this* the putative spouse-on-parade? He doesn't look old enough to play tiddlywinks, let alone know enough about life to entertain thoughts of marriage."

"I'm mature for my age," said the Prince. "You've no call to say that. I am skilled in life. I know all about suffering from my Dostoyevsky and my Balzac."

"You want suffering, I'll kick you in your Balzac," said Miss Yaga. "Anyway, I've come to have a conference with your godfather, so run along to your soldier bang-bang games."

"Silence this creature," said the Tsar, his voice growing ever more gentle and soft. But even now his armed guard hesitated.

"First things first. We've brought you that thingy. Cat, give it to Madame Apoplexy so she can hand it over to the kingpin."

"Well. This night affords its surprises." The Tsar lifted his left hand and once again the guards fell back a few steps. To Elena: "Liberty, only until this reunion is accomplished." To Prince Anton: "I don't suppose *you* arranged this melodrama for *my* entertainment?"

The Prince shrugged. "No, but what an excellent notion."

The great-aunt was rubbing her eyes, trying to follow the train of events. Elena spoke through her resentment and mortification. "Dear Madame Sophia. However hard I tried to behave like a girl from London, I'm only a girl from the farms. In Miersk we apologize even for being alive, and that's the deepest apology I can give you. I've stolen your affection and I've lied to you. I don't ask for your forgiveness. I don't deserve it."

"*Ma chérie*, tell me which part of this is a dream and which is not," ventured Madame Sophia. "I wish there were program notes. Still, I couldn't read them anyway, what with my poor eyesight. So who can complain?"

"You can complain. It's *deeply* Russian to complain," said Miss Yaga. "But if it's spectacles you need . . ." She withdrew from a beaded bag a cloth sleeve with the phrase *Four-eyes!* embroidered on it. "They'll conform to your needs, or I'll stamp upon them with my dainty heels — I promise."

She extracted a little pair of wire-rimmed glasses that unfolded at the nose joint. "These once belonged to Galileo, if I'm not mistaken, and with them he saw the secrets of the stars. That's stars, not 'tsars.' Myself, I rely on the trade journals."

"Some Hotel Bedlam is missing a regular client," whispered the Tsar.

"She speaks the nonsense of the sorely aged," replied the Deputy Sub-Lieutenant.

"Shut up, you two," said Miss Yaga. "I'm starting to remember why I prefer life in my own private hermitage."

The great-aunt fixed the pince-nez upon her nose. Then she

raised her recessed chins and peered through the lenses at Elena. To her credit, she didn't recoil. But the grip of her fingers on the settee tightened. "By Saint Basil and Saint Cyprian. My agitated dreams were warning me, but I thought it was the zinc tonic."

Next she regarded Cat, who had come to stand next to Elena. In the gaslight, even a half-blind raven could see that the two girls looked alike, especially when dressed expensively. But the ways they looked different were striking as well.

Ekaterina, Cat, named for Catherine the Great, stood with her neck erect, her eyes level, her face serene.

Elena, every bit as pretty, twisted her fingers, cast her eyes down. Marooned in this imperial cage, she became more rural by the moment.

Madame Sophia held plump, shaking hands to Cat. "*Ma chérie,* I didn't even know you were missing. I didn't suffer a whit. Thank goodness you are safe."

"To quote a great sage, 'Goodness had nothing to do with it,'" said Miss Yaga.

"She's right," said Cat. "Miss Yaga is my traveling companion and governess now. She saw me safely home, dear *tante.*" She yielded to her great-aunt's embraces with a certain reserve, a reluctance to be on display.

"You can explain later," said the great-aunt. "But if your parents ever learn of this —!"

"They'd laugh and open another bottle. But now, the gift. Miss Yaga?"

Miss Yaga came forward. The Fabergé egg was still in its pocket of straw and dung. "Cat gave it to me first, but I already have one

279

just like it. Only better." She didn't curtsey. Why the Tsar didn't have her arrested for insolence, he didn't realize until later. But it isn't only young ladies who charm.

Prince Anton did the honor of clawing open the batting. "It's like a gilded rugby ball." The size of his two hands clasped. The nest fell, more or less intact, to the carpet. He held up the gift. Its baroque curlicues gleamed, its jewels glistened.

"Oh my," said the Tsar. "But it is porcelain, not cloisonné upon steel. A departure for Fabergé. Can this be genuine?"

Madame Sophia signaled to soldiers that they should hoist her back to her feet. "I asked the studio *not* to duplicate their methods used to create your famous collection of eggs. That would be impertinent. Besides, the Tsar likes novelty, and I thought a porcelain egg would have a reticent sort of prominence of its own. By post, I directed the artisans myself. The separate windows show three beloved stories from Russian folk literature."

The gift was center stage now. Even Miss Yaga fell silent, watching the Tsar receive his tribute.

Both girls stepped apart, and away from each other.

Cat couldn't look at Elena now. By perpetrating the fraud, Elena had helped Cat and betrayed her at the same time. Elena, a mere acquaintance — there'd been no time to become true friends. Cat saw that clearly. So why should this reunion feel so abrasive? She didn't know.

Nor could Cat bear to see her great-aunt's face when she learned that one of the windows — the one with the Firebird — had been mysteriously changed.

Blinking, surely from the night wind, Cat swiveled her head

and looked out at the black river, between the pavilions and the Winter Palace. She must have flinched, because, while all other eyes were on the gift, both Elena and Prince Anton turned to see what Cat had seen.

Dumb Doma was drifting alongside, downstream. Upon the ridgepole the kitten prowled back and forth, a sentinel, a shifting ballast, it was hard to tell.

No party guest was pointing and screaming. No one was shrieking. All eyes were trained on the Tsar and his gift, if near enough to see, or if farther away, on the comedy of comely men and glossy maidens brought to parade before one another. Adults all, they paid attention to adult life. They thought it was fun.

But Prince Anton turned to Cat, and then to Elena, and mouthed an *O*, meaning, roughly: *What is that?*

Elena glanced at Cat, who looked more chagrined than astounded.

The Tsar's exclamations over his gift commanded their attention, so Dumb Doma, rotating in slow circles, passed on by unheralded.

"A Baba Yaga house," he declared. "Such finesse. Look at those dragon carvings in the rafter beams, and each tiny talon on the house's chicken legs! I've never seen the like."

"And where are the skulls on stakes to serve as a single maiden's security system?" asked Miss Yaga. "A little bloody mayhem to make it seem like home?"

Prince Anton revolved the gift so his godfather could squint into the next opening. "Aha. And here is the great ice-dragon."

"I don't know what that is," said Prince Anton.

"A mysterious creature respected and feared by the Laplanders, those people who live north of Archangel and migrate back and forth between the mainland and Nova Zembla. Look at his teeth — there must be two hundred of them, separately carved."

"Yes, that beast is wonderfully handled. Don't you love his eyes? The emeralds are from an Ankara merchant. *Baksheesh* was involved." Madame Sophia crowed, "Oh, do turn to the next; it's the most splendid of all."

Cat squeezed her eyes closed. The Prince revolved the great egg until the final window was opposite the slope of the Tsar's regal nose.

"What is the meaning of this?" The great man's voice was liquid iron.

Vanished

W hat can you mean?" Madame Sophia's knuckles, on both hands, flew to her lips.

"Is this some attack on our national pride? No story of Russian lore features a wasteland like this sorry scene. Is this supposed to be the Battle of Austerlitz? Some other tragedy of military shame?" His brow was dark.

"But —" Madame Sophia adjusted her new spectacles. "I instructed the studio to fashion a Firebird in the third frame. . . ."

"This is no Firebird."

Madame Sophia grabbed the fabulous gift back from him so she could peer closely and see what he was talking about. She nearly dropped it.

"This scene featured a Firebird in a spring woods. I requested it, I approved the design, I accepted the finished piece when it was brought from London for my review."

Oh, but Prince Anton was enjoying this. "What does it look like now?" He meant to write a letter to the editor of *Vedomosti*, the Saint Petersburg newspaper, championing this troupe of actresses. They should all get raises.

The great-aunt said, "Who's disfigured my gift? The green woods is a rotted forest in a standing swamp. A poisoned wilderness, no less than that. And the Firebird has been spirited away."

Miss Yaga: "Nothing spirits away a Firebird. A Firebird is spirit incarnate."

Madame Sophia rounded on Elena. "Could it be you, you changeling? You! You and your . . . your village cohorts? Did *you* do this to my tribute to the Tsar? Ruining my name, and that of my family? Arrest her!"

"She is already arrested." The Tsar was beginning to sound tired.

"I had nothing to do with that," said Elena hotly. "It was never in my possession. Your great-niece had it all the time. It's her fault."

"And she gave it to me," said Miss Yaga.

"I don't believe it. You stole it from her." Madame Sophia turned her ire to Miss Yaga. "And *you* pocketed the lovely Firebird, fleshed with yellow diamonds and canary pearls, and somehow you did over the setting to hide your crime. Who are you, anyway? Some schoolmarm from that miserable hamlet called Miersk?"

"I don't steal," said Miss Yaga. "Be careful, my dear, with your accusations. I can be tetchy when aroused."

It seemed to Elena, then, that the singular Miss Yaga grew. How? Not in stature. The intensity of her menace made her seem more lethal, more ancient. She looked the same, but she no longer

284

seemed a harmless scold. More like an ambulatory bayonet stitched into a size-zero governess's black uniform with yellow wrapper.

Cat pressed her hands together. "Miss Yaga, remember your station."

Perhaps Prince Anton sensed a rising threat, too; he jumped in. "If the Firebird is missing, what about that huge eggshell we just saw? The false guest said *it* was a Firebird's egg." He pointed to Elena.

"That's what I first thought. I was lost and far from home, and beside myself. I mistook some large snake egg for a Firebird's egg. It was a passing fancy that I let myself believe. I know better now how little magic exists in this world."

"Less and less by the hour," snapped Miss Yaga. "Tell us what happened."

"Well . . . at first I *thought* I'd found a Firebird in the forest. When I was trying to escape from the train — I *did* try to escape, you see," she said in an aside to Madame Sophia and to the Tsar. "I plunged to grab the Firebird's tail, to wish this mishap right again. As I neared the creature, a fox flushed a common farmyard hen out of the underbrush. The blasted hen nipped the tail feather before I could get to it. The Firebird expired and burned to ashes, and in its ashes appeared the egg. Which I took. Later, I believed I'd stumbled on an egg and only dreamed that Firebird part, out of fear and hope. I'd been prone to fancy, you see. I'm recovering from that. Still, I gave the woodland egg to the Tsar, in lieu of the Fabergé egg that had gotten, um, misplaced."

"I knew it!" shouted Miss Yaga. "I *knew* there was something amiss with the Firebird. The Firebird breathes spirit, and the land lives; when the Firebird dies, the land dies with it! What do you think your little tchotchke is shrieking at you?" she said to the Tsar, pointing at the Fabergé egg. "Your country-land is sick."

The Tsar listened. His manner didn't change an iota; this is a skill of world leaders. But his words belied his stoic demeanor. "The other egg," he said. "The one the impostor brought?"

"The envoy returned it to the treasury," said Prince Anton. "Remember?"

"I will not suffer to have it touched again," said the Tsar. "Let me go look at it myself." To Miss Yaga: "You come with me."

"We can candle it," she said, "and perhaps see if the Firebird is arrested in there, unborn, or if this egg is the second fraud of the day."

Candling an egg: holding it up before a candle to assess the glowing contents within. I considered this strategy in my study of light upon light, of influence of light.

Miss Yaga picked up the discarded nest from the carpet and somehow stuffed it into her reticule. Then they strode, heel matching heel, the Tsar and — Elena was beginning to guess at her impossible identity — the witch. Side by side. Away from the throne carpet, along the chain of pavilions to the westernmost tent, the treasury.

Madame Sophia struggled to keep up. Elena and Cat took her arms, hauling her along. Prince Anton carried the Fabergé egg. The crowds parted in surprise and silence as the royal retinue made its hasty way.

At the row of six remaining soldiers behind the velvet rope (Prince Anton having been called away from his post), the Tsar paused.

"Has anyone been in the treasury tonight?" he asked the men.

"None but us, Your Excellency," said the captain, a man of dignity and tonsorial excellence. "And your godson incognito among us, of course."

"Guards are posted on the sides to make sure no one has approached from the water?"

"As you instructed us. All evening, sir."

"Good. Bring me the common flecked egg, about so large"— he held out his hands, the length of a small loaf of bread —"that my envoy delivered here a short while ago."

The Deputy Sub-Lieutenant arrived, panting, from a quadrille. He asked no questions, just arranged his hair to look competent.

The senior soldier returned in ten minutes. He had turned ghost-pale; he was sweating from under his moustaches into his collar. "I don't know how to explain this to the Tsar. But the gift in question seems to be missing. Vanished. Vanished utterly." He looked as if he expected to be vanished next.

The Marvels Deliver
Their Opinion

Miss Yaga shoved him aside and entered the treasury. The Tsar and the Deputy Sub-Lieutenant followed her, and Cat and Elena and Prince Anton followed them. Madame Sophia, puffing, found a cedarwood stool from the Levant upon which to collapse.

Besides the mounds of wrapped presents — pots of heirloom roses from Persia, perhaps, or rare illuminated manuscripts, or useful lavatory soaps — a few genuine marvels stood out.

As tall as the Tsar, in one corner, lurked the fantastic life-size matryoshka.

In another corner stood the immense snow globe. Inside the glass was an impossibly correct rendition of Saint Basil's Cathedral in Moscow, submerged in viscous liquid. If you spun the globe with your hand, it revolved on a track. The Prince tried it. Lightweight paper flakes floated up, fluid curtains of December, settling on domes and spires. A hurdy-gurdy melody tinkled thinly.

In a third corner hulked a giant metallic rooster. His wattles were made of fine chain mail; his copper cape overlapped onto a brassy breast. He loomed as tall as the nesting dolls, his strutting male magic looking his female counterpart in her balsawood painted eye.

"It's got to be here," said Miss Yaga. She made her way to the center of the pavilion. There, she overturned her reticule and shook it. All that fell out was the raggedy nest. She set her bag down with the sides folded open, perhaps to prevent a latter suggestion of larceny. Her hands went to her chin, and she turned a suspicious eye on the other people present. One by one.

It seemed to Elena as if the music and charm of the festival was fading, distancing. Becoming a thing of the past. As Miersk had seemed a dissolving village, a village in the act of turning ghostly, the celebration seemed to be ghosting, too.

Miss Yaga, like a good reproving chaperone, examined her charges. All the guards, then Prince Anton and the Tsar. Elena and the Deputy Sub-Lieutenant. Madame Sophia and Cat. Everyone found it hard not to flinch under her glare, which was accusatory and diagnostic.

Finally she said, "All right. I don't believe any of you is lying. So the Firebird's egg must be here. And if it is, I will find it."

They hardly dared move, any of them. The night had a quality of seizure about it, as if laws had been broken and anything might happen. As if magic was disturbed from its safe channels. As if all the dangerous *maybe*s were inching toward *probably*s. Elena's eyes had dried, and her crusty lids felt like sand. Cat's ears rang.

Prince Anton looked as if he had won at Monte Carlo.

"What are you waiting for?" said Miss Yaga. "Everybody,

look everyplace. Unless it finally hatched of its own accord and the Firebird flew away, the egg should be here. And even if it *has* hatched, the pieces of the shell should be crackling underfoot. Where did you see it last?"

"I set it down next to this set of 624 matching monogrammed towels," said the captain. "My companions watched me come in, place it down, and retreat. Perhaps it rolled someplace." But though they all hunted, they saw no sign of it.

"I'll take some depositions," said Miss Yaga. She ran over to the giant snow globe. It was as tall as she was. She picked it up and shook it.

"Look at this!" she snapped. They all hurried to see.

Whether the donor of this gift had been some wizard of the north or djinn of the south, or Baba Yaga's nervous energy was infectious, no one knew. Perhaps the whole tent was under an enchantment. When the witch set down the enormous globe and spun it, something unexpected happened.

As the globe rotated, the snow rose around the delicate model of the colored spires of Saint Basil's Cathedral. It first coated the onion domes with white. Then, somehow, the snow turned to a drizzle of rain, and the flakes dissolved and ran down the building, pooling as runoff. Saint Basil's looked to be planted in two feet of sludgy wastewater. The music, I gather, was cribbed from Gerzhensky's Symphony No. 1, "Blizzard Pastorale"— the plangent andante movement, though all four movements were lugubrious and andante — based on the Russian folk song "Frostbite in July."

"You're going to let your whole country drown?" Miss Yaga bowled the globe aside. Its music sped up until it sounded like shattering prisms of ice. The globe ripped through the loosely strung tenting and drowned in the Neva, bubbling Gerzhensky all the while.

Next she muscled up to the nesting dolls. The largest doll, the matriarch-general in her painted wooden scarf, stared at the golden rooster. "What are you looking at, hussy?" shouted Miss Yaga. "Wipe that smirk off your face, or I'll wipe it off for you." The doll didn't change her expression, which was complacent, assured, somewhat sassy.

"I suppose you're a music box, too? You think you can hide secrets from me? Well, you can't," said Miss Yaga. "When I find your windup key, you'll sing like the rest of them, sister." She reached up and wrestled with the matriarch, whose head came off with a cork-popping sound, leaving the bottom in place. Inside, an identical smarmy doll snugly waited, as superior as her mother if a little less zaftig. "*Your* mouth is painted shut too, dollface?" Miss Yaga decapitated her and handed her head to the Tsar. Before long there were thirty severed dolls. They seemed to have taken a vow of silence. There was nothing musical about them.

"I *know* they know more than they're letting on," said Miss Yaga. "All this revolting motherliness must be good for something." By now she was hauling off a half-dozen heads at a time.

"Better start putting these dolls back together," said the Tsar. "They're taking up too much room." The soldiers started to pair the tops with the correct bottoms, but forgot to insert the dolls within one another in ascending order. So the Tsar dismissed most of the dolls, and his men jettisoned them out the new rip in the tent, where they bobbed in the river, giant ducklings huddled together.

Miss Yaga reached the last doll. This infant came up nearly to

Miss Yaga's knee and was a foot in diameter. It wasn't at all baby-like, more like a little fierce dwarf mother with a grudge. When Miss Yaga opened it up, she found a piece of parchment on which was written: HISTORY ISN'T FINISHED YET. COME BACK LATER.

"No egg here," she admitted. "Sorry about your dollies, Tsar."

"Each one represented a clan or tribe of my peoples," he said. "Now they are all afloat on the flood."

"I think the water is making them swell," reported Prince Anton, who had been sticking his head out of a side flap to watch. "You're never going to pack them tightly together again. They're all the same size now."

"Release them to the wild, and may they live and flourish." The Tsar put his hand on his forehead as if about to indulge in a major headache.

"A lot of this stuff is just junk you can buy on the open market," said Miss Yaga. "I mean, unless there's a nice flying carpet from Samarkand I haven't noticed, it's all ready for the rubbish bin. And I don't see anything else that could hide an egg."

The six soldiers, who had been ripping through gift wrapping as if hunting for a ticking time bomb, paused in their exertions and had to agree.

"I can only think of one other thing." Miss Yaga marched through the sea of crinkly gilt paper to the well-planted legs of the golden cockerel. "What is this, an emissary from Pushkin himself? What do *you* know, big boy? Spill the beans! We have ways of making you talk."

The golden rooster kept his own counsel.

"Oh, you're going to play *that* game. Well, you asked for it." At this the fiendish little woman leaped upon the back of the rooster and sat down as if prepared to ride him across the steppes at the head of a Mongol horde. Her little booted feet came out on either side in an unladylike fashion, and her skirt rode almost up to her hips. Everyone could see that her stockings were laddered. But she was not one to mind about that.

She reached into the tin feathers of the rooster's cape and felt around. Elena thought perhaps she was trying to choke the thing, to force him to confess. But the old woman was hunting for a key. She found it, and inserted it in one of the rooster's ears, and turned it tightly until it would wind no more. Then she let go of it.

The rooster opened his tin mouth and began to crow in a tin voice.

"Oh, the weather outside is rotten.
See how damp the ground has gotten.
But since we all like to complain,
Let it rain, let it rain, let it rain.

Oh, the storms continue pelting
And the polar ice is melting.
Though it has no place to drain,
Let it rain, let it rain, let it rain."

"Whoever gave you this rooster ought to be shot," said Miss Yaga to the Tsar.

"Well," said Prince Anton, "the rooster does have a tin ear."

"I want to know about the egg! Where did it go, Tarnish-breath?"

The rooster filled its mechanical lungs with melody and started a second verse:

"Oh, the weather is so revolting
That the chickens all are moulting . . ."

"Cock-a-doodle-don't," said Prince Anton to the rooster, once Miss Yaga had finished stamping it silent.

When the last spring had finished springing, the last cog had wheeled away and lost itself in the shadows, Miss Yaga seemed to shrink back to the size she had appeared at first. The campaign, it seemed, was a failure. "There's nothing more I can do here," she said. "The first time in my life I've admitted such a thing. Which is even more proof that the Firebird is dead. If this is so, then all that is spirit and magic in the wide world will die, too."

With that statement, a certain buttress slipped, a strut gave way. The sound of the festival reasserted itself. Miss Yaga went to her reticule and pulled out a sunny yellow parasol that hadn't been there before. She opened it up. She alone remained dry as a small, impossible rain began to fall from clouds that had gathered under the tent canopy. She did not offer her parasol, not even to the Tsar. It looked as if Miss Yaga was done with them, done with them all.

Under Arrest

You came here an impostor, and there's been nothing but upset since you arrived," said the Tsar to Elena. "Guards, take her into custody."

Cat wouldn't return Elena's glance. Elena had hijacked Cat's life for her own improvement and had left Cat behind to starve in Miersk or be eaten by a wild kitten.

"Tell them it was all an accident," pleaded Elena. But Cat wouldn't speak in the girl's defense.

Miss Yaga gave Cat a long, contemptuous glare. Then she picked up the reticule, clipped it closed with a vicious snap, and said, "I'm giving my notice, effective immediately." She didn't bow to the Tsar as she passed him. She didn't acknowledge Cat's sputter of surprise, her unchained syllables. They signified nothing to Baba Yaga.

There was nothing more to be done. Elena was escorted away by soldiers. Cat watched her go, and then turned her face.

The Tsar forgave Madame Sophia any part she might have played in the night's proceedings, including being so inept as to have lost her spectacles at an important moment. She managed to regain some composure, barely.

The Tsar ordered the guests to leave the pavilions and come back the next evening, and they'd start over. He sent Prince Anton to his room.

The guests all hove away feeling that they'd been ignored. But they were determined to put all this behind them, return tomorrow, woo the Prince, and astound the Tsar with their own precious gifts.

As they evacuated the premises and surged along the quays, they were amazed to see the navy of about sixteen dozen floating dolls bobbing in the Neva River. Even the guest who had brought them, a merchant from the Ukraine, didn't recognize them, for his dolls had been built to nest, and this set seemed ready to invade Norway.

Ekaterina slipped her hand into her great-aunt's hand as they waited for their carriage. When it arrived, Korsikov's eyes grew wide with disbelief. "So it *was* you all along!" he said. "What happened to my eyes, that I didn't see?"

Cat didn't reply. Generally she didn't talk to staff.

Miss Bristol sat inside the carriage, huddled over an iron box with a grilled lid and hot coals inside. At the sight of Cat climbing in the door, she started. "Oh, Miss Ekaterina!" she cried. "What magic is this, that returns you to our midst?"

"I have had an excursion," said Cat.

"*Quite* the excursion, it seems," said Madame Sophia. "I wonder if I shall believe any of this in the morning, or merely wake up and find myself still marooned on a train in the middle of the countryside." Putting her head against the side of the seat, she fell instantly asleep.

To avoid the congestion of carriages collecting guests, Korsikov looped a long way around, along the English Embankment, the Palace Embankment. The windows of the Winter Palace. All this glory. Cat couldn't really picture Elena being banished to the depths of a prison. She didn't try. She was too tired to examine the matter closely. She just looked out the window of the carriage as the pavilions began to fall back behind them.

In the black water of the Neva River, she could still see the flotilla of liberated matryoshka dolls. Among them, paying little mind, paddled the serene vessel of Dumb Doma, carrying Miss Yaga into some private Russia, a Russia of secret coordinates. Away from these distresses. Away from her.

Later.

ONE EVENING I SAT DOWN TO WRITE TO THE TSAR, NIBBLING some bread I'd saved from breakfast. As I filled my pen with ink, a storm stuttered at some distance.

I watched hidden lightning pulse the clouds with an oily stain. The flare of a passing dragon, were I given to that sort of fancy. Though what actually nipped by was a wren, stopping at my windowsill. It must have been new to the neighborhood, as I was known for my miserliness with crumbs. I was thinking about lightning, and how life can be changed by a slash of brilliance. Almost without meaning to, I broke a crumb off the crust and flicked it onto the sill. The bird hopped forward, looked at me with one eye, pecked the crumb, and left.

Please don't think I was becoming sentimental. I was in the practice of husbanding my crumbs, and to hell with the birds. But as I considered how I came to be imprisoned, I realized how little sense this story makes unless you see both sides of it. Cat's side and Elena's side, too. The side of the rich and the side of the poor. (Let's just say.) A bird sees out of both sides of its head. It can see two stories happening at the same time, on two sides of its world. We humans can't do that very often.

The rain started up. The wren didn't come back. I ate the rest of my bread. And I continued to think about lightning and thunder, about fire and water and ice.

I have tried to see both sides of the story of the Firebird. On the one hand, his bright and liberated life (so different from mine in prison!), and then his smoky death, when he gives up a wish to some plucky child and is reborn in his own egg. It is a magic cycle but a cycle just the same, like the turn of the seasons, spring to summer to fall to winter to spring again.

And when the cycle is broken? What happens to the magic?

What happens to the world?

PART · FOUR

FIRE AND ICE, ICE AND FIRE

A Wasp in the Jam

The following morning, Madame Sophia Borisovna Orlova was decidedly not at home to callers. She'd taken to her boudoir. She hunched herself in a dressing gown and sipped orange tea, and she didn't bother to brush her hair.

She had the canary cage brought in, but Madame's mood must have been contagious, for the canary wouldn't sing.

She rang for Miss Bristol and Monsieur d'Amboise. "Do not speak," she said. "Just listen. You knew that my niece had disappeared into the wild. You knew that an impostor had taken her place. In short order, you taught Elena just enough of the social graces so she could masquerade as a young woman of breeding. On the one hand, I consider that a job well done. On the other, you collaborated with a reckless brigand at the risk of Ekaterina's life and well-being. I should have you brought up on charges of aiding and abetting, or at least sacked without references."

"But I —" began Miss Bristol.

"I told you not to speak."

Miss Bristol fell silent, but Monsieur d'Amboise did not.

"Madame," he said, "I *will* speak. You may accuse us of any treachery you like once you hear our side. But you may not accuse us without allowing us testimony."

"I said to be silent."

"I will be silent, but not yet. The truth is, the accidental exchange of the girls happened several days before we realized it, as the impostor, Elena, kept herself cloistered. By the time we'd discovered the switch, it was too late to do anything useful."

"It's never too late to save a child. I should have you hanged."

"With all due respect, you should have noticed the difference in the girl yourself, Madame."

The contempt in the room, a blinding frost.

"If you call out the law upon us, we will point out that you traveled with the impostor for several hundred versts without noticing she was the wrong child. What does that say about your capacities as a guardian? Or does it suggest you were in on some scheme to infiltrate the court of the Tsar with rebel peasants? That you're a sympathizer for so-called Bolshevist reform?"

Madame Sophia pulled her coverlets to her neckline as if she imagined being hauled to prison herself. "*You* never had a child, did you, Monsieur d'Amboise? You can't imagine how they do grow and change under your very eyes. And I'm a woman with weak eyes."

"You're a woman with a weak imagination. And unless I am mistaken, you never had your own child, either. You never married. Miss Ekaterina upstairs is the grandchild of your brother. Don't presume to lecture me about child rearing."

"Me either," said Miss Bristol, daringly.

"And you her governess!" seethed Madame Sophia. "Go, you are dismissed, leave my sight, such as it is."

"Dismissed from our positions or just to the downstairs kitchens?"

"Do I have to make all the decisions? Just get out of here!"

So they went downstairs and had tea, rubbed raw by the truth of Madame's accusations. But they also felt they had managed, against the odds, to survive their tribulations, at least so far.

Madame Sophia then summoned Miss Ekaterina. Cat knocked, and entered, and stood looking sideways at the mantelpiece. The great-aunt studied her through the spectacles given her by Miss Yaga, that deranged interloper governess, who seemed to have skived off somewhere.

Madame Sophia began. "Your adventure has changed you a good deal. I'm not sure I approve."

"I didn't ask for any of it. Neither to be left behind by accident, nor to be misidentified by my only loving relative."

"Oh, that. I was not myself."

"No, *I* was not myself. I apparently was Elena Rudina. And you never noticed."

"You jump to conclusions. I did notice you were different. I said so to Miss Bristol. But I thought it was anxiety over meeting the Prince and the Tsar. What did you think of the young man, anyway?"

"Prince Anton? He isn't a young man. He's a child."

"Don't be impertinent. If he can be engaged, he's a young man."

Cat didn't press her point. But it hadn't escaped her that Prince Anton, like Elena and Cat herself, had noticed Baba Yaga's izba paddling by. If Dumb Doma was invisible to grown-ups and yet Prince Anton had seen it, that proved he was no grown-up.

But his status made no difference to her. Cat hadn't traveled to Saint Petersburg in order to become engaged in marriage. She'd come at the bequest of her great-aunt, whose need to supervise the parentless girl seemed greater than Cat's need to be supervised. Anyway, what kind of supervision was it, if Cat could disappear for a week at a time and never be missed?

Cat: "Why did you really pull me from school in London? Why did you have Miss Bristol escort me across the English Channel to Paris? Why did you haul me across Europe by train — Paris, Vienna, Moscow, Saint Petersburg? Just to go to a party and to dance with a beardless boy? Was this *really* to improve my prospects in life? Or was it to solidify your own relationship with the court of our Tsar?"

"Don't you talk to me like that. That's what being out in the wild has done to you: it has made you common. I don't need to answer to you, missy."

"You aren't my mother. You aren't even my grandmother. You are using me for advantage."

"Such advantage as I might derive from your shenanigans I could do without. Anyway, you're wrong. I am an old woman mere moments from the grave, Miss Ekaterina. When I die, a stone marker will be put upon my mouth and you'll never hear from me again. But while I live and breathe, I will do what I can for you, since no one else seems inclined to pay you the attention you need."

"That's preposterous. The teachers at school are quite capable —"

"The teachers at your school are paid to oversee you while you are enrolled. That's all. They must be free to care about someone new when you leave. And your feckless parents wouldn't bother about your well-being even if you broke all your limbs and sat upon your own nose. I'm tired of having my motivations questioned. As Monsieur d'Amboise pointed out, quite above his station I might add, I've never enjoyed the blessings of a husband or children. So I've cared for you as if you were my own. Perhaps I have done it in a slovenly manner. In my defense, all I can say is that I would have raised my own children equally recklessly. Bringing you to the royal court is the best I could think of to do, to launch you on your own two feet before I die."

"You don't care about me —"

"Who else thinks of your future? Who else would bother? Not your bottle-blond mother, duchess of Monte Carlo's roulette wheel. Not your gin-sozzled father, selling arms to natives in French Algeria. Criticize my practices if you will, but you cannot question my motives. I only mean to save you from contamination by your closer relatives."

"May I be excused now?"

"No. There is one thing further."

Cat waited.

"What are we going to do about Elena Rudina?"

Cat lost her composure. "It isn't for us to do anything. She's a stupid, scheming girl from Mud Village. She took advantage of my kindness, and she left me to danger when I fell from the train. We owe her nothing."

Madame Sophia put a handkerchief to her eyes. "And her people?"

"What do you mean, her people?" Cat had gone wary — like a cat.

"As I hear you tell it, there's a brother gone off to Moscow as a houseboy of sorts. And another brother conscripted in the army. And what about that sick mother whom, presumably, the 'stupid, scheming girl' was risking her life and liberty to help?"

Cat fell silent. The grip of the sick mother's hand upon her own — Cat could still feel it. It was the most maternal experience she had ever encountered. But in reclaiming her own station, Cat could not be responsible for that woman's life.

"They took you in," pressed her great-aunt. "Even if for just a night. Do you think your mother and father would have taken in Elena, under similar circumstances? When they have scarcely bothered ever to take *you* in?"

Cat's voice was cold. "I've had too little experience of family *bonhomie* to comment. What happens to that family is no concern of ours."

"Oh, my," said Madame Sophia, and suddenly she was hoisting herself out of her bed. She was unsteady on her little pads of feet, and groped for the backs of chairs as she neared Cat. "I should have thought travel might have broadened you a little. I see you are just a little buzzing factory of selfishness, the way most children are. You have become mildew on the sponge, a wasp in the jam. Sooner or later, Miss Ekaterina, I hope you come into yourself more admirably. In the meantime, if you won't care to enquire after Elena Rudina, I will go alone."

"Go? Go where?"

"I shall go to see the Tsar," she replied. "I shall stand on his welcome mat and pound until he opens the door. After all, *ma chérie,* under whatever circumstances, that Elena Rudina was kind to me. She told me stories to while away the long hours on that train. And I have come to care what happens to her. I shall see if I can plead for clemency on her behalf."

"Why would you do that?"

"If only to find a way to thank her family for taking you in on that first night in Miersk. I gather they had little to spare."

"You," said Cat, "have lost all perspective."

"I have not lost my heart," said Madame Sophia, and she adjusted her new spectacles and then slapped her great-niece across the face. "Nor my aim."

Brother Uri

We haven't spent any time considering the Prince. But he was the child to witness what happened next, so here we go.

Prince Anton was supposed to be resting. The second night of the festival would have to be less thrilling than the first, which had ended in a bizarre social disaster. How he'd enjoyed it, though. One girl disguised as another, and then exposed. That old witch stamping the giant cockerel to bits. The magic downpour.

He tossed and turned, despising household law. Who could sleep when daylight came needling between the join of the drapes?

In his stocking feet, he padded about the apartments that his godfather the Tsar had provided for him. The food provided on trays was rich and revolting. The drawers in the furniture revealed no games. Not even a set of playing cards. The only books were biographies of dead Tsars. He tried to kick a wad of clean socks off the baseboards like a rugby ball, but they had no bounce.

At last he peered out into the corridor. A daytime silence. Most of the court was catching up on its beauty sleep. Even the guard on duty to protect the Prince was snoring in a chair, his lance propped against the door frame.

Anton tiptoed around the guard and arrived at a flight of marble steps. All around, gilt cupids were stuck against the molding like flies on sticky paper. He looked down. The stairs fanned out into a gallery before descending several more flights. At the ground floor, the great frescoes of the Battle of Austerlitz were bright and triumphant, but their reflections wobbled in the water that glazed the flooring several inches deep, one room to the next.

The Prince would have liked to try sliding down the railing, but this banister terminated at a marble statue of a warrior with a spear (Courage), and the other at a matching statue of a divine woman with a scimitar (Charity). Both statues displayed a lack of modesty that Anton admired.

As he didn't want to impale himself on naked virtue, he descended by foot.

When he neared the landing, Anton heard voices a few rooms off. He'd been staying with the Tsar long enough to discover the servants' passages, so it didn't take long to find a panel that swung open at his fingertips. He hurried along a musty corridor tiled in white brick, past numbered doors covered in blue felt. Convenient access for the staff with refreshments, he imagined, or assassins with guns. As I said, he was a boy.

After one or two false starts, he found a door into the room where the conversation was coming from.

As it happened, what a lark! He emerged onto the balcony

above the throne room. A court circular, folded into a paper aeroplane, lay on a chair by the railing. Below, Anton could see the Tsar walking back and forth, juggling a couple of oranges. The Tsar was in his stockings, too, and there was a hole in one of his heels. For some reason this filled Anton with joy.

The Tsar was being followed six steps behind by a saintly monk with a long raveled beard. In those days this gentle scholar was an advisor and mentor to the Tsar. His head was clipped in a tonsure like that of some patriarch painted by an Old Master from Siena or Ravenna. I'm told his humble robes stank of cheese. I did enjoy a bite of cheese now and then. And I can still see the afternoon light slanting like broad golden oars through the west windows.

The boy crept forward in the gallery until his chin was on the railing. The great room was empty but for the two men.

The Tsar: "I don't understand what you are getting at, Brother Uri."

"Your Excellency. Your report of the farce that occurred last night has piqued my curiosity. I wish I'd been there. You tell a story to amuse, but I take it most seriously. It's another sign, a sign of dreadful moment."

Little did I know, et cetera.

The Tsar replied, "You can't imagine that the *actual* Firebird's egg was delivered in a carpetbag to my door? You insist that the Firebird is the very fuse of Russia, Brother Uri. How can his egg be packed up like a specimen of beetle found . . . found by Darwin at some picnic! . . . and brought home for further examination? Perhaps I entertained that idea last night; the wine was sublime, an eighteenth-century Bordeaux. But in the light of day, I find the notion capricious."

"Your Highness, I've been studying the lore of the Firebird passed down from the Scythians and other horse tribes of ancient Russia."

"Yes, yes, Brother Uri. You mention your scholarly pursuits every time we meet. But the Firebird is only a symbol. And a symbol is insubstantial, a puff of breath on a winter's morning."

"A puff of breath is proof of life. I tell you, the loss of the Firebird's egg is not to be taken lightly." The monk seemed out of patience. "I'm not talking about symbols. Using principles derived from Leibniz and Spinoza, I've been trying to answer the question: What kind of shadow does a lighted object throw? Say, a lighted candle on a table?"

"A lighted candle on a table throws candlelight across that table, good Brother Uri. Every Tsar knows this, and most nudniks know it, too."

"You misunderstand me. I'll try again. Suppose you were to light a candle on a table in a dark room. Then you climb on a chair above it and light a *very large blazing torch.* You look at the table-top again. What kind of shadow do you see?"

"You would see the slender shadow of the candlestick, I suppose."

"Yes, but what about the *flame* on the lit candle?"

"I've been too busy governing a continent to try. But one doesn't need to read the mystics or the rationalists to conclude that you'd see no shadow of the candle flame, Brother Uri."

"Not with your naked eye, no. I'll grant you that. But perhaps

313

the sun shining upon the bright light of a Firebird casts an invisible shadow somehow — a shadow made of light, undetectable by human eyes. An influence we can infer but not see, just as we know the influence of time and honor upon human affairs, though we cannot see time nor honor themselves."

"Very metaphorical and a bit sensational, if you ask me."

"I'm examining what the shadow of a bright Firebird is, and where it falls. I suspect its influence is essential to the survival of the world."

"Have you been getting into the cabinet with the grappa?"

The monk pressed on. "We need to find that Firebird's egg. If it fails to hatch, we lose the Firebird's influence upon the land and people of Russia."

"Brother Uri, a shadow is nothing but a dark outline. It has no *influence*."

"Tell that to radishes planted inside a box with a lid on it. The shadow of the lid has quite an influence; the radishes will never mature."

"*You* are a radish."

Prince Anton smothered a giggle. He thought the monk called Brother Uri looked more like a bearded parsnip. That boy has a long way to go.

Radish or parsnip, the monk persisted. "You must send out scouts the length and breadth of Saint Petersburg to hunt for the stolen egg. It can't be far."

"You are assuming the gift actually *was* the egg of the Firebird and not a decoy made of papier-mâché. In any case, all my available men are digging ditches to try to run this confounded flood back to the sea where it belongs. I can't afford so much as a footman to scour Saint Petersburg."

"You must afford it. It is said, 'One should see the world, and see himself, as a scale with an equal balance of good and evil. When he does one good deed, the scale is tipped to the good — he and the world are saved. When he does one evil deed, the scale is tipped to the bad — he and the world are destroyed.'"

"Interesting. Who said that, your grandmother?"

"Maimonides. The great Jewish scholastic."

"I didn't know you read Jewish philosophers."

"It is said, 'You must accept the truth from whatever source it comes.'"

"And who said that?"

"Also Maimonides."

The Tsar, who was trying to balance these thoughts between throbs of a headache, turned to the Deputy Sub-Lieutenant, who had come bowing at the door. "Are there other audiences for today?" asked the Tsar somewhat hopefully.

"Two impromptu visitors, each ignorant of the other and waiting in separate parlors. They were both present last night at the festival. I usually send such petitioners off with a warning. But each declares she has something to tell you about the strange events last evening."

The Tsar gave the monk a look.

"Maybe one of them will be announcing a stolen egg and asking for ransom or reward," observed Brother Uri. "May I stay and listen?"

"Very well. Send in one of them," ordered the Tsar.

Anton stretched his cramped legs. He was well returned to hiding position when the first of the visitors was shown in.

"I am Madame Sophia Borisovna Orlova," said the old woman to the Tsar. "The fool who couldn't tell her own great-niece from a substitute. And I am the woman who gave you, inadvertently it must be admitted, that egg which Elena Rudina once imagined to be the unhatched egg of the Firebird."

"We were just discussing that egg," said the Tsar. The monk bowed.

"I can say nothing of that egg. I wasn't there when the peasant girl found it. I haven't come about the egg."

"More's the pity. Still, continue."

"I have come for clemency." The old woman squared her shoulders and balanced her pince-nez upon her nose. "I know much of the history of your reign, Your Excellency, and I do not flatter you with falsehoods when I say you aren't the brute that some of your forebears were. You have, from time to time, shown compassion and even clemency to your subjects."

"Citizens," said the Tsar, "but go on."

"My great-niece, returned to me thanks to that itinerant governess she met in the woods, has told me of her adventures. It seems that some in the circle of Elena Rudina, that peasant child, were kind to my poor Ekaterina in her distress. And the Rudin family is suffering with want of a most severe sort."

"Blessings on them, and the stars look kindly upon them."

Stars, Firebirds, thought Anton: both of them bright and ineffectual, it seems.

"I would rather *you* looked kindly upon that family by

releasing their child," said Madame Sophia. She gripped her hands as if trying to pull her own fingers off. "She is, after all, only a girl yet. I am throwing myself upon your mercy. I would dash myself at your feet if I didn't fear a broken pelvis."

"That child claimed a false identity to gain access to my court and parade herself in front of my godson. Who despite his lineage is hardly canny enough to tell a lark from a lump of coal."

Anton bristled at that. Still, I daresay it wasn't far from the truth.

Madame Sophia waited. An elderly woman's caesura carries a certain authority, but the Tsar was the Tsar. She looked him in the eye.

He stared back lengthily before replying, "I will not release her."

The dowager was ready with another gambit. "There is the matter of her brother. This Elena came to you to ask for his release, so he can help feed the starving family. He was conscripted into your army, perhaps to dig emergency canals. In your goodness you might at least liberate him."

Oh, right, thought Anton. I was supposed to send out for information about that fellow. I thought it was her beau. What was his name?

"Luka Rudin," said the old woman.

"Enough!" roared the Tsar. "Let the peasants take care of themselves; I have a world in rivulets under my soggy feet."

"I beg you to reconsider my requests in the sanctuary of your private chambers." Madame Sophia bent as low as she could manage, and she began to back out of the Tsar's royal presence. Anton began to inch away, too, thinking perhaps he could learn about whether the brother was indeed in Saint Petersburg. He might do that much for the hapless girl who had managed to amuse him at the boring grown-up party.

The old lady was bumped into, from behind, by someone entering without being announced. "I've been kept waiting long enough, I have an appointment later on today to have my toenails examined by a lady podiatrist. What's the holdup?"

"Why, Miss Yaga," said Madame Sophia. Brother Uri's head snapped up.

An Audience
with the Tsar

Anton paused in his retreat and gaped between the balusters.

Brother Uri took a step back. But the Tsar seemed untroubled by the intrusion of this small, urgent woman.

"Whatever diversion you're planning for tonight, break it up," she said. "We've got a serious problem, Mister Tsar of All the Russias."

"I'll see myself out," said Madame Sophia in a husky whisper.

"You may as well stay. We might need common sense," said Miss Yaga. "And I'm not sure the supreme ruler and all his advisors have a clue."

"Oh, linger a moment," said the Tsar to the great-aunt, and to Miss Yaga, "I thought you gave your notice last night?"

"I'm not here as a domestic but as a savage agent in my own right."

"What are you on about, woman? Have you located the so-called Firebird's egg that went missing?"

"I never saw the darn thing," said Miss Yaga. "Though if I fell over it on my way to the loo, I would know it wasn't a party trinket to fob off on the Tsar."

"The woman's lost her mind. I'll summon the guards," said the monk. It is easy to understand his confusion. Witches often work by confusion.

"Brother Uri. You might learn something. Let the woman speak," insisted the Tsar.

"It's my opinion that the Firebird is dying," replied the newcomer. "I would say *dead, kaput,* but some magic is still alert in Russia and for all I know in several neighborhoods abroad, too. Perhaps he is paused in his cycle of life and death."

"Just as I was saying," interjected Brother Uri.

"How would a governess know about magic?" asked Madame Sophia, despite herself. That missing egg was, after all, not her prime concern.

"She's no governess," said Brother Uri. Miss Yaga may have lost her mind, but he had found his. "She is the witch."

The Tsar wasn't sure whether to be amused or alarmed. "*The* witch?"

"The same," said Miss Yaga. As Anton watched, more slack-jawed than ever, he saw her pinwheel her arms. In an acrid backfiring of yellowish exhaust, the woman lost her snug sunshiny waistcoat and her padded shoulders. The neat hair, piled on her head under an off-center toque with a pheasant's feather, exploded into a crinkly mass of dried beach grass. "Baba Yaga, arrived at

320

court at last, and I wish this were a christening so I could cast a few good spells and have some fun, but honeybucket, we haven't time."

Brother Uri grabbed the arm of the Tsar and tried to rush him out of the room. The monk always had the Tsar's well-being foremost in his heart. But the Tsar shook him off, scolding. "You're a scholar of lights and shadows. Here's a walking shadow. Pay attention."

The witch continued. "In my understanding, Firebirds die and are reborn in a matter of moments. Pause the cycle, buster, and the whole experiment is off. Did that conniving peasant girl — Yelena, is she called? Elena?—*actually* find a Firebird's egg? Or is that another lie? Frankly, I don't know the little sinner."

"I saw it," said Madame Sophia faintly. "Well, I saw something."

"That was before I gave you your new spectacles, if I'm remembering correctly. You might have seen a small watermelon whitewashed with lime. And no one else, apparently, looked at the thing closely."

"I saw it," said the Tsar.

"You're a professional potentate, you couldn't tell a goose egg from a gallstone."

"I saw it, too," called Anton.

The heads of the grown-ups turned: the Tsar, Brother Uri, Madame Sophia, the witch. Anton liked startling a quartet of grown-up authorities. "I lifted it out of its box. Remember?"

"Oh. An eyewitness," called Baba Yaga. "You held it? What did it feel like?"

"An egg. I guess. I've never done my own cooking."

"You might as well interview a signpost at a crossroads about which path to take," muttered the Tsar. Anton was tempted to aim the paper aeroplane at his godfather's head, but that might be viewed as an attempt at a coup.

"Signposts can be very conversational if you get them in the right mood," said the witch. "Look, Prince Ants-in-Your-Pants, tell me *one thing* about that *egg.*"

"It felt . . . it felt warm."

"So maybe it was the Firebird's egg, after all," said Madame Sophia. "Maybe Elena was telling the truth." They all looked at her. "For once," she amended.

"That's no proof. There were gas lamps and braziers and about a thousand people there," said Baba Yaga. "Even a corpse would have felt cozy with all that attention. No matter. I have a deeper concern to raise."

Brother Uri came forward. "Witchcraft has no place in this court. This is a house of law," he said. "It is a house of reason and of enquiry."

"As an old friend of mine once said when I brought him some interesting brownies, 'You must accept the truth from whatever source it comes,'" she replied. "Haven't you read your Maimonides?"

"Who *are* you?" asked the Tsar.

"You know who I am. I am the larch root in the spring and the feverwort blossom in the fall. I am the forlorn echo in the dry community well. The tisane that can chase away the blues. I live in isolation for my own protection and for yours. And yet I'm flushed out into the open by a groveling child, some relative of this old hen, and I'm wasting time at the court of a human emperor who doesn't know when his socks have holes in them. It's an indignity. But I endure it because we are *all in trouble.*"

The Tsar's hand on Brother Uri's forearm kept him silent, but the monk was bristling. Professional jealousy. She was getting the Tsar's ear in a way he had failed to do.

She hammered on. "This city is damper than Venice in a monsoon. The largest pastures in the world shrivel and die for lack of rain. Great Tsar, with your considerable resources, unseat this ill, and return our natural weather to us! For nature depends on magic, and magic on nature." An aside to Anton up there: "It's a which-came-first puzzle, like the chicken or the egg."

Anton couldn't help asking. "Which came first, the chicken or the egg?"

"The witch came first," she replied.

"I can't change the weather," admitted the Tsar. "I can't even change my own socks, as you have pointed out. My valet does that for me."

"Well, what about you, master scholar?" asked the witch of Brother Uri.

"You don't scare me," he said. "And we're working for the same team, you and I, so retire your superior tone or I'll smack you on your nose."

"Oooh, a live one at last," said the witch. "And?"

"I've been trying to tell the Tsar for weeks that the problems are a question of influence. Something has come between the sun and the earth, to change the pattern of our wind and water, our winter and summer."

"Something has come," said the witch, "or something that was there has gone. And this has been going on for longer than the

Firebird's paralysis, assuming the child was telling the truth about having seen the Firebird die."

"Elena Rudina is a confessed liar. Accused and sentenced as such," the Tsar reminded them.

"Nonetheless, the young scoundrel may have twigged to something. Peasants are rooted in this land more deeply than Tsars," the witch said over the emperor's objections. "The truth is that she brought words to our conversation today, and today is where we find ourselves. The work of repair begins in common words owned commonly. Starting with the word *help*."

"I've been studying the Firebird's influence for decades," said the monk.

"The winter sky won't snow. The summer sky won't stop raining. A world wound: rot and decay everywhere we turn. I still have some magic resources of my own, but for how long? We have to look for the cause somewhere. The question is, *where?*"

"Elena might know," suggested Anton. "She's the one who believed in the Firebird enough to rescue its egg. Ask *her* where to look for the source of this world wound. It can't hurt." The boy's remark was just faintly taunting.

"No one can speak to her. She's in prison," said the Tsar. "I forbid it."

There followed a deep silence. Out of love for the Tsar and for all the Russias, the monk looked at the witch, looked away, looked back again. Some might have said it was right then, that moment: that's when he began his descent toward sedition. An unholy alliance.

"Elena came into the imperial presence under an alias," continued the Tsar. "Tantamount to treachery and betrayal. She could easily have had a pistol in her purse. Who knows what she might do next?"

"Oh, really. The idea! She's a child," said the great-aunt. "Miss Bristol said she had a doll in her purse, not a pistol."

The Tsar began to walk out of the room. Without turning his head, he raised his right arm and pointed a finger in the direction of the gallery. "And you, young man, are supposed to be in your chamber. You are in serious hot water!"

"Don't you understand?" said the witch. "We're all in serious hot water. I'll take on the quest of searching for the cause of the world wound, but I must know where to look. All directions are the same to me. Hailstones over Hoboken, you manage to misplace a Firebird's egg, and Your Imperial Majesty is too haughty to ask a peasant girl for advice? And don't leave while I'm talking to you. Who do you think you are? How did you even get this job in the first place?"

"Influence," said the Tsar, and left.

The Second Night
of the Festival

C at couldn't sit down. She walked back and forth in the reception room overlooking the street, and then leaned against a French wallpaper that showed pagan temples in Elysian fields. Every eighteen inches, another pantheon in the greenery. A world lousy with ineffectual gods.

From here she could see who came and went through her great-aunt's front door.

Monsieur d'Amboise, receiving a barrage of invitations for Madame Sophia to reveal all about her role in last night's debacle, noticed the girl lurking. "I'd have thought you'd take to your bed all day. Tonight the high drama of the Tsar's festival continues."

Cat looked away. "I'm not going to attend."

"I'm surprised you think you have any choice in the matter. Can I bring you a refreshment?"

She didn't answer. He disappeared to his post below-stairs.

A short while later the front door opened. The driver entered, escorting Madame Sophia on his arm. "Thank you, Korsikov. That'll be all. I'll pause to catch my breath." The great-aunt inched toward the side room, and she saw that Cat was waiting for her.

The girl bowed slightly. "I owe you an apology."

"I accept your apology. Ooomph. I'm too old to be stirring things up with the Tsar. Drag over that little footstool so I can rest my — yes, that's good. Will you ring for d'Amboise to bring me some water? There's a good girl."

Cat did as she was told, and then pulled a chair close to her great-aunt's. "I was wrong not to think about the family in Miersk who took me in, however briefly. I was wrong and you were right."

"That happens occasionally, my being right. What has changed your mind?"

Cat had asked herself the same question. "*Ma tante*, I know that you think I was being hysterical about Miss Yaga being the great witch." At this Madame Sophia waved her hand: *Bygones, bygones, I've moved on.* "But in fact, now that she's left, I realize that the ways she cared for me were motherly ways. I didn't see this at first, having had so little exposure to my own mother."

"I'm sure your mother means well," said the great-aunt, insincerely.

"She nurses her drink better than she ever nursed me. No, I know motherliness, if I know it at all, through you."

Madame Sophia almost relented. "Me? A woman who can't identify an impostor in her nest? That's hardly a textbook definition of *mother*."

"*Au contraire*," said Cat, "it's the best definition. You took care of Elena as well as you've taken care of me. As well as Miss Yaga took care of me. Your concern for Elena extends even after her risky charade is exposed. That's a measure of your character that I hadn't been given chance to observe before."

The great-aunt was silent. One mawkish tear slipped out from some dry old crease. "I will not risk sentimentality by commenting," she brought herself to say. "I'm glad you are restored to me, Ekaterina. I wish I'd been able to liberate Elena, but I failed. Apparently she's in prison for treason."

"But all she was trying to do was help her mother."

"As you point out, she succumbed to lying and impersonation. And in her own self-interest she ignored *your* plight. Had you not met Baba Yaga — yes, my dear, I know who Miss Yaga is, and I think I almost guessed last night — you might have perished in the forest."

"Do you know where Elena is imprisoned?"

Madame Sophia sighed and began to prepare for the assault on the staircase to her room. She needed a nap. "Brother Uri Metchik, an advisor to the Tsar, seems to know how the palace works. I'm not privy to that information, and I left him muttering with the witch. All I know is that Baba Yaga will set out tonight to try to discover the cause of our floods and erratic weather. One thing leads to another: she might save the lost Firebird before he dies, unhatched, in embryo. Wherever he is."

"Do you believe she can do this?"

"Ekaterina, I believe in heavy cream and good manners. I don't know what else to believe. And Baba Yaga doesn't know which way to turn. But once all good children are abed, she said, she leaves by riverboat from the Hermitage Bridge on the Winter Canal, beside the Winter Palace."

Cat stood as her great-aunt hauled herself back onto her wobbly ankles. "Why didn't my parents have more children after me?"

"Oh, my dear. Your parents hardly had *you*; they weren't to be bothered by trying again. Now, get some rest. The second night of the festival starts at midnight. While I'd love nothing more than to stay home, our absence would suggest complicity in these affairs. I'd die of shame. Till midnight, then, *ma chérie*."

Cat waited until her great-aunt had turned the corner of the first landing. Then she pushed open the door to the servants' part of the house and descended to a great busy kitchen. She told the cooks to prepare a hamper with every sort of food they could spare. Breads, crackers, perhaps some cheeses; hams and sausages; pots of jam. The cooks, who had heard their own version of the previous night's proceedings, thought Cat an apprentice witch, and scurried to do her bidding lest she change them all into French-speaking mice.

Then Cat ran up to her own chambers. Miss Bristol was sitting in the corridor, bent over some needlework. "I need your help," said Cat. "I want you to take all these gowns my great-aunt had prepared for me — these, and these too — and find some place to sell them. Collect the money and entrust it to someone who can bring it to the Rudin family in Miersk, to thank them for attending to me."

"That's stealing," said Miss Bristol hotly.

"You're already in over your head. Do as I say," insisted Cat. "I won't need them. These coats, this hat." She rummaged in her dresser for the warmest leggings she could find. She took everything useful and heaped it upon her bed.

"Are you mad? What are you doing?"

"I am rearranging my life. Summon Korsikov. Tell him he must have the carriage prepared for eight o'clock this evening. I am making amends."

Monsieur d'Amboise paused at the open door and knocked at the jamb. "I believe you might be needing this?" He held a Gladstone bag aloft.

"How did you know?" asked Cat.

"I may not be a witch," said Monsieur d'Amboise, "nor am I a mother. But I am a damn fine butler."

Later, at the servants' entrance to the house, Cat turned to them. "What will you say to Madame Sophia?"

"We will say," said Miss Bristol, "that you have followed your great-aunt's example of concern, and you have gone to rescue the world."

As Korsikov mounted to his box, the butler and governess passed the final parcels of food through the windows. Cat, through the open window of the carriage: "Why are you helping me?"

Miss Bristol shook in the rising cold. "Elena was never you, but we took care of her in your stead when you went missing. Wrong we may have been, not to sound the alarm, but we weren't cruel. Now we'd help her if we could. We can't. So we're helping you."

"That's all that most of us who are not Tsars or witches can manage to do," added Monsieur d'Amboise. "Take care of the one at hand. Here's your scarf."

He didn't smile at Cat. He said, "Jane, you'll catch your death."

So Miss Bristol has a first name, thought Cat. Imagine. All this time, I never thought to ask. And he probably does, too. I wonder what it is.

As the carriage pulled out of the forecourt, Cat squirmed

around to see them, possibly for the last time. They weren't waving. They'd turned back toward the house. Monsieur d'Amboise had his arm around the shaking shoulders of Miss Jane Bristol. In the lighted doorway, there was a second valise that Cat thought she had left behind. Then she wondered if that was a suitcase packed for the butler and the governess, and if they were rescuing each other, tonight, together.

The House of
Solitary Confinement

And what of Elena, that opportunist, that fraud?

It still pains me to dwell on the imprisonment of any creature. I shall make as swift work of this section as I can.

Elena concluded that the Saint Petersburg House of Solitary Confinement was inaccurately named. The room into which she'd been thrown wasn't the bastion of solitude she might have expected.

For one thing, three rats either lived in the corner or they were passing through on their way to cheerier lodgings. Their eyes were beads of molten iron.

The chill of underground: a clammy weather evoking no season in nature. The air filled with the reek of mildew. The flat pillow on the cot felt coolly furred, the pelt of a dead pet.

Something made the light flicker. What seemed an ailment in her eyes proved, once they settled upon her, to be moths. She tried to console and humor herself: there weren't as many as might be found, say, in a moth factory.

I will not even mention the word *spider.*

Elena called out to ascertain the number of other prisoners in solitary confinement. The *hello* that echoed back through the barrel-vaulted stone corridors was her own voice, sounding frightened.

She sat at the edge of the bed and considered her plight.

Good fortune had shadowed her steps for so long that she'd begun to mistake it for fate. She'd grown over-sure of herself and her capacity to endure.

In the interest of helping her mother, of finding milk and medicine for her, Elena had let herself become cocky. She had traded simple honesty for scheming.

And, though she could scarcely credit it of herself, she had gone before the Tsar of All the Russias and addressed him on behalf of Luka and their mother.

Let them remember this when they call my name in the roll call of the damned, she thought hotly.

I suppose you could say that Elena deserved to weep; she'd made a royal botch of it. But we all do sometimes. If we're lucky, we weep alone. The one thing captivity can be good for: privacy.

Later, Elena allowed herself to admit the other truth.

She'd taken advantage of the accidental substitution of lives, hers with Cat's and Cat's with hers. She'd enjoyed the experience of feeling full. She'd been able to practice the tricks of elegance that she'd picked up from her traveling companions. She'd become seduced by comfort.

And in comfort, she'd also become aware of the appeal of the constructed world. Not just the things themselves, like well-made food set just so upon the gold-rimmed plate, but the attributes of things. The shape of rooms, the cut of gowns, the color of blossoms in porcelain vases, the elegance of boulevards, the music of unhurried conversation, the allure of foreign tongues.

When, really, the society into which she'd been born boiled down to something much like what she had now: a few mice, a few rats, a few moths, and a colony of mildew. *This* was her home, her legacy. With a common characteristic of poverty. She knew it for what it was now. She deserved it.

Finally she slept, or she slept again. So long susceptible to fancies about the magic world, she didn't have the spirit to dream. She didn't even dream of sitting on a cot in a prison cell.

She didn't dream of walking in a cloud of stars, hoping to find her father, since no one living could help her now and only the dead could beckon her.

She didn't know if it was hours, days, or weeks after her arrival when the sound of the stones snoring turned into the sound of footsteps. A voice said, "Up and on your feet, by the orders of the Tsar."

Though it might be to a chopping block, she obeyed the command.

Between two guards, a monk of some sort stood there, wearing sandals and robes like the mendicants who wandered the country with begging bowls. He shuffled in with a lamp and he said to the guards, "Five minutes," and closed the door.

The man was balding but not elderly. Tall, perhaps spindly; gaunt. He had more curiosity than kindness in his face, I regret to admit.

"We haven't much time," he said. "The wise men with their ancient knowledge are stumped. The witch with her more ancient magic is running hither and yon like a chicken with its head —"

"— intact on its shoulders," interrupted Elena. "I don't like thinking about heads severed from bodies just now."

"I need your help. The Tsar is distracted and dubious. The great and good of Saint Petersburg aren't paying attention. The young prince suggested that I ask you my question. He said you were cannier than the lot. And I suppose, why not? A rural child who believed enough to be granted a glimpse of the Firebird — maybe you have access to the knowledge we need. Access born of your very innocence."

"If I were *very* innocent, I wouldn't be in prison," she pointed out.

"The other kind of innocence."

"Native stupidity? That kind?"

"Let's not argue over definitions. There's too little time. The witch is leaving tonight, but she doesn't know which way to turn. Where should she go? What is your advice to her? The influence of your intuition, please: it's all we have."

Elena remembered Peter Petrovich's old bromide: *Ambition without direction is like milk without a cup.* But Elena hadn't warmed to Baba Yaga. The witch had rescued Cat, but she'd also been the agent of Elena's unmasking. "I am either too stupid or not stupid enough to have intuition. I have no advice for her."

The monk sat down on the edge of her cot. "You are a child of farms and fields. You live closer to the weeping earth than we do. *Think.*"

"I can't *think*. I haven't been trained to *think* in some Happyweather School. Had I grabbed a Firebird's feather, I'd have wished my father to come back to take care of my mother. But he can't. I can't. No one can. I have nothing to give you but my failures."

She didn't want him to see her eyes. Putting the prison apron to her face, she felt the lump in her pocket. The matron had let her keep her mother's doll. "Your court has singing artificial roosters and matryoshkas as large as brown bears. My small life is only this high." She pulled it out. "This is my only inheritance, a plaything for making stories with. I have no wisdom, and few stories anymore, either, except the story of our downfall."

"Does this doll open? What is inside? Has it a clue? Maybe it can tell Baba Yaga where to turn."

"It's a long time since *you've* played with dolls. This toy has a painted mouth. It doesn't speak." She opened the top half of the big mother and pulled out the other six dolls. "They have no secrets."

"Your mother trusted you with this. Show me."

"My mother had no reason to trust me. I've failed thoroughly." She opened the second mother and removed her five descendants.

"These are like eggs, each one holding the future. Show me more."

"The last one is as mute as the others, I promise you." She uncapped the third mother and out slid the four remaining dolls. Then the fourth, and the fifth, and the sixth, in turn.

"Are they telling you anything? Which way should Baba Yaga go to discover the ailment that tumbles the seasons, and floods the world, and frightens the missing Firebird so much that he refuses to be born?" His voice grew hushed. "They will open the door in a moment. I do not know if they will let me take you with me. Is the sixth mother telling you a secret?"

Elena could hardly stand this talk of mothers. "She's saying she's pregnant. The seventh is a baby, and knows nothing, like all babies."

"Ah, babies in their influence. Boy or girl?"

She shook it out. It lay in her palm like a quail egg. Natasha Rudina always called for Luka first. First Luka, then Alexei. Her only daughter was in prison. "It's just a baby. Good luck to it."

"What does it say?"

"It says nothing — it's asleep!" In frustration she shook it at him. They both caught the tiny pin-like rattle. She'd never heard it rattle before. Well, she'd never shaken it. She knew better than to shake a baby.

"What is it saying?" He grabbed her wrist. He frightened her. "Open it."

"The baby doesn't open. It's the last one." To prove it, she twisted the baby's head and removed it from its neck. "Oh. Oh, my. I never knew it could do this."

They both peered at it in the gloom. "Is it a tiny clock?" she said. "Is it telling me it is time to die?"

"No, it isn't a clock. But it is a message, I think. It is a compass."

"And what does it say —?"

"It says," replied the monk with a weary satisfaction, "North."

North

She bade good-bye to the rats, to the mice and the mildew. The moths followed her into the corridor as she, in turn, followed the monk and the two guards. Soon she was standing before a desk in a room with windows. That gibbous moon, stouter than before, swam beyond iron bars.

The prison governor initialed some papers and then said, "You sign here."

Elena didn't know how to write her name. The monk signed for her.

The governor said to Elena, "Our brother Uri Metchik here brings instruction from the Tsar to commute your sentence from imprisonment to banishment. The good monk will escort you as far as the Archangel road. You can't have your ball gown back. You can keep the tunic and leggings and apron we gave you. Pick a coat from that pile in the corner. You'll leave with boots, gloves, a shawl, two portions of Mama Prison's Best Loaf, and a threat of execution should you ever appear within the walls of our soggy city. You're welcome."

"Can't we hurry this up some?" The monk looked over his shoulder.

"I can't express my gratitude." But was Elena speaking in irony or earnestness? She admired a certain tartness she heard in her own voice. At least through her misadventures she'd found that. Not such a bad thing.

The monk was tapping his sandaled foot. "Paperwork. Get on with it."

The governor applied a wax seal and took a ring of iron keys from a hook. Elena followed him and the monk into the courtyard through which she'd arrived. "How long did those papers say I have been here?" she asked the governor.

"Since last night. Oh, but we'll miss you. You cheered the place up with your winning ways."

"Well." She threw back her shoulders. "I'd say I came through that ordeal pretty well. Now to the next one."

"Hurry," said the monk, and the governor took his time. Even so:

The world outside —

She watched it shape itself in the moonlight as the dogs were called back and the gates were swung open. I can hardly write this part, I get emotional. Liberty is costly but so glamorous.

"Saint Nicholas be on your right hand," said the governor to her.

"No need," said the monk. "*I* will be at her right hand."

They paced the quiet streets. The monk said, "Don't dawdle. Don't look back."

"Are you going to abandon me in the wild?"

"We're in luck. Anyone who might be out tonight is at the festival. With such a diversion, you can easily steal away."

"I don't steal anything anymore. I've learned my lesson. But why should we scurry like brigands? No law is higher than the Tsar's decree."

"Indeed. But he doesn't know he has set you loose."

"What do you mean?"

"*Will* you keep up? The Tsar's instruction was forged. He hasn't commuted your sentence. You're now on the run from the law. I risked my freedom and my life to rescue you from prison."

"I didn't ask you to do that! Now I'm worse off than before, a fugitive."

"Worse is to come unless you continue to help. Child, you're the one who found the Firebird's egg. And now you've told us where to turn. Your influence is still required. Hurry."

They crossed a canal behind the palace. The Hermitage Bridge. A musical pressure nearby, chatter and violins in the cold. But they were beyond sight of the festivities, and tonight few people wandered down this side street. The monk stopped. He threw off his cowl. "We're here," he hissed. "Where are you?"

Something in the shadows moved. Elena started back. That section of shadow straightened up and became more distinctive. "Prince Anton!" she said.

"We're all ready for you," he replied. "The League of Freed Prisoners welcomes you on board."

"What? Who? Are you mad?"

The boy hopped to the top of the stone balustrade, stepped off into the air, and disappeared, but Elena heard no splash.

Meanwhile, along the quay, a quartet of soldiers was approaching on some campaign. The monk felt the menace and he helped Elena to scramble up on the rail. "I recommend you follow the boy. It will go far worse for you if you're caught a second time, and bad news for me if I am found with you."

Together

Hurry, will you?" said the boy's voice from below the bridge. As wary of river water as she was of floods, Elena knelt on the balustrade and looked over.

Prince Anton's legs were spread-eagled across the ridge beam of Baba Yaga's house, which was kicking its feet to keep from being pulled out of the Winter Canal—or the Winter Groove, as some still call it—and toward the Neva River.

"This sweetheart's itching to cast off," hissed Prince Anton. "Jump aboard!"

"But I need to go home to my mother," she said. "It may be too late."

"Quick, I think they see us," said the monk. "Jump, jump now, unless you want to return to prison, or worse. Go with them, it's your only chance."

She didn't want that. She could only say, "But where?"

"You know. The North," the monk replied. "Tell Baba Yaga."

He couldn't see Dumb Doma; he was, after all, a grown-up. The monk had to trust the Prince, whom he thought both trying and untried. Entirely clear of a moral intelligence like his own. "From here, may the angels keep you," whispered the monk. He strode across the bridge toward the quay. The soldiers saw him. They didn't come after him yet.

Elena had no reason to obey Brother Uri, but she didn't want to be apprehended by soldiers again. Reaching for Prince Anton's hand, she dropped the few feet to the roof of the izba. Her personal eclipse of moths descended, too. There she crouched beside the boy as Dumb Doma slid from the bridge.

Suddenly a dormer unfolded itself out of the slanting roof. Blurt, slap, jolt, and there it was. Like a soufflé in a magic oven, rising to perfection in ten seconds. *Fwoop!* A casement window opened with a slam, and the head of that wicked creature appeared. Baba Yaga, none other.

The witch: "Get inside. We have no time to waste. If you linger at the souvenir stand, Baba Yaga's Rescue Coach will leave without you. And no refunds!"

"I want to ride up here," said Anton. "Tally-ho, and giddyup, and so on. I need to kick this vessel in the right direction. We'll head for the Moyka River and avoid the fuss on the Neva. Not that there are children out at this hour."

Elena faced the threat of pitching into the river. So, against her better judgment, she climbed in the window.

The witch in Cat's book had been more horrible to look at, but Elena soon decided that the actual Baba Yaga was less reliable — which seemed, on the balance, more dangerous.

Elena followed the witch down a set of steep steps. Sitting

cross-legged on the floor in a corner of the room, with a kitten on her lap: Cat.

"Oh, you," said Elena. "I suppose I've brought more trouble for you?"

Cat, unsmilingly: "No, this time I've chosen trouble all by myself."

"Thank you for joining us at Saint Petersburg," said Baba Yaga. "Depending on your 'advice,' your peasant 'intuition,' as that Brother Uri promises you possess, we'll chart our course and get under way momentarily. Our final destination, which we hope to avoid, is Doom."

"Who are you to kidnap me? This is one captivity exchanged for another."

Cat stood up, dumping the kitten on the floor. "Elena, this is, well, you know by now. Um, and this is Elena Rudina," she said to the witch.

"We were introduced at that boring *soirée*," snapped the witch. "I know who she is, and the boy. And I've taken your measure, too, Mademoiselle. It's a good thing you decided to help rescue your friend. I abhor a stinker. What is the advice, child, that Brother Uri promises you will have for me?"

"I think he's nuts," said Elena, "but he thinks the word is *North*."

The witch turned away to study an upside-down wall map. "Ultima Thule, Ultima Thule, where summers are bummers and winters unruly." The room rocked. The only sound a faint lapping, as around docks when a boat passes.

It's hard to imagine which of the girls felt more awkward. Think about it. Elena, given the chance, had stolen Cat's identity and brashed her way into the Tsar's festival. Then, when Elena's deception was unveiled, Cat had refused to stand up for her, to defend her.

Neither girl liked the truth about herself at this moment.

It seems there is no shortage of regret among the young — but then, they are young, they make mistakes. They have time to correct them and the courage to admit their failings aloud. Adults should try it. But frankly, I think it's a miracle that adults can manage to speak to one another at all, and that the entire species doesn't take a universal vow of silence. Some days I wish it would.

The girls stood square in their opposite quietudes, several feet apart. Cat straightened her shoulders as if a headmistress were chastising her about her posture. Elena twisted her hands behind her back. The first words of apology are the hardest to get out. Elena, who was after all the one with a maternal compass in her pocket, plunged ahead.

"Thank you for coming to rescue me," she said, and added, "and I didn't thank you for that half apple. Back there. In Miersk. Thank you."

"I never asked you what your name might be," said Cat. "If I'd bothered to do that, I might have known you better. I might have cared more about what happened to you."

"You can ask now."

"Elena, what is your name?"

A tickle rose in Elena's throat. She thought it was dust but actually it was a chuckle, a sound so foreign in her own throat that she hardly recognized it. "Lately I've been going by the name of Ekaterina," she replied. "But when my mother was wandering in her mind, she often called me Luka or Alexei. So it doesn't matter.

345

Anyway, she never called for me without asking for her sons first, so my name doesn't signify much. I don't even know what it means."

Cat replied, "Well, your mother called *me* Elena, and she held my hand, and nobody's mother ever did that for me before." And continued: "And she didn't call for her sons first, that time. Just one word that morning: *Elena.*"

"I object to all this sentiment," called Baba Yaga over her shoulder. "It curdles the mayonnaise." They paid her no mind. They had run to each other's arms at last. Their wet cheeks rubbed against each other, finally starting their friendship, and finishing the job of apology and forgiveness that words could not handle.

A certain compass needle swung about, a certain cloudiness started to lift. For the moment, anyway. Though needles always swing again, and storms never clear for good.

The League of
Freed Prisoners

The witch continued to scowl at her map. She took it off the wall and checked the back, on which she had scribbled a recipe for wolf sausage, with the emendation: *Serves one. For a month.*

Elena, to them all: "How did this come about? Why do you bother with me? That monk—he doesn't know me. He pretends I'm special. He's a dunce."

The Prince, clambering down the ladder, began. "Madame Sophia went to the palace, and so did the witch. I eavesdropped. After the Tsar left the throne room, Brother Uri and Baba Yaga concocted a plan to spring you from prison so you could navigate. Since I don't want to get engaged in marriage, I signed on as crew. Anchors aweigh and all that."

Cat continued: "When my great-aunt came back from the palace, she told me that Baba Yaga was going to make an exploratory journey to find out what's unbalancing the seasons. She mentioned the bridge from which Baba Yaga was leaving. And I . . . I had amends to make. So I volunteered, too. Then when I heard Brother Uri and Baba Yaga's plan was to rescue you, I clapped at the idea."

Elena, to them all: "But why aren't you off hunting for the missing Firebird egg?"

Baba Yaga folded up the map. "We have a different agenda now. But if we happen to locate the egg while we're on our voyage of discovery, we get double bonus points. I'm guessing that the Firebird's reluctance to be reborn is a symptom of a vaster concern. If he permanently dies, unborn again, it could mean — I suppose — a deeper death."

"I didn't know there were degrees of death," said Elena.

"Your father is still alive in you, I can see that," replied the witch. "When you die, he dies further."

"You have no right to look at me like that." Memories of Elena's father — they were private. They were hers. She had put them away as deeply as she could. Now they stirred simply because Baba Yaga had mentioned him. Something about Baba Yaga raised Elena's hackles. Elena bucked against Baba Yaga's high self-regard.

"Take no offense, you're just part of a cycle," said the witch. "Lucky you. I have no father and no child, so pity me." She looked anything but pitiable, planning her assault on the North Pole. If Saint Nicholas lives there, thought Elena, he'd better look out.

She changed the subject. She pointed to a nest hovering in midair. "Is that the Fabergé egg again?"

The witch jerked her chin at Anton. "*He* brought it back. As if I hadn't seen enough of it."

"It was the only thing I could think of," he explained. "As a

348

thank-you for taking me along. Besides, stealing it was fun. I might be a thief when I grow up."

Elena turned from the young prince to Cat, and her hands went out wide. "I've no way to pay you. And after all I've done wrong."

"Don't get soppy. We're all in this together," said the witch. "The League of Freed Prisoners, as Anton calls it. Open the window, Mewster, and let's see if we're headed in the right direction. Whatever that is."

"North," Elena reminded her.

"I may be indentured, but I'm busy," said the kitten. "What are you looking at, girl? I'm trying to take care of personal hygiene. Contrary to popular opinion, not all cats are exhibitionists. Somebody else open the window."

Elena gripped the edge of an armchair to steady herself. She knew this was no dream, but the kitten was talking.

Anton was tired of being heartfelt. He began to play rugby with four skulls at once. His opponent was a table with four human legs, which promised a strong defense, but Anton was winning. Cat went to a window and said, "I can see the bloated matryoshka dolls bobbing on the river. They're heading east, against the current. Like us."

"Story of my life." The witch flapped the folded map at a couple of moths. "Everyone always chooses the same picnic ground that I do."

Elena continued clinging to a chair as the house rocked back and forth. Her eyes were becoming adjusted to the murk. The room wasn't large, but it had something she might have called *dimension*. It revealed itself only in glimpses. Where Cat had seen a funhouse mess of a space, Elena saw shadowy walls made of immense carven faces stacked upon one another. Weathered oak, scorched oak, faces like stone, like smoke frozen in place. Their eyes stared and their mouths gaped. Alive, in some sense; watching. Ancestors, or a committee of retired angels on a holiday outing. An outing that was going awry.

It would be curious to know what Prince Anton made of the perplexing chamber. Something else, no doubt. Perhaps he saw rotogravure portraits of Lord Kitchener of Khartoum; Speke, who discovered the source of the Nile; or Wild Bill Hickok; or other saints of an adolescent boy's iconostasis. But I have not concerned myself with that lad, and I can venture no guesses on behalf of his imagination, however pedestrian or heroic. This is not really his story.

In any case, to distract herself from a sense of dislocation, Elena said to the boy, "But, Prince Anton, you have no reason to help me."

"Call me Anton," said the Prince, scoring a goal with the head of Richard III. "Or Antonio, as my friends do at the boarding school in Rome."

She tried it out. "Why, Anton?"

"It wasn't love at first sight, I'll tell you that." He stuck out his tongue.

"That's no answer."

"Oh, well. I was fed up with being displayed like a prize fish on a platter. The Tsar is a good godfather, don't get me wrong. But I don't want to be engaged. I want to learn how to shoot arrows and how to sail and how to draw horses and Lancelot and stuff like that. I want to go to the Argentine and ride the pampas with my gaucho brethren. Or blow poison darts at rhinos in the Congo."

"The Tsar will worry, you running off like this," said Elena.

"Cat got a spree, so did you. You even got arrested. Why should I be left out? It's true that I did feel awful after you were taken away. Oh, and, yes, I kept my promise. I sent out for word of your brother."

Elena put her hands at the base of her neck. "Did you hear —?"

"I learned this much: an influx of soldiers, young and old, was drawn from the hinterlands of the oblast beyond Tyer. That's where Miersk is? They were brought to Saint Petersburg to help dig emergency drainage. But whether a certain Luka Rudin was among them, I couldn't find out in the time I had."

Elena said, "Oh, but that's good enough. Witch, pull the house to shore and let me out. I *have* to find Luka and send him home to care for our mother. That's why I came to Saint Petersburg in the first place. Witch, witch, release me."

Baba Yaga: "I have a *name,* you know. Are you bossing me around? You may have escaped from prison, but I've no intention of letting you go. Have you forgotten what I just told you? We're all in this together. You're the one with a sense of directions, after all."

"That's outrageous." She sputtered. The moths fluttered. "You're — you're inhuman."

"Most days I take that as a compliment." Baba Yaga sneered at Elena. "Look. You may be as stupid as cinnamon custard, but that monk thinks you're setting us on the right course. Now I'll thank you to mind your mouth. We have a job to do, we four, thanks to the accident of congruity. The League of Freed Prisoners."

"I wouldn't join if you invited me," said Mewster, brandishing a cunning set of kitten claws. "I'm a rogue agent. Purrrrr."

"Need I remind you that you're not free?" Baba Yaga asked.

Elena fell into an armchair and began to weep. When the chair put a pair of arms around her to give her a hug, she shrieked. "This house is insane, or I have gone mad. Or both."

Cat tried to comfort her friend. "You'll get used to Dumb Doma soon enough. Trust me."

"Go ahead, snuggle, while the whole world is troubled," said Baba Yaga. "The toy mother says North, so north we must go. Stop all that cozy-cozy, it bothers me."

"What are we looking for, up in the frozen North?" asked Anton.

"A clue as to why it is not quite so frozen?" said Baba Yaga. "I don't know. At any rate, what other ideas do we have?"

Anton shrugged and looked as if he were trying to multiply large numbers in his head. The girls clung to each other. The cat paid attention to a certain pesky mold between his claws. Even the skulls rolled about, slack-jawed and mute.

"This consortium of great minds doesn't inspire confidence," said the witch. "Is it time to strike out across the countryside? We must have cleared the city limits by now." She threw open the shutters on the north wall of her house.

The world beyond, in drifts of moonlight upon scattered clouds, was still as a transfer landscape on a porcelain platter. A design done with a single pot of grey ink, but watered into a dozen gradations. A forested ridge. Lonely farm buildings. A couple of cows in a midnight assignation, their heads close. Perhaps discussing politics, or the price of milk.

Just enough stars visible beside the moon to remind those peering from Baba Yaga's window that all of life itself, however dangerous or wicked, is revealed under a jeweled heaven.

Not far away on the surface of the river, stray matryoshkas bobbed and spun.

"Frankly, they give me the creeps," said the witch.

It all sounds like great fun to me. The League of Freed Prisoners, spinning upriver in Baba Yaga's chicken-legged cottage! How I'd have joined them if I could.

But back in Saint Petersburg, the disappearance of the Tsar's godson had been discovered and, likewise, that of the Fabergé egg. Which annoyed the Tsar mightily even if privately he'd thought the egg déclassé if not downright cheesy.

Then, agents and investigators learned of Elena's unauthorized release from the House of Solitary Confinement.

The Deputy Sub-Lieutenant rushed to the home of Madame Orlova and, after addressing a comb to his flaxen tresses, pulled the bell rope. As there was no butler in attendance anymore, the carriage driver answered the summons. Korsikov was only too happy to spread the bad news. Aha. So Miss Ekaterina was gone, too. Madame Sophia made an entrance and wept in the Deputy Sub-Lieutenant's arms, causing disarray and some damp to his coiffure.

The Tsar's men added up the clues. A conspiracy of sorts, plain as a potato. They turned their attention to me. My remaining hours of liberty were numbered.

The Snow Tornado

The witch stuck her craggy face out the window and barked instructions to Dumb Doma. The house paddled toward the north bank of the Neva River and waded ashore.

Elena was trying to accommodate herself to the notion of a talking cat. "I didn't know chickens could swim," she said politely to Mewster. "If this house can swim, maybe it can fly, too?"

Mewster looked jaded: a normal look for a cat. "Have you ever heard of a chicken who could fly?"

The witch's izba humped itself across fields, following the valley carved out by some tributary of the Neva. The banks were lined with willow trees, tin skeletons in the moonlight, their limbs thrashing in the rising wind.

"How long is it going to take to get where we're going?" asked Anton.

"Since we don't exactly know where we're going," said the witch, "I'd say at least fifteen minutes. Maybe seven years. That's the average term for an apprentice witch. I have parlor games to pass the time."

"I can't be gone for seven *years*," said Elena. "My mother, my brothers!"

"It passes in a flash when you're as old as I am," said the witch. "A thousand years and counting. Table, show us what you got."

The table ambled forward. Its top was covered with a cloth, which the table shook off. The wooden surface revealed landings and pathways for an intricate game designed for four players. Some of the spaces had words written on them. In the middle was a compass rose indicating Northern Exposure, Easter Island, Westward Ho, and Southern Comfort.

"Oh, goody. Let's play Chuckleheads on Parade. I'll deal." Baba Yaga dove into a drawer in the table and fished out the pieces. A set of standard playing cards, an egg timer, and a pair of dice. Four game markers, with faces carved on them: a red Queen, a black goose, a yellow rat, and a blue one that may have been meant as a Commissar of Rents.

Also a revolving arrow mounted on a flat dial that was marked out with a few instructions: Spin Again, Too Late, Quarter the Cash, Lose Your Turn, Home Free, and Chucklehead Challenge.

Finally several sets of cards marked on their backs: CHANCE and DESTINY and WHEN'S YOUR BIRTHDAY?

Baba Yaga snatched up the red marker with the stodgy face on it. "I'll be Queen, and Queen goes first in the first round. Also all the other rounds. On your mark, get set, rumble!" She spun the arrow with terrific force; it whirled so fast the paper dial lifted up in the air like a child's whirligig. When it landed, the arrow pointed to Chucklehead Challenge.

Elena said, "I don't know what this is or why we're doing it. I'm not playing with toys. You're twenty times madder than Grandmother Onna. I'm leaving."

"Don't try me, little peasant girl. You didn't bring me a present, so I owe you nothing. And I play for keeps." She began to hop her marker along a winding path.

Cat said, "Don't be cross, Elena. Within this house Baba Yaga works with finesse, though it's hard to follow her thinking."

"I'm not cross, I haven't time to be cross. Let me out. I'll take my chances."

"I haven't discovered what the Challenge is." The witch pulled a Chance card. *"A Spot of Weather."*

"What's that noise?" asked Mewster. "Is it part of the game?"

"Step out in *that,* will you?" said Baba Yaga to Elena, thumbing at the window. "Be my guest. I dare you. *Bon voyage,* little poor girl."

She leaped up and pulled aside the drape, but the way she drew in her breath startled them. "Crimean Christmas! The card wasn't lying. What is *that*?"

The young people gathered around her. None of them had ever seen the like. Mewster hid under the gaming table.

Against the blackness of night, an apparition of whiteness was hurtling near. It pinpointed upon the ground but broadened in coils as it rose. The top of the monstrous presence spread to the heavens. Though the dainty foot roamed at random like an anteater's tongue, they had no doubt that the heft of ghostly glow and ghastly noise would happen — just happen — to light into them. The entire landscape of Russia stretching out on either side, and this weathery beast would nail *them.* Chance plays rough.

"This is one big breeze!" shouted the witch. "Brace yourselves, kiddos!"

Dumb Doma had been standing still, but now it turned and began to run away. The windstorm, spinning like a top that couldn't topple, bore down upon it. Gravelly snow struck the windows and cracked the glass. As Dumb Doma veered and pivoted, Baba Yaga lurched to slam the shutters closed. "Table!" she shouted. "Chair! Wardrobe! Bathtub! Battle stations!"

The furniture hurried to obey, each large piece throwing itself up against the closed shutters to keep the gale from blowing them open. A chesterfield barricaded the door to the oven.

Dumb Doma loped with longer strides than Cat had known it to manage before. As it left the ground momentarily and began to come down to land again, everyone inside floated in the air, weightless and in slow motion. As if suspended in clear aspic.

Cat realized that the house was being buffeted aloft by the winds. Elena thought the stout faces in the walls looked terrified, when she could glimpse them within the blur and shudder of it all.

"I don't believe it," said Baba Yaga. "Is this some sort of joke?" She sat down upon an airborne stool and began to reshuffle the deck. Perhaps she realized that the others were terrified, and she wanted to calm them by her ordinary behavior. Or maybe she had a card trick up her sleeve.

Mewster had flung himself up in the air and landed upon the floating nest that once again carried the porcelain egg. This seemed to steady the kitten, as the gyroscope of the Firebird's nest held its perfect poise in the mayhem.

Little by little the corkscrew wind caused the witch's hut to mount the air. The pressure upon their eardrums, the irregular gravity. Cat and Elena tried to cling to each other but kept drifting apart.

"An American tornado touring the Russian provinces," said Baba Yaga. "My, the weather is more deeply unsettled than I thought." She put the cards aside and pollywogged through the air, shoving the wardrobe from her front door. "My internal barometer's yipping; I don't want the house to implode. But hang on to something in case I've misremembered my physics."

Anton clung to a swinging chandelier made of elk antlers. The girls managed to kick-scramble toward the carpet, which was itself flying. They each grabbed part of the fringe and floated in midair, like angels supporting a banner that said something uplifting. Well, uplifted they were. The witch said, "Ready, steady, pandemonium."

The unlatched door swung open with a gentle sway. The pressure rebalanced itself, and the travelers settled on the floor. Outside, grim brightness streaked with snow and hail. Every now and then strings of snow would gape apart like twisted lips, as if the black night were a mouth eager to swallow them whole.

Moths

Suddenly Baba Yaga smacked the side of her head. Then she reached for the pieces of the board game, and put her hands upon the dial. She spun the arrow and said, "Come to Mama, come to Mama." The arrow landed on Spin Again.

She did this eight or nine times more. The arrow always landed on Spin Again. "This is rigged. This is cheating. I hate when board games cop an attitude."

"How could it land on anything else?" said the kitten. "We're still spinning ourselves."

Mewster was right; the house was rotating slowly, an unmoored boat in a lazy current.

"The arrow's not going to land on anything else until we stop circling," said Mewster. "You have to stop the wind."

"Ha," said Baba Yaga. "I may be a powerful player in the demi-monde, but nothing can stop the wind."

Anton chirped up, "I heard that if a butterfly flapped its wings in China, by the time that little breeze crossed the Pacific, it could grow into a hurricane."

"What's your point?"

Anton shrugged. "Well, a few moths have been following Elena ever since we picked her up."

It was true. Three or four moths, minding their own business, were inspecting the edges of the carpet upon which the girls had settled.

The witch drummed the tips of her fingers on her forehead. "Do-it-yourself anti-tornado techniques? I'd say don't try this at home, but we are at home. Well, okay. When in doubt, try reverse Chaos Theory. Everybody cup a moth in your hands, and position yourselves at one of the windows."

Elena balked. "You, too, Miss Misery," snapped the witch. "No free rides."

There were just enough moths to go around, since Mewster didn't want to play, and anyway had no hands. Cat, Anton, Baba Yaga, and a dubious Elena: each stood at an open window at one of the four walls of the izba.

The witch began to recite. Her delivery was a little nasal.

> "What's a moth but
> Hinge and bracket,
> Neatly clothed
> In purple jacket?
> Humble agents
> All together

Have the strength
To change the weather.
Help us now
To stem this storm.
Use your influence.
Moths, perform."

Elena couldn't follow the spell. Still, the moth in her own hands began to flutter more urgently. "Don't let it out," advised the witch. "Just knot your fingers and part them. Make a finger-cage, so the breeze can emerge. Then put your clamped fists out the window about a foot — out to the elbow, say."

This the children did. Cat laughed at the soft bump of moth against her tender palms. Elena's teeth were gritted.

A moth is so insubstantial. The wind from its wing flappings couldn't be felt by human hands. Baba Yaga's hands, apparently, were more sensitive, and she hummed a few more lines of guidance to the moths.

"Row, row, row your wings,
Till we can alight, where
Scarily, scarily, scarily, scarily,
Life's a living nightmare."

"I do believe our revolving is slowing down," said the kitten. The table began to walk in circles around the room in the opposite direction, and the other furniture followed it. The legs of the bathtub, Elena noticed, were duck's feet, and those of the wardrobe apparently the stubby cloven pegs of a wild boar. Home furnishings on promenade. The chesterfield betrayed a touch of sashay in its gait.

Above them, in the center of the room, the floating nest holding the Fabergé egg was revolving more slowly, until it came to a stop. Then, after a few moments, it began to turn again, this time in the opposite direction.

"My ears are beginning to pop," said Cat.

"Mine, too," said Anton, and Elena nodded.

"My nose is about to pop," said the witch. "A falling barometer. We're dropping fast. I hope not too fast. Maybe we should all draw our arms in about six inches."

But it was impossible now to control the house. It was circling in the opposite direction, more and more quickly.

"Release your moths!" cried Baba Yaga. They obeyed. The moths from the Saint Petersburg House of Solitary Confinement spun their way into the white-black snowy wind and were never seen again, at least not by the travelers. More liberated prisoners.

The house's descent slowed, but not fast enough. It came to earth in a catastrophic way at the top of a slope. Thumping with a terrific bang, it fell onto its side and began to slide. Snow sluiced through a ground-facing window and built up in a bank, burying Baba Yaga to her chin, which she used as a shovel to start digging herself out.

Elena and Cat tumbled into the open door of the wardrobe and were cushioned from concussion by an assortment of fur coats. Anton landed on the carpet. It rucked up as it slalomed, providing a fabric bolster when he collided with the bathtub, which fell, trapping him.

The duck legs of the tub waggled about in the air. Elena and Cat pulled themselves through the door of the wardrobe. When Dumb Doma shuddered to a stop at last, the front door was facing the ground, the ceiling pointed left and the floor right, and snow was heaped inside everywhere.

Cat and Elena overturned the tub and released Anton, who was raw and scratched from his plight. Then they ran to the witch. Cat and Elena each took hold of one of her hands, and Anton grabbed her chin, which was knobby enough to provide some purchase, and they pulled at her until she popped out.

Mewster was still sitting complacently atop the Fabergé egg, regarding the mess below. He smirked. "Game over," he said to the witch. "But did you win or lose?"

"Where are we?" asked Cat.

They scrambled to see out the windows. The moth-wing magic had worked just fine. It had counterbalanced the snow tornado, which after depositing Dumb Doma on the ground had spun on and eventually tipped over. The remnants of the whirlwind lassoed along the horizon, breaking up into little twisters. Eventually they petered out or were lost in the distance.

"You were asking where true winter went," said Mewster. "Apparently it winters here."

"But I wonder," said the witch. "Have we achieved North, or are we somewhere entirely else?" She turned to Elena. "What do you think?"

Elena consulted the doll. In the impact of landing, the needle had sprung off the dial and could say no more about where they were. "I think," ventured Elena, "we're here."

Perplexity

I've noticed in the stories of saints and their careers, of knights and their quests, a presumption of purity. It seems only the most single-minded candidate qualifies for passage into holy or magic realms, those sanctuaries more inspired than our commonplace worlds of today, yesterday, tomorrow.

Yet I wonder if earnest self-assurance is strictly necessary. What motivated Elena wasn't conviction, but regret and anger. Doubt, too: she was at war with herself: wanting to rush home, wanting to be brave enough to forge ahead. She was hardly stout-hearted. For all I know, maybe Cat and Anton weren't really, either. But it was Elena who was to venture the farthest, so it is her case that interests us most.

Here we see her at the cold dawn of a vision. She twists, she writhes. She is anything but bold. Rather, she's petty and ashamed, mournful and curious, somewhat fouler of tongue than I've allowed myself to write, and her big imagination hasn't served her as well as we might have hoped. She is, in short, a bit of a mess. She is all we have.

I've tried not to weigh in with my own assessment on her character. Who am I to judge? I merely observe her here, a hank of half-brushed hair clouding her left brow. No symmetry, no balance, no grace to speak of. Impatient, affectionate, lately prone to despair. Her bootlaces are untied.

Why Baba Yaga, who eats children, is in awe of Elena is a mystery I cannot answer. But I am in awe of her, too, and I can't explain that, either. Maybe it is simply that the girl has been less cozened into her own character than the others have, less educated to be this way or that.

I don't insist that rural innocence is always superior. It is often stupider. But every raw soul has its own secret advantages. Elena had hers, and those advantages might as well be termed *perplexity*. Perplexity isn't as noble as conviction, but perhaps more good is done in the name of muddling through uncertainty than is done hacking away with the righteous sword of self-confidence. I don't know. And that's my perplexity.

"What are we waiting for?" she said, and flung open the door.

Myandash

"Don't be hasty," cautioned the witch. "Frankly, I don't have the snowiest idea where we are. It looks lunar, doesn't it? I don't believe it snows on the moon, but then I've never been." She rubbed her chin. "Have you *ever* seen a more desolate place? I do believe, honeybuckets, that we're not in Kansas anymore. Or Kamchatka."

It was still midnight — midnight somewhere, though whether this was midnight in Russia or the moon, no one could say. A powder-white world under a black sky riveted with stars. Far off, a swipe of shadow that might be a line of tundra vegetation. The air had a crispness to it that made it feel it couldn't snow here. It was too dry, too brittle.

Elena said, "Well, if we've come to look, let's start looking. I've got to get home. I have a mother to nurse back to health."

"Are you commandeering my mission?" The witch reared back.

"Govern yourself, we have company," Elena replied.

A little bit of Miss Bristol goes a *very long way,* thought Cat, while the house righted itself, not wanting to be seen in disarray. I suppose it was house-proud.

Someone *was* moving out there. It walked upright like a bear or some sort of a snow gorilla. It hulked about on two stiff legs. Then perhaps it noticed them, for it moved closer, growing larger by the moment. A shambling creature dragging its own shadow with it. As if the shadow had weight.

They stared at the creature, wondering if the welcome would be hostile or hospitable. "Who could it be, do you suppose?" asked Baba Yaga.

The children glanced at her. "I'm a stranger here myself," she reminded them.

Anton felt he was about to be harshly dealt with. "It looks like the Tsar. "

"No, more like Saint Nicholas," said Cat, "though he doesn't walk in golden air, as he does in all the ikons."

"It looks like —" began Elena, but she didn't finish: *My father.*

Baba Yaga said, "Perhaps it's that mad Brother Uri who was advising the Tsar about the influence of the Firebird's bright, unseen shadow."

"How could he be here?" asked Anton.

"How should I know? Maybe he hopped an earlier tornado?"

The figure was now large enough to make out as human. He was clothed in shaggy skins so heavy with ice that he clinked when he walked.

"A Laplander shaman, maybe," muttered Baba Yaga. "A berdache? Say hello."

"I don't know languages," said Elena. "Cat, you're glib; you try."

"You think he speaks Parisian French? Or the King's English?" said Cat.

The creature stopped ten feet before the hut of Baba Yaga, at the open door of which — now that it was front and center as it ought to be — the travelers had gathered. He straightened, a giant. His nose looked like a broken adze. His flared nostrils were large enough to store whole walnuts. It made Elena remember taking nuts from the squirrel at the cemetery at Miersk. Where her father was buried in an unmarked grave, unless blossoms scattered randomly should fall upon it.

"This is uncommonly forward of us," started Anton.

The man blinked as if surprised at sound.

"We are newcomers here in, um, wherever we are," said Elena.

The man looked behind him as if to check and see if someone had come up in the lee of his crisp star-shadow. He heard them but didn't see them.

"*Bonsoir, Monsieur,*" tried Cat, and in English: "A very fine evening indeed to you, if you please, good sir?"

He let his furred hood fall back, revealing a woolen cap from which locks of grey-white hair escaped. The cap was knitted all around with images of rust-colored reindeer.

Quite improbably — though what part of this is probable? — a snowy owl perched on his shoulder. The owl blinked at them.

"Oh, bother, I have to do everything," said Baba Yaga. She pushed the children aside and hopped down to the hard snow surface. She marched up to the wanderer, easily three times her size, and stuck out her hand. "Put 'er there, pardner," she said. "When there isn't so much as a doorbell, it's hard to give you notice that we've arrived on your doorstep. But we mean no harm."

He didn't glance down. He closed his eyes, sniffed probingly, and his brown brow furled.

From behind them, Mewster said, "We're not invited, but we come in peace."

Mewster spoke in an ordinary cat voice, but the isolated pilgrim of the snow seemed to hear him. "Where are you?" replied the great shaggy man, in a language they couldn't identify but could somehow understand.

"Here before you, blown into your realm by winds from the overheated south." Mewster snaked between the ankles of the children and jumped down upon the snow next to the witch.

"Oh, suddenly *you've* got diplomatic papers?" But Baba Yaga's voice betrayed some admiration for her familiar.

The shambolic man said, "Lapland does not welcome strangers. The Saami Sámi Lapi do not welcome strangers."

"You are not Lapland, and you are not the people," said Mewster. As he spoke, he seemed to grow larger. Cat had forgotten the lion or leopard in the slushy forests around Baba Yaga's hut. Mewster had some tricks up his own furry sleeves.

"Who are you?" The man's low voice was puzzled but not fearful. "Show yourself to me."

Mewster, growling, paced with nonchalance, like a cat walking through a room pretending not to be the most glamorous thing there. As he walked, his sleek mouse-grey fur took on the sheen of snow-light. He turned, and luminescence bathed him on one side. When he circled back to the ambassador of the North, he was no longer a dust-colored kitten but a great white snow tiger.

Now, it seemed, the man could see Mewster, though the children were pretty sure that he didn't take in their presence,

369

nor that of Baba Yaga or her house. "You stray beyond your territory, cat."

"Cats mark their own territories," said Mewster. "Who are you to complain?"

"I am Myandash," he replied. With his gloved hand he threw off his knit cap. From his head grew a rack of antlers that added another four feet to his height and cast the shadow of barren branches upon the snow.

Mewster couldn't maintain sleek arrogance in front of this creature. "This is your home," he admitted, his voice sullen. "So I ask permission to pace the ice."

"You risk too much, cat. The ice has become unreliable."

"That's why I'm here, to see for myself."

"You are an eastern tiger, an Amur, a Siberian. You are no friend of my people."

"I'm no enemy, nor are my associates."

"I sense others. Where are they?"

"Here with me. They are young, so invisible to you."

"I'm not that young," whispered Baba Yaga, "but I'm young at heart, so maybe that counts. Let's not quibble."

Myandash spoke over her. "How many are you?"

"Legions," said the cat.

"My people, the Saami Sámi Lapi, belong to this land. From Nova Zembla to the North Sea, the reindeer people hunt and fish and migrate with the weather. There is nothing here to support a delegation of legions. Go away."

"We are legion in possibility," Mewster explained. "The young, who are fruitful, carry their future coiled in their living lives."

"This is no place for your young," said the reindeer-man. "Our own young see their world threatened and their future evaporating before their eyes."

"We know. We have come to help. Did you call us here? Did you bring us here on that stack of wind?"

"I do not push the winds around; I do not break the ice nor heal it. I pace to observe. But I do not expect to see a snow tiger so far from its homeland."

"The world is sickening," said Mewster. "The ailment affects snow tigers in Siberia and humans in the cities. It beggars the boll weevils and shrivels the winter wheat. It dances the figures of ancient belief out of their stories and even threatens the renaissance of the Firebird."

Myandash looked uncertain, but he nodded, slowly. "I had not known the trouble was so widely felt."

"We know the effects, but not the cause."

"Ah, the cause." The creature bowed his head. "That's why you have come, to investigate?"

"To investigate. To help, if we can."

"Armies of men young enough to father children can be no help against this calamity, this wakeful fuse. This aberration."

"Myandash, you see whatever there is to see in the land of the Saami Sámi Lapi. But we come from beyond your territory, and our army is mighty."

I do hope he's not talking about us, thought Cat. She glanced at Anton, who was throwing his shoulders back, being a warrior. Cat couldn't tell if she liked Anton at all or found him juvenile. Perhaps both at once.

"First tell us where we are; then tell us where we are going," said Mewster.

Myandash was silent for quite a while, considering whether to answer. He sighed. "You find yourselves beyond Archangel, in the region of tundra that gives onto the pack ice. An hour or two north by human tread, you reach the place where the sea should not be at this time of year, but the sea is there. And the wakeful sickness sinks hot jaws into the bay. You risk everything to proceed any farther than you are."

"Tell him, out of our way," snapped Baba Yaga.

"We ask your permission to venture north," said Mewster.

"This year and last, I have herded my people to the western edge of the Murman Sea, to the lands that usually claim them only in the summer," said the reindeer-man. "North from here is too dangerous for living creatures now. But I will not forbid you, nor will I allow it. I am no longer the spirit guide here. I, too, am losing my strength."

With that, Myandash turned away from Mewster and the invisible others. He began walking to the west. Though he put on his cap and drew the hood back up over his head, the shadow of his antlers trailed after him still, like great blue cracks in the polar ice. He walked with the heavy step of someone in mourning.

The Sneezing Cave

Perhaps for cloven-hoofed reindeer, the edge of the most northern sea in the world was a two-hour trek. For Dumb Doma, it took almost five hours. The house kicked up sprays of chalky snow. Once it fell through a drift up to its hocks. It had the deuce of a time climbing out.

The snowy owl from Myandash's antlers accompanied them. Perhaps she was leading them, perhaps just keeping an eye on them. It was hard to tell. She flew ahead, flew back, occasionally perching on the roof.

Something like sunrise began to show.

Though Mewster had returned to being as cute as a carved toy, Baba Yaga fumed. "At this point in my career, to be upstaged by a common house cat! Who would've been eaten by some marten or . . . or . . . some *skunk,* if I hadn't come to the rescue! And now, the *airs*! I'll thank you to remember your place."

"You aren't the only raisin in the pudding," replied Mewster. "I've done you a service you didn't request. Maybe now you'll let me go?" She ignored him and went stomping about, abusing the furniture, shutting up her skulls in a valise. Evidence, Cat guessed, of the witch's mounting fear of losing her strength and vivacity. In any case, Baba Yaga was so busy being annoyed that she wasn't in the mood for chatter.

So the two girls and the prince did what children do. They paid no mind to the ill-tempered adult and got to know one another by horsing about, making the adult more ill-tempered than ever.

Cat was finding herself more comfortable with Elena. She wasn't sure why. She guessed that when they had been Mademoiselle Ekaterina the Privileged and Elena the Peasant, the differences between them had been too vast. They had both worn their circumstances upon their shoulders like disguises (Elena's like a wooden yoke, Cat's like a Liberty scarf). But they'd traded places, and now, in Baba Yaga's hut near the top of the world, the differences in their backgrounds seemed less extreme.

The presence of Anton helped, too. He evened things out somehow, maybe because he was having so much fun. Though in station he was superior to Cat, he was anything but stodgy. An amiable sort, Cat decided. And pushed around in his life no less than Cat had been in hers, and Elena in her own. He favored a little choice.

What a spree, he told them, to be free from studying girls arrayed before him as possible fiancées. His parents believed the Tsar had organized the midwinter festival to distract the nation, what with another war with Japan always threatening and the capital city sinking in its own juices. But they had made Anton go along with the campaign anyway. The Tsar is the Tsar.

Cat described her own parents, how they flitted from Scottish golf courses to New Orleans riverboats, all the playgrounds of the rich and bored. Anton wanted to know if Cat missed them at all. The girl answered, "No," with such acerbity that both Anton and Elena wondered if she was telling the truth.

As for Elena, this campaign seemed another prison. Less dank and lonely than the former, but still she was trapped in this venture, which shifted her further away from her real ambition. Which was no more complicated than to try to find a cup of milk for her sick mother.

Increasingly, Elena suspected that her mother must be safely dead and out of pain by now. She couldn't have lasted this long. Elena felt cold and safe in this belief. It was better than having to picture Natasha Rudina still suffering while all three of her children had seemed to forsake her. However, a failing body will choose its own time to give up the ghost. Today could be Natasha Rudina's last day, last breath, right now; or tomorrow. Would her ghost pass, to say good-bye to Elena?

Sorrow is so often invisible. Elena fell silent while Cat and Anton laughed. Perhaps the *bonhomie* of that pair offended their hostess. "We've gotten somewhere," muttered Baba Yaga with the sour wisdom of her thousand years. "The end of the line maybe."

They pushed to see. The light had strengthened by degrees; the sky was the color of cabbage soup. An orb swam behind hanks of obscuring clouds. It was too bright to be the moon, but how unearthly, a cerulean sun.

A sea curved ahead of them. The Arctic Ocean, if Myandash

had been telling the truth about where they were. Its horizon was vaporous, indistinct. Near the shore drifted a fantastic city of glacial cathedrals, warships, minarets and caves, small mountains.

"How perfect," cried Cat. "They look soft as cloth. Or as if giant heated knives have smoothed out imperfections. Like carvings in ice at fancy parties."

"Probably sun and wind have done the work," said Anton. "Look, do you see that one with the series of bridges? A boat could sail underneath."

"It's like the Tsar's pavilions, except with bears rather than people," said Cat, pointing. Sure enough, on one floating island, a party of white bears was nosing about.

It's too far, it's too strange, thought Elena. I know black hens, not white bears. I want to go home. Mamenka, if you die, don't fail to say good-bye. I may not recognize a spirit in the blown snow, passing by me, but bless me one final time.

Baba Yaga: "At this time of year, the ice isn't supposed to calve. It's irresponsible, breaking up like this. Forcing polar bears to go visiting their relatives whether they want to or not. This is what Myandash was talking about. Let's go investigate."

She threw open the wardrobe door and hauled out over her head a supply of great fur coats. The children husked themselves in pelts and stoles, and fell off the porch of Dumb Doma into the snow.

"You know the rules. Don't let anyone in, Mewster," said the witch.

"You and your rules," said the kitten, with admirable East Asian detachment.

With the owl leading, they hurried. It would quickly become

too cold, and they would have to go back. To the east, as far as they could see, the sweep of shoreline was flat. To the west lifted a series of snow-covered hills. Pewter in the pale light, brownish-rose in the shadows.

"Well," said Baba Yaga, "not much to see here. We might as well go back to Dumb Doma. There's got to be *some* clue as to what is going wrong. We'll move along the shore and look for it."

But when they got back to Dumb Doma, the door wouldn't open. "Darn, where's my house key?" The witch checked all the pockets of her fur coat.

"I don't think the door's locked," said Anton. "It's frozen."

"Yes, but my key is made of lightning." Still, whether Baba Yaga spoke in hyperbole or fact, no key could be found. If Mewster heard them pounding on the door, he showed no sign of it, and kept dozing. They could see him snoring as the window continued icing over. "Traitor. Ingrate. Wake up or I'll tear those claws out of your paws! I'll take you to the vet and have you neutered!"

"You told him not to let anyone in," said Anton.

"A cat and his schemes," she seethed. "He's been *waiting* for this moment."

"Baba Yaga," said Cat, "*we* can't wait. We need to find other shelter."

"You're right. Much more of this, and we're toast. I mean, frozen toast. Let's climb this hill and see what's on the other side. Perhaps some laggard from Myandash's tribe will provide an extra tent of fur. At any rate, we can take cover in the lee."

They could think of nothing better to do, so they set out in single file. Anton went first and the girls next. Baba Yaga brought up the rear.

377

The snowy owl circled the headland of the promontory but wouldn't come nearer. Nor did it fly away, but rounded in the sky like a sentry.

Near the base of one of the lower mounds, Anton spied a distinction in the coloring of the ice. "There, that shadowy smudge may be a cave. We better take shelter." For the wind was picking up smartly. Snow blew in muslin curtains.

They tried to hurry. Ice was rimming their eyelids. The steely cold made lateral stabs in their chests as they breathed. The skin inside their nostrils felt prickly and brittle.

It only took them a few moments to reach the opening that Anton had noticed. They scrambled up chunks of broken snow, scattered like rocks at the side of a river canyon. At last, out of the wind. Moreover, the cave was warm.

"Hot springs in the Arctic?" said Baba Yaga. "Elena, don't dawdle." The girl was looking at the snow gusts, studying them for character, blessing. Who *really* knows what the specter of a departing spirit looks like? Mama, Mamenka.

They could just about stand up straight. The edges of the cave doorway were smoothed, probably by wind. Thin enough in places for a pale porphyritic light to bleed through. It made the snow wall into alabaster.

Soon they warmed up enough to remove their fur coats. They folded them and sat upon them, and looked out the cave at the churning black sea and the expressive formations of ice that passed by. "A teapot," said Cat, pointing at one.

"Two boots, one atop another," said Anton, indicating another.

"That one looks like the young Dante, when he was dating

widely," said the witch. "He was *lots* of fun at a pig roast, believe you me."

Elena's mind felt frozen. She said to the witch, "Why should you live for a thousand years when you're so awful, and a normal mother dies like a rose in winter?" Some despair was rising in her, unbidden. Tears froze on her cheeks. It wasn't fair. She pulled out the small matryoshka, kissed it with cold lips.

"Don't you cross me, too," said Baba Yaga. "I've had it up to here with insurrection today. You get what you get in life. Rotten eggs."

"Don't fight," said Cat, who had a sense of the witch's temper.

"No, I mean the stink in this cave. It's like rotten eggs," replied the witch. "Don't you smell it? Maybe that's why Myandash's owl won't come near."

Now it had been named, they knew what she meant. There was something strong and organic and perhaps unhappy in the air in the cave. "Maybe," said Baba Yaga, "we should evacuate this cave before it evacuates us."

"Why? What do you mean?" asked Cat.

"I mean that I think the cave may be allergic to us. It is shortly going to sneeze us halfway across the North Pole."

As she spoke, the floor of the cave slithered beneath their feet, and they fell to their knees. "Crawl! Crawl for your lives!" cried the witch, and crawl they did.

Žmey-Aždaja

The four castaways somersaulted forward. The walls of the entrance, lilac-veined a few moments ago, were now running with dark inky cords, patterns coursing through marble. The two sides of the cave entrance had retracted. The opening was narrower, too, focusing.

They tumbled down the crusty scree. The sections of slope that, upon their approach, had seemed to be a hill of milled flour, smooth and unblemished, were now broken terrain. Tosses of ice like the kind of boulders you see at a harbor's edge, used as a breakfront against erosion.

"Don't look back," yelled Baba Yaga as they slowed down.

Cat and Anton did look back. So did Baba Yaga. They didn't, therefore, see Elena lose her balance, and then her grip on the matryoshka. The doll dropped out of her hand and went slaloming ahead of her. Before she'd quite righted herself, she lunged after it, afraid it would bury itself in snow and be lost.

A horizontal volcano was erupting above them. Only the trajectory of the explosion kept them from being scorched to mere bones. The sulfurous, flaming material shot over their heads. Most of the rainbow spray of filth landed in open water. Where it slopped upon an ice floe, though, it melted that ice as neatly as acid might dissolve a sugarcane ballerina. Leaving only a lopsided pencil of snow, which tilted over and disappeared into the boiling sea.

They skidded to a halt in several ignoble positions. "First tornados, now volcanoes," muttered the witch. "What next? And that *stench*. Aggravated sewage. Fish mousse come down with a serious virus."

"Are you all right?" asked Cat. "Anyone hurt?"

"I'm not," said Anton, mopping up blood from his brow, "but Elena might be."

They craned to see where Anton was pointing. Elena had been thrown upon a broken tableland cantilevering over the sea; her head lolled back across the edge. Two feet more and she'd have been dunked, drowned by now, an instantly frozen corpse.

They couldn't see her face. But they didn't like the angle at which she'd been tossed.

Baba Yaga beat the others to Elena's side, scrambling like a fat furry spider down the tilted plinth of ice. In one scoop she rescued the doll from the water, then tucked it into a pocket of Elena's borrowed coat.

Cat clambered beside the witch and said, "Let me." She pulled off her mittens.

Her friend felt warm enough, but her color was pale. Her eyes remained closed and her lips parted. Cat said, "Elena, Elena." There came no answer.

"We've got to get her somewhere warm," said Anton. "She'll freeze to death."

"Don't look at me," said Baba Yaga. "It's she who was supposed to be good with directions." The snowy owl descended through depths of wind, and landed with its talons upon the shoulder of Elena's coat. "You've come to pay your respects? You anticipate. Go away," continued the witch. "She's a member of the League of Freed Prisoners, but she's not *that* freed. Not yet."

Cat said, "You must have some idea." So the witch tried an all-purpose bromide for emergencies like this.

"Hey diddle diddle, I need a little
    Help."

The ground began to shake. The slope upon which they had fallen shifted, a clockwise motion. Segments of ice floor, broken up like peanut brittle in a skillet, slid this way and that with an angry grinding sound. The witch leaped to avoid a six-ton slab while Cat and Anton hauled Elena to safety.

Safety, for the moment anyway, seemed to be at the level part of the landscape, where the frozen tundra looked as much like a sandy beach as it could manage. Flat, though cruelly windswept. The snow dunes continued to heave, throwing off cladding like roof tiles. The highest brow of the hill contorted in a motion not unlike Mewster having a stretch, the back part hoisting itself first and then the front.

And then — Cat was almost glad that Elena was unconscious — a side of the slope fell like a collapsing rock face. A plate of ice five times the size of the Thunder Stone that serves as a base for the famous statue of Peter the Great. Behind that plate a swelling, possessed of a thick but lively light, its surface an angled black slash swimming in emerald-gold.

The tapered oval blinked at them. "Cor blimey," muttered Cat, sinking back to school slang she and her classmates used when the proctor was out of the room.

"What is it?" said Anton.

The witch didn't answer. She stood alert and quivering, not from cold but from the thrill of something unknown. How much of this world could be fresh to a thousand-year-old witch? wondered Cat. What a novelty for her.

"Žmey-Aždaja is awake." A voice issuing from what was left of the mountain. One of the near ridges was yawning open. The mouth of hell, black and hot. The voice sounded multiple, accompanied by its own echoes. "I am Žmey-Aždaja." Every word was a labor, produced from a throat some distance away from the mouth. It spent its words frugally.

"Žmey-Aždaja," said the witch. "You sound like a savory paste, possibly made of aubergines, suitable for spreading on crackers."

The being did not reply. Perhaps it saw through the lunacy that Baba Yaga so often reeled off to disguise her intentions.

"Would you tell us what you are, Žmey-Aždaja?" Anton's voice cracked. Hardly an adventurer's bold challenge, but he spoke bravely through the wobble.

Cat saw the ridge above them lift and settle. The cave in which they'd taken shelter was leaking a tarry spume. It was paired with a second cave on the other side of the ridge. Together they looked like nostrils. The golden bulge high above them was an eye. She knew, then, what the creature would say next. She'd traveled far enough to believe in everything.

"Žmey-Aždaja," it said. "The dragon of ice."

Baba Yaga: "So what Myandash said is true. 'The wakeful fuse . . .'"

"The third figure," said Anton. "The Fabergé egg showed three creatures: Baba Yaga, and the Firebird, and Žmey-Aždaja."

"Baba Yaga," said the ice-dragon, stretching out the name for half a minute, practicing it against the pale iron landscape. "Are you still alive?"

"We have no time to exchange social niceties. We've come to bargain," said the witch. "But Žmey-Aždaja, we will freeze before we start. We need your help."

"Talk, talk. Voices." The creature cleared its lungs. A lick of heat pulsed from its nostrils and settled upon them for a moment. Bliss.

"Since you ask," continued the witch, "I am alive enough for *my* purposes. But while we're on the subject of survival, the Firebird hasn't hatched from his shell. Even the egg has disappeared. With your big eye you might happen to know where it is. The land is dying, Žmey-Aždaja. We've come from the Tsar's court to find out why."

"I make no answer to humans."

"That doesn't cut it with me; I'm human on the outside only, and you know it," said Baba Yaga. "I speak to you as force to force."

"You are ten times older than the oldest human ever was, Baba Yaga. I am ten times older than you. I make no bargain."

"Please," said Cat, remembering her Happyweather School manners.

"What could *we* give you to help us?" asked Anton. "We're just meager human children, not magic at all." He began going through the pockets of the fur coat.

"Humans give nothing to me." The creature sounded almost amused, but also irritated. "Humans, *bfahhh*. A mere pox upon the world. A noisy disease, nothing more than that. Their human complaint hums over the horizon. It gets louder by the season. Let the race die out and the human clamor cease."

Shadows upon the talcum slopes drew the musculature of the dragon. The hills shifted. It was clear now that they were segments of the sprawled body. Ice-dragon couchant. Baba Yaga, standing by one of its snow-clad paws, looked like a cricket scraping near the paw of a German shepherd.

"Why should humans cease their human noise?" Baba Yaga asked.

Žmey-Aždaja replied, almost as if talking to itself, "During the months of long nights, I like to close my eyes and rest. I am used to sleeping for half a year. Only when the long days of light return do I wake enough to breathe fire and stir the ocean free of pack ice. That is how it goes, for thousands of years.

"But now," the ice-dragon continued, "this wail of human need stirs me from my winter hibernation. Every hour every day, *I want, I want.* Crying human voices. These sounds, in both ears, they whine, they ring. They never stop. When human voices halt their cry of *want* and *want*, then I will sleep again."

"Why should they?" asked Anton. Cat whirled in surprise at

his voice. Bolder than she'd guessed, now. "All creatures want. It's normal."

"The world is enough. It fills all needs. It has snow and salt, sameness and surprise, change and return. Animals manage. Spirits manage. But every year humans *want* louder and louder."

Cat thought of Elena at the train track, diving for that half-eaten apple. She said, "Wanting *more* and wanting *enough* aren't the same thing."

"There is enough world for everyone. But everyone cries in want of *more*. I want nothing, just the same sleep as before."

"No wonder you're cranky, poor thing. You need your nap. Don't listen to human voices," said the witch. "Let them scream themselves hoarse. They'll never get what they want. They never have, they never do. That's what makes them charming. And fickle. And inventive. And maddening. Just tune them out." She was adding it up for them all and wagging her bony finger at the hillside. "By staying awake, Žmey-Aždaja, you're burning the Arctic winter away. The cities are flooding and the plains are baking. You aren't helping. As the crisis gets worse, the cries will only get worse, too."

Žmey-Aždaja said, "Even you, you come all the way here and you *want, want, want.* My eye doesn't care, my ear doesn't care. If enough ice melts, I fly free. I eat the world. You will be as dead as that human girl who was thrown onto the ice. I don't care. Silence, soon enough." The ice-dragon closed the eye facing them. The ocean burned.

The Starry Crown

The only daughter of Natasha Rudina and Maxim Rudin, treading the margin.

The world was made of ground-up stars, but it didn't scorch her feet. She felt neither cold nor hot, though she wasn't wearing so much as a blanket. She was naked as a maiden doing her spring bathing on the day of her wedding.

She wondered at the loss of her clothes. She didn't think she needed them now. Maybe someone else who could use them had found them. She hoped there weren't too many holes in them.

She didn't remember that her most recent garment had been a fur robe from the wardrobe of Baba Yaga, to cover the prison tunic, apron, and leggings supplied by the prison matron. She could only think what she had worn when she was about seven, a pretty skirt with golden stripes across flourishes of green. Sun on new wheat.

She looked around her. She could almost make out buildings and cows and carriage sheds. The air was clean and keen; you could see through the invisible threads of it. Yet the buildings remained unseen. Hulking in a fog, losing proportion, orientation.

Here was the chapel with its rustic spire; here was the grave-yard where her father was buried. She could see neither rusty gate nor bell tower nor gravestones. She sensed only the thump of space that implied the chapel, as if she'd indicated it with her hands, describing it to someone. "See, the chapel was here, and over here, the three better homes in the village, the ones that were sometimes painted, and here, the train track ran through the village, back when I was a little girl. The place was called . . ."

She wasn't really speaking, but even so she couldn't recall the name of the village.

"And our home, of course, was, well, here. In the middle. Right where I am."

"And I was called . . ." But she couldn't think of that, either.

She was standing in some idea of her home, though she was under a toss of bright and bitter stars. She'd never seen so many stars, not in all the nights of her life put together. They hung over this state of night that felt formal as a sacrament.

And my mother was here, somewhere, and my brothers, the older one and the other one. I don't remember their names.

Right in this space they were, standing. Almost inside me, all of them. Everything else was outside, but they were inside.

She looked about some more, feeling more alert and just mildly fretful. The echo and implication of a terrain rather than the terrain itself. The echo of an echo, and it was fading. In reality there was nothing but stars and ground.

Then she began to sense upright stripes, beyond the distance that might have housed her village. Irregularly spaced, they pulsed from the ground to somewhere above her head. Perhaps these were tree trunks. Carven over with faces one upon the next, monstrous or loving, but in any case attentive. Hadn't the world been bracketed on all sides by woods? These vertical bars, then, the world forest. Or echo of forest.

She turned slowly and looked. The space between the bars was subtly different in three distinctions. One was pale blue-red. That was where the horseman of the rosy dawn was passing. One was yellow-green. That was where the horseman of the high noon was passing. The third one was cold white blackness. That was the horseman of midnights. All the days and nights.

The trees, if they were trees, reached up. Their branches, if they were branches, were groins of vault arching overhead. Into the branches the stars came to roost, in swoops and chirping clusters. Like everyone else, stars have families. Little by little the stars arranged themselves in a sparse light cloud, blurring out thoughts of village or of people or of a home, or of trees. Stars close overhead. Stars in an airy thicket all around her, down to the ground. Only stars around her. She was in a nest of light.

Near enough to touch, if she had needed to touch them. There were few needs left now.

Then she knew what it was. A crown of light. Larger than Saint Nicholas could ever wear, or any Tsar in any century of Russia. Large enough to sit upon the whole world. That's what stars were: that's what they did. Crown the world.

A movement, it expressed itself beyond the starry postern. Something made of the clean darkness, a more pertinent if obscure shape.

A creature walked through arches in the crown of stars. It put down its head, and its antlers almost touched the ground. It looked about, saw her, came nearer.

You have come to the border, it said. Are you ready?

Am I ready for what?

Are you ready to cross?

She couldn't see anything to cross, but she didn't want to be rude to a reindeer.

Who are you? she asked.

Who are you? it replied.

When she found she couldn't quite answer, he nodded. You are nearly ready. But it would be better if you were to be sure. Wait here.

She had no plans to go anywhere else. After the reindeer had disappeared and been gone for some time, another shape began to take place at a different point outside the crown of stars.

A man walked in. He stood where the reindeer had stood. She now saw there was a thin trickle of water between them, a mere thread. She needn't drown; she could just step across. The narrowest threshold. That was all, and it would be easy.

He didn't hold out his hands to her, but gripped his hat as he might have done walking in from the fields to the overseer's office in the great house of the báryn.

Papa, she said.

Why have you come here? he replied. It is not your time.

I have not chosen the time. I would not know how. Did you choose your time?

He relented. I suppose no one chooses the time, he agreed.

Come home with me, she said. Mamenka needs your help sorely, and I am not managing well. I have lost my way.

I cannot go back, he said. But you can.

I am failing, she said. You left me with a task, and I can't fulfill your request. I seem to have run away from home, and gone to prison, and now I am banished to the northern wastes. I am as far from Mama's bedside as I could get.

I asked your help to comfort her, he said, not to change her path among the stars. Please go back. There is more you can do if you do not lose heart.

Tell me what I must do.

I cannot.

Tell me where we are.

I will not.

Who is the reindeer?

It is the guide.

She tried to think of something else to say. There was so little in her head except love.

Then she thought to say, and said, Where do the stars come from?

He put his hands together and did not answer.

Then she felt she could see him more clearly, somehow. He had her father's face. She remembered how his nose was something like a rock and something like a plum, and how his eyes had several depths of glint, depending on if he was angry, or frightened, or feeling wide love for his daughter. Now as she looked at him, his eyes had all their glints at once. She never wanted to leave him again, but she sensed his fear.

Stars crown the world, she said, but the lights in your eyes, those are stars, too.

They make up your crown, he said.

I am no queen of anything.

Something too few of us know while we are alive, he told her. We are all crowned with glory. Peasants no less than kings.

She understood, but the understanding was momentary. Here in this nowhere that had suggested a small village to her, then a world forest, then a crown of stars, she really had nothing. Just black emptiness outside the archways of stars.

Such memories had been planted in her own share of days, however. Planted by actual buildings, convincing sheds, recognizable fields and graveyards. Bells that could really peal, woods to get lost in, lordly suns to cross the sky, moons to rise and diminish and return. Birds and sorrow, acorns and arguments, supper and washing up, spruces and ladybugs, and the one shared schoolbook the village so prized. She had been queen of that world, standing in its very center as now she stood in a crown of stars.

What must I do if I go back, she asked again.

I cannot tell you, he reminded her. I have no compass, even now. I can only tell you one thing.

What is that?

How I cherish you.

Papa, she said, and she could not touch him, for while she felt an improbable absence of shame or modesty, she was still naked. And to embrace him she would have to step across the string of water. So she simply raised her hands out to him as if holding up a bouquet of posies. Papa, if I go back, I will need to know something.

Yes?

What is my name?

My future and my past: your name is Elena.

Oh, she said. Her vision swam with water. What does that mean?

That you have a name means I named you. The word *Elena* means "light." Now go back. I beg you. Be Elena. Be born. Be light in your world and in your days and nights. There is time enough to be star.

Papa, she said, but he was gone.

So she went back to be born. The snowy owl, whose presence she hadn't noticed till now, led the way.

Still Later.

THE ICE-DRAGON GRINDS HIS TEETH AND CAN'T SLEEP FOR human suffering.

The egg of the Firebird has gone missing.

The League of Freed Prisoners has convened in the North. While they've nearly lost Elena Rudina, it seems she remains among them.

The eyes of a snowy owl flash images to the inside of my own dead eye. I write what I see.

I see this: There is a certain energy and inevitability to decay. An axle on a train starts to rust through; nothing in the world, not even Baba Yaga's magic, can convert the rust back to strong iron. The vibration of a wheel begins to loosen the nut on a screw. But even if the wheel should run backward, the nut will never tighten by itself.

Certain kinds of repair require agents to become involved.

The Tsar had heard me natter on for years about the Firebird and what the shadow of light might be, where it might be found. He remembered I had been in the room when Baba Yaga declared that, if she could find out which way to go, she would investigate the causes of calendar mayhem. The Tsar's godson had disappeared; the Fabergé egg had been taken. The Tsar told his bodyguards his suspicion. They did the rest. They came to my apartment in the palace.

I had only time to cap my bottle of ink and reach for a few extra pens. I preferred the ones with steel nibs, for their clean line. I put them in a front breast pocket of my outer coat.

In the struggle at the top of the stairs, I fell against the wall. One of my attackers grabbed me by the lapels, thinking I was trying to escape. The unbuttoned greatcoat rode up in his fists as another man punched me. The instrument that blinded me, driving into my eye, was one of my own pens. Not even the better one among them.

Later, later, I was able to bend the tip back. It's the pen with which I have been writing these notions.

You know what happened next. The prison governor identified me as the one who had submitted the false order to release Elena Rudina from captivity. I think the term is "forgery." I — who have tried to use a pen to tell the truth! — stabbed both in the eye and in the heart by the same pen. But never mind.

I had thought the Tsar might require an audience with me.

Question my actions. For so long he had trusted my thinking. But the man had come to his own conclusions. He was starting to see sedition everywhere.

And perhaps he is right to do so. Once decay and corruption begins, who can stop it? Though I declare now and unto my dying breath that I had nothing but the good of the world and of the Tsar's beloved Russia as my heart's desire.

The Tsar didn't call for me, didn't even name my crime. He left that for me to do for myself. And that's what I tried to do in my daily letters to him, what I've been trying to do in these pages, too.

I had been to the House of Solitary Confinement, to spring Elena from her captivity. I expected to be delivered there myself. Perhaps beaten, maybe executed.

Instead, my head swaddled in such bloody bandages that I could see nothing from either eye, I was put in a horse and carriage and carried away under cover of night. I don't know how long we traveled. From the loss of blood, I swooned. I can't guess whether we rode for three days or thirty.

In time we arrived in some trading village at a muddy cross-roads. A medical man enduring a hardship post examined my eye, and declared he couldn't save it. A few days on, we reached this stone tower on the edge of an endless steppe. When they forced me up the stairs, I felt sure they meant to push me over the para-pet. But I would not die, I told myself. I would open my wings and fly.

As you realize, they didn't kill me, nor even try. They settled me in a room at the top. One high window, with a bracket outside it, rigged with a rope and a pulley and a bucket for the delivery of food, letters, necessaries. This square stone room with a rough-timbered ceiling, one mattress and three blankets, one desk and one chair, one chamber pot. In the morning I tipped my night soil into a chute in the floor. Presumably it spilled from some vent in the wall far below, for after the first day or so I wasn't bothered by the odor.

It took me only a week to realize I could trade sight in my dead eye for the visions of birds.

How this happened, I don't know. It wasn't vodka, as I had none.

In my more superstitious moments, I think perhaps Baba Yaga hexed me with this happy talent on that one afternoon when we met in the Tsar's presence and we made common cause, breaking the Tsar's command out of love for his realm.

Other days I believe perhaps I always had the talent, but the richness of personal sight in two eyes had blinded me from realizing that I might attend more closely to the lives of other people around me.

Too late perhaps, this is what I've been trying to do.

PART · FIVE

HOME AGAIN, HOME AGAIN

The Teeth
of the Beast

T hey had to bring Elena to warmth. But how? Two or three versts away from Žmey-Aždaja, the chicken feet of Dumb Doma were sinking in the drifts and freezing there. The witch, Anton, and Cat, working together, couldn't dislodge them, couldn't break through the iced windows. The doorknobs were lost under snow solidifying like Portland cement. And the ice-dragon wouldn't help warm them; it was done with them. Human noise!

"Hens and dragons both have warm blood," said Baba Yaga. "Warm blood melts the ice. They sink deeper. It's why the dragon seldom moves."

"Like when you stand in bare feet at the edge of the beach at Monte Carlo?" asked Anton. "The waves come in, and though you don't move, you sink until you are stuck. Then you must wriggle to get out."

They had to do *something* to keep Elena warm. She looked as if she might be turning to ice herself. The sky was a glass dome, too few clouds etched upon it. A fresh wind kicked up off the sea. Proper conditions for freezing to death.

Cat and Anton dragged Elena as best they could between the immobilized legs of Dumb Doma, where at least she would be somewhat out of the elements. Baba Yaga tucked her fur coat around Elena like an extra blanket. "This won't do for long," she said.

"You'll freeze to death yourself," said Anton to the witch.

"Nonsense. I thought I'd take advantage of the sun and improve my color. Anyway, witches are cold-blooded. Mind your own business."

"Might we at least build a break, something to keep the wind off Elena?" asked Cat.

The witch grunted, shrugged, nodded. "Might buy us a little time."

"Look," said Anton. "Over there. Those icicles by the edge of the water. Maybe we could stack them into a break? Or drive their points into the snow and make a kind of stockade fence. Like Fort Apache in the color supplements."

Since no one had any other ideas, they wandered back to the edge of the iron sea. Anton was right. The frozen shore was broken. All about lay dozens of stalactites of ice, averaging four feet long. They were portable, hadn't frozen together.

The witch: "Very nice dripstones, these, highest quality. My question is, where did they fall from? The moon?"

The ice-dragon had not spoken for a time, but at the mention of the moon, it opened its eye again. "They belong to me. Leave them alone." It breathed a pinkish plume of air that turned the color of rot against the albumen sky. The sun had gone halfway along the rim of the world and was starting to descend. "Those are my old bones. When I can't sleep for all those tides of sound, I chew ice. Teeth break off." Its snout scraped along the shoreline as if to demonstrate. The jaw opened. A sight you'd prefer never to have seen, and it will not be described here.

The witch tried to drive a bargain. "A fat lot of good they're doing you outside your mouth. Once a tooth escapes its prison, it's a free agent. Anyway, we need these. I know, *I want, I want.* But we'll pay you for them. Set your price. We'll talk."

Žmey-Aždaja scraped its head along the shore, but made no effort to bite them. It was still frozen in place against the coastline. "Dragon teeth are tools of danger," it warned them.

"In my experience, dead teeth don't bite." Baba Yaga hoisted the curved tines in her arms and beckoned Cat and Anton to join her. They could manage only two at a time. Huffing and weaving with the effort, they hauled their salvage over to where Dumb Doma was trapped, shivering and coming as near to knocking its knees together as it could, considering it had no knees.

"Whoever plants dragon teeth on a night of a full moon reaps trouble," snorted Žmey-Aždaja. A moon began to shoulder up over a forlorn section of the horizon. At first glance, this moon looked just about full. Naturally.

"What is the moon but the egg of the world," said Baba Yaga. "An awfully long gestation period, but when it hatches, alert the wire services. Žmey-Aždaja, you don't scare me. Finders keepers, losers weepers. Lost teeth are the bones of history. Simmer down, you're distracting us. We may not be able to persuade you to settle your grievance with the human race, but don't stop us from trying to save this specimen child."

Anton said, "I remember about dragon teeth from our classics professor in Rome. Jason and the Argonauts. In ancient Greek myth, Jason planted the teeth of a dragon, and they sprouted into an army of warriors."

"Any relation?" Baba Yaga asked the ice-dragon.

The creature lowered its lids halfway — its expression reminded Cat of Mewster in hunting form. That focused, abstracted look before a pounce . . .

"I don't believe in that farrago," said the witch. "A dragon-tooth army? Sounds like a public relations campaign to keep poachers at bay. The sun is setting, the wind is picking up. I think your teeth are past regeneration, frankly, but we'll have to take our chances."

The ice-dragon's rage made small avalanches powder the air; it spewed another noxious fireball into the sea.

"Honeybucket, you need some other hobby than chewing up the shore and melting the ice cap. We have your best interest at heart. But first things first. We have to save this child."

"We *have* to save her?" asked Cat. I suppose she looked shocked at the witch's apparent tenderness.

"I meant to say we're *going* to save her. Since I know she's your friend, blah blah blah. After all, Elena's the one who got us into this mess, what with her doll compass. We might need her to guide us homeward." They lifted the first dragon's tooth. It might have been mistaken for the rib of a whale. The pointed end drove into the snow neatly, stabilized at about the halfway point. Baba Yaga added, "Elena stood up to me, and without taming me with a house gift. Few children manage that."

"Tribute is your custom?" said the ice-dragon, in sulfurous

smolder. "Yet I get no gift. Who steals my bones should submit a tithe."

"You know," said Baba Yaga, "dragon voices are as vexing as human ones. Cat, Anton, why don't you recite verses from the Georgics, or sing some barrelhouse blues, anything to drown out our ungracious host?"

She had only been dashing off a mean remark. Nonetheless, Anton and Cat looked at each other.

Cat said, "Baba Yaga, maybe Žmey-Aždaja needs a lullaby. Something to distract it from the sound of human suffering and greed, and lull it to sleep. It wants a token of our thanks for its teeth. What about the Fabergé egg?"

The witch propped her elbow on the top of a planted tooth. She scratched her chin. "You gave it to me, then I gave it to the Tsar. Then Anton stole it and gave it back to me. Now you want me to regift it? Whatever for?"

"When it's wound up, it plays a lullaby. Didn't you know that?"

"A music-box melody will last about a minute, tops."

Cat clapped her hands, to warm them. "Maybe Žmey-Aždaja can rewind it?"

Baba Yaga said, "Dragons aren't known for their small-muscle coordination. Let the ice-dragon hum to itself if it wants to drown out sorrow. We better get this breakfront done before the night winds come, or we'll *all* be ice-dragons by the morning."

Still, Cat thought about it as she worked. On long weekends when other girls went home to be with their families and she alone was left in the dormitory, she'd have given anything for someone to sing her a lullaby. Anything.

Anton, for his part, was thinking things he didn't say because of the ice-dragon's keen hearing. What if they used the ice-dragon's own teeth to kill him? Could they stab him to death? Bite him with his own teeth? Žmey-Aždaja couldn't escape; he was frozen in place. If he was dead, he wouldn't be chewing the shoreline, melting the ice, flooding the world, changing the seasons.

Baba Yaga knew how boys thought. She looked at Anton slant-wise. "Don't even think about it. Even a worrywart ice-dragon has a place in the world. If Žmey-Aždaja *didn't* wake up every spring-time, what would happen to our summers?"

"Human voices," said the creature dully. He heard but he didn't understand.

So they fell silent, each thinking private thoughts. They worked without ceasing, dragging every tooth they could find over to the hut. There weren't enough teeth to make a full round of fence. But the teeth made a nice jawline, a semi-circle in the snow a few feet beyond the corner of Dumb Doma.

The last tooth was only half the size of the others. "A baby tooth," said Baba Yaga, hammering it into place with a certain vengeful glee. Then the witch, Cat, and Anton hurried inside the stockade wall. They couldn't talk anymore. They lay under the house, close together, all around Elena, all in furs. Even the witch was turning blue-white.

The ice-dragon lapsed into a ruminative silence. The sound of its breathing was like the beginning of every thunderhead that boasts its way around the world.

The night seemed to happen in slow motion and racing speed at the same time. The aurora borealis, mute and indiffer-ent but gorgeous, spanned the heavens like bolts of shimmering green and gold gauze. The sun was gone. The moon was up. As it rose, it became like an iced orange. It bowled along the horizon for a while. Shortly — or many frozen dreams later — it began to sink again, and disappeared beneath the edge of Žmey-Aždaja's forehead.

When the pale blue sun made a nominal return appearance, the League of Freed Prisoners began to stir. They didn't even know if they'd slept. Frost-coma and sleep feel much the same. Ice glued their lashes shut until they rubbed it away.

A windless dawn, a soundless earth. Baba Yaga sat up, the breakfront behind her, and watched the morning light play upon the devastated shoreline, the ice-dragon's articulated forehead. Then she knelt up. "Are you awake?" asked the witch, rubbing the shoulder of Elena, kicking gently at Cat and Anton.

"Yes," answered the soldiers.

The Dragon-Tooth Boy

C at sat up at once. Anton raised himself on an elbow and turned. The witch knelt at the edge of her coat with her knuckles on the ground, an elegant chimpanzee. Elena didn't stir. Arms crossed upon her breast. A stone maiden on a medieval tomb couldn't hold more still.

Beyond her, the teeth were gone, replaced by an army of soldiers. In the dim light they appeared at first like a hedge of fir trees grown together, their shoulders and the skirts of their broad coats covered in windswept snow.

Baba Yaga whistled. "Well, how *do* you do?"

"How do we do *what*?" they replied in unison.

As the light strengthened, they became easier to see. They weren't snow-covered fir trees. Something more like Bavarian nutcrackers. Though their faces were almost identical, they looked human enough. Not retired army men, these, but seasoned, ready for the next engagement.

Anton was impressed and hoped for battle. To be a soldier!

The regiment wore black caps with sprigs of evergreen poking from hatbands. Pine-green epaulets, pine-green sashes and belts, and military trousers trim in the Prussian style, fitted snugly in black boots. Brass-buttoned ivory coats flared at the hip.

"I suspect you are just as stuck in the snow as my house is." But Baba Yaga was wrong. The soldiers kicked up a knee-level blizzard. In a moment they were free and standing at attention, waiting for orders.

Baba Yaga crawled out from beneath Dumb Doma and stood up. Anton and Cat followed, rubbing their creaking limbs and yawning. "How many of you are there?" asked the witch. "Have you multiplied during the night?"

"We don't know how to multiply," they said, "nor divide. If you ask us to split up, we can't. We are an army. We are the army of Žmey-Aždaja."

"I'm not," came a new voice. The soldiers didn't turn at the sound, but the witch and her two young companions did.

At the end of the row was a boy. He was dressed just as his compatriots, except his clothes were sized to suit his stature. "I'm not a soldier yet. I am the dragon-tooth boy," he said.

"Aha," said the witch. "That short one."

He looked younger than the others. In human childhood years, he might be about ten. He didn't seem to have a remark to make about why he was different.

"Trust me," said Baba Yaga. "Regimentation is not for everyone. If you want to avoid the military life, you came out in the nick of time. We'll call you Nikolai Žmey-Aždajavich."

"He is not one of us," said the army.

"Not yet," said the dragon-tooth boy.

"Not ever," they replied. "You will not grow any bigger. Milk teeth don't."

The boy blinked. "I object. I am intended for military service."

"You speak independently," said Cat, to change the subject.

Baba Yaga said, "Everyone else is talking lockstep, and Nick has got a private voice. So that's something to be said for youth, I guess."

"We are the army of Žmey-Aždaja," insisted the soldiers. "We put ourselves at your command." It was like hearing a great wind speaking aloud. A single voice with many strands of personality in it. There must be two hundred of them, thought Cat.

"First things first," replied the witch. "Help us free this house from the snow, so we can get inside and warm up this frozen girl of ours, assuming she's in a condition where it's better to be warm than frozen. By the look of her, I'm not sure."

"Wait, witch," said Žmey-Aždaja. The ice-dragon hadn't slept, of course. Fretting, it had chewed more ice at the edge of the harbor. Then it had begun to work at the ice casing upon one of its forearms. Its anger at the appropriation of its infantry was getting the better of it. Its crenellated crest, engorged nearly obsidian, marked its backbone, like a parade of awkward tombstones on the brow of a hill. "My army is stolen from me. Take it under your leadership only at your peril." At this, a front claw suddenly shook loose, and four curved talons unsheathed in such a flash of light, they seemed to appear out of nowhere. The sound was like the clanging together of bronze shields. The talons, down-arching sickles, plunged in unison into the ice and gripped it into wedges the size of stallions.

"I'm not *sure* if this is the right time for a lullaby," said Cat. "But maybe?"

"Time is against us," said Baba Yaga. "If you're right, we need that Fabergé egg in Dumb Doma. I doubt a lullaby will work, though 'music hath charms to soothe a savage breast, to soften rocks, or bend a knotted oak,' according to Congreve, who couldn't carry a tune to save his life. We always made him turn the pages of the sheet music on choir night."

The witch's digression had no effect upon the ice-dragon. It wrenched its wrist laterally, releasing a pummel of snow boulders.

Baba Yaga said to Cat and Anton, "Are you paying attention? Charm it somehow, before it's too late. We'll start on the house. Men, move out." She gestured in the direction of the army, which marched after her to the base of Dumb Doma. Soon a screen of flying snow all but hid the house from view as the army set to freeing the pair of chicken legs.

Cat and Anton put their heads together. They knew no common lullabies in English, French, Russian, or Italian. The only song they could come up with was one that Cat's friends at school sometimes sang on their precision march through Kensington Gardens.

"She's only a bird in a gilded cage,
   A beautiful sight to see,
   You may think she's happy and free from care,
   She's not, though she seems to be,
   'Tis sad when you think of her wasted life,
   For youth cannot mate with age,
   And her beauty was sold,

411

For an old man's gold.
She's a bird in a gilded cage."

"Whoever *she* is, she needs to join the League of Freed Prisoners," called Baba Yaga. "At the rate we're going, Dumb Doma will be eligible to join soon, too."

Žmey-Aždaja had gone still. Its talons gleamed like hoops of nickel, but they didn't scrape. Its one visible eye was fixed upon them piercingly.

"Don't stop now. Verse two," suggested Baba Yaga.

"I don't know one," said Cat.

"I'll improvise." To divert attention from the army at its civil engineering assignment, she began to invent a verse of her own.

"I'm only a witch living all alone,
   A miserable sight to see.
   You may think I'm scary, thus free from care,
   And I'm not, though I'd like to be.
   I don't have a child to boss around,
   A young one to call my own.
   Since they think, 'It's transparent
   She'd stink as a parent,'
   I'm a witch living all alone."

By the time Baba Yaga was done, Dumb Doma had been freed, and it was beginning to scratch at the snow as if looking for grubs. It stepped away from the form of Elena—corpse or Sleeping Beauty, no one yet knew. Marbled in morning light.

Still, the door of Dumb Doma remained frozen shut, and the windows opaque with their icy shutters. Baba Yaga ordered the house to stand still so she could pull and push at the latch. She grunted, tugged. She couldn't budge it an inch.

"More music," said the ice-dragon, "or my army turns against you."

The army stood at attention, awaiting the superior command, whomever it came from.

"Do I have to do everything?" panted Baba Yaga. "I've nearly got this door. Somebody else make up a verse."

Cat couldn't make up words on the spot, nor Anton, of course; he was a prince. So they were surprised when the dragon-tooth boy took a shot at it.

> "I'm only a boy born a dragon's tooth
> In the nick of time, sad, but true.
> No father or mother, just two hundred brothers
> All telling me what to do.
> I want to belong to the two hundred strong,
> Yet here is the dismal truth:
> I'll never get older
> Or grow up a soldier,
> I'm a boy born a dragon's tooth."

Well, thought Cat, watching the ice-dragon react. Here's one for the record books. Mother and Pater never paid attention to what I might need. And here, a legitimate monster bothers to notice the needs of *its* offspring.

413

For a tear the size of a hot-air balloon, a bath of hot bile, was falling from the ice-dragon's visible eye. Wet fireworks. When the tear struck, ice melt flowed seaward in great spreading sheets.

"Congreve had his finger on something," murmured the witch. "Never underestimate the power of cheap music, as he used to remind his wife, a lion-tamer in the local circus." The ice-dragon didn't mean to be useful, but emotion is involuntary. A convulsive warm front gushed toward the group. Summertime breezes off the Caspian Sea.

Elena rubbed her eyes. *Be born. Be light.*

The snowy owl, who had disappeared overnight, stood again on her shoulder. Elena tried to sit up but couldn't manage.

Cat fell upon her friend. Where her tears trickled across Elena's cheeks, they drew tracks of pink in the light frost. "Oh, so you haven't . . . ! I was so afraid you had left us."

Elena was too exhausted to speak, but the ice at the corners of her mouth crinkled. She looked around. She didn't know about Žmey-Aždaja or the army of dragon's teeth. The dragon-tooth boy, a surprise, too. Truly, this world was just as mysterious as the crown of stars from which she had emerged.

The ice-dragon, lying there in a long heap, foothills to headland. It made her think of the world in curtains, a bed-nook world she used to imagine existed. And it did.

The Part-Time Hero

Mewster must be becoming a teenage cat. He's rebelling against authority. He's barred the door. I'm working on this lock." Baba Yaga sounded nonchalant, bored, as if she didn't want Elena to notice her relief. "Dumb Doma got frozen over. We had a little problem getting inside. No biggie. Thanks to these soldiers standing against the windchill, you made it through the night."

"Have you tried the trapdoor?" Elena replied.

"You and your sense of direction. What trapdoor?"

Elena cleared her throat to build strength for a longer statement. "Lying on the ground while you were all singing, I stared up at the underside of your house. I could see your cellar door. It looks as if it might open easily enough."

"I don't know what you're talking about. A house on legs can't have a cellar."

Elena said, "Oh. I thought you might use trapdoors to come and go at a moment's notice."

"I never would. Cheap stage tricks. House, come here."

The house was high-stepping with a certain *joie de vivre.* Soon enough, however, it obeyed.

The witch explored its undercarriage. "Well, well. My little Dumb Doma has been remodeling again." She thumped on the trapdoor. It swung open. A small ladder unfolded to the ground. From the shadowy top step, Mewster peered down.

"Trying to sneak in after a night of high jinks? It's about time you got home," said the kitten. "Out gallivanting till all hours. Drunk and disorderly, no doubt. You ought to be ashamed of yourselves."

"Why didn't you let us in? We could have frozen to death."

"You always say don't open the door to strangers. Who could be stranger than you?"

"I'll wring your scruffy Siberian neck. Move aside."

The human children climbed out of snow glare into the comfortable dimness of the cottage. The dragon-tooth boy stood below the izba, uncertain.

"What is that?" asked Mewster, twitching whiskers.

The witch said, "His name is Nick-o'-Time, but we call him Nikolai. Don't just stand there, honeybucket; come inside."

"Take it from me," said the kitten through a big fake yawn, "unless you've brought the old harridan a present, remember not to eat any food. Or you'll be sorry."

"I think dragon-tooth boys don't eat," replied Nikolai, climbing up the ladder. The trapdoor shut and bolted itself. An area carpet skittered over it, and a small overwrought table hopped forward and settled itself on the rug, looking pert.

"I am betrayed by my furniture." The witch sighed. "Also my house pet."

Mewster snarled, "Serves you right. Question *my* ability to handle a high-level negotiation? A tiger is no domestic animal. So maybe now you'll let me join the League of Freed Prisoners and release me to the wild?"

"You still have time to serve. Don't bother me. We have to plan."

Benches drew themselves up to be sat upon. Cat rummaged through the supplies she'd brought from Madame Sophia's kitchen, and served up a steaming pot of hot cocoa. The witch poured it out into chipped cups. Nikolai didn't take any. Still, a certain vigor bloomed in his face, which was less waxen than rosy now, like the other children.

They didn't speak for a moment, taking stock. Surviving another hour. Cheeks were apples; clothes were dripping. The smell of wet wool. Baba Yaga stoked the stove. Cat and Elena and Anton looked Nikolai over. All at once they started laughing, all four of them. I cannot begin to say what they thought was funny. I am too far from my own childhood, if ever I had one, to hazard a guess. But even the furniture shook with glee while Baba Yaga's back was turned.

Rejoining them, the witch said, "First things first. Nikolai, a proposition. Would you be willing to stay here by the ice-dragon and rewind the music box until that old insomniac nods off? Mind, it could take some time. That creature has an agitated sensibility."

The dragon-tooth boy straightened the sash across his chest. His face had returned to solemnity. "I'd like to stand my post, of course. Like my brother soldiers. But I'm young to decide on a permanent calling. I hope there might be more to being a soldier than turning a key in a music box."

The witch said, "You may have a point. Still, we're in a pinch. I admit, the hours are long and there's little by way of a salary. Yet you'll have the satisfaction of staying near your old dada, who grew you out of his very own gums and bit you off by accident and spit you out. That's sort of, um, touching."

The dragon-tooth boy thought about it. "I don't know why I should. *I* didn't wake him up with noisy fretting over milk and supper and bread and being married to princes and wanting adventure and abducting children out of loneliness."

The witch's left eyebrow raised. For a new student to their dilemma, he was catching on fast.

Cat said, "You didn't wake the ice-dragon up; that's true. But what choice is there? We can't stay here to do it. We're flesh and blood as well as bone. We'd freeze to death."

Anton liked the newcomer. "It does seem a rum deal, Nick. But as long as there's someone to turn the key when the mechanism winds down, the music may distract the ice-dragon from the noise of human fretting. It can drift back to sleep, and stop chewing ice and breathing fire upon the ice cap. The floodwater can retreat, and the weather drift back to normal. Crops can grow in their usual way."

"And you'll go off and explore the source of the Amazon in the Andes," said Nikolai to Anton. To Cat, "And you'll go back to school and learn how to marry a prince if you ever meet one again." He turned to Elena but just shook his head at her. "In any case, I'm to be excluded from your League of Freed Prisoners." His face was figuring out how to pout, a skill that comes naturally to the young. "I get to be the hero. Lucky me."

Cat said, "Nikolai has a point. I think heroism is one of those things that can be shared without diminishing it. What about us?"

The witch examined her fingernails and said in a distracted, ordinary grown-up voice that belied her interest, "What do you mean?"

Cat stared at the ceiling, hunting for words. "Part-time heroes. If Nikolai is willing to help, so should we. As we can."

The witch spat on the floor. "Doing precisely what?"

"Well . . . I don't know yet. But we can think about it."

"Trust the young to imagine they can improve on human nature. Let me tell you: Sudden understandings at the end of an adventure are a sorry farce. Beware the shattering idealism of the young. Cute, and deadly."

"Maybe," said Nikolai. "I'm not human, Mama Yaga, so I don't know."

The witch raised her hands to the rafters. *Mama Yaga?*

"But all right," continued the dragon-tooth boy, "I'll help. I'll start. If the others agree to join in, I'll put a half-year to start. I'll stay here till the summer solstice. Give my new friends a few months to see if they can do *something*. Something real, to reduce the human complaint. I'll turn the key to the music box shaped like an egg, and I'll lull the dragon to sleep."

"Just for a few months." The witch nodded. "The ice-dragon is *supposed* to be awake for part of the summer. That's part of his nature, too."

"Summer is four months away, enough time to start on setting things right. And though I'm only a milk tooth of a dragon, I have my own life to discover."

"Well, I like a child who knows his own mind," said Baba Yaga. "As far as I'm concerned, it's a deal. Here's my contribution: I'll come back at the summer solstice and liberate *you.* Then you can join the League of Freed Prisoners. We'll see if these three chuckle-heads can make any difference in the world by then. Either way, you'll have put in your hours. A part-time hero."

"What will we do then?" asked the dragon-tooth boy. "When summer arrives?"

The witch looked if she thought she might be coming down with something. She chewed her words like a gum arabic before speaking them. "My other visitors are going to have to go home eventually. After these adventures with them, I may find my old life as a hermit somewhat lacking in smack. Boring, even. So I've been thinking it might be time to have a baby. I was going to call it Baby Yaga. But maybe I'll just adopt. Would you be my new boy?"

The hummingbird dropped dead, and Mewster was too shocked even to pounce for a bite. The table got down on its knees. The wardrobe door flew open, and the mirror showed a reflection of Baba Yaga with a fistful of balloons on strings and a basket of candy canes, toy soldiers, gingerbread dragons, and pistols.

Cat looked put out. Anton mouthed the words, *It's not fair.* But Elena was relieved at the thought of being released to go home.

The dragon-tooth boy said, "A dragon for a father and a witch for a mother? I'll think about it, Mama Yaga."

"Hey!" Even Mewster was sputtering. "What about me?"

"You," said Baba Yaga, "I'm not even talking to you yet. I'll let you loose in the wild when I'm good and ready. Gather your hairballs and let yourself out. I need you to pull Dumb Doma home." The witch snagged the floating nest from midair and retrieved the Fabergé egg from it. "If we're doing this, let's finish it before I get soppy. Here you are, Nikolai. You know where the door is."

The dragon-tooth boy stood at attention. He *was* only a boy, after all. But he accepted the Fabergé egg from the witch. He examined it. "I see your house, Mama Yaga," he said, "and here is my father, Žmey-Aždaja. And here is the Firebird's egg."

They all peered. In that window where recently they had seen deadwood and rot, a little porcelain egg rested in a patch of porcelain ferns.

Nikolai inserted the key in a slot in the wooden base and wound up the music box. The egg revolved. Firebird, witch, ice-dragon. A plinkety melody sounded and sounded again.

The dragon-tooth boy bit his lip and blinked a couple of times, quickly.

"I shall not forget you," he said to them all. "This egg will remind me all through my springtime. And I shall try to do my best."

The three human children promised to do the same.

But what *was* their best? What actually did they mean to do? Three young human beings not yet reached the legal age for marriage? How to be a part-time hero when you were still young enough to be sent to your room for misbehavior?

They didn't know. It had something to do with trying, though. Trying to limit their own greedy *I want*s. Maybe trying to help satisfy someone else's needy *I want*s. Do without their green silk gowns, sell a palace or two, supply some fretful infants a honey-bucket's worth of goat's milk. Give away some of the nuts and mushrooms found in the forest. Offer someone the extra length of cotton, the spare broom.

Sharing by turns or sharing by portions or sharing by common holding — or they'd do without, and share the nothing equally.

All they could do was make a start. Then, when the Fabergé music-box egg finally broke, maybe they'd have reduced the chorus of *I wants* just enough for Žmey-Aždaja to sleep through the winter as an ice-dragon ought. Help return the cranky imperious world to its own cranky imperious balance.

A tall order. Probably impossible. An irresponsible fairy tale.

But I want it to turn out to be true. I do. *I want, I want.*

A House Has Its Secrets

B aba Yaga clicked her fingers. A staircase unfolded out of the wall. She rushed up the steps and rummaged about in an impromptu attic, returning with a set of leather reins stitched with jingle bells. Suddenly no carping or comedy, all business. "Let's wave our good-byes to the North. Farewell, Nikolai. I hope the key in the egg doesn't break."

"Of course it will," said the dragon-tooth boy. "Anything that can happen will happen, sooner or later. The question is whether or not the world can be made ready."

Then he bowed formally, for his green-and-white wool uniform was stiff with newness. He took the glossy egg that Madame Sophia had ordered for the Tsar. He didn't look at the humans as he marched to the door.

They grabbed their fur coats and followed him. The sun was nearly behind the horizon. Quickly outpacing his shivering friends, he marched toward the menacing creature, and he didn't look back. Soon they could hear the tinkling sound of the music box in the icy air. Music over snow is like prisms tinkling from some drafty dining room of long ago.

As Baba Yaga used the reins to hitch Mewster to the front of Dumb Doma, the children walked a few feet away to catch a last look at Žmey-Aždaja.

A great Russian writer remarked that once you have looked closely at the drawing in which an artist has hidden some objects to be found, and you've discovered them, it is impossible to un-see them. Now that the children knew what they were looking at, it was hard to believe they hadn't recognized the great hump-backed ridge as an ice-dragon lying against the shore of the harbor.

The short northern day was nearly done already. Žmey-Aždaja was close to dozing, frosty flanks gleaming against the coming night. The slope of his snout was angling toward them now. He seemed to be curling up more tightly, like a borzoi on a hearth rug.

For the first time, they could see both of his eyes. They were heavy-lidded. Only a deep glow, the sort one might mistake as a reflection of sunset, betrayed the life in the hillside.

Žmey-Aždaja didn't speak again. It seemed to Elena, though, as if he nodded the most discreet of acknowledgments. Perhaps she was succumbing to being fanciful again. She should watch out for that.

Still, Elena supposed that an ice-dragon has little practice in thanking guests for presents. This, then, was something of an effort. She waved. The part-time hero was already stepping over the other side of the dragon's forearm, distributing the lullaby of the porcelain egg. He looked forlorn. A toy soldier set out upon a snowbank.

The fate of the world shouldn't rest on a single set of shoulders. The others would have to get to work. So, with Cat on one side and Anton on the other, Elena returned to the front doorstep of Dumb Doma.

"I don't suppose that when a large wrong has been set a little right, everything else sorts itself out in perfect order," said Cat to Baba Yaga.

"I don't know," said the witch. "I signed up for a correspondence course in dental hygiene, which taught me that careful brushing removed the rust from my iron teeth, but I never did receive any invitations to the Friday-night barbecue at Marie Antoinette's. One's bite, for good or for ill, doesn't change much through life. One gets what one gets."

Elena said, "But we have a chance now. Don't we?"

"Well, there's always a chance," said the witch, "if you believe in chances. I myself am governed by destiny. And it hasn't escaped my attention that the Firebird's egg is still missing. What that means to the spirit of Russian magic, who knows. Cat, when you get back to London, remember to look up Sherlock Holmes and engage him to solve the Case of the Purloined Egg. Get inside, honeybuckets. It's time to go."

"Where are we going?" asked Anton, his face falling.

"Back to Saint Petersburg. If this strategy works, you three can claim you helped still the floods, at least for a time. Maybe in thanks, the Tsar will issue a pardon to Elena."

"How are we going to get back? Even you can't hail a passing tornado."

"Mewster will pull us." She went to the front door and called out, "Mush, baby, mush."

425

"Mush yourself," called Mewster, tangled in reins. "Which way should we go?"

"How should I know? I couldn't find my own house if I didn't bring it along with me wherever I went. Elena?" The witch looked at the girl, who took the matryoshka out of her pocket. She didn't open it, just stroked the doll's head.

"Which way?" replied Elena. "Home."

So Mewster swelled to the size of a great white Siberian snow tiger and began to pace along the rim of the harbor, looking for a dip between hills in which he could turn to the south.

The ride was bumpy. Dumb Doma had to run to keep up with Mewster. Anton mentioned that skiing in Switzerland was a smoother ride than this. Baba Yaga agreed. "Giant chicken feet aren't designed for cross-country marathons. I must have a pair of skis somewhere." She poked about in a cupboard, but all she turned up was a tennis racket, its strings chewed out by mice. "This is no good. We'll have to make a sled. Wardrobe, come here; your time is done. I'm going to take you apart with this hammer." But the wardrobe ran and hid its face in the corner and wouldn't come out.

"Tarnation pudding," said Baba Yaga. "Well, honeybuckets, help me unscrew this trapdoor we just noticed. We'll slap it on the ground and Dumb Doma can balance on it, and it'll work as a kind of toboggan."

She ordered the table and carpet to scurry away. Then she passed around screwdrivers and a crowbar. They went to work at the stubborn door. "I have the most . . . opinionated . . . household," grunted the witch. "Home ownership is not for the timid. On the count of three. One . . . two . . ."

She didn't say *three,* and the children said, "Oh!"

"Well, looky-looky," said the witch.

When the trapdoor flew open, a brightness seared their corneas. You can guess what they found, not hanging in midair but nested in a wooden cradle beneath the house, like a secret box slotted underneath a tabletop.

"That drawer wasn't there when I was lying under the house," said Elena. And it seemed to her that the obscure figures that sometimes haunted the walls of Dumb Doma, figures mounted upon one another in stacks and columns, opened their mouths not in horror but in relief.

Anton said, "But my godfather sent the Firebird's egg to his treasury. How did it get here?"

Cat figured it out. "Don't you remember? Dumb Doma drifting downriver beside the pavilions. We saw her — but no one else did."

"I bet it was that cat," said the witch. "I bet Mewster made a leap, and slipped under the awnings of the treasury tent, and made off with the Firebird's egg while we were all chewing the fat with the Tsar. Why didn't he tell us?"

She ran to the front door. "Mewster! We found the Firebird's egg!"

The great cat was laboring to drag Dumb Doma upslope. On either side, the army of dragon's teeth was marching along as sprightly as possible given the deep snow. Short of breath, Mewster managed to growl, "You couldn't find honey in a bucket, honeybucket."

"It's not my fault I don't have my best spectacles anymore!" she screamed. "But why did you take it?"

He answered, "*You're* the only one who wants a companion? You kidnap me and hold me hostage — you filch children lost

427

in the woods — and you think Dumb Doma doesn't also have a maternal instinct in its wooden chicken-hearted breast? After all these years, it was feeling broody. It wanted an egg to sit on. So I found one. So what?"

"But you could have upset the balance of the universe!"

"So could we all," he replied. "You too, witch."

Baba Yaga wanted to candle the egg and make sure the Firebird was in embryo therein, but the egg was almost too warm to touch. Maybe that was a good sign.

The witch called the Firebird's nest from where it hovered near the ceiling, and the nest took the glowing egg as if it was purpose-built to hold such a relic. Which it was.

"Now everything is perfect," said Baba Yaga. "Someone sing a fatuous victory anthem, and we can all go home."

"Not so fast," called Mewster through the open front door. "Weren't you making a sledge for the house? I'm already exhausted, and we haven't even made it up the first slope."

"Oh, right," said Baba Yaga. She lifted the hatch from where they had set it. The floor had already healed over. There was no evidence of a secret entrance. No hidden drawer. She sighed. "This house needs therapy." Then she ran to the front door and slapped the trapdoor out onto the snow. "Dumb Doma! Roost on that rectangle of wood and keep your balance, and we'll all have an easier time of it."

The dark had swept in for good by now. They caught a glimpse of the full moon that, the previous night, had raised up an army out of the planted teeth of Žmey-Aždaja. The marching was slow.

Those soldiers were made to fight, not to wade through three feet of snowdrifts.

"What's that?" asked Elena. She pointed ahead.

The horizon had become lumpy, a moving silhouette, like gear teeth laid on a long curve. The teeth weren't sharp, but rounded. Was it the ice-dragon's tabbed spine? Had Žmey-Aždaja changed its mind, broken loose, circled around to ambush them? More and more shapes rising over the brow of the slope, the huge moon behind them providing both contrast and glare.

As the moon rose higher and the light strengthened, the hulking, bobbing shapes came nearer. They weren't a single backbone but separate entities. "It looks hostile for a welcoming committee," said Baba Yaga. "I doubt it's the Saami Sámi Lapi, who are a peaceable people. Maybe it's a battalion of some sort to keep us from returning. We'll get closer and have a better look."

By their hesitation, it seemed that the indigenous tribe had noticed the awkward sledge of Dumb Doma pulled by Mewster, and the army that flanked them on either side.

The brigade began to swarm down the slope toward the League of Freed Prisoners with wild, high-pitched ululations. It chilled the blood to hear it.

Armies Meet
by Moonlight

A little light," said the witch. "Where are my skulls? Caligula and Robespierre! And Benedict Arnold, Tallulah Bankhead, whoever you are, I can't remember. Open your lighted eye sockets, we need your help."

The skulls rolled out from underneath the bed. The witch said to the children, "What are you waiting for? Come on, grab a noggin. We'll repair to the roof and see what we can see."

A folding ladder obligingly unpacked itself from the ceiling. The children and the witch scrambled up. They found themselves on a narrow landing facing a gable with a casement window. "So this is where my window seat went," said the witch. "I can't decide if Dumb Doma is treacherous or just forgetful. Come on, out we go."

They clambered over the cushions and through the window. Once there, they inched around the gutters and trim until there was a sentry stationed at each corner of the izba's steep roof. The witch called, "At my command, lift your skulls high and hold them out. We'll blind these newcomers, giving our army the advantage."

"I hope they take it," said Anton. "They've had no military training."

"They're born soldiers. They'll know what to do. Ready, steady, go."

They each lifted a skull.

The radiance from the bony eye sockets grew in strength and became beacons. The wailing of the approaching army mounted to a higher key. It was joined by the roar of the soldiers, readying for the fray.

"Oh, mercy cut us a little slack," shouted Baba Yaga. "It's those pesky matryoshkas, come to plague us! Let loose an enchantment, honeybuckets, and it stays loose. It wants to follow its own track. *I want, I want* in the magic kingdom. Watch out, the battle is joined now!"

The dragon-tooth army was pelting forward through the snow, falling on their knees in their haste. They threw down their bayonets in favor of making snowballs, and pitched them at the bevy of matryoshkas. The snowballs fragmented into snow dust before impact. Fully risen but one tip still grazing the horizon, the moon now looked like the supreme snowball of the galaxy.

The dolls drew nearer, sliding with verve and control. Their rounded bottoms skidded over the top of the ice and didn't break through, didn't hobble their progress as the men's was hobbled.

"I have a nasty feeling about this," said Baba Yaga. "The strategies of this sort of war are inappropriate for young eyes to see!

Close your eyes, kiddos!" Did any one of the children obey? I ask you.

In his harness, Mewster turned and growled up at the witch on the roof. "When hearts collide . . . Where's your fiddle, witch?"

"I don't do *romance!*" cried the witch. "Never could stand the stuff!"

"Oh, yuck," said Cat. "We barely escape from the marriage market that the Tsar was running . . ."

"You said it. From an engagement ball to a rodeo at the Kissypoo Corral."

The battle was being joined. The cry of the matryoshkas wasn't a battle alarum but a shriek of delight. Nor had the soldiers been roaring to give themselves courage under fire but to return the signal of approval.

Now that they'd been out in the world a few days, the matryoshkas had become differentiated. Though they were still shaped like pins for a game of skittles, with no arms except those painted on their curved sides, the colors of their garments varied, and their faces had grown individual. This one had a blond curl painted across her forehead; that one had more hooded eyes, smeared with kohl. A third had a serene expression like an ikon of a saint; another featured a saucy wink.

Each of the dragon-tooth soldiers met a Russian doll he found toothsome. Each soldier threw his arms around the neck of the doll where her pear shape began to taper into her rounded conical head. His fingers just met around the sides, and a wild northern dance of matrimony began. Sometimes he was planted on this ground, his booted feet spread wide and turning, and he was hoisting his partner in the air, her lacquered bottom shining red and black and blue in the skull-light. Then she was planted again in the snow and spinning, and her soldier wheeled about, legs in the air like fringe, revolving around her. Their joy was contagious, at least to the children, who clapped and hollered. Baba Yaga jeered.

The Immortal Hen
of the Tundra

Once the moon went down, the dragon-tooth soldiers and their matryoshka brides stopped dancing. The League of Freed Prisoners and the witch watched as the soldiers lifted off the heads of their chosen dolls and climbed inside, pulling the doll heads down upon them like lids upon a jar. The dolls fell in line behind Dumb Doma.

The stars came out. A host of spangles: yellow, periwinkle blue, white.

They made Elena mindful of something, but what, she couldn't remember.

Anton wasn't given to flushes of emotion. He didn't think of stars as beautiful, administrative, or celestial chemical accidents. He thought of them as background to adventure. Maybe the only suitable background.

Cat thought of being packed off back to school, and the stars didn't help. You couldn't see stars very well over London.

"We're off," said the witch, and they went inside.

Only a little more need be said about their return journey. Often enough, Mewster was able to find frozen slicks along valley floors. Now that Dumb Doma could balance on its trapdoor sled, Mewster could make impressive speeds. The army of matryoshkas carrying their cargo of husbands whisked along behind. Now and then, overturning on a curve, the dolls would squeal in joy but bob back up and hurry on.

Baba Yaga stoked the furnace with birch wood and sat down nearby. With a dainty set of embroidery scissors, she went at a sheaf of brightly colored origami papers. The shreds tangled in Mewster's whiskers. The witch said she was snipping a portrait of her son's personal history, the circumstances in which he had come to be born. She would lay it under an oval of glass after the glue was dry.

The missing window seat had obligingly reappeared opposite the stove, so the children squeezed themselves onto it. They wanted to harvest every last glimpse of cold and mystery before it was gone for good. They didn't speak for now.

Once, Anton tapped his finger on the glass. He pointed, and the girls peered. They thought they saw the figure of Myandash at the base of a snowy knoll. A figure like a totem, like a tree trunk topped by a rack of antlers. The figure raised one arm in a sort of salute. At the end of his fist sat a snowy owl.

Myandash may only have been gesturing to Mewster, but three children each put a palm on the glass, three lifelines.

Little by little, the North became far away again. So does all memory, unless you write it down.

They didn't know how near they might be to Archangel, and whether Mewster would try to skirt the outpost or lead a dawn invasion of dolls through the streets of that city. At first light, as Mewster dragged Dumb Doma and her passengers around the brow of a low but wide-flung hill, they saw in the distance what they took to be an ice fortress.

"One prohibition after another," said Baba Yaga. "Does no one want us to return? Why has the Tsar caused an outpost to be built in this barren hinterland?"

They drew nearer. As the sun rose, they saw that the structure wasn't as big or solid as it had first seemed. It looked like an armory of snowballs for the next playful skirmish between the soldiers and the matryoshkas.

"What fresh caprice is this?" asked the witch. She opened Dumb Doma's door and shouted to Mewster, "Let's have a look, but be careful in case there's someone treacherous behind that mound of ammunition, waiting to ambush us."

Mewster slowed his pace. They saw no sign of life as they drew close to the ziggurat of artillery. Then Elena let out a cry. "I do believe I know who that is. Up top, can you make it out?"

Cat and Anton and the witch strained to see. The black fur cap of a lone soldier peering out from behind the ramparts? Then they realized that the cap was strutting by itself and that it wasn't a cap at all but a small, homely creature. Looking proud of herself.

"Is that a *hen*?" asked Baba Yaga. "In the frozen North? However possible?"

"It's the hen of the tundra." Elena, laughing and clapping her hands: "Those aren't thousands of snowballs, but eggs! Her eggs! I'd recognize that hen anywhere. So I *didn't* imagine it. She's the one who was flushed out of the forest by the fox. She zipped into the clearing as I was trying to snatch the Firebird's feather, and . . . and she took hold of the feather with her beak before I could get there. She was in the jaws of death, and she must have made a chicken wish . . . to live long enough to lay one more egg."

"If these are all hers," said Anton, "then she's lived to lay about ten thousand more eggs. She's a very busy little hen."

"Yes," said Baba Yaga, "but 'one more' is always the *next* one. So she'll always live to lay one more egg. And then one more. And then one more."

The chicken had laid about six eggs while they were watching. She didn't seem at all tired or bored, just tidied the eggs into her stockpile.

"She's still young. She won't be able to lay at that rate forever," said Baba Yaga. "But it seems that she'll always be able to lay one more."

They came to a halt at the bottom of the wall. It was time to get out and stretch their legs. A spicy clarity in the air, redolent of the fir forests to the south. The tree line wouldn't be far away now.

"Little hen," said Elena, "are you from Miersk originally? One of our own? You were lost in the woods and chased by a fox, and you found the Firebird. And now we've found you." She put up her hands, a gesture of family feeling.

The hen regarded Elena with a dubious eye. She began to back away, making the hawking, embarrassed chuckle of a confused hen — the only kind of hen there is. Then she cocked her head and noticed Dumb Doma.

The house was dancing up and down on her giant chicken legs. Snow came flying off the roof in great puffs. Dumb Doma preened and scratched. The hen of the tundra hurtled off her giant storehouse of eggs. She tumbled down the slope and approached Dumb Doma as a chick will race toward its mother.

"Dumb Doma wanted an egg," said Mewster. "That's why I took the Firebird's egg for her. But it seems she'd be happy to adopt."

"So our party grows," said Baba Yaga. "Well, Madame Hen, you're welcome to join us. But we haven't got room for your warehouse of eggs."

The hen didn't seem to mind. She roosted upon the makeshift sled between Dumb Doma's feet. She stared at them, conveying little in the way of an opinion, twitching her head in that staccato way of hens worldwide, and perhaps universal, for all I know.

What did she see in them? I don't know. Birds are my eyes, but hens are inscrutable.

So Baba Yaga corralled the children, and they climbed back into the izba. Then the house on chicken legs, and the witch with iron teeth, and the four skulls, and Mewster the enchanted snow tiger, and the army of matryoshkas bearing their beloved cargo of dragon-tooth soldiers, and the unborn Firebird in its glowing egg, and the immortal hen of the tundra living to bear one more egg, and Anton Antonovich Romanov, the distant cousin and godson of the Tsar, and Ekaterina Ivanovna de Robichaux, the wealthy French-Russian girl being schooled in London, and Elena Maximovna Rudina, a peasant girl from Miersk, prepared to leave the world of ice magic behind.

The Norway Geese

On the outskirts of Archangel, the company paused.

The city huddled brown and grey against the plain. Human roads again, and clutches of low gnarled trees struggling to stand upright against the wind off the steppes. It was very early morning either the next day or the next after that.

Clutching a scarlet plush tarantula, Baba Yaga was snoring in her trundle bed.

The children were already awake. They felt the end of their adventures approaching, perhaps the end of their friendships. They wanted to treasure every moment before the magic evaporated and they were dumped back on the several floors of their hard lives.

Cat and Anton agreed that their lives had promise as well as perplexity.

Cat: "I wasn't interested in meeting any cousin and godson of the Tsar, even though my great-aunt thought it might be my ticket of rescue from a life of abandonment by my parents. I thought the Tsar's godson would be old and fat and leering, and smell of cherry pipe tobacco. If I was unlucky, he would like me and propose to take my hand in marriage, and I'd have to accept. When, really, I see now I'd rather go back to school in London."

Anton: "My parents insisted I participate in that marriage market. I was hoping I'd wiggle out of having to make a commitment somehow. I'd rather travel and have some adventure, though no adventure I can imagine could match the one we're on now." He grinned at Cat. "The Tsar wants me suitably promised to some young woman far enough away from the throne that I could never be a threat. It's how royal families operate. But I'd rather decide for myself how to live my life. Maybe I could come visit in London sometime?"

Elena braided her hair in the way she'd always worn it in Miersk. She could feel the reality of her village origins rising to claim her. How many peasants from Miersk had ever gone to Saint Petersburg? Dr. Peter Petrovich Penkin alone, as far as she knew. Well, and Luka. But even they had never continued to the far northern shores of the vast Asian continent. Even leaving aside the congress with Russia's magical energies, Elena knew she'd already had the adventure of a lifetime. There'd be little left to her now but sameness and worry and hunger.

So she didn't speak, though her friends could see the weight of her limited future occurring to her. The way her shoulders dipped, her eyes lowered.

"*Is* there any way we can avoid the futures they have set out for us?" asked Cat, putting her hand on Elena's knee.

"We have a job to do. Žmey-Aždaja has told us this," said

Anton. "So nothing can be the same. It can't go on as it always has. We can't be as we thought we would be. We must change ourselves."

"We must change our ambitions," said Cat, nodding, "and that will change us."

They looked at Elena to see if she agreed with their aspirations, if she would join their cordial society.

She was too honorable to pretend. She smiled at them out of affection, perhaps even love, but she didn't speak. She didn't lie. She didn't think there was opportunity for such as her.

Her silence sobered the other two. They sat in stillness in a ring on the floor, knees nearly touching, as the house rocked slowly back and forth. Mewster's pace was slowing down. As soon as the roads became more mud than ice, he would have to come back inside and be a kitten again.

The quiet was broken, then, by a rack of distant cries. As if to break from submission to Russian fatalism, for they were too young to embrace it fully, the three friends scrambled to the window. Baba Yaga yawned herself awake.

A great cloud of Norway geese was sweeping upon them. It was impossible to count the number, but it was in the thousands: five, eight, nine thousand geese.

They took no note of the company of travelers beneath them. The wind pulled this way and that. No one could say what forces caused the current of geese to dip and sink, to wheel away and veer back. But every time they turned a certain way in the dawn sun, the cloudless sky became a skin like fish scales, blinking. It seemed a language, a set of signals, if they only knew how to read it.

The shadow of their flight upon the ground, a word inscribed upon the earth.

"They are off somewhere, on some campaign," said Baba Yaga, joining them. She took screws of cotton wool out of her ears and stored them in the heels of her slippers. "Surely it isn't the time of year for their migration."

"Are they going south for the winter? If so, they're late," said Anton.

"If north for the summer, they're early," said Cat.

"They're going east, toward the dawn," said the witch. "That isn't their habit. They'll have to learn their traditions again, if you three can manage to keep your promise to the ice-dragon, and reduce the degree of human wailing."

"We three?" said Cat.

"*I'm* not human. I've made that clear enough. It's none of my business if your kind survives or not."

"I found the Firebird's egg," said Elena. "I rescued it until Mewster and Dumb Doma rescued it again. It's still alive inside its shell. Isn't that enough?"

"It's more than I did," agreed Baba Yaga. "Still, the curse of being human is that there is always something more to do, while you are alive. Me, I'm just about immortal, so I have all the time in the world to pick up the niceties of bridge."

"They shouldn't go east at this time of year, though," said Anton. "They must behave as they should, or we shall never right the world."

"They are wild things," replied the witch. "When did a wild creature ever obey an order or keep a promise? Or a child, for that matter?"

On the Bridge
Near Archangel

A half an hour later, the Norway geese were nearly gone. Smoke was beginning to arise from the chimneys and hearths of Archangel. Roosters crowed.

"We'll skirt the town," said Baba Yaga, and directed Mewster to take what looked like an orbital track around fields of broken stubble and halfhearted fences. They kept Archangel to one side.

Then they came to a stone bridge across a narrow but swiftly moving stream. On either bank, bare trees leaned. Ahead, the track rose up a slope, and there was mud and runoff in the road.

The company of matryoshkas was lagging behind the izba, shaking merrily and silently. "I'm going to have to send them downstream," said Baba Yaga. "I don't think they can slide across mud as easily as they can slalom over the snow."

The matryoshkas didn't wait for Baba Yaga to say more. One by one they rocked down through the stands of willow and plopped into the water like so many balsa-wood ducks. They spun and eddied at first, but their soldier husbands gave them ballast. Doll by doll they caught the current and began to ride the rapids.

Anton and Cat were waving good-bye. As Baba Yaga unhitched Mewster from the reins, she said harshly, "So many *fare-thee-wells*. You want to go, too? How about you, Mewster? If this is the season for good-byes, let's get it done with all at once."

"You'd abandon your guests halfway? They can't get back to Saint Petersburg on their own." Mewster was scandalized. "And I haven't served my sentence yet. You aren't famous for freeing any serfs. Are you coming down with something?"

"Furniture!" bellowed the witch. "Table, bathtub, the lot of you. It's time to go out in the world and seek your fortunes, if that's your hope."

There was a crashing sound as all the furniture went and tried to hide under the bed, and the bed tried to hide under itself.

"The League of Freed Prisoners is taking new members for the next five minutes, then the rolls are closed," she continued. Mewster chose this moment to take a nap. I like to imagine that at least a dish ran away with a spoon, but even the kitchen implements stayed in their places, either devoted to Baba Yaga or terrified of freedom.

Elena came to Dumb Doma's front steps and picked her way down them. She was carrying the Firebird's egg. "All right, then, freedom it is. I think you're right. This doesn't belong to the Tsar," she said. "It belongs to Russia. And Dumb Doma has her own hen now. She doesn't need this."

No one spoke — perhaps they didn't dare — as Elena proceeded to put the Firebird's egg in the water.

"Live your life," she said. "Be born. Be light."

The egg followed the last of the matryoshkas, spinning softly and glowing with its own interior fuse.

Now the Firebird's egg was drifting around a screen of trees and rocky riverbank. Now it was lost to sight.

A moment after it disappeared, the granite pink of early morning near Archangel became transparent with a shudder of white power. This lightning began at the earth and flared heavenward. The Firebird reborn.

Though the skies were still clear, a snow began to fall over the North. A solid, steady, full-bodied flurry of flakes from nowhere. See that Archangel blue sky as a background, and the snowflakes turning in the frigid air. Where they landed on the ground they were white, but in the air? Snowflakes cold as cold brass, snowflakes like cold copper, and saffron, and cold gold, in all those shiny colors of a Firebird, and more colors besides, colors that have no names. Winter at last, before it was too late.

The Kitten's Advice

A matryoshka army, an immortal hen, a resurrected Firebird. You will think this a string of nonsense. Perhaps
you have never been far enough from home. You leave
home, I have learned, counting the trip day by day. If you ever get
to return, you count the trip miracle by miracle.

But now the journey began to seem unending. Elena thought,
The real world is starting to reassert itself. I have to get used to
what I will find next. Perhaps a return to prison, since I've helped
do away with both the Fabergé egg and the Firebird's egg.

"Why such a long face?" asked Baba Yaga.

Elena didn't answer. She had seen that the witch was pulling away
from them. She no longer made any pretense of trying to prepare
them supper, but sent them out to beg for bread. Then they had eggs
on toast for supper because, of course, there was no shortage of eggs.

For hours at a time, the witch sat at a surprisingly ladylike little
escritoire, with sheets of paper and pots of ink. She ran the plume

of her pen across her noble nose. She was making notes on how to be a good mother when the dragon-tooth boy came home for the summer, but she burnt the pages every evening in the flame of a taper. "I'm writing them," she snapped when Cat asked. "I didn't say I want anyone to read them. Myself included. I don't pry. They're none of my business."

It was hard to believe it, but the weather *had* grown colder. The mushy winter thaw that had characterized the day that Elena and Cat had first met — that thaw had lifted. Snow almost daily. They'd liberated the matryoshkas and their soldier husbands too soon, they realized. The bobbing dolls *could* have continued to zing alongside Dumb Doma.

But Mewster was domesticated again, a pretty kitten at the saucer of milk or sleeping aloft in the airborne Firebird's nest. He refused to pull Dumb Doma on the toboggan any longer.

The day came when Baba Yaga snapped at the children, "We're getting too near Saint Petersburg. When the Firebird of Russia was missing and presumed dead, I sucked it in and made my appearances. I have no need to do that again. I hate crowds. But there's the road, there's your life. Go find dinner, and don't come back to give me any. I'm done with sharing. Anyway, I'm not hungry. This is toodle-loo, honeybuckets. Don't bother to write, because I get no postal delivery where I'm going."

"We can't leave just like that." Cat was appalled. "Where can we find you if we need you again?"

"You can't. Listen, Little Drear, I hate saying good-byes. I have a good strategy for avoiding them."

"What's that?" asked Anton.

"I eat my guests. Better keep moving while I'm soft-hearted and have given you a chance to get away." She flourished a hand in the direction of the four skulls, which were sitting along a baseboard all pell-mell, like discarded boots. But by now the kids saw them for what they probably were: learning aids for medical students, made out of some chalky composite and bought wholesale.

They could see through Baba Yaga, too.

The fiendish glee had gone. Her face looked ancient, betraying that she saw worries behind her eyes as well as in front of them. This campaign had changed her, too. Or maybe it was the stress of fretting over her son, off at his first job and no word from him yet. Elena realized she felt sorry for the old witch. Baba Yaga reminded her of Grandmother Onna, hovering near the well, uncertain if the current disaster was serious enough to take a plunge.

They gathered their things. There wasn't much. The witch said they could keep the fur coats and such. "Souvenirs," said Cat in a cold voice, wanting a gesture of some sort, a ceremony, a more potent talisman than mittens.

"You brought me a Fabergé egg, twice, and then we had to give it away twice. I'm out double," replied the witch. "You don't get so much as a comb from me, for that. It's the thought that counts." The first migraine of parenthood deepened upon her brow.

Anton leaped down happily enough. Adventure begins with not knowing what comes next. But Cat lingered at the door. Cat wouldn't accept this rude dismissal; her great-aunt's moral rectitude arose in her. "Really, all this, and you're not even going to say *good-bye*? I hardly think that's fair."

"If you need someone to abuse, go find your parents. They're shirking their duty by taking themselves out of the line of fire. I have my own obligations, and I haven't time for your nonsense." The witch slammed the door behind them and began cursing up a storm, banging frying pans and rolling pins. Elena caught Cat's hand and gave her a corner of her apron to wipe her face with.

They could hear a sound from Baba Yaga that they'd never heard before. No one could bear to admit what it was. The young can never stand the tears of the elderly, and woe betide us if the elderly in question is more than a millennium old. They looked about, they avoided comment. Anton kicked at stones. Elena gripped the matryoshka for comfort. Cat just stared at the hard, hard world the way it was, the way it would always be: a disappointment. Here was Dumb Doma. Here was Mewster on a sill by the open window, perhaps also trying to escape the maelstrom of a witch's grief. Here was the immortal hen of the tundra, having no luck pecking for grubs in the snow at the feet of Dumb Doma.

"Why doesn't she let you go, too?" Cat's voice was steel, as if she was jealous of the kitten. "Are you the last one not to belong to the League of Freed Prisoners?"

"That's between her and me," said Mewster. "That's our story. It runs on a parallel track. Everything doesn't get fixed at once, no matter how simple or sentimental you are. Go find your own story, and stop interfering in mine. Anyway, she needs *someone* to berate, or she'd lose her marbles. And then where would we all be, if she got crazier than she already is?"

Saint Petersburg was promised by a sign. They turned to walk down the road in that direction. Dumb Doma followed for a few tentative steps until the witch bellowed from inside that Dumb

Doma was to stay where it was or she'd come out and chop off its legs. So the izba paused, and stepped in place, as if unhappy to see its passengers walking away. But there was nothing it could do.

A moment later Mewster called to them. He was prowling on the roof with little dainty steps. "Haven't you forgotten something?"

They turned. The kitten said, "Little Miss Cluck Cluck?"

"But . . . but that's Dumb Doma's baby," said Elena.

"To hear you tell it, that black hen was a citizen of your village before she set out on her own adventure. Maybe she wants to go home, too. In any case, she's a grown hen giving out more eggs than you can count. And in the grain crib, she's left a half-dozen downy live wires who are busy stealing Baba Yaga's patented magic oatmeal. Dumb Doma will have her family."

"That's kidnapping," said Anton. "Let's try it." He ran back and scooped up the hen. "I hope this is good advice."

"Little advice is good," said Mewster, "but look: maybe Baba Yaga will come hunting you for revenge, and then you'll get more of that excitement you crave. Now, you'd better hurry away before she discovers her loss."

Dumb Doma was distressed; they could tell by its hopping up and down, three feet in the air. The sound of crashing furniture and the shrieks of the witch followed them almost a verst. But as soon as they rounded a curve in the road and disappeared from view, the sounds stopped. Dumb Doma didn't have much of a memory. After all, if it couldn't keep track of where the furniture and windows were supposed to stay, it probably couldn't tell the difference between an immortal hen and her chicks.

The Word of the Tsar

Saint Petersburg was thick with human noise.

They found their way through the maze of neighborhoods to the street where Madame Sophia lived. When they rang the bell, Monsieur d'Amboise answered the door.

Cat: "But I thought you and Miss Bristol left."

"We lasted two days. We were haunted by the thought of your great-aunt grieving over your second disappearance so soon after having been reunited with you. We thought we could bear it, leave her sorrow behind us, but we couldn't. So we came back. We persuaded her you'd return. Today you've proven us right."

Anton and Elena waited downstairs while Cat went up to visit her great-aunt. When she returned an hour later, she was much shaken. "I can see she's relieved that I'm home," she said, "but the toll upon her has been serious. She should travel to the south, to get some sun and rest, and I should go with her, if I'm not detained by the authorities for my part in this affair. London will have to wait."

Then they set out by carriage to see the Tsar. Korsikov clacked the reins, and Monsieur d'Amboise accompanied them. "We don't need a chaperone *now*, after all we've been through," said Anton. But the clammy ordinariness of life was back upon them, and his protests were ignored.

From the opposite seat in the carriage, Monsieur d'Amboise studied Elena's face. "I see you, too, have been through a great deal," he remarked.

"Can you see *what* I have been through?" she asked.

"No one can see that," he replied. "Evidence of life, yes, but not the life itself. That is private until it is shared."

She was in no mind to share, though she appreciated his observation.

They turned onto the quay along the river, heading for the Winter Palace. The pavilions had been dismantled or had drifted out to sea. The river was now frozen over. "A sudden cold snap at last," growled Korsikov. "Makes the digging of the emergency canals harder to handle, but the water level hasn't risen much in the past week. So maybe the worst is over.

"For now," he amended, being Russian. "But worse still is yet to come."

Whole populations of the city were out on the ice, skating with abandon. Elena and Cat and Anton itched to join them, but the work they had to do next was more important.

Monsieur d'Amboise and the children were invited into the palace and led to a chamber hung with silk panels. It wasn't long before a monk came to the door. Rangy, mangy, and intense. "I am Brother Grigori Rasputin," he said. "The Tsar's new advisor. I replace Brother Uri, who has been — called away."

Monsieur d'Amboise didn't want to release the children to his care, but the advisor to the Tsar overrode his concern. "Don't fret. I'll return and tell you what His Imperial Majesty has decided, when the time is right," said the monk to the butler.

"It's strange to see a holy man devoted to poverty making himself at home in such surroundings," observed Monsieur d'Amboise.

"It's a penance I endure for my Tsar."

Brother Grigori led them through room after well-appointed room. Great windows overlooked the Palace Embankment on one side, and the shine of winter sun off the frozen river danced over gilt and velvet. "You have severely troubled your distant cousin, the Tsar," remarked the monk.

"That's none of your concern," said Anton.

"It is. Though newly elevated to my post, my concern is the well-being of our leader, about whom I care in every way I can."

The boy only said, "He wanted me to be engaged to someone who could never qualify as Tsarina, should accidents happen that put me in line to the throne. He wanted me out of the way, accounted for, and shunted off the stage."

"He wanted you out of the way," said the monk, "for your own sake."

"I don't know what that is supposed to mean."

Brother Grigori glanced at Anton, and then at the two girls who were walking several paces behind. "I do not betray confidences of the Tsar," admitted the monk, weighing his words. "But I think I can say this: Not everyone who must wear the crown does so willingly. The burdens of state are just that: burdens. Even though you're but a distant relative of the Tsar, you are his godson. Our emperor would rather see you safely removed from the obligations of ruling Russia than have you remain in danger of being brought forward as a reluctant Tsar. Should something happen to him and his heirs. You want a life of adventure? I understand this. I was a boy once. To be Tsar is to have all the wrong adventures, all of the worries with few of the joys. He can't liberate his own children from the obligation to rule, but if he can protect anyone else, should something happen to his own line — well, as a godfather, he's doing what little he can for you."

"I see," said Anton. He wasn't sure he believed what Brother Grigori was saying. There was an argument for anything.

The monk delivered the children to a doorway, where the Deputy Sub-Lieutenant bade them wait until they were announced. The monk melted away. In a few moments, a maid came out and held the door open so they could enter.

They met the Tsar in a room that looked like an ordinary study. An interrupted game of cards on a table with a green felt cover, improbable greenhouse blossoms dropping their summery petals on the windowsill. Several books were left facedown at the pages on which they'd been abandoned. The Tsar looked tired, but his face opened up at the sight of the children.

"There you are!" he cried, and opened his arms. Anton did not dart to them. The Tsar embraced him anyway. "You wretched child. Why did you run away from all I was doing for you?"

"I do not care to become engaged," he said. "I prefer a life of uncertainty."

"I wanted you accounted for," said the Tsar, "and you proved to manage precisely the opposite. Your parents are beside themselves with worry, but I've already sent a messenger to tell them you are returned. They'll arrive at the palace to greet you within the hour, I'd warrant. Now, tell me where you have been and what you have done."

They could see his head was full of doings all over Russia, from the Bering Strait to the Baltic Sea, from the borders of Prussia to the Mongolian reaches to the Himalayan khanates. So, though they hadn't discussed a strategy, they colluded by instinct and didn't reveal everything to him.

Anton told about the approach to the North. "You couldn't have gotten there and back in such a short time," said the Tsar. They didn't tell him about the snow tornado.

Cat talked about Žmey-Aždaja and why he was being kept awake all winter, the rattle of human suffering, and that they had placated him for the time being, but not forever. The Tsar: "What *I* want is peace and succor for my people; I assume that's a noisy desire, too." Playing along, as if he couldn't imagine that the ice-dragon of old legend was a real creature coiled around the edge of a harbor. Belief, like everything else, ebbs and flows.

All Elena said was "We found the Firebird's egg. Now that there's a chance of winter when there should be winter, and a chance of spring and summer in their own turns, we could release the egg to the wild. And we did. The Firebird hatched."

"Ah," said the Tsar. "I once had an advisor who studied the Firebird. He is now, um, retired. He has written me bits of what *he* thinks may have happened. I don't know how much of your story is fanciful, how much is bald lies. But I hope the Firebird *has* revived itself in time. The wildness and plenty of Russia is not dead."

"The plenty needs to be shared," said Cat, "so that Žmey-Aždaja doesn't wake out of turn again."

"Easier said than done," said the Tsar, picking up a crystal bell and ringing it, a signal that the interview was over and the children should be ushered away.

"Wait," said Elena. "I came to Saint Petersburg to ask you to release my brother Luka, who was conscripted to help dig new canals around this great capital and drain the unseasonable floods."

"I'm lifting my decree of your imprisonment," said the Tsar. "Don't push me."

"I promised her I would find him," said Anton. "Do it for me."

"Don't tell me what to do. I'm glad you're home, but you're still young enough that I can give you a caning for insolence. I can't release one young soldier boy among many. Every conscript has a family who needs him. Russia needs him more. Without these canals, our capital city will drown."

Anton, furious, turned his back to the Tsar and walked to the windows.

"But we've told you. The floods will recede now that Žmey-Aždaja isn't melting the harbor ice out of anxious insomnia," said Cat.

"I know about anxious insomnia. Go," said the Tsar.

The double doors opened. The maid curtseyed, ready to escort them away. Anton shouted, "Look! Look! On the ice!"

The Tsar sighed. He crossed the salon to join the children glancing up and down the frozen river in front of the Winter Palace.

From the right, from that branch of the Neva River that flows from Lake Ladoga to the north, a colorful swarm of life-size matryoshkas came skating along. The citizens of Saint Petersburg cried aloud in shock and delight, as if they'd suddenly found themselves in a storybook. The matryoshkas weaved and bobbed and made elegant figures among the crowd, and came to rest at last in several square formations, like chocolates arranged in a gilt box. Ten across and twenty deep, they lined up on the river ice in front of the Winter Palace.

At some signal that no one could hear, the heads of the dolls came off, and the dragon-tooth soldiers climbed out, replacing the heads of their substantial wives and standing at attention, each next to his jolly Russian doll.

"There's your army," said Anton. "*They* can dig your emergency canals and reservoirs. Those conscripts from the farms and the fields, like Elena's brother; they can be freed. They can go home."

"I still hope you never have to be Tsar," said the Tsar, shaking his head. "But should it happen, I think you might make a good one."

"Will you release Luka? Will you give your word?"

"Do you ask for the word of the Tsar?" he said. "I am the Tsar; I am the word."

As they watched the soldiers and their partners, then, right before their eyes, it seemed that the toy roundness of the swollen matryoshkas gave way to a more ordinary human lumpiness. The soldiers began to look only like the next horde of immigrants, newly arrived from some part of the country infrequently remembered. The swarms of city dwellers coursing up and down the esplanade took them in, ignored them, went about their business.

The influence of magic only lasts so long. This was now a new population from the provinces to feed and to house and to line up for work. Despite the aggravation to his existing headache, the Tsar began to give his orders.

All Aboard Who
Are Going Aboard

I t was meant to be celebratory, a visit to Saint Petersburg's first ice-cream parlor. The new delicacy was so popular, though, that the establishment had sold out of its top choices: chocolate, vanilla, and strawberry. All they had left was potato, cabbage, and a flavor called winter, which tasted like balsam on ice. Madame Sophia paid. They ate in silence, looking at their spoons.

Then at the reopened Vitebsky rail station.

Anton stood in a serge suit, belted at the back. A schoolboy's felt cap was jammed on his head and a red scarf wound around his neck. His chaperone, a brute with arms like a stevedore, was there to keep Anton from boarding the train at the last minute, slipping away to find another adventure. The very existence of a railroad station was agony. All those beckoning whistles, those clouds of steam.

Travelers hurried through the concourse, presenting their platform tickets to attendants. The porters hauled luggage on wheeled carts, groaning. Shipping trunks suitable for ocean travel, matching luggage of Italian leather, the occasional crated piano-forte intended to grace some dacha in the country. Plumes of ostrich feathers, and cologne; courtesy and the lilt of easy laughter.

Most travelers, though, wore shapeless coats of brown and grey and charcoal. Boots of leather, if they were lucky. If not, rank claddings of felt, laced with strips of hide. Every female traveling in any class other than first wore a head scarf, even baby girls. Elena was no exception.

For the time being, she'd forsaken the fur coat that Baba Yaga had bequeathed her. She didn't know how to mount a third-class carriage wearing a coat that would be the envy of her fellow passengers. They'd assume she'd stolen it. But it was stored in some lengths of brown paper and wrapped in twine to which Luka had attached a handle made out of a twig, for easier carrying. It would make a warm blanket for Mama, if Mama was still alive to need warmth.

Yes, Luka was there. Changed from his adventure, too; changed in ways that Elena couldn't yet understand. Perhaps she never would. In a few short weeks, he'd grown to a man. His face was now more guarded. Some hunger lines had been erased, and he looked fuller, pinker. There were new lines around his mouth. Lines not of hunger but, perhaps, anger. He didn't talk much. But he'd greeted his sister with a shout of delight, that human sound of a human bell.

The Moscow train was scheduled to leave at seven in the evening. They would take it to Novgorod, then transfer to a trunk line as far as Borsky. From there they'd find out if another train was heading toward Tyer or Plinsk. If not, they'd get a lift on some farm carriage, if one was passing, or shoulder their burdens and walk.

The night had fallen, the conductors were shouting for

stragglers to board the train. Madame Sophia took Korsikov's arm and retired to her carriage at the kerb, waiting there for Cat.

"We must go," said Elena. She set down the basket with the hen of the tundra in it. "There is little chance we will meet again, but we must not mind too much."

Cat: "Don't say that. No one can know what will happen next. This escapade began by a bolt of lightning striking the bridge north of Miersk, throwing us into each other's lives. We didn't call for that lightning, nor did we recognize it for what it meant to us. How can we think we know everything now?"

"We've talked of this already." Elena was too brisk, thought Cat. "Someone like me isn't made to live in the wide world, but in the scratchy nest of a village. I must take care of my mother, if it's not too late, or mourn her and live in her memory. I promised my father I would. If Miersk is even still there."

"If you should depart Miersk for any reason, leave word where you are going. When I am grown up some more, and Madame Sophia and my parents are no longer organizing my days for me, I'll hunt for you. *Ma chérie*. This is not the end."

"This is good-bye." Elena threw herself into Cat's arms. She didn't cry. She clutched as a drowning child clings to a savior. It seemed she was shuddering for everything: for the departure of her worldly friend, for the life that Cat and Anton would probably make together, for the evaporation of the fantastic from her days, for the relief of securing Luka's release, and — she knew — for fear of what she would find when she finally made it to Miersk.

Cat's eyes ran, more out of sympathy than worry. She enjoyed a larger imagination for possibilities. For her, it wasn't a question of when, but how.

"We promised Žmey-Aždaja," she whispered. "We haven't yet worked out how we will do it, but it's our job to try. That part isn't done yet."

Elena couldn't speak but she thrust her mother's matryoshka at Cat. In lieu of a token from Baba Yaga, maybe. Better than nothing. If the needle no longer pointed to NORTH, any direction ahead was possible. Without parents or brothers to care for her, or even Baba Yaga, Cat needed it more than she did.

Anton didn't lean in to embrace Elena. As she paused on the step of the train to look back one last time, he saluted her, one general acknowledging another.

"We're off," said Luka gently, pulling his sister to his side.

The train whistle blew, scattering pigeons, and a steam from train engines rolled in to divide the company, to leave them remote and isolated.

Curtains closing at the end of a drama.

Then forward Elena and Luka went, or backward, to find if they had done enough. If they had done it well enough. If the good doctor and Grandmother Onna and the others had been able to tend to their sick mother. If, if, if. Each *if* a magic spell all its own, portending separate new worlds.

Elena leaned her head against her brother's shoulder and closed her eyes. She pictured herself on the arrival, and lights in the snow, and the astounded villagers gathering to hear their story. And she pictured a few eggs from the hen of the tundra, and a cup of milk heated in a pan, to warm the weary, to settle the stomach, and to help with sweet dreams.

As the lights of Saint Petersburg grew smaller behind them, twinkling and then indistinct, and as the train rocked through fields snowier than they'd been upon Elena's arrival, she thought:

But how do we know if the good we've managed to do is enough?

There is always more to do.

She put her face in her hands to save her brother from having to see her wince. Being able to conceive such a notion — that there is always more to do — was both a challenge, she supposed, and a proof that, in some respects, she was no longer a child.

The window by her seat was blotched with spots of rain dried into spearheads of dust. The world beyond — it was just a few fields right now, under the darkening sky. A farmer shrugging at snow to be cleared from a stable door. His hand on his head, scratching his hair. A donkey nearby, tied to a limp old cherry tree in no shape to bloom again. But it had to bloom again. Hold on, dear world, she thought. We're coming.

The Graveyard
in Springtime

I t would be unseemly of me to try to picture for you too spe-
cifically the moment of Elena and Luka's return to Miersk.
After so much time in isolation, I do not quite trust my own
emotions.

There was something to hope for. Miss Bristol and Monsieur d'Amboise had followed Cat's instructions, given on the
night she'd left for the North. The butler had sold some of her extra
clothes and sent some food to Miersk — though who knew if it
ever got there. All along the route it would have traveled, people
needed food.

And before the departure, Madame Sophia had provided for
Elena a selection of modern cures and traditional physics in
twists of paper. She was to hand them to the doctor. And, hidden in his boots, Luka had some military pay with which to buy
a cow that the whole village could tend. Now that Luka knew the
ways of the world better, he was braver, and he'd go farther afield

until he found a cow with enough breath and milk left to merit the expense. They'd need milk whether their mother had died or not.

Train service had not yet returned to anything like normal, and in fact it took them more than two weeks to organize their connections. They slumped and slumbered on old trains that broke down constantly. Finally, Elena and Luka were set down at the edge of the oblast, their own homely old district, and they had to cross the final stretches by foot. You must remember that no train regularly passed through Miersk. The Tsar might have been grateful to Elena for her contributions to the nation, but not so grateful he was going to charter her a private train. She was, after all, still a peasant.

So here they are, can you see them? It's late morning on a day in early spring. The calendar hasn't been fully realigned, if ever it will be. So the trees are all afresh with nubble and frowze of bud and flower. Birds have finished their morning chorus and are flicking about the verges of the track, their breakfast extending into lunchtime. Luka and Elena are carrying their coats over their shoulders.

Now they are recognizing a few outbuildings.

Now, around a rise, they see the spire of the chapel of Saint Veronika.

Now someone is shouting their names.

Yes, someone. Which someone?

He throws himself into their arms almost before they can believe it. Alexei, of course. Late in this tale, but who cares: this is what life is like. There's always someone new coming down the road, through the door.

Here he is, gasping, grown taller since they saw him. *What, what,* they sputter, and also: *When? And How?*

It's quite simple, really. When Elena disappeared, Peter Petrovich realized he couldn't manage to tend to Natasha Rudina on his own. Grandmother Onna was dotty, his own leg was becoming infected, and so on. So he wrote to the báryn in Moscow and explained the situation: Luka drafted into the army, Elena run off to rescue him. The landowner may have been overly concerned with his own well-being, but he wasn't a devil. He sent Alexei back.

"I set out after you." Alexei to Elena, laughing, holding her hands. "*I* wanted to rescue *you*. I got as far as Plinsk before I gave up. I was afraid I'd get lost, and then we'd all be lost separately. I realized I had to come back and tend to our Mamenka. *Somebody* had to. The doctor couldn't manage anymore."

Elena was overcome. She hadn't conceived that someone might try to rescue *her*. But this is how it goes, she thought. As Mewster said, always there is someone else's life running on a track parallel to our own. "And Mama?" she said, when she could speak.

"Oh, Elena," he said, his eyes a pattern of bright confusions. He looked from Luka to Elena and back again. "You will find her in the graveyard. No, no!" he shouted, darting after his sister and brother. "We'll go together — wait for me!"

With their dropped luggage, he struggled to rejoin them as they ran up the low rise to the front of the chapel. The belfry was still scorched, the broken bell listing where it had been hauled to one side. Ferns unfurling at its chipped rim.

They breached the rusty churchyard gate and flung themselves through the garden of stone memorials to the paupers' field beyond.

She is standing up. She doesn't see them yet. She is terribly thin. Her hair needs a good soaping. She carries an old saucepan, the one with the hole in the bottom. She has filled it with flowers, blues and whites and now some yellows. Not sure exactly where her husband lies, she is tossing handfuls of petal to fall where they might. Some will fall on his unmarked grave. Yellow, white, periwinkle blue. Curtains of blossom, opening.

Now she is turning. Now she sees them. The petals in the air surround her, surround them all.

The Doctor's Advice

Later, I won't say how much later, the three Rudin children are in the doctor's surgery. Such as it is. Clothes, little bottles, notes in scrapbooks, powders and vials. Dust everywhere, even mold. Foul smells competing for attention. Hardly hygienic, possibly even toxic.

Other villagers are here and there, outside, at their jobs of eking out a subsistence living. Only Grandmother Onna is in the room with them. She had been planning a squash pie, but she's fallen asleep with her head on the table, almost into the rolled-out dough. They could make a death mask of her if they wanted, using the pastry crust.

It isn't Grandmother Onna they've come to see, though. It is Peter Petrovich.

He is the one in need now. Whatever happened to his leg has seemed to hop to his heart. He isn't breathing well, and he can't sit up. He lies on his side. His knees pull a little toward his beard. He wears a knitted hat in bed.

"What can we do for you?" one of the Rudin children asks. They've all come to the same side of the bed. Elena sits on a stool close up to his side, as she used to sit playing at her mother's sickbed. Her brothers stand nearby.

He can hardly see them through the pain, but he tries.

"I look at you," he says. He points to Luka. "You are the most beautiful person I have ever seen." Then he points to Alexei. "And you are the most beautiful person I have ever seen." And Elena. "And so are you. The most beautiful. I've ever seen."

"There must be *something*," says Elena. "Another pillow. A glass of water?"

Luka cannot speak. He pushes aside the curtain so a little more light comes through, while there is time.

"I see the world," says Peter Petrovich, though his eyes have a filmy, milky look. "I see the maple tree and the cow. I see the hen and the egg." He pulls for breath as if breath is thick honey from a deep, heavy bucket; it resists him. "I see the spring riding . . . in over Russia . . . more powerful than Napoleon's army. It is so beautiful. I cannot bear to leave it."

They don't need him to declare the special name of this day. They know it.

"What can we do?" This, now, is Alexei.

The doctor pulls back his pointing finger and grasps his own hands, makes a loose fist the size of his heart, the size of a Firebird's egg, and pumps it a few inches at them, for emphasis. They know what he is saying, they hear it without words, they understand his

468

instructions to them. The same thing Elena's father said to her in the starry crown, and what Baba Yaga will say to Nikolai, come summer.

Live your life.
Live your life.
Live your life.

After.

ON A DIFFERENT PIECE OF PAPER, FROM A DIFFERENT WINDOW in time and the world, I finish my examination of these events.

On the thousandth day of my imprisonment, when I pulled up my pail of breakfast, I found therein two things.

One was a key.

The second was a letter from someone named Brother Grigori, writing on behalf of the Tsar of All the Russias. It contained one sentence. It said:

You are now a member of the League of Freed Prisoners.

I thought to myself: Frankly, honeybucket, it's about time.

I broke my breakfast bread into crumbs and left the whole thing on the windowsill for the birds. Then I unlocked the door and felt my way down the staircase, and I returned to life.

The wind wasn't a soothing hand against my hoary cheek. It stung, it bit. The light was invasive; there was a smell of drains. A donkey was braying a few fields away. In three years I had forgotten: Yes, freedom is magnificent. But freedom is hard work.

I never did return to the service of the Tsar.

The study of Firebirds is nothing more or less than the study of life.

I have lived in devotion to the rubrics of my congregation. I have turned aside from worldly pleasures to try to learn what can be known of the spirit of Russia. What I know about the time the Firebird's egg nearly failed to hatch is incomplete. What I could not imagine, even with the help of my companions, the birds, I've had to fill in with guesswork.

Still, some years after the events recounted herein, I found myself in a district of Moscow you could hardly call prosperous. It was a warm summer evening. I'd spent the day at an errand on behalf of an elderly brother in my order — a brother more elderly than myself, I mean, which by now is a rare creature indeed.

I'd become weary. I was in need of sustenance before returning to the dormitory in which I'd been granted a bed for the evening.

I should add that the years had been full of upheaval, and nothing in Russia was as it had once been. Where great wealth had been concentrated in some hands, it was now concentrated in others. The poor and the needy, though, hadn't benefited much in the process of transfer. History rarely favors the lowly.

Looking for a place to find some supper before continuing by foot back to my lodgings, I turned onto a side street. Laundry hung on lines across the alley. Cats and dogs and urchins fought for such scraps of edible trash as could be found. High up in a tenement, some mother was singing a tuneless lullaby to some baby. Ah, lullabies. The air was pleasantly cool, appropriate to an evening at the end of a warm summer's day.

It had been a long time since I'd served as advisor to the Tsar of All the Russias, may he rest in peace. I was an old man by now, in need of a place to sit. I asked a comrade on the street if he could spare a hank of bread or a sip of potato soup to settle an old man's stomach.

He shrugged; he had nothing to offer. "But try around the corner," I was told. "A small establishment near the end of the street. There is a sign out on the pavement. You will not miss it. It is called Egg & Spoon."

"Is there no place else? I am a man of the cloth," I told him. "I have no coin to sit in a café or a restaurant."

"You will not be turned away," he replied.

I continued on and located the place of which he was speaking. I went down a few steps to a room below street level. I found that he was right.

If I am not mistaken, the ancient woman sitting at a wooden table near the door was someone I had once met. She had been called, back then, Madame Sophia. Now she was too frail to rise when I came in, and thin and bony where she had once been buxom and broad. But her smile was immediate and welcoming. She didn't recognize me, but gave me leave to enter anyway, and sent me to a table along the side of the room.

I sat amid a crowd of the poor. They were all eating peasant fare, a substantial if plain meal of eggs and slaw and black bread. Served with a swallow of vodka or, if there were children on the laps of their mothers, milk. I saw people come and sit down, and argue and joke, and clear their plates, and others take their places. Sometimes people left coins in the jug on the table where the old woman sat. More often they only left their thanks, and their *good-evening*s, and their hope to meet again the next night.

To my table came a strong young woman. I ought to have pretended that I didn't recognize her. Nevertheless, I said to her, "Miss Ekaterina?" She didn't hear me. The clatter of settling trays and the laughter of children with their parents, of workers with their mates, drowned me out. I didn't speak again. I simply watched her.

She moved with efficiency and grace among the tables, delivering meals and wiping down tables. From time to time, she went to the door of the room in back, from where the food was coming, and called out a request or a question. I am almost sure I heard her address someone in the back as "Elena."

Or was this only the poor hearing and the lively hopes of an old man?

I wanted to ask after Anton. Had he found adventure, had he changed his mind about marriage? I wanted to ask after the dragon-tooth boy. I wanted to know if any of them had ever seen Miss Yaga again. But their work was too important to interrupt. I comforted myself with watching Miss Ekaterina, the Tsarevna of the charitable hall, seeing everyone fed as well as she could manage.

I suppose she was calming the storm of need, sharing what she had — her time, her friendship with Elena, and maybe the eggs of that immortal hen!—thus, in her small way, helping the ice-dragon sleep when the wintertime came in.

As I left the establishment, I said, "I have no coin to pay."

The old woman said, "Give us your blessing, good father. And peace be with you on the street tonight."

I left then, and I never went back. But as I walked along the alley, I listened to the sound of children playing in the gutters. These children had been fed enough, this one night at least. The sound of their common joy made a kind of magic in the neighborhood. The setting sun spilled long drifts of light behind them, but as the children turned in its splash, I could see their laughing eyes.

I believe it was that night that I made my final stab of understanding about the Firebird. I had long since stopped wondering if the great sun could cause the illuminated Firebird to cast a bright shadow. The Tsar's skepticism had nearly beaten my faith out of me. How *could* a flame be cast as an impression upon the earth?

But whether as divine inspiration or as a bit of old man's folly, that night I came to a conjecture that I have never proven and yet never abandoned.

Yes, I decided. A Firebird flying across Russia in the strength of a noonday sun does indeed cast a shadow. Nothing that is spiritual can fail to shine. Of course we can't see it directly, because the shadow it casts is just another kind of light. You have to look sideways to see it, but once you see it, you can never un-see it.

It is the light you see in the faces of children.

"The eggs — the eggs are teaching the hen," the count said through happy tears . . .

— Leo Tolstoi, *War and Peace,*
translated by Richard Pevear
and Larissa Volokhonsky

In memory and honor of Maurice Sendak.